# Ways of the Wolf

## by

## Cheryl Starr Munger

*T.I.T.A.N. Series*

**Ways of the Wolf**

Contact Information: info@thewildrosepress.com

Cover Art by *Debbie Taylor*

The Wild Rose Press, Inc.
PO Box 708
Adams Basin, NY 14410-0708
Visit us at www.thewildrosepress.com

Publishing History
First Edition, 2022
Trade Paperback ISBN 978-1-5092-4240-5
Digital ISBN 978-1-5092-4241-2

*T.I.T.A.N. Series*
Published in the United States of America

Since I've met you, I have yearned to take you to bed. God knows I wanted to, but I couldn't do that to you. I had to be sure about how I felt. Yes, maybe I didn't understand it all at first, I've never been in love before.

"And yes, I have laid awake at night and imagined every way possible that I could make love to you. I go to sleep thinking about you, I dream about you, and I wake up in the morning thinking about you. But I never once thought of you being a one-night stand. I want you to go home with me, so that I can, yes, protect you, if it were anyone else with your qualifications, I'd let them stay, but it's not, it's you, and you are the one I want to protect.

"I must have that as a man, as a *man*, Kara. Do you understand that? It's also the way of the man who loves a woman as passionately as I do you. You are the one and only one. I've fallen madly in love with you and want to be with you every day of my life. In fact, I can't think of a second of being without you. So, yes, please come back with me. He paused and turned away, then turned back. "But if you want to stay…"

# Dedication

This book is truly dedicated to my wonderful editor, Lill. You've taught me so much! Your patience with me rivals that of a slug crossing the Mojave Desert, sometimes I don't know how you do it. You have always been there, day, night, week-ends, and through the pandemic, and not only have you been a great teacher, but I also consider you a great friend. It's been so much fun working with you and getting to know you! I hope we will work together way into the future!! Hugs and love!! (Oh, for those pesky comas, space, delete, coma, coma, start over…rewrite…lol)

Also, a shout to my wonderful husband, whose words have always been to me to keep going and keep writing. Especially during those moments of doubt on my part. Thanks, honey, for your support. It means a lot.

## Chapter One

Kara waited at the edge of the empty warehouse with her Glock 22 in hand. She stood ready with her heart pounding having just rounded the last corner. The wind picked up and whistled through cracks of the tattered building. A crow called overhead, flew low, then up, and circled. White puffy clouds in an endless blue sky moved quickly. The whole area felt eerie and seemed to step on her already taut nerves.

Snippets of the last time she was in this position swept through her memory. Her fiancé was killed, and it was all her fault. She shook her head. She'd been through the psych classes she was made to endure, and with a deep breath, she used her tools to try and quiet her heart and mind.

She smelled oil and grease coming from the old, abandoned warehouse and scrunched up her nose. She leaned against the corner of a nearby smaller building. She slipped her gun back in its holster. She'd checked all corners of the warehouse, no one was here that she knew of…yet. The windows around the top were broken out, they probably all were at one time, but someone had replaced them around the lower edges where anyone could crawl through.

Whoever replaced them hadn't bothered to take the tape off the outside announcing they were new. She looked around the strange area and took note of all the oddities. There were places on the building missing some sheet metal, and she could hear pieces flapping in the wind. It wouldn't be long, and a rough breeze would pull them off entirely.

Who would fix half a warehouse? Better yet, who would want to have a warehouse in the middle of nowhere? She glanced at her watch keeping track of the time. The one or ones she's waiting for should be arriving soon. She stood in a good place for seeing anyone coming in.

She glanced over the empty parking lot. The tar appeared old and cracked like the mighty Thor had taken his hammer to it. Small tiny plants were reaching toward the sun coming up through the crooked veins. Down at her feet she watched a couple dandelions bend with the breeze and felt for the beautiful tiny flowers. "*Sometimes you just have no say where you come into the world and what conditions you are made to live in.*"

She bent down and brushed the two tiny flowers with her fingers and smiled. Sighing she stood and closed her eyes trying to get a feel for the place. Sometimes this resulted in a vision but this time…nothing.

She wasn't sure if they had the right place after all and wondered about their informant, Tanny Albright. His name was really Terrence, but everyone called him Tanny. He looked like a Tanny; the tall skinny man fit his name. Until now, she'd say he'd done a good job helping them. She leaned against the edge of the building and adjusted the small mic on her collar. "Tell me what you see, Carl." She waited. "Damn it, Carl speak to me."

"Not now," gasped Carl.

She could hear fast moving footsteps. Carl or someone else running? She heard creaky wooden steps being stomped up. "Silent much?" she asked Carl. "What about the rest of you?"

"Eyes on the west end, captain," announced Samantha.

"Get ready to move in, Sammy," said Kara. "Tom?"

"Inside east end," said Tom, his tone nonchalant. "This place is dead, and I don't see any large shipment of drugs."

"Pay attention, Tom, doesn't mean they aren't there. This isn't a drill," said Kara.

"And this isn't the army," said Tom.

"That was a low blow to Kara," said Sammy. "You really are an SOB," she said into her mic.

Kara took the remark in stride, perhaps everyone knew the circumstances of her leaving the army. Although it did make her adrenaline spike, his words brought back the memory. She'd better get used to being ribbed about what happened in the service. She was told time was the finest of healers, but it had been a year and she still thought about it often.

A pang of loneliness hit her, and if she had been home alone, she knew she'd collapse in tears again. She was still having nightmares over it. His bloody body lying in the street. An expression of terror frozen on his face. It came back to haunt her. Work is good she told herself, then didn't believe it. If she'd just pulled the trigger, he'd still be alive. She leaned her head back and sighed. "*Pull it together Thomas,*" she told herself. "*Right now.*"

Her thoughts quickly went to the people she was in charge of now. She was new and still working on her place within the group. They'd lost their previous Captain to a heart attack. Someone she knew they had loved. It would take them awhile. The comment was aimed at her military service, but she didn't care.

Right now, she was anxious. The whole thing didn't feel right to her. The big guy running this drug ring was smart, and they had it on the good that he'd be here today, around this time, with a large shipment of drugs. This was the only place she could see everything and where she could remain hidden. Someone would have to get by her to get into the warehouse.

"Just looks like fertilizer," said Tom. She could hear him scuff his foot on the cement. "None too clean about storing it either. The shits everywhere."

He no sooner said that when she got an instant vision of fire. A huge explosion in her mind. She saw it all in a split second and she knew. This was a set-up. Shock went through her system and her military training took over. Adrenaline coursed through her veins, and she bolted.

She took off running holding her collar up to her mouth. "Abort!" she shouted into her mic. "Abort! Get the hell out of there, now! All of you! Set up! Get back Sammy! Move!" She moved as quick as her feet could take her but kept yelling. She felt it before she heard it. Heat hit her and it felt like a gale force wind punched her in the back as the warehouse exploded behind her. She was picked up and thrown into the empty parking lot and slammed against a light pole. Then everything went black. Her last thoughts were about getting her people out alive…and losing her fiancé.

*****

*A mile away…*

Cain slowed his silver '64 GTO and glanced at the computer on his dash. Ansen Horn had to be close, but where? He looked at the blinking, nonmoving green dot on the screen. "What's this asshole up to anyway," he asked of no one. He spun the wheel hard left and made a sharp U-turn. "He's got to be close," he mumbled. He gave the car some gas and felt his back tires give way making gravel spin out from under his car before catching the pavement.

He was in no mood for this game of chase. This idiot had taken him on a wild goose chase to Florida and back. Well, it wasn't a total loss, he told himself, he's sure that they'd found another piece of the puzzle in Miami. He fell deep in thought about the last couple of days as he passed the same scenery for the second or third time. He kept missing the small road that led off the main one. When he drove, he could think, and he was deep in his thoughts.

He wanted to know who Horn met with.

He no sooner had that thought and his cell went off. He pulled it from his shirt pocket, glancing at the caller ID. "Yeah, Damian," he answered. "Perez? You sure? That figures, there's been some noise about him lately. I was afraid of that. Okay, let me know if anything else comes up. Yep, soon." He clicked off and returned the phone to his pocket.

He knew whoever Horn met with was big on the drug scene, but Perez? He shook his head. Bigger than he first thought. It pissed him off and he slammed his hands against the steering wheel. Horn had his fingers in too many damn pies, and he was ready to cut them all off himself.

His thoughts traveled to his boss, Christian Keller, who thought Horn was the mastermind behind this drug ring that supplied, Arizona, Texas, New Mexico, and California. Now with his jaunt to Miami, Florida it proved Colombia was somehow tied up in it too, especially since he met with Perez. He saw the connection in the beginning of the west coast and its states, and that had taken him three years to put together.

How far did these people from Colorado go? They weren't easy, and he didn't think Horn was smart enough to be the mastermind. If he were a mastermind of such a large intricate operation, he wouldn't get his hands dirty by being sighted at some of the sites of crime.

He slowed down again as his thoughts took him to the different crimes and drugs he was sure Horn was involved in. He wasn't watching where he was going and he passed the small road for the third time. There were no other roads or paths within the mile that he could have taken. He knew Horn pulled off somewhere within this mile. He had to, he'd had him in plain sight and lost him. Looking at the small computer screen displaying the tracker he saw Horn stopped, and he was close. He slammed on his breaks made another U-turn and headed back to the overgrown dirt road off the main one

More like a path. He grunted as he spun the steering wheel hard-left maneuvering back around. He was angry over the whole mess, but this was his job, and he took it seriously, after all he was a TITAN, and on top of that, he was the alpha male of the pride of the Silver Sables. He was also part of the United Clans for the betterment of all. He had huge responsibilities. He didn't have time for games.

Horn was a half breed, half Lycan half witch. He knew because when they almost had him in New Orleans, he caught his trail and his scent. He could smell him. There was a derogatory name they used for them, Salmagundi, Gundi for short. They got the name because eventually they all went crazy. He didn't much care for it, but it sure fit this man.

In reality, he felt sorry for the ones who were changed. He knew some sorcerers that worked for TITAN, and he liked them. They were intelligent people and helped run TITAN, and boy could they come up with spells. He shook his head and hoped they'd soon find a cure.

He felt sorry for the half breeds because once changed they were headed for a meltdown of the worst kind. Then it was up to the Lycans to take care of the problem, because their bite had caused the problem in the first place. He felt the guilty weight of it all.

He slowed down and pulled off the road. He carefully maneuvered back behind a large outcropping of rock and some aspen. He felt hidden enough. He shut the rumbling engine down and got out. He patted his car, his pride and joy, Silver Slayer, and looked around. "Seems to be no one around," he said to no one. "But he *has* to be within a mile of here."

He looked around and sniffed the air. Yep, he's going to have to do this the hard way. Through his wolf. He pulled his hand down his thick dark hair, rubbed his face with a sigh, and pulled his T-shirt over his head. He would begin his search here. He quickly undressed, threw his clothes in a duffel bag, pitched it in the trunk, locked the car, and put the keys under a rock.

He stretched his legs, arms, and neck, then rotated his head getting ready for the change. "*Mutatis Mutandis.*" He said the ancient words that enabled him to change. He immediately felt the tingle, the first part of the change. The hair on his body sprouted, his jaw elongated, his bones twisted and turned, and his canines grew. For a split second his blood felt like acid running through his veins then warmed. He dropped to four padded feet.

His vision became sharper, and the smells of the crisp mountain air invigorated him. He stood, his black as night fur with a silver stripe down his back glistening in the sun. His icy yellow eyes sharp as a tack. He felt the familiar feeling of freedom and let out a long howl announcing his presence. He wasn't close enough to home that his call would alert his own, he was in Arctic Pride territory, the neighboring clan of Lycans. His howl announced his arrival as a silverback in the white wolves' territory. It was the polite thing to do.

He looked around but didn't see any of the pure white wolves. He was alone. That was all right. He'd love to come face to face with the asshole he was after, just the two of them meeting. He knew Ansen didn't know him, not yet, but he would when he put him away for good. The man was rich as sin and has the attorneys to prove it. But more than that there was someone with power backing him, he was sure of it. A great many innocent lives were lost because of him. The man thought he was above the law.

He stood and sniffed the air. He couldn't smell the gundi, but it didn't mean he wasn't somewhere around here. He sniffed the ground, smelled the strong scent of rabbit, he lifted his head and looked through his wolf's eyes at his surroundings. He dropped his inside eyelids, the thin membrane that allowed all wolves to see halo's. He could see recent energy paths of small animals, but that was all.

The energy trails they left behind was like a halo, an aura, a faint light, but there wasn't any recent activity.

The halo, as the prides called it, was dimming. He retracted the inside lid that acted like a prism and took off in a run toward where he last glimpsed the car on the road. That's where he'd start. He ran across the meadow and up a small hill, then stopped.

He was looking toward the west when he heard the explosion. His head snapped to the north where he saw smoke and the tips of flames above the forest trees. He took off in a dead run toward it splashing through a shallow, slow-moving river, and into an open area. When he got closer, he slowed. The fire was so hot that if anyone was in the building, he was sure they were dead.

He went around the blazing parameter getting as close as he could sniffing the ground. He could smell the strong odor of sanitizer, acetone, and fertilizer used to make explosives. Homemade. Accident? He didn't think so, he felt, no he knew, Ansen had to have had something to do with it. He sniffed some more and ran across a pile of charred bone. Human, dead, burned to a crisp. He found two more dead and traveled on.

He was busy trying to differentiate smells when he heard a moan. He raised his head and looked to where he thought it came from and trotted toward it. He could smell human, different from the three charred bodies he smelled at the other side of the building.

The air was so acrid he coughed. He heard another moan, coming from the parking lot. He padded closer and saw the woman lying face down at the base of a light pole, judging from the bend in the pole, she'd hit it.

He quickly went to her and with his teeth he rolled her over putting out the lingering flames, another moan escaped her mouth, then she was silent. He could hear her heartbeat, erratic, thready, and by how badly she was burned, he didn't think she'd live long. He had a decision to make, save her or let her die.

Her face was beautiful, and peaceful looking. If she was awake, she'd be screaming from the burns. Could he bite her to save her only to add to the pain of the burns? Should he just let her die. Hell no. If it were him, he'd put up with all the pain of change and the burns to survive. He pushed her head aside with his nose exposing her neck, the quickest way into her blood stream, and he bit.

As soon as he bit her, he knew. The blood touched his tongue and he tasted it. "Damnit," he thought to himself. *Witch*. Why didn't he smell it right away? The damn chemical smell was overpowering. Now it was too late. She would only have ten to twenty years at most before she'd go mad. He should just do away with her.

The questions cycled through his mind quickly. He didn't have the luxury of time to ponder them. He turned and searched the area for any sign of life. None, he turned back to her. In addition to the bad burns she was bleeding from where he bit her.

The change would be very painful, but when finished, the burns would be gone, she'd be healed. Well, maybe they'd find a cure in ten to twenty years. Who was he kidding? They'd been looking for a cure for as long as he could remember.

One thing for sure, he couldn't leave her, she'd be changing soon and that was on his shoulders. He repeated the words "*Mutatis Mutandis*," to himself. He changed back to human form and stood naked looking at her. He quickly scooped her in his arms and took off running. She was his responsibility now. He'd have to follow Horn another time, but he did need to call and report in to his boss.

He didn't live far, and he had a fast car. He could be home in minutes. He was going to be in so much trouble. He reached the car, pulled out his keys, opened his back door, and laid her on the seat. He popped the trunk, pulled out a blanket, and put it over her. "Well, it's as comfortable as its going to get until I get you to my house. I hope you stay out until I can get you settled." He grabbed his clothes out of his duffle and was pulling on his pants when he saw her eyes snap open. She screamed.

"Perhaps that was the wrong thing to say or wish for," he said. He leaned in the car, one leg in his pants and the other fighting to get down through the material. "Hey, you're going to be all right." He almost tripped over his pants. He took a step away. He patted her leg and she screamed louder. "Please," he shouted, finally pushing his leg through the pants. "You're going to have all of Denver here if you keep screaming like that."

"The paaaaiiin!" she gurgled.

"You're going to be all right. It's going to get a lot more painful before it gets better." She looked at him and he saw pure terror in her eyes. And what eyes they were. They damn near bowled him over. He grabbed the edge of the car.

She screamed again then passed out. "Thank you powers that be," he said with a huff zipping up his jeans. He was out of breath, mostly because her screams scared the bejesus out of him, and because he'd been fighting to keep his balance with only one pant leg on. He threw on his T-shirt, hopped in the front seat, and started his car.

He was afraid the rumbling engine noise might stir her, but she was still out. He drove in silence, Ansen Horn almost all forgotten, for the look in her eyes would be forever burned in his memory. She had the greenest eyes he'd ever seen, and although they showed the excruciating pain she was in, it didn't diminish their beauty.

He mentally kicked himself for the thought and grabbed his cell from his shirt pocket. He speed dialed his boss and got the dreaded recorded message. He waited patiently for it to finish. "Christian, I'm up here in the Rockies off dirt road 22 at some type of large building or what's left of it, warehouse maybe. There was an explosion. There are freshly charred bodies. Get Stone up here to check it out before the P.D. gets wind.

"I have a sneaking suspicion Ansen had something to do with it because I followed him up here. I had to change the lone survivor to save her life. I have her in the car now on my way home. Call as soon as you get this." He ended the call and threw his phone on the seat next to him, then kicked in the gas pedal and headed home.

With that taken care of, his thoughts went back to the burned woman in his back seat, worry setting in. What was he going to tell everyone? It was against the law and morals to turn a witch. It was basically a death sentence for the one turned.

He went back and forth in his mind. He should have let her die, but he gave her ten more years of life, but she will go crazy, so sad, she was really beautiful... Wait what was he thinking? Well, she is beautiful. Doesn't make it right. Maybe they'll find a cure in the next ten years. Hadn't they been trying to do that for hundreds of years? *There was no cure.*

"There could be," he said out loud. He slammed his hands against the steering wheel and made a left turn that would take him to the back road to the lake. He couldn't wait to get home, he'd been gone long enough, but he was nervous about taking the woman there. He didn't like leaving his home, but someone had to do his job. Besides he enjoyed it.

He turned onto the gravel road that was essentially a very long driveway, flew down it, and ended up in front of his house, slammed on the brakes, and quickly threw the car in park. He didn't bother to garage it like he usually did. The garage wasn't attached, and parking here gave him quicker access to the front door. He hopped out and opened her door and stared at her for a second. "Please don't wake up yet," he pleaded in almost a whisper. "Shit," he said. "I have to unlock the front door." He quickly went and unlocked the door, opened it, then hurried back.

She hadn't moved a muscle. He tried to be as gentle as he could with her back being in such bad shape. He'd get her inside, look her over, clean what he could and wait for her to make the change, that is, if she didn't die first. She was burned over twenty-five percent of her body as far as he could tell.

He'd have to get the chains from the basement. He didn't like the idea of having to chain her up, but there was no other choice, it was painful going through the change for the first time and in the throes of it anything could happen. Her body's bones had never changed shape before, neither had her blood. Her blood would feel like acid running through her veins the first time, something that happened to them all. It was hard enough going through the change being in good health. Ergo the chains.

Four chains attached to a thick iron collar that would go around her neck. She could hurt herself, and would, and she'd probably hurt him too. A change would make the wolf exceptionally strong, and she wouldn't know what she was doing. She could destroy his log home in a matter of seconds.

The chains had to come out, he would chain her to his bed. It was made to withstand the change. He had an iron bed, but it wasn't a wimpy delicate one. He had it made with the intent of bringing a human there to change. A human woman who would become his wife. It wasn't meant for a witch. His life wasn't meant for a sorceress. He didn't know that much about them.

After getting her settled he went and got the chains and chained her to the bed. Then he set about to cleaning her wounds. Some areas were just too raw to touch. He hit a spot and her eyes flew open. She screamed bloody murder, and he thought his ear drums exploded. He reared back. Her eyes turned bloodshot red, and he knew the change had begun.

Her blood was moving at a rapid rate, he knew her heartbeat had accelerated, and her bones were beginning to change. They would be malleable then hard and switch back and forth until all the changes took place. It was all extremely painful, and all he could do now was stand and watch. To get near her would be a disaster.

He watched in fascination as her body went through the changes. It was the first time he'd seen it for any length of time. She became distorted, screamed, and screamed some more. As her bones changed shape, he watched different colored patches of hair sprout then recede. He wouldn't know what breed of wolf she'd be until she fully changed. Her coat would determine the pride she'd belong to.

He spent the night by his bed watching over her.

Midway through there were times she'd quiet and then times she screamed so loud, he felt she could be heard all the way through the city. He never could get used to a new wolf and the change process. He avoided it whenever he could. He couldn't remember his own other than pain unlike anything else he'd ever encountered.

He thought about the first time he was approached and asked to become wolf. He was a human and chosen by Christian and two others to become part of a pack. He'd known Christian in WWII at Pearl Harbor when it was bombed, and he'd become his friend. They said they needed him and pleaded their case. At first, he thought it was some elaborate joke being played on him by some friends from the Navy.

He was one of the early TITANs. He worked out daily, ran, exercised, and stayed on top of his game. He listened to all they offered, and after he saw Christian change in front of his eyes, he couldn't turn it down. Living five hundred plus or minus a few years was a definite advantage, but not the deciding factor. No, the deciding factor for him was better sight, smell, and strength. That's what sold him.

Come early morning she'd become hoarse from her screams and finally calmed down. It seemed like it had taken an eternity. He was sure it felt that way to her. He waited now because she would fully transform, and he'd see her wolf form for the first time. Once she fully settled down, he put the words she needed for transformation into her mind. Since he was her sire, they were connected mind to mind, it was his duty now to be her guide.

With eyes still closed she whispered. "*Mutatis Mutandis*." He waited patiently as her bones twisted and popped, her jaw elongated, and fur grew. With great surprise he saw her change into a silver sable with the most beautiful coat he'd ever seen. She was pure black with the silver stripe down her back, but she had a white chest that was absolutely striking and a white tipped tail. He'd never seen another like her.

She was one of his kind and that humbled him. A jolt of happiness ran through him, but it was short lived when he remembered she was also a witch. He'd have to face his clan and the Sorcerer's council with the news at some point. This was something that was kept within the two different factions. It wasn't TITAN business, and it certainly wasn't human business.

*"Where am I and what ha...hap... happened to me?"* she asked with her mind. He could hear, see, and feel her frantic emotions.

*"You are now wolf as well as a sorceress. A beautiful Silver Sable."*

She looked at him with shock, he could feel her shock. *"What the hell are you saying? You aren't making any sense."* Her head bobbed, but her eyes darted about the room like she was about to bolt. He knew she was going to go into shock he'd seen it in others before. He had to try and calm her.

*"You know you are already a sorceress. Well, now you are also Lycan."*

*"Are you crazy? Are you calling me a witch, and a wo...wolf? A sorceress? Wolf? This can't be, I'm human. I'm just human!"*

She was getting ready to snap. He had to tell her the truth, but he also had to calm her down before she hurt herself. He sat on the edge of the bed and put a hand on her.

*"Think about what you just went through."* He

began softly. *"You were burned over twenty-five percent of your body. Look at yourself right now. Go ahead look. You know what I'm telling you is truth. Besides you would have died had I not changed you."* He was frustrated but he kept his voice soft as he gently stroked her head. The very last thing he needed was to be a sire of a newbie, but he couldn't take back anything, besides he didn't want to. Still, he was somewhat angry with himself for changing her. He always promised himself he'd never change a human, he'd never bite one, he didn't want the responsibility that came with being a sire.

That was saved strictly for only one, his mate, she would be the only one he'd change. He didn't have time for this. He didn't have time to train her. Damn it, He stood and stepped a few steps back. *"Change back,"* he commanded. He knew a newbie had to do whatever was commanded of them, and only the sire could make a command. When one was made there was simply no choice.

*"Mutatis Mutandis,"* she said, and she changed. He stared as she changed, and he found himself looking at her naked body. Good God, he thought as he swallowed his tongue, the beautiful curves the woman had made his mouth water. Then he remembered what he'd done and that she was also a witch. The guilt settled in his gut.

"I heard that," she said with a look that could kill.

"Sorry, I couldn't help it," he replied, turning his head away. "Won't happen again." He slammed his mental wall up. "I have to unchain you and find you some clothes." He went to the closet and pulled down a blanket and quickly threw it over her.

"Better?" He glanced at his bed and the mess she was sitting in the middle of. There were bits and pieces of her clothing strewn across it, some burned, some ripped. He shook his head and rolled his eyes.

"Oh gods, the explosion, my crew...did you see...I was burned...the pain...oh gods the pain. I don't feel any of it anymore. Why? What happened? What the hell did you to me? I must be hallucinating. Am I dead? I'm dead right and this is hell?"

She was heading into panic again. "I'll explain everything after I get you unchained and some clothes on you. You'll want a shower no doubt."

"Let me out of here, I have to find my crew." She yanked on the chains. "Why am I chained up? Please get me out of these. What the hell is going on here and what did you do to me? Did you give me a hallucinogenic? Did I dream that explosion?"

He sighed. "No, and no. What you think was a hallucination actually happened." He took the key and began unlocking the chains. First the four at each corner, then the one around her neck. "Listen to me, there was no one alive other than you at the fire." He gathered the chains and laid them in a pile on the floor, then grabbed his robe off the back of the bathroom door and tossed it to her.

"I...I'm going to put the robe on," she said, as if she needed to announce the fact. She flicked her hand toward him motioning for him to turn his head.

He quickly did as she asked, but not before he caught sight of bouncing breasts as she dropped the blanket.

"That can't be...my crew..."

He stood with his back to her. "If the three that I found were part of your crew, I'm sorry they are dead. You were the only one I found alive."

"I'm decent," she said, a little deflated.

His first thought was, better than decent. He had to quell those thoughts right away. What the hell was wrong with him. He went to his dresser and pulled out a white T-shirt and some jogging pants with a drawstring.

"They will be big on you, but they will work for now. The shower is through that door. Go shower, and we'll talk when you come out. There's an odor that comes with the first change and no one likes smelling it. Scrub up and meet me in the kitchen. I'll throw this bedding away, then I'll put on some coffee."

"You are awful damn bossy," she said grabbing the stuff to her chest.

He stared at pieces of her long dark hair, at least what was left of it. A lot had been singed off. She'd had most of it on top of her head at one point during the day, because some was still there. Now, a lot of it was everywhere and in knots. He looked at her large, emerald green, cat eyes, and was almost drawn in.

She looked damn beautiful sitting on his bed all disheveled. He mentally smacked himself. This was not going to happen. She was a half breed. Even though he felt extremely sorry for her and for what he'd done, he wanted no part of it. "I'm your sire, I have every right to be bossy. You'll do as I say until I release you."

"I have a job to go to. I'm a captain, Denver, P.D. It's an important job, and I'm in the middle of a drug case."

He raised his eyebrows at the words. The first thing that came to mind was the man he was after. "You won't be going back," he said with finality. He quickly left shutting the door behind him before she could respond.

When he got to the kitchen, he called his boss and

filled him in, then he went through the motion of making coffee, not paying any attention to what he was doing. He wanted to know more about who she worked for, how they were involved with his case, and who okayed it. If she was local police, they should have been pulled from the case and not allowed near it.

It was too big for them. Besides they could have blown all the work he and his partner had been doing the last three years. He slammed a coffee cup on the counter. He was going to be thoroughly pissed if his mission was in any way jeopardized. He'd know soon enough.

One thing a sire had over a new Lycan was power. They could use mind control if a new change refused to listen. That was for the safety of all. He slammed a second cup on the counter. His stomach was beginning to sour. He leaned back against the counter and glanced at the calendar. "Damn," he said as he quickly went over to it. "Full moon in three days. My luck keeps getting better and better," he said sarcastically.

"Well, I'd say your luck is better than mine today," she said, as she entered the kitchen. She had a towel over her hair and was rubbing it dry.

He quickly snapped his head toward her and did a mental wow! The woman cleaned up good. "It's going to be a full moon in three days."

"Yeah, so." She threw the towel around her shoulders then picked up a cup and went and poured herself some coffee.

He watched her. All other women waited until he handed them their cup. Now he was comparing her to other women. He was an idiot. "All Lycan change on a full moon whether we want to or not. It's the closest to wild we'll ever get. We hunt and we eat animals. That's why our packs live in National Forests. We are protected here, lots of area to spread out in, and we can hunt.

"Deer, rabbit, you get the picture. We keep the population from getting out of control. If you're new, you could run across a human and eat them. Now that's against the law. So, until you can control that urge you are under my command."

"That's ridiculous. I'm vegan. I don't eat animals let alone humans." She took a sip of coffee.

He snorted. "Not anymore, you're not. You will eat meat, and you'll eat a lot of it."

Her eyes narrowed over her cup as she stared him down. If looks could kill. "I *said*, I don't eat meat."

"Suit yourself. You'll see." He poured himself a cup of coffee. "I forgot to ask. You like cream or sugar?"

"Do you have any vanilla cream?"

He preferred black coffee, but he did keep stuff like that for visitors. "Help yourself, look in the fridge."

She found some and pulled it out. "You shouldn't eat so much meat," she said as she poured her cream. "There must be six steaks in there and four pounds of hamburger. I didn't see one leafy thing."

"I eat meat."

"Apparently lots of meat." She put the cream back in the fridge and turned toward him. "So just tell me." She took a long drink of her coffee.

"First of all, you're a witch…"

"Now wait right there, buddy. That's the second time you accused me of being a witch. I am not a witch. I don't practice the art. I never have. I don't mean that in a negative way either. I don't judge anyone else for the practice, but I've never been involved. I know nothing about it. I told you that."

"I don't think you have a concept of what kind of power true sorcerers and sorceresses have. There are powers that I have no concept of. I for one, highly respect who and what they represent. I just think you are afraid of who you are. So, trust me they are very real, and it is not any hokey pokey running around under a full moon naked kind of thing. At least I don't think that's involved, could be, I wouldn't know. Anyway, I will grant you that I can't smell it on you, but I damn well tasted it in your blood."

"What do you mean tasted? You bit me?" she squeaked.

"I was wolf, and that is how I saved your life." He went to the pot and poured more coffee. "You?" he asked holding the pot in the air.

"Sure, I could use a warmup," she said looking inside her cup. She got up from the stool and handed him her cup then went to the fridge to get the cream. "Yes, I suppose you are right. I am afraid. I have no idea what being a witch even means." She went and sat back on the stool at the bar.

"Well, wolves and witches or warlocks don't really talk to each other about who and what they are, but I can say, the ones who work for TITAN are very intelligent and talented in what they know how to do. I just know very little about them otherwise."

She glanced around at his home. Log, open concept. She sat at the bar looking into the two-story great room and glanced at the large stone fireplace with a three-inch-thick long wood mantle. It took up most of one wall. "Nice place," she said with a sip of coffee. "Very rustic." She set her cup down and fluffed her drying hair.

He couldn't help but admire what he was seeing. "I

like it. It's woodsy, and I like woodsy."

"I can tell," she said. "My crew…"

"I'm sorry they are dead. I found the charred bodies."

Tears gathered in her eyes and ran down her cheeks. He could see the sorrow and loss etched across her face.

"Look," he said. "I don't know if it will make you feel any better, but there was nothing you could do. From what I could tell nothing was your fault unless you set the blasts."

She looked up at him and squeezed her eyes shut. "My crew…my fiancé…"

"Your fiancé was in the blast?" he asked.

She opened her eyes. "N…no, just something I was remembering."

"Wanna talk about it?" he asked concerned. She shook her head as if she were afraid to speak. She took a long drink of coffee. He didn't think she'd answer. "I know it has to be hard for you to lose your people, but back to point. Your parents didn't teach you about being a witch growing up?"

She shook her head again then must have trusted her voice once more. "No, I was adopted."

"We need to speak to your adopted parents."

"No, you can't."

"Look we have to get to the bottom of this. You have ten to twenty years before you go completely mad."

"What do you mean go completely mad? Are you saying I will go crazy?" She jumped from her stool almost knocking it over and began pacing. "What is it that will make me crazy?" She paused in thought. "If I am what you say I am, and I am magic, isn't there something I could do to keep that from happening to me?

Don't they have some kind of potion they can take? She sat back down and stared at him. He noticed her shaking.

"Sorcerers have been trying healing spells for as long as I can remember and so far, nothing. If I were you, I'd be asking them about where you came from."

"Well, I can't do that because they are dead."

"Didn't they leave anything for you?"

"I have their home."

"Have you found anything that may help find your biological parents?"

"No, but I haven't looked either. I haven't touched my dad's study and my mother's room is still the way she left it. To tell you the truth I haven't had the time to go through anything, and I'm not sure I want to."

"Is it the time, or is it, you are afraid of what you might find? The only thing I can think of is that your powers could be bound. Heard of that once. Do you do anything unusual? Like make it rain?"

Her eyebrows shot up. "Make it rain?" She jumped from her seat again. "I don't chant and do any dances if that's what you're asking."

"If you're a true sorceress you don't need to."

She was quiet for a moment. "Well, there is this thing," she said shyly. "But I don't know how weird it is." She put her finger to her lip and sat back down.

"Try me. What thing?" he asked. He took a seat across from her and looked in her eyes seriously. She quickly broke his gaze and looked away.

She stared into her coffee as if all her answers lie at the bottom of her cup. "I get visions sometimes of things happening just before they happen."

"A seer?" he asked with surprise. "There hasn't been a seer that I know of in hundreds of years. They are extremely rare. Wow. Anything else. Sorcerers usually have three specialty powers."

"Nope, that's it. I always thought it was weird. I've never talked about it. I didn't want anyone to think I was crazy." Her face dropped and it appeared like she'd just lost her best friend.

"What?" He was beginning to feel sorry for her.

Her head snapped up and the determined look was back. "And now I am a wolf?" she asked.

"Yes," he said.

"I *am* crazy," she said squeezing her eyes shut.

"No, but you are my responsibility until I release you. I must teach you our ways. If there's ever a chance you could become wild, because some have, you will be put down."

"What do you mean wild?"

"As in, you are wolf more than not. You hunt a lot and humans are included. You break the laws."

"I'm all about protecting laws. What exactly are your laws?"

"You're in human form more than not. You hunt occasionally, mostly on a full moon cycle. You don't eat humans, and all the other laws that are also included in the human world, are in ours as well. Oh, you can never change a witch or warlock because it's an eventual death sentence for them."

"Oh, you mean like you surmise you did with me?"

"Accidents happen. I'll deal with it."

"But you saved my life. That should account for something."

"In all reality I should have let you die. I could have called for an ambulance, but you wouldn't have made it. You were close to being gone when I bit you."

"I guess I should thank you, then." She stood and held out her hand. "Names Kara Thomas. M.P. Sgt. Kara Thomas, honorably discharged after an accident."

He took her hand. "Well then. Hi, I'm Cain DeLucci. AD-8 TITAN. You were with Military Police, huh? Your expertise?"

"Criminal investigation, counter-terrorism, physical safety," she said as she took a sip of coffee.

"What happened? Where were you stationed? Ft. Leonard Wood?"

"I see you are familiar with the military, and that's a good guess. But I don't want to talk about it," she said with finality. "I work with the Denver Police Department now as a chief detective and my crew was killed in the blast."

"A little below your pay scale, I'd say."

"I like the job. I had people, and now they're dead, just like my partner. I should give up." She sighed, leaned her head back, and closed her eyes.

"It wasn't your fault there was a bomb in the place you were at. I think you were set up."

She quickly sat straight and looked at him. "Oh, I know I was. Damn informant. Everyone said he was reliable. I should have done more research on *him*."

"Check twice, I always say."

"I did. He's been giving us information for years. He's done some good work."

"It sounds like he was as set up as you were." He felt his cell vibrate against his chest. "Hey, hang on I gotta take this." He turned and pulled his cell from his jacket pocket.

"DeLucci." All right Christian, I'll be right there. Tell him I'll meet him at the site. " He hung up his phone and turned toward Kara. "That was my boss. I had to call in the explosion, and he wants me down at the site to meet with my partner, Stone. He calls me boss even though he's my partner. He's a dash five and I'm a dash eight so I'm always lead on investigations, and he has to listen to me. The ones with more seniority bring up the ones below them. That's how we partner at TITAN. Just so you know.

"The local P.D. shouldn't be involved in this case. How did you get ahold of it anyway? The ones responsible are too powerful for local P.D. You aren't equipped."

"Our informant. He said if we wanted to put a dent in the drug situation that we could catch a big fish at the warehouse at noon. He gave us the address. We didn't have a name. There was supposed to be some shipment of drugs in that old warehouse. There wasn't, just a bomb."

"You should have cased the place first," he said with a frown.

"What do you think we were doing?"

He went to grab the cups off the counter and evidently Kara had the same idea. She grabbed a cup, and he grabbed her hand. When he did, he felt a surge of warmth travel through him. A foreign feeling enveloped him, for a second, he transcended time and space, and it was just the two of them on the planet. The feeling frightened him, and he jerked his hand back.

At the same time Kara took a sharp breath. She picked up the cup and he noticed her hand shaking. Her being a half breed went through his mind and a door slammed shut on his feelings. He quickly stood back.

"I shouldn't be taking you with me, but I can't leave

you alone."

"I'm fine by myself, but I'm going with you, I *want* to go with you. I might be able to help. Besides I need to know about my crew, so just get over yourself."

He looked at her. "When we are finished, we are going to your place for clothes. You might want to get a haircut at some point. I also need to make sure P.D. is stopped from interfering in this case. I've been working on it too damn long to have the P.D. muck it all up. Three years I've got into this investigation."

"Three years and no bust?" she asked raising her eyebrows. "You should have him or them by now."

"It's bigger than you think. We are thorough. We want them all. We will get them all."

"How big?"

"West coast and evidently the east coast as well. There's someone very big involved and that's the guy I want. To hell with his pansies. They are a dime a dozen and easily replaced." He zipped up his jacket and went to his closet and pulled out another. He threw it at her. "Put that on, it's chilly out. Spring is always chilly."

"I enjoy the chilly weather," she said laying the jacket on a stool.

"Put-the-jacket-on," he said through his gritted teeth. "It's chilly."

She quickly picked it up and put it on. "Stop doing that to me. I hate taking nonsensical orders."

"Then do what I tell you as soon as I tell you."

She rolled her eyes then zipped up the jacket. "You really do have to get over yourself. You aren't as macho as you think."

"You don't know what I think.

"I know some, I heard your thoughts in the bedroom.

28

She gave him a quick smirk.

He ignored the comment. "Let's go," he said, as he threw open the door.

## Chapter Two

Kara stood at the edge of what was once the building. The morning was overcast, drizzling, and it was chilly out. It went with her mood. They found three bodies. Her crew. She was still feeling a bit crazy walking around in almost a daze. She couldn't believe she was now a wolf and a witch, but she couldn't dispute what had happened to her. Her mind was in a whirlwind as she tried to make sense of it all. She didn't sleep well. She couldn't quit thinking about it. She had paced the bedroom she was in back and forth all night. A foreign place to her. Nothing seemed right anymore. Her world had come crashing down and worse her parents were gone, and she had no one to talk to.

She was relying on a stranger. Someone she didn't know if she could trust or not. Strangely enough she found herself thinking she could. He seemed strong and she was attracted to that strength. Somehow it gave her courage. She glanced over at him and watched him speaking to the man that was his partner. She knew about TITAN, but not how it worked. She just knew the police, even the army seemed to bow down to them. The impression she got was that they were intelligent and good at what they did. They had to be good if they were TITAN. She caught enough words to know they were deep in conversation about the fire. Cain was gesturing with his arms and she supposed telling him his side of what happened. She thought about the people who died with sadness. She couldn't save them. If she had only had the vision sooner, perhaps they'd still be alive. She should be dead on this ground right along with them. Cain must have picked up her thoughts because he left his partner and came over to her.

"What do you remember about yesterday?" he asked.

"Not much to remember. We weren't here but fifteen minutes and the thing blew. Why?" She wasn't going to let this get the best of her, not this time. She'd taken on other jobs where she had been the hero. It wasn't until her fiancé that it put her in a mental state. She just wasn't going to let it happen again. She had tools now and she knew how to use them.

"Ansen Horn must have found out you had some information on him. He works that way. If anyone gets close, they end up dead."

"You're still alive."

"I'm smart. I have a lot of patience. I was following him yesterday and lost him off the main road. I pulled back and took to my wolf. I was just cresting the hill when I heard the explosion. Came as quick as my feet could get me here."

"I guess that was good for me. I need to report this to my department."

"Not about Horn, but the explosion they already know. I talked to my boss this morning while you were in the shower, and he said he'd talk to them and get them off the case."

"Did you mention me?"

"Yes, I didn't tell him everything. He knows you are wolf now and that you were burned over twenty-five percent of your body, and that I changed you to save your life, but I didn't mention you were a witch and I want to keep it that way for now. He said he'd get ahold of your department and let them know you resigned. At some point you will have to talk to them. They have orders to step away from this one."

"Hey," said Stone walking over. "Awful what happened here, huh? Those poor people burned to a crisp." He stopped a few feet from them, and Kara could feel his gaze as he looked her up and down. He finally spoke. "Who's this pretty lady?" he asked with a smile.

"This is Kara Thomas. She was here yesterday when this happened. I found her unconscious and burned. I turned her. Kara this is my partner, Stone."

Kara watched the change in Stone. He smiled wide and put his hand on her shoulder in a very friendly manner. The man was handsome she'd give him that, but she was in no mood to be flirted with, and she definitely got the impression he was doing just that.

"So very nice to meet such a pretty lady," he said.'

She held out her hand to shake, and when she did, she quickly moved out of his touch. "Mr. Stone," she said icily.

"Uh, just Stone."

Kara noticed his blush and thought maybe she'd hurt his feelings with her coldness. Maybe he was just being nice. She was definitely still jumpy and couldn't trust her instinct, so, she smiled and tried to rectify her rudeness. "So, just Stone, you are Cain's partner?"

"Technically my name's actually Domizio Ferrari, pronounced Doe-meet-see-o and Ferrari like the car, but Stone is what I go by, and technically Cain is my partner, but he's also my boss. He's dash eight, and I'm dash five.

He's lead on all investigations…and you don't need to know all that. Nice to meet you."

"Nice to meet you too, Stone. Did you find anything here that might help?"

"No, I just got here seconds before you both did. Christian told me very little of what happened. They were taking the bodies away when I got here. I did find this." He stepped up to Cain and handed him something small. "Isn't it a kind of a pagan sigil?"

Cain took the small piece of punched metal and looked at it closely. "Sure is." He handed it to her. "Do you know anything about this?"

"I told you, I know nothing about pagan practices." She grabbed it from his hand. Before she could look at it her eyes rolled back, and she had a very sick feeling go through her. It was so quick Cain didn't catch it. She quickly gave it back to him, her hand a little shaky. "I have no idea what it is."

She didn't know what she felt, and she never wanted to feel it again, but she did want to know what it was. She watched as the two men walked away from her. She glanced over at Cain who was now standing beside Stone talking in low tones.

She looked at the two men side by side. Cain was dark with dark arched brows over the most beautiful honey golden eyes she had ever seen. He had high strong cheekbones, and a square chin with a dimple in the middle. He had a curl over his left brow and every once and awhile he'd unconsciously push it out of the way. His thick dark hair just curled over the top of his ears and around his collar. He was taller than Stone and a might bigger.

Alone, Stone looked like a linebacker himself. He

had blonde hair, cropped short, blue eyes and she supposed he was handsome to look at. They were both striking in opposite ways, but she thought Cain was by far the most handsome of the two. Perhaps it was the testosterone he put off. His high energy was almost tangible and electric. She had to admit to herself, he was damn macho.

She wasn't going to tell him though; she knew it'd go to his head. She supposed a lot of women told him he looked good. She knew the two of them could walk into a bar alone and leave with whoever they wanted without even trying. She wasn't going to be one of those women.

"I don't envy you taking on a newbie, Cain. I understand why you did it, but there will be consequences. You're not supposed to change anyone so close to a full moon and without planning it."

"I didn't plan it, Stone, damn it," Cain spit out. "It happened. You don't need to tell me there will be repercussions."

"Hey, 'her' is right here, don't talk about me as if I'm not."

"So, you know there's rules for wolves?" asked Stone.

"I was perfectly happy just being a regular 'ol human being doing human being things. I didn't know any of this existed until this morning. I didn't know what was happening to me yesterday other than I was in excruciating pain. The burns, my blood, my bones, I wished I was dead."

"It can make you feel that way," said Stone. "I bet you feel different now."

"I feel like I could conquer the world," she said, smiling.

"You haven't let her run free as wolf yet, have you?" Stone turned toward Cain.

"No, not yet."

"You better acquaint her with it before the full moon or you'll have your hands full."

Cain rolled his eyes. "You don't need to tell me my duties as sire, Stone. I know what needs to be done."

"No, I don't, you're right. I'm wrapping up here and leaving. Sounds like you have a lot on your plate for the next month or so. When are you going to report what you've done?"

"Not until I have to… And Stone…"

"Yeah," Stone turned back around.

"Don't you mention it to anyone either. I already told Christian, but I just don't want it out there yet."

"You're the boss, boss," he said with a salute. Stone jumped in his SUV and she and Cain got in his car and started it.

"I meant to tell you. I like your car. '64?"

"Yep, my baby. This thing will shit and git."

"I've never heard that one before. I had a '67 Chevelle once. She was my baby. Now, she would shit and git."

He laughed. "Wow, she knows about classic cars."

"Women have been known to appreciate fine cars." She smiled up at him. He caught her grin and smiled back. She quite enjoyed his little lopsided grin. It made her feel warm inside. His golden eyes sparkled with a mischievousness which made her giggle. She quickly squelched her thoughts because she knew she had to keep her distance from him. He didn't care to be close to someone who might go crazy in ten years. She sighed.

She blew off men long ago anyway, her partner in

the army being killed just reinforced her commitment. She never wanted to feel such pain again and she wouldn't. She did not want a man, not now, not ever. They were just too complicated, and she didn't care for games. She turned and stared out the window. It seemed like it took forever but they finally made it back to main roads.

"I live just west of Denver at the edge of the mountains on Clear Creek just three miles off the Lariot Loop. My parents have a small ranch there."

"That's where we are headed," he said. He pulled onto I-25 South and sped up.

After a few seconds of awkward quiet she turned to Cain still trying to wrap her head around what happened to her. She wasn't sure she wasn't still in shock over it. "I'm not sure how this has happened to me, but I need some answers. I don't know anything about being a witch and I never knew a human could be turned into a wolf. How the hell does that happen? Why does one go crazy after ten to twenty years? Is there a reason for it?"

He slowed the car and glanced over at her. "We believe it has to do with the mixing of blood. There's an inoculation given to changed witches or warlocks to help slow the process down, but so far there is no cure. It doubles the life span. Ergo the possibility of twenty years instead of ten. It's almost a guaranteed ten without it. That's the best anyone's come up with. We should make an appointment as soon as possible. It doesn't really matter when you get the shot in the ten years, but I believe the sooner the better."

"I've been thinking about it since you told me. Something doesn't sit right with me about it."

"What do you mean?"

"You can change a human into a Lycan with no fear of it happening to them, correct?"

"That's right. Go on."

"It has to do with blood. My blood is as human as any other human's blood. I'm O-negative, a little rare, but still a common blood type. It just seems strange to me."

"Well, I'm not a doctor so I couldn't say one way or another. History proves that eventually a turned witch or warlock will go mad after ten to twenty years of being bitten by a wolf. When it happens, they must be put down. The only way to do that since the wolf is so strong and heals easily, is a silver bullet through the heart. We can also die by chopping off our head, but that's a little messy. When they become mad, they become very dangerous to everyone."

"Have you...have you had to put anyone down because they went crazy?"

"There's a special squad for it. I couldn't do it. I've had to kill before in my line of work, but I've never had to do an execution."

"There's no medicine to help with the symptoms?"

"Like I said, there's an inoculation you can get that is to help prolong your mental stability, but no cure."

"Why change them at all then?" She was getting confused.

"There is a law against it, however, as in your case you were about to die, that is the one and only exception and there's still pros and cons about it. I could have let you die, but I had the ability to do something about it, so I did. The only thing I did was prolong your life for ten to twenty years."

"What's the average life span of the wolf?"

"About five hundred years give or take a few. Some have lived as long as eight hundred years, but it's rare." He glanced at the signs above the freeway. "Is this our exit coming up?"

"Yes, take it and head west. It's not far, maybe nine or ten miles from here."

He did as he was told, and they drove for a bit. There was a large steel building going up with a sign, *Future home of Dalton Memorial Hospital*. "Wow, another building for Reid Dalton. I swear that man is made of money," said Cain.

"He does a great deal for Denver I have to admit. I think he owns more than half of the city. He is donating the land for the hospital and he's sinking a great deal of his own money in it. I see his name in the paper at least once a week for something he is doing. Great guy."

"Didn't he just finish a project downtown? He fixed one of the old brick buildings up and turned it into a public library?"

"Yes, Dalton Library, then there is Dalton Elementary School, Dalton Middle School, Dalton High, there's also all the Dalton Pharmaceutical Companies he owns around the world and I'm sure there are more, I just don't remember all of them. I think that's how he made all his money."

"Hmm, that gives me an idea. I think I should plan a visit with Mr. Reid Dalton. He seems to have a great deal of influence over the city. Perhaps he can help me find the one in charge of the drug and gun running problem I've been working on. That is if I can get the busy man to find time to meet with me."

After being up all night and going back and forth about what happened she was still nervous. Her mind kept going back to it. He seemed to notice.

"Are you okay?"

She was trying to keep it together and she thought she was at least on the outside, but Cain wasn't buying it.

She watched his face go from passive to concerned so she answered truthfully. "No, I'm not okay. You tell me I am witch and also a wolf and because of it I am doomed to go crazy in ten years. Do you know the sound of it is ludicrous? If someone would have told me this was possible yesterday, I would have had them committed. It's going to take me a bit to let it all sink in." Her voice rose and she was ready to fall to pieces again, so she immediately went to her quiet place to calm her nerves. She clenched her fist and looked out the window.

"Look, I know it's a lot to take in. Eventually you will come to terms with it, hopefully sooner rather than later. You have to because during the full moon you become wolf whether you want to or not. I will try and help you process it, so if you need to talk or anything? I do understand how you feel because I remember what it was like for me to find out. Although in your case you weren't told about it before you changed. It's not bad what's happened to you, and eventually you will accept it, perhaps even be glad."

She felt the tears well in the back of her eyes. She quickly shut down the conversation. She couldn't talk about it anymore, not and keep it together. She wanted to talk about other things to keep her mind off what had happened to her. "The first dirt road you come to take it to the right," she mumbled.

"It's pretty back this way. I don't think I've been out this way in a long time. You say you're on the river?"

"Yes, our property runs along both sides of it. There's fifty acres."

"Nice," said Cain.

"Yes, it is. Here we are, that's our drive."

He drove slowly down the long driveway, and they came to a two-story large white Victorian farmhouse with a large front porch nestled amongst some trees.

\*\*\*\*

"Nice place. Big house."

"I love it. It's filled with antiques that have been handed down through the family. This place has been in the Thomas family for three generations. The first generation built it. I am the fourth to own it." She suddenly became quiet.

"What's the matter?" Concern etched his brow. He felt like he was walking on broken glass, one wrong move or comment might send her right back into hysteria and he just couldn't deal with that right now. He waited her out giving her room to tell him things at her own pace.

"I was adopted. I've always known that, but I have no idea who my biological parents are."

"Perhaps we can find some clues. I'd be happy to go through your father's study to help you find anything that might help."

"You don't need to do that." She frowned.

"Look, I have to stay stuck like glue to you until I am sure I can release you. It's a serious matter becoming wolf and it takes a very strong person to control their wolf."

"When do I turn into wolf?"

"Tonight, I will take you to the forest and you will learn to properly hunt. If we run into any humans, you better hope you are strong enough to control your wolf and not attack or eat them. You will learn how to read energy halos, learn different scents, and how to hunt and track."

"Like I told you before, I don't eat meat, I'm vegan."

He snorted. "You'll eat meat. Our job right now is to get you some clothes, look through your father's study, and hopefully find out why your powers are bound. Someone went to a lot of trouble to bind them, you are, what…twenty-five, thirty, and you never knew you had them, not to mention neither did anyone else. Well, perhaps your adopted parents. Were they sorcerers? Did they ever do anything that seemed unbelievable to you?" Did she really know nothing about her background? The idea was strange to him, but he believed her. He'd never run across any wolf or witch who didn't know at least something. This was just getting stranger and stranger. He would give her the benefit of the doubt for now.

"Not that I know of. I never saw either one of them do anything out of the ordinary. I'll be thirty in a few months. When I told my parents that I could see things sometimes before they happened, they told me to keep it quiet and never mention it to anyone, so I never did. They didn't seem surprised. I was very young when this began happening to me. I don't have any control over it, but it happens. Usually, it is when something bad is about to happen."

"Have you been able to thwart disaster?"

"Not on important things. I never had enough time to do anything to change the circumstances. My partner in the army was killed, and I couldn't stop it. My crew was just blown up, and I couldn't stop it. What good are having visions if I can't do anything to stop what's about to happen?"

"If your powers weren't bound and you had proper teaching you could learn to control those visions and how to bring them on." He paused, chewing his bottom lip. "So, you actually saw the explosion before it happened?"

"Yes, just a few seconds before the building blew up. I only had time to run and yell for everyone to get out. Didn't do any good, though."

"Don't beat yourself up, it wasn't your fault. These people we've been watching are cunning and smart. So far, they've stayed one step ahead of me. I've been putting this together for the last three years and I won't stop until I have everyone."

"You say you belong to the TITANs? What does that stand for?"

"Tactic, Intelligence, Target, and Neutralize. We are the law enforcement of the supernatural kind."

"Sounds like a military group or a type of SWAT team."

"Sometimes we are called in to aid either SWAT or the FBI. With your military experience you could probably hire on. I'm sure you are intelligent as well as in good shape."

"Well, thanks for noticing, I think. Not sure I want to join, I'm not sure I should with my track record."

"I don't know what happened to your partner in the army, but I can say the bombing that took your crew was not your fault."

"No matter how you paint the picture, Cain, it remains the same. I was their captain and the only survivor. I should be dead with my crew."

"But you aren't, so like I said before, don't beat yourself up. Shit happens to the best of us."

"Easy for you to say, you are a man. It's hard for a woman to work her way up in a man's world."

"I'd say it's getting better all the time." He shut the engine down, opened his door, got out, went around, and opened her door. "Come on, we've work to do."

She saluted him and got out. She pulled her keys from her purse and let him in through the front door.

Once inside he let out a large breath. "Wow, nice antiques," he said looking about the foyer. There was a large stairway leading upstairs, dark wood banister, a closet under the stairs for coats.

A walnut stand stood under a carved walnut framed mirror, two hand carved mahogany Victorian style chairs, and a long, oval, colorful, handwoven rug over highly polished wide plank oak wood floors.

"I really like this place. I always liked old Victorian style and antiques."

"I do too. Follow me to the kitchen and I'll put on some coffee."

They passed through a dining room that had a ten-foot mahogany table with six matching chairs. There was a fireplace on one wall, the other wall held walnut drawers and doors with beveled glass. The same glass and shelves framed the French doors leading into the great room. Beside the fireplace was another pocket door that led into the kitchen. He followed her into the kitchen.

It was a large country kitchen with a bay window at the end and a round oak clawfoot table and four chairs in front of it. The numerous all wood cabinets went to the ceiling. Left of the oak table was another door. Cain was impressed with all the natural wood finishes. "No paint on the cabinets, I like that," said Cain. She walked through the door beside the table, and he followed her into a butler's pantry holding more built-in shelves and drawers over a long counter. She retrieved coffee, sugar, and cream from a second fridge.

Opposite the door was another that led onto a large back porch. Cain stood there in the doorway and glanced into the porch. There were hooks for coats and an old church pew beside the door which sat under a set of double windows, where one could sit and put on or remove shoes and boots.

He glanced over the cubbies for boots and over at the windows beside the back door. "I could get lost in a place like this," said Cain. "I've always appreciated natural wood and how it looks. Nowadays everyone paints everything. It's nice to see it like this. I like that the rooms seem so spacious as well.

Kara chuckled "If you like this part of the house, then you'll really enjoy the rest of it." She set about making coffee and after she had it on, she went to the counter where there was a large cookie jar in the shape of a chicken. She removed its head, grabbed about a dozen cookies, and set them on a plate. "I don't know about you, but I could use a good dose of sugar."

"Going through a change makes you very hungry. If you think you are hungry for sugar now wait until tonight when you'll be hungry for meat…I know, I know, you are vegan, you don't eat meat." He grinned widely. He knew she was going to eat meat, it was inevitable. Wolves needed it in their diet regardless.

"While this is brewing, I'll go pack some things, you are welcome to come along if you like."

"I like. Lead the way."

She led him through to the back porch where there was a secondary staircase going upstairs, it wasn't open like the other one. She opened another door off the back porch. "This is where the maid slept." He glanced inside the large room with two windows. Not bad he thought. They continued on, she closed the door, began going up the steps, and he followed.

Once upstairs there was a long hallway. On one wall there were paintings of family members. He looked at everything with interest. Against the other wall were more delicate antique tables with chairs beside them and mirrors above them. She walked further and he followed her to the third door down. They walked into a large bedroom holding a four-poster bed, two matching dressers, and a row of nicely decorated windows with window seats underneath.

Kara went and pulled a suitcase from under the bed, went to the dresser and began taking things out. He didn't pay attention to what she was gathering, instead he went to the window and pulled back the sheer and looked outside. He could see the river from the second floor and an assortment of trees.

He gazed out over oak, hawthorn, tree lilac, and hornbeam, and some scattered aspen. Down a small path was a large red barn. "You've had a good life here," he said turning toward her.

She had her hands still in a drawer and stopped what she was doing to glance at him. "Yes, I suppose I did. At least I have no complaints. As a child I rode horses, swam in the river, and climbed trees. I had a great childhood here. I just wish I knew more about my background. Especially since you tell me I'm not only a wolf now, but I'm also a witch."

"I have friends who are such. They are great people, and they do amazing things. You should be proud of who you are and what you're capable of."

"I get the picture." She threw a couple sweaters in her suitcase with the rest of the stuff and forcefully closed the lid. She picked it up and he took it from her. "I can carry my own suitcase," she said with a frown.

"You're welcome." He headed for the door. "Anything else you need to take?"

"How long will I be at your place?"

"As long as it takes. We can always come back for more if you have need."

They went down the main staircase and he set her suitcase near the door. "Now, how about that cup of coffee and let's go see what we can find in your father's study."

\*\*\*\*

After they each had a mug full of coffee, she said, "Follow me." She wasn't sure she wanted to see her father's study. She hadn't been in there since they died. Her heart started racing the closer they got. They walked down a hall and into his room. There was a large picture window with a large solid oak desk in front of it, floor to ceiling books, a spiral stair that led to a second story loft filled with books. There was also a stone fireplace and a couple of overstuffed recliners with another antique table in between.

"I can see why this is his study. This is better than a man cave. I can almost smell a good Cuban cigar."

"He smoked in here. Mom wouldn't let him smoke any other place in the house. This room always smells of Cuban cigars and brandy. He loved good brandy."

"I say we check the desk first for any clues." He tried to open a drawer and it stuck. Kara walked over to a silver box, pulled out a key and opened the center drawer which allowed the other drawers to open. "That was handy," he said. "I'll start on this side you start on that one."

Her heart calmed down and she found it wasn't as bad as she thought. Actually, she was more excited at the prospect of finding out anything that might tell her something about herself. She began pulling stuff out of the drawers.

There was a large file of paid bills, letters from an old war buddy, letters from relatives, old newspaper clippings, and other various papers. There was a carved box that held a pocketknife, and an old pocket watch with the initials D.T. for Darrell Thomas, her adopted father.

"I remember playing with this watch when I was a little girl. I especially loved the winter with the snow-covered hills and trees outside. Inside there'd be a fire in the fireplace, and he would be smoking his Cuban cigar and sipping brandy." She closed her eyes for a second. "I can almost smell the cigar and his warm brandy breath."

She could see the flicker of flames from the fireplace in his glasses as he chuckled at her. Her eyes welled with tears. This was why she didn't want to go through their things. It hurt like hell to know they were gone.

"There has to be something here," said Cain. "Something you should know. I feel it. Where would he keep secret papers, important ones?"

She wiped a tear from her eye before he could see, then turned toward him and cleared her throat. "Well, there is a safe."

"Why didn't you say so?"

"Because you wanted to look in his desk." She got up and went to a wall that had a painting of a waterfall and deer drinking from a river and removed it. Behind it was a safe.

"Great, it's not combination. Where's the key?"

"I don't know. I never saw him open it."

He started looking at the sides of the drawers of his desk, pulling them as far out as they would go. Nothing.

"Wait, that reminds me. I did see him under the middle drawer one day and asked what he was doing. He said someday I'd have to do the same. I thought it weird at the time but look under the middle drawer."

He moved his hand under the drawer then stopped. "There is something under here." He pulled the drawer out and emptied the contents then turned it over. On the bottom was a stapled envelope and inside was a key. "Viola!" he said.

He went to the safe and opened it. Inside were some papers and a book. He pulled it all out and set it on the desk. "This is definitely meant for you."

She looked at the book. "Humm, *The Oracles*." She opened it and leafed through it. "It seems to be a book of spells."

"Here's a letter to you."

She opened it up and noticed her hands were shaking.

*My Dearest Kara,*

*If you are reading this, then I'm gone, and it's before your thirtieth birthday. It's up to you to carry on. Your powers are bound for a reason, and that's to keep him from finding you. There is a prophesy involving you.*

*It comes from your biological grandmother and yes we knew of her and of your mother. We knew a great deal but couldn't tell you, even now as you read this, I won't mention who he is because of his power. You must figure it out for it will prepare you for what you must do. He mustn't know about you until its time, because of his power. You may be of his blood, but you are also the only one who can stop him. Perhaps I am saying too much, but I also feel the need to help you. It's been hard knowing what you are and not telling you, but it was the only way to keep you safe.*

*You must stop him.*

*Become familiar with the book of spells, learn them. We've gone to great lengths to keep you secret. Your aunt gave her life so you may live, and your mother lost hers in giving birth to you. You have a job to do.*

*Your mother and I could never tell you what to do, but we were thrilled when you joined the military police. The training will surely help you.*

*Good luck and know even though you were adopted by us, we've always thought of you as our daughter. We love you very much and could not be prouder of you.*

*Love, dad*

"What in the Sam hell does this mean? Who's he? Why all the nonsensical parables?"

"Well, it's as plain as the nose on your face your adopted father couldn't tell you. Whoever *he* is, he's powerful. Perhaps *The Oracles* has an answer, at least for what you are holding in your hands."

She went through the book a little more slowly, turning page after page. She flipped fast until she hit the last page. On the back cover there was another note taped to the inside back of the hard cover. She pulled it free and carefully opened it.

*To an end…* (it began)
*On a clear dark night*
*As the full moon wanes*
*Greed and evil*
*runs through your veins*
*By the silver light*
*of an ending moon*
*Silver from a furry hand*
*Shall stop you soon*
*Tis blood of your blood*
*Be wary and fright*
*For in the dark shadows*
*Your life ends this night.*
*So, mote it be…*
*So, mote it be…*
*So, mote it be…*

Cain was looking over her shoulder and reading what she was looking at. "It appears to be some sort of spell, or prophesy."

"Why is it taped here? It's so yellow and the handwriting so shaky. How old do you think this is?"

"Judging by the color of the paper, it's very old."

"What do you think it means?"

He scratched his head. "It's so vague, but if I had to guess, I think it is meant for you but about someone else. If you combine this prophesy with the note from your father, I believe you are meant to stop someone very powerful."

"Who? Who am I supposed to stop? Stop from what?" She felt her heart racing once again.

"Hmmm. He leaned back against the desk and crossed his legs. He closed his eyes and tapped his chin with his forefinger. His eyes snapped open. "Blood of his blood…Blood of his blood. I would say you need to stop your biological somebody. Uncle, father, brother. I don't know. Whoever *he* is."

"Well, don't you think I need to know. I don't know anyone I'm biologically connected to," she squealed. She went to the safe. "There aren't any more papers in here. There are no adoption papers. There's nothing." She ran her hand to the back of the safe and ran into something. She put her hand around it and pulled it out.

"What did you find?" He walked up to her.

She opened her hand and in it was a silver bullet. "Why is this in here?"

"I don't know, but I'd say it's pretty important. Let me see it."

She handed it to him. "It's a silver bullet."

"It looks like an executioner bullet. Why is it in the safe? There has to be a good reason. This is so strange. There is no number on it. There should be a number. What a puzzle."

"I don't like games. I detest them."

"I don't think this is a game, Kara. I think your adopted father would have told you if he could have. Didn't you see? He could scry and find out about you. That tells me he is a sorcerer and a very powerful one. That's a start. You are supposed to be kept a secret. I would say by the prophesy you are the only one who can stop him. This is bizarre."

"Another seer?"

"Well, the way I understand seers is they run in families. I think because you are a seer, there is someone in your family who was one. But I heard the last one died off a couple hundred years ago and there hasn't been one since. Until you. They are rare."

Who's him?"

"I think that is what you are supposed to find out. Bring the spell book with you. For now, let's put this bullet and the letter from your father back in the safe. I need to think on the bullet for a bit and figure out what we should do about it. No one should have a bullet like this, they are kept under lock and key, and only an executioner can have possession of one. They are also numbered so they can be kept track of. Another mystery. Anyway, it will be safer in the safe for now. We can come back if we need to."

"No, put the bullet in your pocket. I don't know why, just don't leave it behind."

He looked at her with a confused look. "Do you know something?"

"No, just a hunch. I don't feel right leaving it behind. Sometimes I get hunches and I'm getting one now. Before there was the explosion and before I had a vision of it blowing up, I had a hunch. The whole thing didn't feel right to me, and I should've listened to my gut. I guess that's where I failed."

"I believe hunches can be as powerful as any sight you may have." He sighed and stared at her. "That's why you should have been taught since you were young. All right then. Did you say you wanted to go through your mother's room?"

"Yeah, but I'll go through it another time."

"We can do it now if you want."

"No, I have things to process. I think this is all my heart can handle in one day. I'll do it another time."

"Okay, then, let's head back. It's getting late and I need to take you out as wolf."

"That's what I'm afraid of."

"Of being wolf? It's quite freeing and nice. I think you'll enjoy being wolf."

"It's not that, it's about eating meat."

He grinned. "I see."

Then she couldn't believe it, he actually had the audacity to snicker.

Chapter Three

Kara sat nervously while Cain drove his SUV further up the mountain and pulled into a small clearing behind some trees. "This is where I like to come and let my wolf out. There are hardly any people who come through here. Sometimes I run into a few, but this is the best place for you to experience your wolf. Signs in the area prohibit camping during a full moon. That helps. When you change, I want you to stay close to me and not take off, I need to keep an eye on you."

"I told you, I won't kill any animals, nor will I eat the meat."

"Yeah, and I'm tired of hearing it." He threw it in park and opened his door. He climbed out and so did she before he could go around and open the door for her. She was excited, but at the same time reticent. She couldn't bear the thought of killing any little wild creatures.

"When you are wolf you become primal. The wildness takes over and you must learn to control it and not let it control you. Remember that. It will be hard."

"Yeah, yeah, you mentioned it a hundred times. You forget I was wolf at your house even if it was only for a few moments. I didn't try and eat your face off then."

"Don't get smart. You just went through your change you didn't have time to let the wolf sink in, nor the energy for it. Besides I didn't give you time."

He opened his trunk and pulled out two duffel bags

and threw one to her. "You'll put your clothes in there."

"I am not stripping down to my underwear out here in the woods in front of you."

"No, you'll remove that too" He sighed as he nonchalantly undid the zipper to his jeans.

She caught a patch of dark hair leading down like an arrow and caught herself staring at him. She realized what she was doing, felt the blood rush to her face, and quickly turned her head. "This is crazy."

"No crazier than you being a witch and not knowing about it. Your underwear too, unless you want them torn to shreds, then you won't have anything to put back on when we are finished."

"You can change into wolf while you're dressed?" she asked glancing back at him. "You to...took all your clothes off," she stammered. She couldn't help it she looked the full length of him and noticed what a fine specimen of a man he was. She quickly looked away. She felt the heat rise in her cheeks and knew by the feel they had to have turned crimson. This man stood naked in front of her like it was no big deal. Perhaps to a wolf it wasn't. She didn't know whether she should be insulted or if this was natural. Well she wasn't carved from that kind of cloth so refused to look at him.

"Yes, I did, and so will you. You can change into wolf while dressed, but you'll rip whatever you're wearing to shreds. I won't watch, just get undressed and put your clothes in the duffel and throw it in the back. I'll lock up when you are finished." He turned away.

Perhaps he did have a sense of dignity after all. She moved to the other side of the vehicle and undressed and did as she was told. Glancing over the top of the car to check and make sure he wasn't watching. He wasn't.

"I'm ready."

"Remember stay by me. We can communicate telepathically once you change. I can command you as human and we can join thoughts, but humans usually erect a wall around their thoughts. If you run into a wild wolf you might find their thoughts broken, like pictures really. You will be able to communicate with them as well but not command one. Once you learn more about yourself you will be able to command them as a human. You'll learn."

"Why teach me at all when someone is only going to execute me in ten to twenty years."

"Enjoy what time you have, Kara. It's all any of us can ask for. I don't mind taking the time to teach you."

"I'm sorry, that was a childish remark on my part. I guess I'm feeling sorry for myself. I don't know how to act, what to think, I don't know what I believe in anymore. I want to scream but I'm afraid if I do, I will fall apart at the seams. I'm holding on to a thread of sanity and it's unraveling as we speak."

"That's okay, you're allowed. I think I know what you are going through. It's a great deal to take in on such short notice. I will be with you all the way. " He smiled, and her heart melted. "You're doing quite well, considering"

She liked his smile...a lot. "Thank you." She was still nervous and shaky, but she put on a front. She had to learn and get through this. She couldn't fall apart.

"Say the words that call forth your wolf."

"*Mutatis Mutandis*," she whispered. She felt the heat in her veins first, then her bones began to reshape themselves. It wasn't near as painful as the first time, in fact she was quite surprised. The pain hit, but it didn't last long at all. It seemed just when she recognized the pain it went away. She could handle that. Not near as bad as she first thought it would be. She felt herself become shorter and her jaw elongate. Hair sprouted from her skin and then she was on four paws. She raised her head and howled, and for some reason it felt okay. For all of her surprise, this seemed right.

He repeated the words and changed a bit quicker than she did. *"Look carefully at your surroundings. You have an inner eyelid you can drop. Do that."*

She blinked a couple of times then thought she felt what he was talking about. *"I think I have it."*

*"Do you see the halos of other animals left behind?"*

*"That's what the streams of light are?"*

*"Yes, focus, you'll be able to tell which animals have come through here. In due time you will be able to tell how long ago each animal traveled through and what they are. You can begin to hunt that way. Breathe deep."*

She did and smells inundated her. She could smell water, the earth, rabbit, and deer, even the water in the air. She found it fascinating. She could vaguely smell the different animals She raised her head and howled again. He did the same.

It was getting dark, but she could see as if it were day. She was amazed at how good her sight was. She glanced at Cain, then did a double take. He was absolutely beautiful as a wolf. The largest canine she'd ever seen, striking yellow eyes, and a thick shiny black coat with a silver stripe down his back. It must be what she looked like. He did say she was a Silver Sable like him. *"You look good as wolf."*

*"So, do you. Are you ready to hunt?"*

She didn't catch the last part because she caught site

of a rabbit in the bush. Excitement ran through her and she pounced. She scared the rabbit out and it took off, and so did she. The chase was on. She wasn't paying attention to Cain anymore. She completely forgot about him as she ran through the trees. She completely forgot about being in shock. She was different. She was wolf. She caught site of a deer across the brook, and she forgot about the rabbit and headed after it.

She was so excited she didn't know what she wanted to do. She wanted to do everything. She wanted to chase everything. Deer were much faster than rabbits and chasing them was more fun. She was having the best time of her life and she laughed inside her mind. For the first time since her fiancé was killed, she was enjoying herself.

She could smell the fear on the deer, and it triggered something in her. It was a strange sensation to be able to smell fear, but she knew that's what it was. She was anxious, happy, excited and...what? Then she realized, she was hungry.

In fact, she was downright famished, starved for meat. She was no longer thinking vegan. She could smell the blood of the deer and she could hear the blood pump through its veins, and it seemed natural to her. She could feel the saliva drip from her jaws as the hunger took over, the muscles in her legs bunched, and she leaped toward the deer. It reared up, turned, and took off. She ran after it, completely forgetting that Cain even existed.

She followed the deer leaping over a fallen tree and through the river. She jumped over a couple of squirrels barely catching a whiff of them. She was focused on the deer, the kill, and the meat. It went one way as she veered another so she could head it off. She saw a thicket just ahead and came upon its flank steering it toward the large thick brush. The deer was quick and avoided getting caught in the trees, turning on a dime and leaping over her.

Damn the thing was quick as lightning, something she wasn't expecting. It ran through the river and slowed them both down. They came to a clearing, and it took off with phenomenal speed, but she wouldn't let it get away. They were in a thick forest but there were paths they could take, animal paths. She saw a number of trees ahead that made a U shape and the perfect place to guide it. The woods were dense, but the patch of trees formed a great natural trap. She was gaining on the deer now.

She lurched and managed to bite its hind leg, but it didn't stop. It came around like she thought it would and she leaped into the air and latched onto its neck. It was all pure instinct.

She heard it bay as she took it to the ground. She sank her teeth deep and the blood ran over her tongue and fueled her for more. The smell of blood reached her nostrils and she bit down again. Hunger etched her stomach, she was wolf, she was primal. The deer thrashed, but she held on.

Pure adrenaline pumped through her veins, her sight acute, her olfactory senses heightened. All her senses were as sharp as a razor blade. She felt unstoppable. She ripped at the flesh in its neck until it bled to death. Then she dropped it to the ground. She didn't have to stop and think of where to go on the deer she knew. She was famished and quickly pulled the meat away with her teeth and eating as quickly as she could, swallowing blood, meat, and even bone.

She thought she'd feel disgust at taking the life of an

animal, but instead she understood. Suddenly Cain was beside her. He sat quietly watching her and she glanced at him and growled loudly.

*"I'm not going to interrupt your meal."*

Civil words to a wild mind. They sunk in and sobered her. She realized how she must appear to him. Like a wild animal.

*"Right now, you are a wild animal."*

She narrowed her eyes. *"I'll share. Come, you are welcome to share this with me."* She instinctively knew this was proper wolf etiquette to invite another wolf to join in the meal. She understood if he were to kill the deer, she couldn't eat without being invited, especially since he was an alpha. Wolves were very smart. They were very civilized toward each other and communicated well. Wolves had a hierarchy the alpha the head of it all. It wasn't words they sent to each other, more like images. There were rules and she was learning them. It was amazing. Cain was right, this felt very freeing, very wild, very exciting. She loved being wolf. It was like she had woken from a very long sleep and was now finally alive. As if she'd been reborn. She glanced again at Cain still sitting patiently. *"Come eat with me."*

*"It's nice of you to offer."* She knew he was making sure it was what she wanted. He joined her and together they made a meal of the young doe. When they were both sated, Cain ran to the river and buried his face in the water. She followed suit. *"Even wolves like to stay clean."*

She understood. *"It is so other wild animals don't smell the blood on us, right?"*

*"You're learning."*

She heard snarling behind her, and she glanced

back. Other wolves were making a meal of what they left behind. *"Hey."* She growled.

*"Leave them, Kara. They are wolf all the time. Let them eat. They are hungry."*

She felt selfish and put in her place, but it was short lived. She found she wanted to run more, so she took off running higher up the mountain. She chased a few rabbits but felt no hunger, just playful.

She sniffed around in the bushes and smelled a ground mole. She could hear it digging underground. It felt like an invitation. She dug frantically in the dirt until it was uncovered, and it quickly dug back down. She let it go because she wanted to run some more. She loved this play. Hide and seek of the wolf kind. She heard Cain behind her snicker in his head. He'd read her thoughts. She thought it would be fun to try and lose him. She knew he heard her thought because she caught the whisper of him laughing. She took off running.

She dodged behind trees and hid behind rocks. Hide, sprint, then run. When he found her, she yipped, startling herself. He laughed in his head and her own laughter bubbled through her. He was enjoying this cat and mouse game as much as she was. She followed alongside the river for quite a distance then took off toward higher ground. She must have gone a mile when she smelled something in the air.

She came around a rock outcropping and into a clearing with a small firepit and a tent. Beside the fire sat two men eating with their fishing gear by their side. She smelled the fire, and it triggered a deep fear in her.

Then she smelled the humans. They smelled good. Their blood smelled sweet, and she wanted to taste it more than anything. She wanted to taste them...no she had to. She crouched low, then sprung.

They saw her just as she leaped. She made it midair when she was hit in the side and taken to the ground, the air knocked out of her. She glanced at the object that hit her. It was Cain and he was not happy. He growled at her and bit her shoulder hard.

One of the men had a rifle and she felt the shot before she heard it. A bullet hit her in the shoulder.

Cain pulled her into the bushes. *"Does anything feel broken?"*

She stepped down hard trying to see what hurt. *"No, but my shoulder hurts."*

*"Of course, it hurts. Don't pay attention to the pain and run back down the mountain. Now!"*

The command struck hard in her mind, and she took off running. She felt frightened, scared out of her wits, so she ran hard. She feared the men, and she feared Cain. She could feel the stabbing pain in her shoulder but did not slow down.

Cain was right behind her. She kept going until they reached their vehicle. When she got close to it she dropped to the ground panting. She'd lost some blood and the pain in her shoulder was excruciating.

Cain came up behind her and commanded her to say the words that would change her back.

*"Mutatis Mutandis,"* she thought, and felt herself go through the change. She lay on the ground naked. Cain said the words and quickly got the key from under a rock, he opened the back and pulled the two duffel bags out. He leaned down and inspected her shoulder. "You idiot you could have been seriously hurt. Didn't I warn you about humans? You were supposed to avoid them at all cost for this very reason. Do you realize you could have

killed one of them? Or both? It's the part of the wild you have to learn to control and tonight you failed miserably."

"My shoulder," she whined.

He looked it over, then turned her and looked at her back. "It looks like a twenty-two, there's no exit wound, so it's probably lodged in a bone. Yes, it's going to be sore, hurt like a son of a bitch, but being a Lycan you will heal. Your body should push the bullet out as you heal." To show her what he meant he pinched her shoulder where the bullet was, and she screamed out.

"Why the hell did you do that?"

"Because you were being stupid. Let this be a lesson and I mean it in more ways than one.

"I can feel my body working on pushing it out. It burns." She completely ignored what he said about humans. She changed the subject completely. "I ate meat. She closed her eyes. "And the horrible thing about that is that I loved it." She gulped and felt warm tears fill her eyes. She'd failed everything tonight. She even failed her own rule; she ate meat. Not good.

"Yes, I told you, you would," he said with compassion. "It's part of who you are now." He sounded almost apologetic.

He could have yelled at her, but he didn't. She expected it, but instead he stayed quiet.

He took a bottle of saline out of his duffel and poured some on a cloth then wiped at her shoulder. "I won't bandage it. It should be healed by the time we get back. Let me help you get dressed."

"Oh, God, I'm naked in front of you" She looked at him. "Oh, God you are naked in front of me." She couldn't help as her eyes traveled the full length of his body and again she liked what she saw. She couldn't hide the blush rising in her cheeks. She felt the blood rush there and her face heat.

"I saw you naked the night you changed. It's not like I've never seen you naked. Come on, I'll help you get dressed then get you in the SUV."

"You get dressed first then you can." She turned her head away from him, but not before she caught his grin. She felt like hitting him.

He didn't say anything afterward. In fact, he didn't say anything to her the whole way back. She wanted to scream. The air felt so thick and heavy, anything just to break the ice, but she didn't. She kept her mouth shut. She knew when the bullet worked itself out because she felt it against her sleeve. She reached up inside her sweater and felt around until she grabbed it.

She also felt her shoulder. Where there should have been a hole there was only new skin. She was amazed by it and wanted to say so to Cain, but she caught a glimpse of his face, and could tell by his stern look and tight jaw, that she shouldn't say anything. She could only guess what might stream out of his mouth if she did.

Once back at the house she found she was exhausted. "Where am I supposed to sleep? I'm really tired."

"You're really tired because your body had to heal." He walked away from her, pulled his hand through his dark hair, put his hand on his hip, and looked toward the floor. He quickly turned and strode back. He stood inches from her. She wanted to back up, instead she stood there determined, but gave away her nervousness by gulping.

She lifted her chin in a daring manner. This man

confused her, made her nervous, gave her goosebumps, and made her feel all kinds of crazy. He stood there like a statue and his golden eyes stared at her forever. She could feel his warm breath on her face. Finally, he spoke.

"*Damn* it, Kara, I *warned* you about humans and your wild. You should have stayed away. You knew you were supposed to avoid humans. You should have it ingrained in your mind by now. Even the wild wolves know to avoid humans. No, instead of avoiding them, what do you do? You head face first, smack dab, into trouble. What the hell were you thinking? Were you going to bite them? Eat them? I told you…Never mind, it's partially my fault, I should have commanded your wolf and I didn't. I didn't think we'd see humans the first time out and you took me by surprise."

He paced and she could see he was trying to keep from losing his temper. She would have lost hers. She felt like an idiot. She thought from her army training she'd be strong enough to do what she was supposed to, but the wild in her was stronger. She had to be more careful.

"Look," he continued a little softer. "I know I have to repeat myself and I don't mind. If you don't get it under control by the full moon, we're both going to be in a hell of a lot of trouble."

"Why, what does the full moon have to do with it?"

"It's the only time we have no say so over our change. As soon as it gets dark, and the full moon rises, we change, no words, no command, we just change, and once we do, we can't change back until morning. If you think your wild was hard to control tonight, wait until the full moon. It's the closest you'll ever be to a full-blown wild wolf."

"So, what's the big deal about not having any say so over our change or being wolf. It would be like tonight."

He snorted. "You think? You think! *Damn* it, Kara! On a full moon you are fully wolf. There are no decent thoughts in your head, just shattered pieces of humanity, you can't talk yourself out of things. If you don't train yourself now, on a full moon you will kill a human, and if you do, you will be put down, no questions asked. I might not be there next time to stop you. But I'm not sure I could.

"I will be spending my time trying to control my own wolf. I won't have time to try and control yours. You think the wild took over tonight, you were civilized compared to what will happen on a full moon. Usually, a change on a person is planned with a full month to train before a full moon, you have only three days. I'm not sure you'll pass and it's my head on a stake if you don't. Do you understand? That's the only reason I'm pressuring you so hard. You *have* to learn it."

"Oh." She knew the dam was open and he was going to tell her what he thought whether she wanted him to or not, exhausted or not. "I'm sorry, Cain. I didn't have time to think. I just smelled and the smell…"

"Is your first sensation," he finished. "Then comes the urge. That is why you must get ahold of yourself now. We will be going out every night until the full moon. I may have to chain you for this first full moon. If I must, it will be torturous for you, and you'll tear yourself up. I don't want to have to do that, but I can't, I *won't*, take a chance of you killing a human."

"I'm sorry," she said and meant it.

"Don't be sorry, just get ahold of yourself and do what you were told. You didn't get into the military without having a strong will. Use your will to ingrain the need to stay away from humans. It's something only you can do, and you must do it. Find your center and drive it into your mind that humans are to be avoided at all cost. If you kill even one, it's a death sentence for you. Add that to your thoughts and it will help."

"Give me a chance. I know I can do it," she said with conviction.

"I know you can. I truly believe it. If you can't and you kill a human, then it's your head, then it's my head."

"Why would it be your head? You wouldn't be the one to blame for me doing something wrong."

"I'm your sire, Kara. I am totally responsible for you until which time you are released."

"They would execute you too? That's ludicrous!"

"No, worse. They'd blackball me. I'd lose my job, my status as alpha male of the Silver Sables, our clan, our pack. I've worked very hard as the alpha male and at my job. It's my whole life, and I take it all very seriously. I can't have you mucking it all up. I won't."

"I see." She lowered her head. She felt like a complete idiot. She sighed. "I have a question.

"Why *did* you change me? You could have walked away and let me die. I wouldn't have known. Your people wouldn't have known."

"Because I couldn't let you die. There was no time for an ambulance or to get help from anyone else. It was the only choice I had, that's why."

"You could have just let me die."

"But I didn't," he said then turned away. "Come on. I know you are exhausted. I know what it takes to have your body heal. You will probably sleep a good twelve hours tonight." He headed for the door. "I'll be right back. Stay put." He went out the door and came back in carrying her suitcase. "Come on, I'll show you to the guest room."

She felt like if she were wolf right now, she would be following him with her tail between her legs. She didn't think she could feel any lower. She let him down, she let herself down. Maybe it was because she was so tired, but she didn't think so. She felt like a piece of crap and felt that way through a shower and right up until she crawled into bed where she cried herself to sleep

Chapter Four

Cain woke up at daybreak and decided to go for a run. He knew Kara would probably still sleep for a few more hours and he hated waiting. A good run would make his morning brighter. He stretched a few times then silently let himself out the front door just as the first red of the sun shone on the horizon over the lake. He took a deep breath and smelled the dew on the fresh pine of the trees. There was a swirly mist above the lake. It was a beautiful morning.

It was a new day and he felt rested and ready to tackle anything. He started off at a slow jog but the more he thought about what was happening in his life his speed increased until he was in a dead run. He liked thinking while running. If he had questions. they would usually be answered while running. It was invigorating and he felt relatively good this morning, despite the night before.

He wasn't sure what to think about Kara. It was true he never changed anyone before and even though he knew all the rules of being a sire, he never wanted the responsibility. Now he was stuck with it. And what about Ansen Horn?

He was a thorn in his side and if it was the last thing he ever did, he'd see him behind bars. If he could get to where he could catch him with a big shipment coming in, he'd have him. On the West Coast most of it probably came through Texas and California from Mexico. He didn't know the specific drop spots. He'd found an old, abandoned tunnel and watched it for months, but it was truly abandoned. They probably switched between places and had several drop spots. Hell, the drugs could be trucked in, flown in, or they could be brought in through a tunnel, or even over the border.

The thing was, he felt the mastermind was somewhere here in Colorado, because of Ansen Horn and where he lived. He remembered when he first found out about him. They discovered drugs coming in over the border and he was with his men waiting in Arizona. They got the bust all right, but Horn got away and if he hadn't had a photographic memory and caught sight of his license plate number, he wouldn't have found his name.

The guys they busted weren't any help at all because every damn one of them took a cyanide pill and killed themselves the second they were trapped with no way out. What kind of drug smuggler kills his own men? Better yet, how do you talk someone into doing such a thing? It seemed like prison would be preferable. It was possible they could be under a spell, but sorcerers for the most part were good people. At least the ones he knew were. There was the possibility there was one with bad blood, it had happened before, so he couldn't rule out the possibility there was some magic involved. With any species there are the good and the bad. He knew that.

They simultaneously took the pill and dropped at the same time. It was so quick none of the officials could stop it. He was lucky he caught Horn driving away from the scene, even though he was in a line of stopped traffic, he caught a look on his face as he went by, that just screamed to him he was part of it. He knew in his gut he had something to do with it, and he was right. Proving it was another thing altogether.

He was at his wits end, and he needed some help. His nerves were on edge, and he was running short of patience. Perhaps it was because he had the added burden of being a sire. And to top it off, she was a witch. He saved someone who was going to go crazy in the end. *"Great job,"* he mouthed as he ran.

His thoughts drifted back to Kara. She was beautiful. Her smile intoxicating, she was funny, and her little habits made his heart flutter. Hell, he felt it even now just thinking about her. He wished she wasn't a witch, if she wasn't, maybe he'd think about…no he chided himself, even if she wasn't, he wouldn't. He was her sire only. He pushed his thoughts back to his job and to the man he was after. He concluded he indeed needed the help.

He couldn't very well put an ad in the paper, *"wanted, informant for drug bust"*. They made a few small arrests and some of them talked, but they could only get as far as the sellers on the street. After that it was dead end. He was running out of ideas and options.

His thoughts vacillated back and forth between his case and Kara Thomas. *Sgt. Thomas*, he mouthed correcting himself. It made him smile to think of her in the military giving orders. Now that he'd like to see.

He reflected on the trip to her parent's house. *Her house* he reminded himself, it was hers now. He remembered seeing the sign for the new hospital and Reid Dalton. If he remembered rightly, he had some big thing coming up. He'd either read about it or his boss mentioned it. Then the idea hit. He needed to talk to Dalton, he wanted…no… needed his help.

With a plan formulating in his mind, he turned around and headed back home. He let himself in quietly so as not to wake Kara, but he was surprised as he closed the door behind him. The smell of frying bacon, fresh coffee, fried potatoes, and eggs enveloped him.

The warmth and the smell made him feel something he couldn't put his finger on, perhaps nostalgia, his mother used to cook breakfast. Whatever it was, it felt good. His mouth instantly watered and realized he was famished. "I guess you are awake," he shouted, as he took off his running jacket. He threw it over the arm of a chair and headed for the kitchen.

"Yep, I'm awake. I heard you leave. I'm a light sleeper, and since I glanced out the window and saw you take off jogging, I knew you'd be back and you'd probably be hungry, sooo I took it upon myself to make breakfast. Are you hungry?"

"Hungry isn't the word for it. The smell is making my mouth water, I'm famished." He noticed her hair was wet and figured she must have showered before she began cooking.

"Good, because I'm making a large breakfast. Eggs, potatoes, bacon, and hotcakes."

"You can cook all that at the same time?"

"In case you didn't notice, I was raised on a ranch. I was brought up on large breakfasts, even learned to cook them." She turned to him with spatula in hand and elbow on her hip. Her green eyes sparkled, and it warmed his heart. Her dark hair was all a skew and it almost made him laugh.

Her hair looked like a lopsided old-fashioned mullet from being singed and he felt bad for her. He loved her smile and he'd like to see more of it. He was going to have to make an appointment to get her hair done. It might make her feel better. He'd surprise her and take her after he checked in at work. He smiled.

"You have a nice smile," he said. "When you smile, which isn't often."

"Do you always end a compliment with something negative?"

"Well...I...I didn't know I did. It's that you smile little, and it's a very nice smile."

"Thank you, I think. I haven't had much to smile about lately." She turned around and flipped a pancake. "Grab the syrup from the fridge and pop it in the microwave please. Add a little butter. You don't want cold syrup on your pancakes."

"Yes, ma'am, right away," he said, smiling wide. He quickly went to the fridge and grabbed the syrup and butter then went to a cupboard and retrieved a small pitcher. He poured some syrup in it, threw in a hefty slice of butter, and stuck it in the microwave. "How long?" he asked.

"Thirty seconds should be enough. Don't you ever heat your syrup?"

"I hardly ever cook unless you count steak on the BBQ. Now there I'm a damn good cook. But, in the kitchen? Well, that is whole different story. My kitchen is allergic to me, just ask my housekeeper. No, my specialty is a fine cut steak on the barbie. Maybe even some added shrimp or prawns. I can peel and cook those too."

"But you have all kinds of meat, and your shelves are stocked. Do you have a cook come in?"

He could feel the heat rise in his face. He didn't want to tell her he kept things stocked for when women spent the weekends with him. Which was usually every weekend unless he was busy on a case, but he also had a cook come in. She must have guessed because he saw the immediate change in her expression.

"Is there someone who would normally be here?" she asked.

"No," he answered, not lying. "I sometimes have a cook come in. There's one I can call at any time. Twenty-four-hour notice of course, but there have been the occasional emergencies."

"Ah, I see," she said. "It's for your weekend women. You keep things stocked for them or is there just one woman?" She turned and flipped the pancake in the air, then took a fork and moved bacon around in the sizzling pan, avoiding looking at him. Then she stirred the eggs. She went to the toaster and threw in four slices of bread and pushed the lever down, a little forcefully he noticed. She was waiting for his answer.

How was he supposed to respond? Careful, he told himself, you want to see more of her smiles today. He felt like a jerk after last night when he berated her. He'd heard her crying later. He remembered his first time out as wolf. He didn't run into any humans, and that was good, because he probably would have killed one or more.

As it was, he killed three deer, four or five rabbit, chased a coyote, and killed a ground hog. He ate most of the first deer and the rest was for fun. Of course, he wouldn't tell her that, it was too embarrassing. Since then, he only killed for food and just chased other animals for fun. He was a little mad at himself for the way he treated her the night before, but damn it, he wanted her to succeed. He knew she could.

"I cook sometimes," he answered. It was the only thing he could come up with. Well, it wasn't a lie; he did cook sometimes. Maybe twice a year. He always had to call in his housekeeper when he did because when he was finished it always looked like something blew up in the kitchen, and he hated cleaning, especially doing dishes. Maybe that's why he seldom cooked anything but steak on the grill.

She looked over her shoulder at him and if looks could kill. He knew he'd been had, but she didn't say a word. The timer went off on the microwave. "Saved by the bell," she said. "Get out a couple of plates and pour us some coffee, don't forget the syrup. Please."

"Yes, ma'am," he said with a salute. He quickly did as he was told as she scooped scrambled eggs from the pan on his plate then some on hers then put the pan in the sink to be washed. She put two slices of bacon on her plate and the rest on his, looked at him with the expression of don't you dare mention bacon. Then she set down a plate with a stack of pancakes and went to the toaster and pulled out the finished four pieces of toast. She quickly buttered them and put two on his plate and two on hers.

"Let's eat, I'm starving," she said. She didn't say anything more about women and the food he kept at the house. He was glad for that. They sat in silence while they shoveled in the food. She got up once and grabbed some cream from the fridge and poured some in her coffee.

"You?" she asked. He shook his head, no. He glanced once at her while she was eating bacon and didn't say a word. He knew she was no longer vegan but didn't want to mention it. She did, however.

"I forgot how much I love bacon," she said as she took a big bite. "Oh, and ham. I loved ham. Do you like ham? I make this killer glaze for ham. I almost forgot about that. It was my mother's recipe. Maybe I'll make it for you sometime."

"I'd like that," he said with a full mouth. He took a drink of orange juice then cleared his throat. "I'd like that a lot. I'm a fan of ham myself. If your glaze compares to this breakfast, it will be the best ham I've ever tasted."

"Thank you," she said with a blush.

He could tell it made her feel good. He enjoyed making her feel good because most times she seemed sad. Her beauty shone when she smiled but it was apparent even when she didn't. The dimple in her cheek only appeared when her smile was wide and it added to her adorableness. She was probably the most beautiful woman he'd ever met. He wanted to know more about her, what made her tick. "Tell me Kara, why'd you decide to become a vegan?"

"I couldn't see taking the life of an innocent animal just to feed myself, especially when our bodies don't need meat to survive."

"How do you feel now?" he asked. He really wanted to know, and she must have picked that up, because instead of any snide remarks, she told him the truth.

"I feel different. I feel like I've been asleep all my life and now I'm awake. I feel more energized than ever before. I'm thinking clearer, sharper...like I'm smarter. I don't know, but I do know, I'm no longer vegan, and you can say I told you so."

"No, I'm not going to do that. I was just trying to help you to understand yesterday."

"I know, you were trying to help me, and I

76

appreciate that. I also appreciate the fact you went out of your way to save my life when you never wanted to be a sire. I appreciate you taking the time to teach me what I need to know. I'm sorry I didn't listen about the humans. And that I almost attacked one. I should have known better, done better."

"It's very hard when you are first turned. To tell you the truth, I killed three deer, some rabbit, and a groundhog. If there would have been a human around, I don't think I would have stopped, I would have killed him and probably would have eaten him. Either that or Christian would have killed me first."

"You ate all that you killed?"

He laughed. "Good God no, to tell you the truth it was the hunt that drove me. I'm sure I left plenty for the scavengers."

"I understand that now. I understand all you were trying to tell me. Who was your sire? Was it Christian? If you don't mind me asking. I don't want to get too personal."

"I don't mind at all. My boss, Christian, yes. Christian confronted me and asked me if I wanted to make the change."

"You mean some people are chosen and asked?"

He chuckled. "We don't go around waiting for people to be mortally wounded if that's what you're asking. We take our time, research ones we think would be a good fit, then when we are ready, approach them."

"Is there a certain amount you select, or how does that work?"

"We do have a quota."

"How do you know what pack someone will belong to?"

"That's something we don't have an answer for. We must wait for the change to see where they will belong. In its own way it seems to naturally keep everything even. Each pack has about the same amount of people."

"How very interesting."

"Natures like that," he said, and smiled.

"What about marriage and children. Do women have puppies?"

He was taking a drink of coffee when she asked, and he spit it out coughing. Gagging he asked, "Did you really just ask that?" He took a napkin and wiped his face and took another to wipe the table where the coffee hit.

She giggled. "I just wanted to see your reaction. But really, how does that work? Can children turn into wolves?"

"Wolves only marry other wolves. If a wolf falls in love with a human, they are asked to change. In fact, they must change if they want a family. All children are born human. They don't change until they are around sixteen. Both parents have to be wolf if they want children, it's the only way they can conceive. If a witch turns wolf and marries a wolf and has children, which is highly advised against, all children are born wolf. It's dominant of the two.

"They are taught early about their background and the parents ready them for their first change. The father usually commands the child when the time comes. He is literally their sire. If there's no father, which can sometimes be the case, the mother takes over. Both are prepared for their child. In the case where a male child needs help with something more male related there is always an uncle or male member from the pack assigned to step in and help. It's worked out that way for centuries, and it's worked well."

"I bet some kids try at an earlier age," she said and took a bite of her toast.

"It's like with any family. Teenagers are teenagers whether human, wolf, or witch. The words for changing aren't often talked about for that very reason. I imagine if a sorcerer and sorceress marry and have children, they have their ways to teach their children. I'm not privy to how they do that. I do know they school them much differently than humans do."

"I wouldn't know, I was never taught," she said sadly.

"You have the book. You can study it, and today would be a great day. I have to see my boss early this morning and you have to go with me."

"Why? I'm not going to do anything untoward. I can stay by myself, stay here, and go over *The Oracles*."

"Not gonna happen. We have rules, laws, and we all abide by them. It used to be they could leave newbies alone, but some thought they'd try being wolf and accidents happened. Our clan law went into effect hundreds of years ago and it's worked great so far. I can't leave you alone until I release you, and I won't release you until I feel you are completely ready. If I let you go too early and something happens, I'm responsible, and I am punished along with you. You are my responsibility until I say otherwise."

"I see," she said sipping her coffee. "I thought it was a dumb macho thing, but that makes sense. After last night, I can see why."

"We'll go to my work this morning and this afternoon you can study the book. I have things to do in my study, some paperwork, so it will work out perfectly."

"Are we going out tonight as wolf?"

"Yes."

Chapter Five

The morning was beautiful, the sun was shining, and even though it was chilly, Kara was enjoying the ride into Denver. She was going to meet Cain's boss and she was a little nervous. She was afraid he'd be able to detect her being witch and wolf. If he did, Cain would be in a lot of trouble for changing her. She didn't want that for him.

She liked Cain as a person and appreciated him saving her, but that was it. A couple of times she found herself attracted to him and she had to remind herself she had sworn off men. Especially a man who carried a gun or wore a uniform. Besides she didn't sense any interest from him. Either way, she didn't want another relationship—ever. She could accept being lonely the rest of her life more than experiencing another loss like she had.

She watched the scenery speed by her as she sank into her thoughts, not really focusing on anything. She thought about the man she had planned to marry. Cal was tall and thin, sandy colored hair, and blue eyes. He always had a happy air about him. When she first joined the army, she was afraid of facing off with men, but he encouraged her.

It was because of him she decided to join the military police. He asked her all kinds of questions about what she wanted for her future and how she saw herself getting there. Those conversations helped her decide to join and she was glad she did. She was top of their class. He took her to dinner to celebrate. Physically she could keep up with most any man and her superiors recognized her skill. She traveled up in rank rather quickly, she felt she owed that to Cal too.

Cal was the type of man who never got angry, at least to the point where he'd lose his temper. The only way she could tell he was angry was a tightness in his jaw. He was methodical and planned out everything. In fact, he had his whole life planned out. She could never do that. She knew herself well enough to know she'd probably change her mind about one or more important things in the coming year.

She couldn't plan one year let alone her whole life. But the structure and the security were what led her to join the military in the first place. You had to make decisions and stick by them. She could do that now after learning how. The military sure taught her that.

Her thoughts turned to the fateful day Cal was killed. She should have taken the shot, but she didn't. Now he was dead. All because of her.

She was deep in her memories when Cain stopped the car and put it in park. "We're here, North Capitol Hill," he said. "You were quiet on the way. What's on your mind?"

He seemed genuinely concerned. She could see it in the look on his face. He's probably thinks she's having trouble processing everything happening to her. She couldn't talk about Cal, not yet, it was still too painful. "I was just enjoying the ride. The sun is bright and the day beautiful. I love Colorado in the springtime." She wasn't lying about that.

"I do too. There are some places that are beautiful in the mountains, waterfalls, and great places to hike. If you enjoy hiking, I can show you some."

She smiled. "We'll see."

His expression turned sober "Are you ready to go in? Christian won't bite, I promise."

"What if he can tell I'm witch and wolf? What do you call people like me? Salmagundi?" She could tell this surprised him. "I heard it in your mind when I went after the humans."

"I'm sorry you should have never heard me say that. It is a derogatory name, and it shouldn't be used. I used it on Ansen Horn because he's corrupted, and he deserves to be called that. I don't feel that way about everyone who is changed.

"It's a term used on them because they eventually go mad, but I don't normally call anyone names. I always felt sorry for the ones who ended up that way, and each year I hope it is the year they find a cure. I hope there is a cure for you."

"Well, thank you, but I'm afraid your boss will be able to tell."

"Eventually I will have to tell him, but I don't want anyone to know yet, because your powers are bound. The smell of witch isn't on you, it's cloaked. I want to know why. Someone went to a great deal of trouble to keep you hidden. Who are you really?"

"I'm hoping I can find some answers in The Oracles."

"We need to go back to your house and see if there are any other clues that we missed. There may be some in your mother's room. There may be some in The Oracles we missed too. It will do you good to go through

83

it."

"All right. If you think we need to go to my house, we can. I think I'm ready to tackle mom's room.

"Then it's on our to do list. Ready?"

"Lead the way." She took off her seat belt.

She followed Cain into the tall brick building. It was a beautiful area of the city, and she was impressed. "This place is better than the P.D. station," she said.

"We're on the ninth floor. My office is next to Christian's."

They walked into a busy office. There were several people standing around talking. They all stopped and looked at them. She felt eyes on her, and she supposed they already knew Cain had a newbie. She tried to pick Christian out of the group but didn't see anyone who fit the man she imagined, until a tall, blond-haired man came through another door emitting high testosterone levels. She was sure it was him. He glanced at Cain, smiled, and immediately came over.

"Cain. Come into my office. I want to hear about your trip and everything that's happened." He glanced over at her and looked surprised. "You must be Kara Thomas?"

"And you must be Christian," she said and smiled. She liked his smile. She held out her hand and he took it and shook it. "Come tell me everything. Stone told me very little."

They went through a door and down a short hall into another office. There was floor to ceiling windows and a great view of the city.

"Nice office."

"Thanks, Cain is right beside me with about the same."

"Mine's a little smaller. Not complaining, just a fact."

"You have the biggest office after mine. That's because he's the best man for any job." Christian smiled at her. "So, bring me up to speed."

She listened to Cain tell Christian about his trip and how he followed Ansen Horn to the spot where the warehouse blew up. He talked about how he found her on fire and why he changed her. He never mentioned she was a witch and Christian didn't seem to notice. She let out the breath she had been holding. It was going to be okay.

"Listen, Christian, I need a favor."

"Go on," said Christian. He raised his eyebrows and rolled his eyes. Giving her the impression it was something he might do frequently where Cain was concerned. She bet Cain always pushed Christian to the breaking point and then some. She almost giggled but refrained. Instead, she sat quietly and smiled. She enjoyed listening to them and she found out right away Christian was a pushover where Cain was concerned. It was obvious he adored Cain, but on the same token, Cain adored him.

"You've met Reid Dalton and are on a first name basis. I've never met the man. There's some big thing coming up. I can't remember what it is. I either saw it in the paper or you told me about it. I want an invitation."

"Why? Why would you bother Reid with anything? He's a very busy man and he's constantly doing things for the city. He's a great man, but hard to get a meeting with."

"He has people all over this city. He knows practically everyone. I want to talk to him about catching

Horn."

"Good Lord, man, have you lost the few marbles you have in that ball on your shoulders? You don't want to bother Reid with problems concerning Horn and what he's mixed up in. You could get him killed."

"He didn't get where he's at by being stupid, Christian. There's someone else working with Ansen. I know it. I feel it in my bones. I just want him to put some feelers out and have some of his people snoop around. He's smart, he won't get killed. Besides, he doesn't have to go out on the streets. He has people to do that. At least let me talk to him. If he doesn't want to help, he can tell me himself."

"Not this again. I told you, Ansen Horn is the mastermind behind this."

"What if he's not? What if he's working *for* someone? This drug thing is huge. A lot bigger than you or I thought. For Christ's sake, he met with a Colombian Kingpin in Florida. Then he went to New York. I checked with New York and their drug problem has tripled in the last five years, and I know damn well it has to do with Ansen. The big fish for the U.S. is here in this state, in this city, I know it. Just let me talk to Reid. If I can just meet him and set an appointment with him, talk to him, I'm sure he'd help."

Kara watched Christian's expression. He had a deep frown on his face. She thought he was going to flat out say no, but he surprised her. He went back to his desk and pulled out a drawer.

"It's a black-tie affair. The benefit gala is for the new hospital going up. This invitation is for one, plus one. You'll have to take a date." Christian looked over at Kara. "It's the day after the full moon. Are you ready for the full moon?"

She knew he was asking about her. She glanced over at Cain and swallowed hard and held her breath. She knew he didn't think her ready.

"We'll be fine going the day after the full moon," said Cain, surprising her. "Things are going along very smoothly."

"I'm glad to hear it. I was worried when I heard you sired someone just when this investigation was heating up and with three days until a full moon. And need I mention you have never sired anyone before?"

"I'm not worried. Kara was an M.P. Sergeant in the army. Anti-terrorism was just one of the qualifications. She's actually been a great help."

"Wow," said Christian. He turned his attention to her and smiled. "We could use someone like you on our team. When Cain releases you, come see me."

"I'll think about it. I'm not sure what I want to do yet."

"Think about it and let me know. Of course, I will want copies of your records with the military service. You know experience, yada, yada, all the good stuff."

"Yes, well, we'll see. I appreciate the offer." She really wanted to say yes, but something in the back of her mind held her back.

She was glad when Christian handed the invitation to Cain dropping the whole *come see me for a job* thing. "I didn't want to go anyway. I hate things like that, and it seems I'm always drawn into them. Can't turn them down you know. Make my excuses. Tell him I had a prior engagement and that my contribution is in the mail."

Cain smiled. "Thanks, Christian."

"Don't thank me, I still think it's Horn we need to get. If he's shut down, the whole mess will be over with."

"Not so sure about that."

"I'm waiting, Cain. Prove me wrong."

"I will, I will. I'll let you know how it goes."

"Yes, you will. Now get out of here. I have work to do. Nice to meet you, Kara."

"You too." She held out her hand and he shook it, and then they left.

**** 

Once back at the house Cain went to his office and left Kara reading The Oracles. She'd been quiet on the way to Denver and the way back. Something was on her mind. Christian didn't pick up the smell of witch on her and he thought that maybe is what bothered her. She was probably worried about his boss finding out.

He scratched his head. He didn't know what was in that pretty head of hers and he couldn't spend his time thinking about it. Of course, even with her walls up he could force himself into her mind, but he wouldn't do that. He'd leave her to her privacy unless he felt the need. Right now, he didn't.

He had work to do. He had to fill out a report about his trip and he had to think about how he was going to approach Reid Dalton. He knew the man loved Denver and the people in it, so he just had to plead to his sensibilities. He was sure he could gain his help.

He sat down and powered on his computer. While he waited for the computer to warm up, he looked at the invitation in his hand. Black and gold, shiny, fancy letters. Funny how this little piece of card could get him an audience with the most important man in Denver. He opened his top drawer and slipped in the invitation.

Black tie, he'd have to get a nice new suit. The only other suit he owned was about twenty years old, he needed a new one.

He sat in front of his computer and let his mind wander. He felt for Kara knowing that in a few years down the road she'd begin to go crazy. He'd seen what happens to sorcerers and wolf and it wasn't pretty. Once it started it continued until the person went completely insane. If they had coherent thoughts, they remained alive. Most having to have help from family members. But once they totally lost their mind they were put down like a rabid dog. He didn't care for it, but supposed it was for the best.

They were given a sedative and then shot through the heart with a silver bullet, never knowing what hit them. Bullets are numbered and made by TITAN and kept secret. The numbers were matched with the executed wolf. Strict records were kept. A silver bullet after all could kill any wolf if shot in the heart.

He thought of Kara being wolf. All in all, she did well her first night out. He thought she did better than he did, but he wouldn't tell her. Of course, Christian was with him his first time as wolf. If he had to say he had a best friend, it would have to be Christian. For all his bark he lacked the bite to back it up. He was really a marshmallow, but he was strict with his people.

He was from Arctic Pride, the Alpha male, a huge white wolf, and the most beautiful of all of them. Christian was hoping he'd turn out Arctic Pride, but he was Silver Sable and now he was Alpha male, leader of the Silver Sables. He was glad he turned out that way, He loved his pride of wolves. Wolves saw beauty in each other. In the world of wolf there was a hierarchy and they treated each other with great respect.

Humans wouldn't see it because they just didn't know. Hell, he didn't know before he became wolf, but there was a complicated world out in the wild. Wolves treated each other better than humans did. He understood the world of wolf and being wolf he understood all of nature better.

He glanced at the screen in front of him, put in his password which allowed him into his work system and pulled up the report form. He hated this part of his job, but he supposed it had to be done. He sighed. Time to get to work.

An hour later he finished his report and decided to tap into Florida and New York's police system. The TITAN's had more clearance than most police, even access to parts of the military system. He could look up anything he wanted and get answers. He wanted to see how many deaths there were in Miami and New York due to drugs and guns. He was shocked at the increase.

He'd already studied California, Arizona, New Mexico, Texas, and Colorado, and it was unbelievable the crime rate surrounding drugs and their increase over the last five years, and Ansen Horn had something to do with it. He clicked from Florida to New York and lost himself in reading statistics. Damn it he hated what was happening to kids.

Guns did not belong in the hands of teenagers, yet here it was, they were getting their hands on automatic weapons. That didn't even include the deaths caused by Cocaine and Heroin. There was a mixture of the two and it was deadly. In five years, it had increased by five hundred percent. Staggering. He might be only one man, but he felt he had to do something to stop it.

Before he knew it, it was two hours later. He stretched his back and switched his computer off and he thought he'd go check on Kara and see how she was doing with the book.

When he found her in the kitchen, he froze in shock. There was Kara, her back to him, hovering in the air, feet off the ground, she had a yellow light about her, and her hair was flying out like she was filled with static electricity.

When he heard her say the words, *to break this binding spell*…He shot across the room and slammed the book shut. The light dimmed, her hair went down, and she landed back on the ground. He saw smoldering green stuff smoking in a bowel, and three lit candles in front of her. He noticed blood dried on her hand and wondered what she'd done to bleed.

"What the hell do you think you're doing?"

"I was breaking the binding spell on me. I wanted to know who I was."

"Don't you dare, not until we find out why you were bound in the first place."

She swung her arm out like she was going to say something, but he found himself blown across the kitchen and slammed up against the wall. Stunned he shook his head and let out a cough. "What did you just do?" he asked after catching his breath.

"I…I…I don't know. I'm sorry. I just thought I didn't want you angry with me and I wanted you out of the kitchen. I didn't do it on purpose. I'm sorry."

"Did you finish breaking the binding spell?"

"No, I was only half-way through it."

"Well, you must have opened a door. At least we know what your second power is."

"What?" she asked.

"Obviously, you can move things with your mind. You are lucky I came in when I did. If you get your powers back without us knowing anything, someone else could sense it and come after you, possibly kill you. There has to be a good reason why they were bound. For God's sake Kara use your head."

Her expression dropped and she became very quiet.

He realized his words hurt her. "I'm sorry. You frightened me. I shouldn't have reacted the way I did. I'm trying to do all I can to keep you safe."

"You were right, I should have been more careful. I just wanted to know who I was, and I thought if I unbound my powers, I would know. I didn't think. I was so happy to see there was a way to break the spell, I couldn't wait to try it. I found all the ingredients I needed. I thought it was a good thing to do," she said her lip trembling. A tear fell down her cheek.

\*\*\*\*

Cain walked over and put his arms around her, and she leaned into him and let the tears flow. She thought he'd understand, but evidently, she screwed up again. She was about to her breaking point. He rubbed her back, and she felt safe and warm. She got lost in his arms and when she looked up into his golden eyes she reached up and kissed him. It felt so natural to do so, even more so than it ever did with Cal.

It startled him and he jumped back, and she took it that the kiss disgusted him. She quickly broke away. "I'm sorry, I wasn't thinking."

"No, you weren't. I'll put this book away for now."

She turned and went quickly to his guest room and closed the door. She went and sat on the bed and broke down in tears. She felt like she was mucking everything up. She felt like she didn't belong anywhere, and it made her feel isolated. What the hell made her kiss him? She knew he didn't want to get near any half breeds, yet she still kissed him. Hell, she didn't want another relationship. Her mind was going crazy and the rest of her right along with it. She thought about her parents. She really wished they were here so she could talk to them. She really missed them, and she didn't realize how much until she was in her dad's library. She sobbed over the loss of her parents. She was doing things she knew she shouldn't, and it terrified her.

She thought about the people who were in her care and were now dead. This was the last straw. She no longer cared about living. She shouldn't be alive anyway. There was only one thing to do now. It was the only way, she thought...for her, but especially for Cain.

\*\*\*\*

Cain stood outside the door feeling like an ass. She was crying and he had made her cry. He could hear her sobbing. He didn't know if he should try to talk to her or leave her alone. He opted for leaving her alone for now. He needed to think about what happened. When she kissed him, something deep and unexpected happened. He didn't understand it. It was like he felt when he entered the house, smelled breakfast, and knew she was there. He was excited to see her. He'd never been excited to see any woman except for sex. He couldn't wait for them to leave in the morning.

He'd never wanted a woman in his house before, but he looked forward to having Kara there. A warmth traveled his body and once again it was like they were the only two in the world. He felt protective of her. He felt his heart open, and a warmth settle in his soul, a sort of knowing. It was like he'd known her his whole life, possibly lives before this one if there was such a thing. It was a strange feeling. He didn't even know how to explain it to himself, or how to handle it, it literally shocked him.

Whatever it was, he felt like his soul melded into hers and they became one, and it wasn't because they could share thoughts, or that he was her sire and was connected to her. He'd been through many women, bedded them, and not one ever made him feel anything close to what he just felt from that one simple kiss. It turned him inside out.

He desired her so much that it scared the living shit out of him. He shouldn't have jerked away, but damn it, it startled him. Besides, he reminded himself she was a witch. He felt sorry for them, even respected the hell out them, but wolf and witch didn't mix. The truth of the matter was she would eventually go mad, and he knew himself well enough that it would tear him up if he were to love her then watch her go mad and have to eventually be destroyed. He wanted marriage, a family, and to live a long life with his wife and children. He couldn't think about her. He couldn't. He didn't dare.

He shook his head and went back to the kitchen to retrieve the book and put it away. He'd have to be more careful in watching her. He took it to his bedroom then changed his clothes. He wanted to take Kara to buy a dress and he needed a suit for the benefit gala.

A while later he gathered himself and went to her door and knocked on it. He didn't hear any more crying, a good sign. He waited for her to answer, but she didn't. He knocked again. "Kara, we need to get some new clothes for the banquet." He waited…nothing. He turned the door handle and opened the door. The window was wide open, and she was gone. His heart dropped to his toes. On the bed was a note. He went over and picked it up and read it.

*Dear Cain,*

*I'm sorry for all the trouble I've caused you. You've been more than kind and I appreciate all you've done for me. Thank you, from the bottom of my heart. I'd like to make a ham dinner for you sometime…as a payback for your kindness. Perhaps someday we can be friends. For now, I need to figure this out on my own. I will leave you alone, as I don't want to cause you any more trouble. Have a good life. I'll always remember you.*

*Kara*

He saw red. He crumbled the note in his hand making a fist. "Damn it to hell! Where the hell, did she go?" He quickly went out in the other room, grabbed his jacket and keys, and slammed the front door behind him. He had to find her, especially before the full moon. She wasn't ready for it, damn it, and he had only two nights left to take her out. This was totally insane. He'd never again have another newbie.

He hopped in his '64 and took off down the long drive. He could only hope she'd stay near the roads, and he could get a glimpse of her. He knew in his heart of hearts she turned wolf so she could travel faster, he hoped she hadn't, but he knew better. So, instead of looking for a dark-haired woman running down the road he had his eyes peeled for a black female wolf with a silver stripe down its back.

At least she was in Silver Sable territory. He had to find her before she reached a highway or the public. He rounded a corner and crossed a creek and out of the corner of his eye he caught sight of a black wolf. She was coming close to the dirt road but when she saw his car she turned around and ran.

He pulled off the road, threw it in park, had his shirt off before he got out of his vehicle, and was dropping his pants. He left his clothes where they fell, and he said the change words before his pants were fully off. He quickly changed and he took off in a dead run toward where he saw her.

He followed her scent for about two miles before he caught sight of her again. Once he saw her, he had her. She was slowing, most likely tired, but he had too much adrenaline to slow down. He finally caught up with her. He stood on large boulders looking down at her. She didn't see him. He pounced and sunk his teeth in her shoulder and took her to the ground. She howled. He ordered her to make the change back. He could tell she didn't want to, but she didn't have a choice. He did the same.

His mouth was on her shoulder, and she lay naked beneath him. He let go and looked at her. "What the hell do you think you are doing?" he asked her.

"I don't want to be a bother to you any longer. I can take care of myself. I've been doing it for years. Good God you're naked. Get off me!" she squealed.

He held tight to her as if he didn't hear her words. "You don't understand. I'm responsible for you. You haven't been through a full moon yet and you aren't ready. You can't just take off. Besides we are joined mind to mind until I release you.

"You couldn't have stayed away for very long, because your mind would have brought you back, our minds will be locked together until the release. It's my job to teach you the ways and we've barely scratched the surface. There's so much you don't know yet."

"Don't you have some kind of book I could just read?"

"Well, we saw how it went with The Oracles. Even if we had such a book, which we don't, I'd be afraid to give it to you. You seem to dance to your own tune."

He suddenly realized he was laying naked on top of her. His body already had ideas about it. Kara must have realized it at the same time because he saw her gulp and her face turn bright red. He felt himself grow painfully hard against her side. My God, he desired her. Her body felt perfect. She smelled so damn good, and he would love to taste a kiss again. She quickly broke into his lustful thoughts.

"Do you think you could get off me now?" she whispered.

He thought of every mundane thing he could think of to cool off, he was afraid to move, afraid of what might happen. "Do you promise not to run away again? I'm your sire, you cannot lie to me."

"I don't lie to anyone, if I wanted to run, I'd tell you. But no, I won't run. Good God, Cain, I didn't want to cause you anymore trouble. I seem to be doing everything wrong."

He slowly pulled himself up and sat next to her as she sat up. She quickly put her arms over her breasts as if they'd hide them. He could have chuckled over it, but he was being serious. "You would cause me more trouble if you ran without me releasing you. I'm responsible for you, if you came up missing, it would be my head. It would be worse than you making a mistake. Please don't do that again."

"It seems this last year I have been making a lot of mistakes. I don't trust myself right now. I don't trust anyone or anything. I don't belong anywhere, and I don't know who I am…"

"Why don't we go back to the house and talk, okay? As your sire, I should know everything going on with you. I wanted to take you shopping for a dress for the gala, get your hair done, and I need a new suit, but we can do that tomorrow. I think right now we need to have an in-depth discussion. I want to know what is going on in that pretty little head of yours."

She looked away like she might cry, and he felt he may lose it if he saw one tear come out of those beautiful green eyes. The last thing he wanted to do was make her cry. "Kara you aren't making any big mistakes, in fact you are doing better than I thought you would."

She looked at him hopefully. "You are still naked."

"You don't have any clothes, do you?"

"No, I didn't think to…"

He smiled. "I have an extra set of sweats in my duffel in the car. They'll work until we get home. Come on. I'll pop a bottle of wine and we can talk. Just talk. Okay?"

"We'll see, I don't know what I can or cannot talk about. Some things I haven't talked about, and I don't think I can."

"I won't make you talk about anything you don't want to, but I do need to go over why it's important for you to stay with me until I release you. We have rules, laws we go by, and they must be followed for the protection of all."

"I understand," she said meaning it. "I just knew I

didn't want to cause you any more trouble."

"Kara, you haven't caused me any trouble at all. Well, not much trouble anyway. For what you've been through I'm amazed at how well you've held up. I wish you would understand. I know why you were doing what you were doing with The Oracles. I would probably want to do the same. Sometimes people on the outside looking in can see things a little clearer. It wasn't wrong of you to do that, but until we find out why your powers were bound, we should leave them that way.

"I'm not trying to keep you from knowing about yourself, I'm trying to keep you safe." He noticed the little quiver to her lip, and knew she was trying hard not to cry. He smiled at her and slapped her butt. "Come on, I'll race you back to the car." He hopped up and held out his hand. She took it and let him pull her to her feet. He couldn't help it, he gazed at her beautiful body and damn near swallowed his tongue. He squeezed his eyes shut for a moment and tried to clear his thinking. Kara took off running.

He chased her and couldn't help but laugh. He enjoyed staying behind her because he loved watching her round butt wiggle with her quick stride and leaps. He couldn't get over how perfectly beautiful and graceful she was, both in human form and wolf form. She was something songs were written for, poetry written about.

She was the most beautiful woman he'd ever met. He literally loved her body and gazing at it made his stand to attention. Another reason he stayed behind her. It was hard running with his thing smacking his legs. He tried hard to think of other things, but it didn't work. But by the time they got back to the car he had himself under control and he was glad they were back.

He picked his pants up off the ground and quickly put them on then grabbed his shirt off the front seat. He'd even left his door open, and he never did that. He popped the trunk and pulled out his duffel and handed her his sweats then turned his head as she got dressed. He wanted to be angry with her, but he couldn't. He was just happy to have her back.

He'd been frantic thinking she was gone from his life, and it was more than just being her sire and keeping her out of trouble. He felt for her. He had some things to think about, but right now he wanted to get back and have a deep discussion with her and he wasn't going to let her get out of it.

At home, and as promised, he brought out a bottle of good wine. While she was getting dressed in something of her own, he pulled the cork to let it breathe. He grabbed two wine glasses, went to the fridge, and took out the three different cheeses, got his favorite crackers and arranged them on a plate. He grabbed a jar of baby dill pickles, a pickle fork, and a small dish and scooped some out.

He wasn't sure she'd like pickles, but they were there if she did. He enjoyed them with cheese and crackers. After he set it on the coffee table, he lit a fire in the fireplace, and pulled the shades across the lower windows. He felt comfortable and hoped she would too. If he could get to the bottom of what was bothering her, maybe he could help her.

He sat on the couch and poured two glasses of wine. Lit the three candles on the table and popped a cracker in his mouth.

"Wow," said Kara as she entered the great room. "This is very nice. Makes the place feel cozy."

"Yes, and I love a good fire in the fireplace," he said and smiled.

She sat at the other end of the couch and crossed her legs. He knew by her body language she was distancing herself. She probably didn't want to talk about anything important. The wine was a very good vintage and he hoped it would do the trick and help her open to him. If it didn't, he had three more bottles to back this one up. He was set. It was probably just the changes she was going through. Whatever it was, he was going to get to the bottom of it.

He handed her a glass of wine. "Thank you," she said.

He took the other glass. "To us wolves," he said and raised the glass. She touched hers to his.

"To us wolves, and the sorcerer in me," she said and smiled. They both took a drink. "The taste is wonderful," she said. "What is it?"

"*Cantina Tramin Kellerei*," he said.

"I think I'll remember this wine. It's very smooth. I enjoy a good wine. In fact, it's the only type of drink I partake of. I don't care for any type of mixed drink. Occasionally I will get a craving for a beer or two, usually when I'm working up a sweat."

"The same for me. I don't like scotch or any other type of alcohol, though I do enjoy a beer when I cook on the BBQ, or during a good football game. I don't drink very often, but when I do, I like something good and palatable. There are also crackers, swiss cheese, sharp cheddar, and colby if you like, and dill pickles. Not many people like dill pickles and wine, but I do."

"It sure sounds good to me." She reached down and grabbed a cracker and some swiss cheese.

Cheryl Starr Munger

"So, tell me, Kara. What happened in the army that made you want to leave the service?"

"Way to open a discussion, Cain. I was afraid you'd want to know. The one thing I don't wish to discuss."

"If it's too deep and hurtful you don't need to say," he said, giving her an out.

"I guess it's time," she said with a sigh. "I've never talked about it, but I think you should know, you deserve to know." She took a long drink of wine and stuck the cracker in her mouth.

He nodded his head and waited. He knew she was trying to formulate what she wanted to say so he wasn't pushy.

"My partner was killed, my fiancé as I mentioned earlier, and it was my fault."

"I'm sorry for your loss. I doubt it was your fault but tell me what happened."

She got a faraway look on her face and munched her cracker and took another drink of wine to wash it down. Then sat back and got comfortable.

"Cal and I were escorting an important dignitary and his wife who were visiting from Spain. Ambassador Miguel Hernandez and his wife Valentina. It was our job to protect them while in the U.S. They were seeking help concerning the Catalan Crisis. It was a true political crisis, and they needed our help. We weren't expecting any trouble, but it found us anyway.

"We were just getting out of the car at their hotel when Ambassador Hernandez was shot at. I had a good clear shot at the shooter, but there were innocent people around and I didn't dare fire. I should have, if I would have, maybe Cal would still be alive. The first shot rang out and Hernandez grabbed his wife and I pushed them down beside the car.

"Like I said, I had a clear shot, but there were people around, so I didn't take it. He shot again and it would have hit Perez or his wife, but Cal jumped in front of them, and the bullet hit him. He had his vest on, but unfortunately, he was hit in the head. He died instantly. Miguel and his wife were unharmed, but I lost my best friend, lover, and fiancé. I swore in that moment that I'd never again get close to anyone."

"I'm sorry, but truly it was not your fault."

"That's what the army said too, but I couldn't let it go, my time in the service was almost up so instead of quitting the army they offered me sort of a retirement package which I was grateful for. I went to counseling for a year, another requirement. I was going to stay on until that happened.

"My plans were to retire from the army. Since then, the whole thing has played through my mind over and over. I should have done something, anything to stop it. I was trained for it. Time and again I feel I should have taken the shot. He would still be alive if I would have."

"No, Kara. You did the right thing. An innocent person could've moved into the line of fire and been killed. You made the correct decision, it may hurt, but in the end, it was still the correct decision. I'm sorry to hear you lost your fiancé, but you did what you were trained to do. Even the army knew it. You would have been dishonorably discharged if it weren't the case. Instead, you got an honorable discharge and a severance package."

It was abundantly clear to him why Kara was having trouble. It was weighing heavy on her, and he wanted to make her see it wasn't her fault. What if she took that shot and an innocent child got in the way? He knew that would devastate her more. His heart went out to her, and she was holding up damn well considering all she'd been through. He was quite impressed.

"Then there's the fact I joined the Denver P.D. and what happens? My whole crew gets killed. Just when we were feeling comfortable with each other. I feel like I'm jinxed."

"God, Kara, you aren't jinxed. Horn had it planned to destroy you and your people. The man is smart and he's manipulative. He had to have found out you had something on him, so he set it up to take you all down. You couldn't have known. I'm sure the informant thought he had something good for you and he planned that too.

"I've been watching this guy for three years and have yet been able to get him in a position where we could take him down. It's been hard for me to get around him without him finding out. Like I said he's smart and cunning, he's no fool. Because of guns and drugs, the man is rich as sin. He's got the best attorneys money can buy so even when we do get something on him it has to be good, or his lawyers will tear it apart."

"Do you really think so?" she asked hopefully.

"No, babe, I know so. You are a strong woman, and I can tell, smart. None of it was your fault and you need to quit beating yourself up over it. Like Christian said we could use someone like you on our team. You can't go back to the P.D. Wolves don't work for them that's why we have the TITANs. I hope you'll think about joining. We really do need someone of your background."

"What about me being a witch *and* wolf. I'm going to go crazy in ten years. What's Christian going to think and say when he finds out. I bet he won't be asking me to work for him then."

"You may have twenty, besides they may find a cure by then and you won't go crazy at all." He looked at Kara and he could see the tears gathering in her eyes. One fell out and traveled down her cheek and she quickly wiped it away. It broke his heart. He went and sat beside her and wiped her cheek.

"Don't cry, babe, please don't. Like I said you are a strong woman. You didn't get your position in the army by being weak or dumb. You had some dumb luck and that's all. Try to remember all the good you did."

She looked at him and swallowed hard. He pulled her in his arms and held her close. "Cry if you want. I shouldn't have told you not to. You need this and it will make you feel better."

That's all it took, and she broke down and sobbed into his shoulder. He felt like his heart had been put in a vice and tightened. He stroked her hair and her back and let her cry. One of things he did was investigate her military record. She was top of her class, physically she kept up with most all the men, she was a sharpshooter, she had a good sense of the criminal mind, and she had several commendations for her bravery.

He felt her crying silently into his shoulder and he tightened his hold on her. His own emotions were getting the better of him and he didn't understand it. He just wanted her to feel better. He felt like his heart was being twisted like a wet wash rag being rung out. He wished she could see herself the way he saw her. She was a strong woman, intelligent, and beautiful in every way possible.

When he thought she finished crying he leaned back

and lifted her chin and the way she looked at him with those large sparkling green eyes melted his heart. Then without thinking he leaned down and kissed her. It wasn't a peck on the cheek or quick kiss, and he didn't jerk back in surprise, he kissed her deeply and hard. In that moment he wanted her, all of her, and he felt desperate about it. He found he wanted her so bad he was shaking, and he never shook.

Just as he deepened the kiss even more, his cell phone went off. He realized what he was doing and regretfully pulled back. He didn't want to stop the kiss because he was enjoying it immensely. It felt so right to him, she felt so right to him. But it wasn't meant to be because the moment was broken, and he could tell she shut down.

She moved away from him and seemed instantly cold. He wanted the warmth she provided back. He wanted that peaceful feeling that settled down deep in his gut. He wanted her to give over to him again, the feeling of her letting go and letting him in. He didn't want it to end. It was a feeling that made him feel whole. Instead, he glanced at her staring away from him, so he grabbed his cell off the coffee table and looked to see who was calling.

"It's Christian, I have to take it."

"I understand," she said. She brushed the hair back off her face and looked toward the window.

"DeLucci," he said into the phone. He hit speaker so Kara could hear their conversation.

*"It's Christian, Cain. It looks like your man is on the go again. He left his home in Washington Park and it looks like he's heading for Cherry Creek. I need you to follow and see what he's up to."*

"The wealthiest place in Denver? Maybe he's looking to go up a rung on his ladder."

*"I doubt it. Follow him and see where he's headed. This may be our chance."*

"On it, thanks," he said and hit end.

He looked over at Kara. "Ansen's on the move. Come on, we're to go see where he's going."

"Hang on and I'll grab my jacket," she said and stood up.

"You aren't going to try anything…"

"Funny?" she finished. "No Cain, if I would have thought, I wouldn't have tried it earlier. I haven't been thinking straight lately."

"Understandable. We'll finish our conversation when we get back. Right now, I'll be in the car."

**\*\*\*\***

Kara quickly went and retrieved her jacket and slipped it on. She noticed a set of keys in the front door. "You want me to lock up?" she asked hollering at him. She was glad for something else to take her mind off where the conversation was going. And what about that kiss? When he pressed his lips to hers, she couldn't pull away. She found she didn't want to. She forgot about everything except being in his arms. It felt so real, so right. She'd have to think about how he made her feel.

He rolled his window down. "Yes please, lock up." She did and got in the car and handed him the keys. She watched him push buttons and turn on the car's computer screen.

"You have a way to follow him?"

"I do. While we were in Florida, I had a chance to put tracking device under his car. So far, he hasn't noticed that it's there. Let's see where this guy is going, shall we?"

"You bet," she said and smiled, then her smile died. "If he's responsible for getting my crew killed, I want to be there when he goes down for good."

"I'll make sure it happens. He started his car, turned it around, and headed down the long driveway.

It didn't take them long to get close. "He's stopped."

"Do you know where?" she asked.

"By the map, it seems he's at the country club."

"Maybe he has the day off or is having lunch."

"I doubt it. Let's see if we can catch him and see what he's up to."

Just as they pulled up to the country club, Ansen left. "Shit. He's on the move again."

"What are we going to do, chase him?"

"What would you do?"

"Since he didn't stay long enough for lunch, I'd say he met with someone. I'd try and figure out who and why."

"Exactly my thoughts," he said with a smile. "Seems like we think alike."

"At least on this we do." She smiled back.

"Let's go see what we can find out." He parked the car and they got out. They went to the restaurant and Cain went to the reception area. He pulled out a badge and said, "Names, Cain DeLucci this is my partner, Kara Thomas. We're with TITAN. There was a man just in here. He didn't stay long. I'd like to speak with the person he spoke with."

The woman looked up and didn't seem very happy. "We protect our client's privacy here, Mr. DeLucci. You won't get anything from me. Besides men come and go all day long so I have no idea who you are looking for."

"I'd like a list of everyone having lunch."

"Do you have a search warrant?"

"I can get one quick enough."

"You do that Mr. DeLucci, then I'll give you a list of names," she turned and dismissed him.

"Wait," said Cain. She turned around. "What's your name?"

She frowned and held up the name tag she was wearing on her lapel. "Can you read?"

He squinted. "Perhaps if you were a bit closer. You're too far away."

"Carol," she said, and kept walking away from him. "Come on, Kara. We're leaving."

"That woman doesn't seem to be having a nice day."

"Let's see where he is headed next."

They followed him downtown to an area with a row of nightclubs. By the time they caught up to him he was on the move again. "Damn it, why did he stop here? Most of these places are closed during the day. What is the man up to?"

"I don't know, but I'm getting some bad feelings." And she was. She had a muddy, murky, feeling. It was like the one she had the day of the explosion. She almost shrugged it off, but instead stopped herself and tried hanging onto it.

Cain snapped his head around and looked at her. "What do you mean bad feelings? Like you had at the old warehouse?"

"Yeah, like that."

"Enough where I should have Christian keep these businesses closed all evening? Can you pin-point which place makes you feel it the most?"

"I feel it down this whole stretch of buildings. I can't

pin-point it. Maybe if we walk a ways I can get a better feel."

"Let's check it out. Get closer to where you feel it's the strongest." He got out and she followed.

They walked past a couple of buildings and she stopped. "I don't know, Cain, the longer we're here the worse this feeling is."

They walked down a block passing different night clubs. When they reached the middle, she stopped. Right here. This is where I feel it the strongest."

"Are you sure? We didn't finish walking the full length of clubs."

"I'm sure Cain."

"All right." He went to the front door and tried it. It was locked. He tried looking in through the window and all was dark. "Let's go around back. There's usually a backdoor. We'll try it."

They walked back toward the way they came and went down the side and into an alley where there were trashcans and dumpsters. Two trash cans were turned over and a screeching cat pounced out of one hissing when they walked by. The two brick buildings were two stories and had some windows, but they were covered with green shutters.

Other than the cat the place was dead still and quiet. She didn't like any of it and the feeling was only getting worse. She stopped and closed her eyes trying for a vision, but she got nothing. She wished she had some control over it, but she didn't. Cain stopped and turned toward her.

"What? Are you seeing something?" He walked back to her.

"No, I was trying to, but I can't just make it work."

"You'll have better control when you get your powers. Come on, I'm starting to feel nervous, and I never feel nervous.

They made it around to the back of the one she felt the strongest feeling from and to the back door, but it too was locked. "He can't do much if he can't get inside. There's nothing here."

She hadn't noticed the skies darkening, but she did when it started raining. Then in seconds, it poured.

"There's a basement over here, Cain, with an overhang," she hollered at him. "We can get out of the rain for a bit and maybe check it out."

They rushed down the steps and under the overhang. He tried the door, and it was locked, then he leaned against it, Kara doing the same. She looked out at the rain then wiped at her face. He stood there and sighed. "It seems everything is locked up tight." He moved closer to her and tried to block some of the wind and rain. He looked around at the rain, the doorway, and then up.

She watched him glance around and saw his face change expression to one of surprise.

"Oh, Christ," he said squinting his eyes. "I hope to hell that isn't what I think it is."

"What?" she asked. She tried to brush the rain away so she could see better.

"We need to call the bomb squad." He stepped back and squatted leaning up against the wall.

"Wait…what? The bomb squad?" She could barely hear him for the pounding of the rain or was it the pounding of her heart? Did he say bomb?

He turned his head toward her. "In five hours and fifty-eight minutes this thing is going to blow," he shouted. "Just about the time everyone comes out to play. Look up there." He pointed.

Just under the overhang, tucked neatly in the corner of the building, was a bomb with a timer. She could see the green screen with the time showing in neon red and she watched as the seconds ticked by. It reminded her of her old digital alarm clock. "God, Cain, you think Ansen did this?"

"I'd bet on it." He pulled out his cell, hit a button, and she could hear it dial out. "Hey, Christian, we need a bomb squad downtown in the nightclub district as fast as they can get here. Five-o-eight twenty-first street." He paused. "I said five-o-eight twenty-first street."

She couldn't hear what Christian was saying, but she bet he was up in arms.

"No, right now. It's going to blow in five hours. I know it. Everyone will be out by then. If we hadn't found it a lot of people would die. Okay, we'll wait here for them." He paused, then continued. "Kara found it." He glanced at her and smiled. "When? Okay, I'll let you know." He clicked his phone off and stuck it back in his pocket.

When the first of the bomb squad arrived, the rain subsided to a sprinkle lightening her mood. It didn't take long at all and the street was filled with police, the bomb squad, fire department, and E.M.S. One of the cops came up to them.

"Who found the bomb? Oh, hi, Kara. I heard what happened. I'm sorry for your loss. You all right?"

"Hi, Jeff. I'm fine, and no, I don't want to talk about it."

"Who found the bomb? And why were you down there to begin with? Everything is closed."

"We were walking downtown looking at all the

places when it began to rain heavily," said Cain. "We just ran down there to get out of the rain, and I happened to glance up and see the bomb."

"Just on a leisurely stroll, huh?" asked Jeff. He had a very curious look on his face. She knew Jeff didn't buy it for a second, but he kept it to himself. She wouldn't have bought the story either, but she let him have it.

"That's what I said."

"All right, that's what will go in my report. I think it's pretty coincidental you find a bomb on a leisurely stroll of downtown."

"Yes, coincidental," said Cain with finality.

She wondered why he didn't mention Ansen or about being a TITAN, but then she remembered what Cain said earlier. Horn was Cain's puppy and he'd be the one to bring him down and the P.D. needed to stay out of it.

She wondered why anyone would want to blow up this strip of nightclubs especially filled with young people. Possibly hundreds would have been killed. It was a Friday night. Probably one of the busiest. Judging by the size of the bomb this whole block would have gone up. It was rather brazen if you asked her. If it were her, she would want to speak with the owner of the club first thing.

It was a couple of hours, and they were finally finished with the P.D. and the bomb squad and they were allowed to leave. Cain told the same story repeatedly and when she was asked, she said the same thing. She almost believed the story herself it was told so much, but they stuck as close to the truth as they could without giving anything away.

She knew it was because this was Cain's case...but

she was the one who felt something wasn't right in the area, and they couldn't tell anyone else without giving a whole lot more away. She was beginning to see the differences of being wolf and witch and she couldn't just blurt out everything. It was the first time in her life she kept secrets, but they were important ones.

They just got settled back in the car when Cain pulled out his cell and called Christian. She knew he'd want an update on what had happened.

"Hey, Christian, Yep, all done. I need you to find the owner of *Frenzied*. I want to speak with him as soon as possible. Where he lives would be best, but yes, I want his number and address. I'd rather speak to him in person." He paused and nodded his head. She could only guess what Christian was telling him. He nodded again as if Christian could see him. "There's got to be a reason why he wanted to blow a city block. Call the Chief of Police and make sure they get back with you on any fingerprints."

She could only hear one side to the conversation, but she could fill in the blanks easily enough.

"No, I don't think they'll find anything either." He paused again. "Of course, it was Horn, he was here, but he met someone at the country club. I need a warrant to see who was eating lunch there. No, probably tomorrow, it's late now and I'm not sure the same person will be working. No, it doesn't matter, but it would be easier if I talked to whoever was working at noon. Get it to me by tomorrow morning, please."

She wondered what Christian was saying to him. "Kara sensed it. She gets these feelings and has learned to follow them. No just that something was wrong. You know, we get them occasionally ourselves."

She looked out the window. She knew Cain was trying to be truthful to Christian without saying anything about her having any kind of powers. She felt like a kid trying to hide something from her mother. She liked Christian and she was uncomfortable not telling him the truth, and that feeling came from what she learned in the army. Being truthful with your comrades was very important.

"Yes, in the morning. I'll be there. Yes, I know day after tomorrow is the full moon. We're ready, no worries. Yep, 'k." He ended the call. He turned toward her and took a deep breath and let it out in a sigh. "You did good today. You need to listen to your hunches as much as any visions you get."

"I never really thought about it, but you're right. I had a hunch before the warehouse blew up, but it's hard to tell your crew to abort on a hunch."

"You didn't have trouble after your vision."

"Right again, but the visions always come true, not so with my hunches. Besides there isn't any clarity with a hunch. What am I supposed to say? Hey, I have a hunch something isn't right?"

"No, but better to go with them and be wrong than to ignore them and suffer the consequences."

"So, I'm finding out. Where to now?"

"Back to the casita and the bottle of wine waiting for us. We have a couple of hours before it gets dark. Day after tomorrow is the full moon and the day after the benefit gala. I have to get a new suit and I'll get you a new dress and have your hair done tomorrow."

"I can get it. I have money, just because I turned wolf and you are my sire, doesn't mean I can no longer take care of myself."

"I never said you couldn't. I was just trying to do something nice for you. Since you've gone through so much, I thought it might make you a bit happy to have someone take care of you."

"Oh," she said, feeling put in her place and a bit embarrassed. "Well, then, I think a thank you is in order. So, thank you." With that she smiled at him, and he smiled back. It did make her happy. It had been since Cal that anyone offered to do anything nice for her, so yeah, it felt damn good.

She enjoyed the ride back and the small talk about Colorado. It felt comfortable. Before she knew it, they were back. He held open the front door for her and she walked in and took off her jacket and hung it up in the closet. He'd already filled her glass of wine and he stood by the kitchen sipping his.

"My turn to cook," he said jovially.

She looked at him with a bit of shock. She knew he didn't enjoy cooking, so it took her by surprise. "What are you making?"

"My specialty. Steaks on the grill. How do you like yours?"

That's right he did mention he could cook steaks on a grill. "Well before I liked steak well done." She noticed his grimace. "I take it you frown on well done?"

"Got that right. Destroys all the flavor."

"Well, since I've been vegan for the past ten years, why don't you fix it as close as to well done that you'll allow, and I'll try it." She took a sip of her wine and felt very comfortable. "I'll help, what can I do?"

"Since you didn't look past all the meat in my fridge perhaps you should pull out the two drawers below. You might find some green leafy things in them to make a salad with. Note the salad dressing in the door."

She opened the fridge and pulled out the two drawers. "My bad. I guess I shouldn't assume. So, you do eat salad?"

"My human part enjoys a good salad with steak, but if I had to choose between the two, I'd live on steak. However, I do have a weakness for homemade pie. You will find blueberry and cherry pie rotting somewhere here in the kitchen."

"Rotting?"

"Yeah," he said blushing. "No one can make a pie like my mother did, but I keep trying to find one. I usually eat one piece and throw the rest away. I can't ever find any as good as hers was.

"So, your favorite is blueberry and cherry?"

He paused. "They are my second favorite. You've probably never heard of it," he said with a faraway look. "It's called golden raisin pie and she made them with golden raisins and fresh walnuts. She used to crack the nuts herself. Since she died, I've never had it. No one makes it that I know of."

"That's sad. I have things my mother made no one else can make. So, I know what you mean. Actually, the sound of steak does make my mouth water."

"I think you'll enjoy it."

He leaned by her to grab the steaks off the second shelf and brushed up against her, and she felt a warmth travel through her. It felt like bees buzzing through her blood. The muscles in her stomach tightened and she realized she was utterly and completely attracted to him. She wanted to grab him and throw him up against the wall and kiss him till he was crazy. And his smell? God, he smelled good. She could hardly breathe.

She gulped, and when he had ahold of the steaks he turned and looked in her eyes and they locked. Time stood still. She was drawn into the smooth honey tone, and they warmed to a darker shade. She was lost and felt like she was riding a current of water ready to breach the top of a cliff and tumble over.

Her world was topsy-turvy. She was at the precipice of something new, something exciting, and for the first time in her life, she wanted. She wanted with a passion. She wanted him. His body let off so much heat. She felt like she could wrap him around her like a blanket.

She'd love nothing more than to be cocooned in his warmth and just let eternity pass her by, and she could almost feel his naked skin next to hers. She felt a twitch and rubbed her thighs together, then breathed deep and caught a pleasant whiff of his cologne and his dark male scent. Since she'd become wolf her sense of smell heightened considerably as a human and right now that was a definite plus.

Testosterone came rolling off him in waves and she was as attracted to that as a bee was to pollen. His masculinity fairly screamed at her. She gulped. She swore he felt the same. He just stared at her with what seemed forever but was only seconds. He slowly pulled the steaks out not taking his eyes off her. She thought she could clearly see lust there. Just as she was ready to throw caution to the wind and lean down and kiss him, he cleared his throat, pulled the steaks out quickly, and said, "I'll start the grill."

That certainly threw cold water on her heated blood. She couldn't form a word if she tried, so she nodded her head in answer. The moment was broken, and she was glad. She had decided after Cal she wouldn't fall in love ever again, but this felt different, this was nothing like she felt for Cal. Cal was stable, dependable, and he never invoked anything near what she just felt for Cain. She was ready to take Cain in his own kitchen, everything else be damned. What on earth had gotten into her?

When she had sex with Cal it felt preplanned just like his life and it was always in bed, the lights off, and it was always missionary style. They tried oral sex a couple of times, but both times it didn't seem to do anything for either of them, and they ended up back in their regular positions anyway, so they just stuck with that. The last two years with him it was maybe once a week.

The rest of the time they were too tired to do anything. Sex was all so clinical to her, and she thought that was what having sex with anyone would be, just a way to procreate. Or at least what she thought before she met Cain. She supposed if sex with him was anything like she was feeling she had a good idea it'd be hot wild sex, and the thought had her whole body heating up and tingling.

No, this man was unpredictable, exciting, attractive, and gave her goosebumps. She found she wanted to do things to make him happy, bring a smile to his face. It played havoc with her feelings of never wanting to become involved ever again. Perhaps it was just a sexual thing. Cal would have never thought of buying her a dress or having her hair done for her, it was always simply going out to dinner for any celebration. She cursed herself in her mind as she pulled the last of the vegetables out. She had to quit comparing the two men, they were completely different from each other.

Then it dawned on her. Cal was safe, that is why she

thought she loved him. He had his life planned out, he'd be stable, and is that what she really wanted in a relationship? Safe? Dependable? Reliable? She still wanted dependable and reliable, but wasn't Cain as well? Why did he seem so different to her? She really had to think about what she just felt. It was all so new to her.

Is that what falling in love felt like or was she falling in lust? She still wanted to jump his bones. Then why when she was around other men, she'd never felt this way? She didn't have time to analyze it all right now, but she would just bet when she pulled the covers over her tonight Cain would be in her thoughts until she fell asleep.

She turned around with the carrots and almost hit Cain in the face with them. "Uh, oh, sorry. I wasn't paying attention."

He laughed. "I can see." I was just getting the grater out of the drawer for you. Carrots are better grated up, don't you think?" He asked standing upright.

She looked at the bag of carrots that she forgot she was holding. "Ye…yes, I always grate my carrots." What a dumb thing to say. She put the carrots on the counter by the sink and began washing them. She noticed he had a cutting board out with a knife on top sitting on the other side of the sink. He's quick, she thought.

She could see past the great room the shades were again pulled back and the sliding door open. She could smell the BBQ smoke from remnants of his cooking before and it smelled good. He came back in with an empty wine glass and she glanced at hers. It was empty also. He grabbed the bottle poured her some, and did the same with his, then set the bottle down and grabbed the steaks. He walked back out. "It's about ready to go on the grill, how are the veggies coming?" he yelled, as he opened the lid to the grill.

"Just about there," she yelled back. She put her mind to cutting up the vegetables and put him to the back of her mind, or at least tried to, but he kept sneaking back, and she couldn't for the life of her, quit smiling about it. He excited her, and how exciting was that? She shook her head as she chopped up green onions. Man-o-man, she thought, her feelings were all over the place. One minute she felt like dying and lonelier than she'd ever been, the next she was laughing, or sexually attracted to Cain. What the hell was wrong with her?

She found plates, salad bowels, and silverware and set the table. She grabbed all the dressings out of the fridge and put them on the table and set the large salad out. She wasn't sure he liked grated cheese on his salad, so she set a bowl of it to the side. She found a salad fork and spoon in the drawer where he got the grater, then stood back and looked at her handy work. It looked good but was missing something. "Ah." She went into the living room and grabbed two of the candles and brought them back and lit them. Now it looked ready.

"Wow, nice job," he said carrying in the steaks. She breathed deep and the smell of the steaks made her mouth water.

"Those steaks look scrumptious. And they smell divine. I didn't know I was so hungry. Usually after a breakfast like we had this morning, I'd eat light the rest of the day, but I feel like I haven't eaten at all."

"It's because a wolf's metabolism is a lot higher than a human's. You'll find tonight after we eat and turn wolf you will be hungry all over again. When I said you'll eat lots of meat, I wasn't kidding. Just turning wolf will eat up all the energy you produce from this meal. You'll be starving again."

"Wow, I can hardly believe that." She sat across from him.

"It's true. Wolves eat a lot throughout the day, they don't have breakfast, lunch, and dinner, they just have, *hungry*."

She laughed. They had a lot of small talk during dinner, mostly about when they were kids. She couldn't help it, she caught herself staring at him and hanging on his every word. She was enjoying herself immensely and she could tell he was too. She thought him quite funny talking about his childhood mischievousness.

She hoped when she turned wolf tonight, she would do what she was supposed to. She didn't want to spoil the evening doing something stupid again. She told herself to be sure and think when she was wolf and wondered if she could take her own advice. She shook her head.

"What? What are you shaking your head at?"

"At myself. I was giving myself advice for later when I am wolf. Now, I'm just wondering if I will take it." She looked at him and smiled.

"Surprisingly it's one of the best things you can do." He set his fork down and took a drink of wine. He wiped his mouth with his napkin, chewed on his steak a couple more times, swallowed, then continued.

"When you are wolf, as you know the wild is in the forefront. However, you can control your wild to a certain extent by ingraining your domestic, human side, to take control of the wild. When you tell yourself something it somehow gets back through when you are wolf. I know I kept telling myself I couldn't eat humans.

My first time seeing one as wolf, those words screamed to the front of my mind. I ran away before they could see me. So, by all means, give yourself advice. It works."

She chuckled and took a bite of steak. "This steak is perfect. What is it medium rare?"

"Close," he said with sheepish grin. "It's rare, just seared on both sides."

"Oh my God. I'd never eat rare, but this is so…" She leaned her head back and moaned. "So perfect." She chewed then opened her eyes. He was staring at her. She felt her body temperature climb and her blood flow to the places it had never gone before. What the heck was he doing to her? She had to look away from those golden bedroom eyes before she did something embarrassing. She glanced outside. "Did you remember to turn off the grill?" She watched the smoke rolling out from under the lid.

"Oh, shit! I always forget to turn it off." He jumped up and ran outside. He turned the knobs on the front of the grill, opened the lid and a cloud of smoke came wafting out, coughed a couple of times, then closed it and returned. "Well, that used a half tank of propane." He chuckled. "I have to fill the tank every time I turn around. Good thing I keep a spare in the garage."

"I can remind you." She caught herself as he looked at her funny. "I can remind you…while I'm here. Maybe if I remind you a couple of times you won't forget." Nice save, she told herself. Then she thought about what she'd said. It was as though she meant she'd be here for a long time, a very long time. For a second, she felt that way, she felt at home, and it was just something she couldn't get used to. She mentally kicked herself. He must have blown it off because he filled her glass with wine, then his own and didn't say anything.

She realized she hadn't been sad all night and she wasn't missing Cal. The realization surprised her. It was the first time in a long time she wasn't dwelling on it. She felt together for the first time since his death. No, she just had fun, plain ole fun, and she enjoyed herself, immensely.

"Yeah, maybe, I don't know, it's something I always forget doing. Have a couple of habits like that."

"Huh? oh yeah, so, do I," she said getting back into the conversation. "I have a habit of putting all my bills in one place, then I forget about them. I usually get a past due then I sit down and fill out checks for all my bills and pay them."

He chuckled. "I have direct deposit, and the companies I have to deal with as far as bills go automatically debit my account each month. It saves me all the paperwork. But it's something I always take care of right away. I don't like owing."

"I don't either, but I still forget. I'd like to do it the way you do with automatic debit, and I keep telling myself to set it up, but I procrastinate."

"Funny how humans prioritize things in their life." I enjoy a clean house, but I don't clean, I have hired help."

"I like a clean house. But I also don't mind the cleaning. When I clean, I think, and it's during those times answers will come and always when I least expect it." She glanced at the clock hanging over the window above the sink. Seven o'clock.

He noticed her glance. "Yes, we have to eat up it's going to be dark in another hour and we have a long night of being wolf."

The magic of the evening still lingered in the air around them and Kara hummed as she cleared the dishes and put them in the dishwasher. Cain covered the salad and put it in the fridge and threw the bones from their T-bones in the waste compacter. He put the empty bottle of wine in the garage, and they finished what they were doing in a few minutes.

"We work well together." Cain brushed his hands together. "Ready for another night?"

"I wish I could say I was, but I don't feel very ready."

He handed her jacket to her and slipped on his. "You'll be fine."

Kara found herself enjoying the ride as she watched the trees become denser and more reclusive. They seemed to be out in the middle of nowhere. "I haven't seen a single soul up here. It's beautiful. I've lived here my whole life and have never been up this far."

"There aren't as many campers out this way. This is the most remote area I visit. I wanted to take you to more populated places to try and cram your training in, but I saw how that worked. I want to play it safe tonight." He opened the trunk and pulled out the two duffle bags. She caught the one he threw at her.

Kara went to the other side of the car and began stripping down. Cain did the same on his side of the car. He threw his duffel in the trunk, and she did the same.

"Why the duffels if we just put everything in the trunk anyway?" She asked.

"Old habits," he answered. "Sometimes I have had to hide my clothes in the weirdest places. It's just easier with a duffel. There's also a gym in the basement of where I work, and I sometimes make use of it."

"Makes sense."

"Ready?" he asked.

"As I'll ever be," she answered.

They said the words needed for change and both went down on all fours at the same time. Cain howled and Kara answered with her own. He turned to her, his tail wagging and came at her. He jumped on her back playfully and she could almost hear him laughing. She turned on him and nipped his side then took off running.

She was lightning fast, but Cain was just as fast and closing in on her. She leaped over rocks and boulders, and dodged trees, only slowing if she had to. The moon was almost full, and it was bright out. She could see like it was daytime.

She wasn't looking where she was going, and she tripped over a fallen branch and went tumbling down a steep hill. Going end over end she came to a stop at the bottom and laughed. Cain ran down and pounced on her and poked her with his nose.

She felt freer and happier than ever before. Quickly turning around, she playfully nipped at him again. He took off running and she followed him. They were so into their little game of chase they ignored all the little animals near them.

They finally stopped to catch their breath as they stood below near the river.

*"What do you call those small lines of light again, that I see?"*

*"I'm so glad you asked. I can elaborate more on your lessons. Those are halos. At least it's what we call them. You have a second eyelid. To see the halos, you can drop them and retract them at will. It acts somewhat like a prism. They are purely by instinct, but I want you*

*to be aware of how this works. Pick a spot on one of the bands of light you see, and stare at it for a moment."*

She saw maybe three or four streaks of light and was amazed, and she did feel the secondary eyelids closing. If he hadn't told her, she might not have known she was using them. As a wolf everything was much different. Somehow everything seemed cleaner, clearer, even the smells inundating her nose were crisp and clear. She definitely felt more alive, and she didn't feel so lonely, which wasn't so much a surprise anymore.

She did as Cain suggested and searched the area, in one spot it looked like several streaks intersected. Two of the rays were much dimmer than the others. She picked the brightest and stared at it. When moving she didn't notice them as much. They were almost nonexistent, probably due to the eyelids, but when she concentrated, she saw them much clearer.

Once she focused, all the rays became separate, some thicker, brighter than others. She was staring at one closest to the ground when a shadow of a racoon came into focus. It was like a cloud of light in racoon form. *"Is that a racoon?"* she asked.

*"Yes, it came through here and you are seeing the energy field left behind. The trail of energy shows you the way it went. You will learn to do this quickly when you hunt for food. It will help you track."*

*"What's the larger one that is the brightest?"*

*"You tell me."*

She stared at for a moment and a large animal started to form. It looked like some type of deer, but it was much larger. *"Is it a deer?"* she asked, not taking her eyes from it. *"It seems big for a deer. It has horns, but they are too wide for deer."*

*"It's Rocky Mountain Elk. What you see is one who is their scout. If you go further back into the trees, you will find a well-worn path the elk take, as well as other animals, it's where the path is more secluded. If you are hungry, we can follow their path. Also, smell helps. With the smell and halo together we can hunt, but you need to know elk can be very dangerous. They can kill a wolf if you get into the middle of them."*

*"I want to go."*

*"Pick up a scent on the ground and once you do, follow it. The stronger the scent the closer they are. Go ahead. I'll follow you."*

She sniffed the ground and found many different scents. She picked the thick dark musky smell along the ground and followed it. Once in a while she would look up and see the halo and that helped. She was becoming accustomed to what she was doing and began trotting faster as the scent became stronger. They went through a grouping of trees then to an open area and on the other side of the river stood the herd of elk.

*"Do not go into the herd,"* he warned again. *"They might not be able to kill us, but they can cause damage that will make us hurt like hell for a long time. They can crush bones very quickly. They can kill a wild wolf and have."*

She searched the crowd of elk and found a stray toward the back of the group.

Immediately the elk sensed them. One of the elk bayed a warning to the others and they quickly took off. She could hear their hooves hit the ground her hearing was so acute. She noticed her senses were stronger at times, or maybe she was just becoming used to everything. Wolf instinct took over, and the wildness came to the forefront. She saw a smaller elk and took off after it. It was the one she'd seen earlier lingering at the back of the herd. Maybe it was ill.

*"Be careful with the elk. Remember they can strike a wolf and kill them."*

She cornered the elk and it tried just that. It reared up and came down heavy with its hooves, but she dodged them. When it dropped down Cain came in from the other side leaped and bit its neck. She bit its leg and together they pulled it down. It neighed as if calling to the rest for help, but she knew none would be coming. Cain still had ahold of its neck. He released and bit again sinking his teeth in an artery. It quickly died. They were in full wolf form, their nature, their actions, and their appetite.

True to Cain's word, she was hungry, even famished again. The steak did little to curb her appetite. They had a veritable feast. She was enjoying this meal when she heard a wolf growling. She looked over her shoulder and saw several wolves sitting next to each other.

None of them were silver sable. They were all snarling. She watched as more wolves came out from under the brush. They must have smelled their kill or heard the elk baying. She noticed their heads were slightly lowered and their focus almost scary.

*"That thought is exactly true. You really are learning fast."*

She could almost feel pride in the thought. and it made her happy, but she was still hungry. Cain immediately stopped eating and raised his head and looked over at the wolves. *"They are wild wolves. They're hungry. They could fight us for the meat, and they will probably try."*

"*Let them try. I'm not quitting until I'm full.*"

The alpha male of the pack of wild wolves lurched toward her and Cain intervened. The next thing she knew the two were in a heavy fight. She was afraid for Cain and immediately wanted to help.

"*No, stay back! Don't interrupt!*"

She followed the order but didn't like it. She was afraid Cain would get hurt. She listened to their growls, snarls, and the snapping of teeth. She watched in fascination as the two went at it. She discarded their meal and went over to where they were fighting. With pictures in her mind, she gave over their meal to the other wolves and the alpha male quickly stopped what he was doing. Cain snapped at him, but he was already thinking food. Cain stood panting heavily.

"*You all right?*"

"*I'm fine, a couple of scratches. I would have won the fight, but I also feel for their hunger. Those wolves are very hungry. They haven't eaten in a while.*"

"*Then I'm glad we gave it up.*"

"*But you didn't want to.*"

"*I could've eaten more, but when I realized how hungry they were, I knew I didn't need it as bad as they did.*"

"*There's certain etiquette amongst wolves, amongst all the animals of the wild. I would've given our meal up as soon as I heard their first growl, because it was the growl of hunger. We were full, and they needed to eat. It's probably been a couple of days since they ate last.*"

"*Why? It's been easy for us to hunt and get food. Isn't it easy for them?*"

"*They think in the wild, Kara, we have common sense and the ability to think ahead. It's almost like we* have two brains, except on a full moon. It's the closest to wild you will ever get. It's hard to keep your human thoughts going. The rest of the time we are strategic. We can plan out what we are going to do. Wild hungry wolves can't do that. They plan somewhat but not near on the same scale as we can."

"So, they plan as well."

"Only to a small extent. Their stomachs take over their minds and it's what they think with. Don't get me wrong, wolves are very intelligent, but they let their hunger get the better of them sometimes and they lose the catch they are after.

She nodded her head in understanding then took off running leaving the wild wolves to their meal, and he followed. They came to the ledge up over the river, a waterfall was off to her right and a large pool down beneath her. "*I think I want to swim.*" Cain came running up behind her. "*Wolves do swim, don't they?*" She could hear the chuckle in his thoughts.

"*It's more like, wolves can swim if they have to.*"

"*Not just for something to do, or like take a bath and clean up?*"

"*Not usually. In the wild, the way wolves react to each other is by their smell, so they keep their old smell instead of washing it away. Now, it's not to say they stay away from water. They keep their faces clean of blood, like you have already noticed.*

"*Occasionally a wolf will swim on a very hot day because it cools them off. But normally, they avoid fully going in the water. They won't hesitate to cross through the water if they want to get to the other side of the river. It all just depends. To swim in it the way you or I do, is very unlikely for a natural wolf.*

She looked back toward the river and thought she'd love a swim, so she jumped off the edge and landed with a plop in the water. When she broke the surface, she began paddling around then she felt something hit beside her and realized it was Cain. He jumped in after her. "*Are you all right*?" She giggled. "*Why you…*" he shouted.

"*Hey. You could have landed on me and hurt me.*"

"*Well, I didn't, did I?*" he asked mischievously. He began paddling around her as she treaded water. He tried to splash her with his paw, and it didn't work. Then he commanded her to turn back into her human form.

Kara said the magic words quizzically and turned back. She treaded water in her human form as she watched him change back.

"I thought this best for our swim." We can enjoy it more."

She shuddered. "It's so much colder in human form," she said her teeth chattering.

"Perhaps this wasn't such a good idea." He began swimming to the edge.

She watched him then decided she wanted to make it to the bank first. She didn't know why she wanted to turn it into a game, but she did, and quickly swam past him. He began swimming faster catching up to her and she squealed. They made it to the bank at the same time and crawled out. They were both laughing. It was fun. She sat on the grassy part, crossed her legs, leaned her head back and sighed.

She wasn't as bashful being naked in front of him anymore, but then again, he'd caught her naked so many times he'd probably seen every inch of her body. He came up next to her and sat. She couldn't help but watch him. She thought she might melt.

He sat and stretched his legs out in front of him then crossed them his thigh covering up the bare part of his masculinity. She wanted to lean over so she could get a better look. Then chided herself as if she were a teenager. She quickly put a wall up in her thoughts, one that wouldn't let him know what she was thinking.

Her and him? It wasn't going to happen, so she just better accept it right now. Besides, she didn't want anyone who wouldn't want her back.

She knew his thoughts about wanting a family and living a long life with a wife. It was a great dream, one that was accessible for him, but not for her. She felt the same way at one time when she was going to marry Cal. Now that wasn't possible. Even if she could have a family, she could possibly go crazy. She couldn't fathom it, so she wouldn't think it. The thought of it depressed her.

"Are you rested?" The question pulled her out of her reverie, and she glanced over at him.

"Huh, what?"

"Have you rested? Are you ready to return as wolf?"

She suddenly felt very tired. "Can we call it a night?"

"Wh…well, yes, if you want. But we still have some night left, you won't have that choice on the full moon."

"It's okay, I'm tired. I'd like to go back if you don't mind."

He must have picked up the weariness in her tone. "Okay, call your wolf back and we'll head back to where we are parked."

She said the magic words and made the change. He followed suit. She felt him probe her mind, but she put up a wall and didn't feel like letting him in. She'd be able to hear his thoughts if she wanted, because he stayed wide open. She certainly didn't want him hearing her thoughts. They were raw and personal and about him.

****

When they got back, they mumbled goodnight to each other and went to bed. After Cain crawled in bed, he couldn't help but think about Kara. The whole day had been great. He couldn't remember ever having so much fun. What was it about the woman that enticed him? She made him feel giddy, young, playful. It had been years since he felt that way. It was a natural joy, not an alcohol induced one.

He couldn't figure it out. He wanted to take her to bed in the worst way. So why didn't he act on his desire? She was beautiful, but he'd had plenty of beautiful women for a one-nighter. Some even called him for more and sometimes he obliged them. He knew he didn't want her for a mate, but what about two consenting adults just wanting to have sex, no strings attached? He could live with that, hell he'd been doing that his whole life. He knew she knew he didn't want her for a mate, so maybe she just wanted sex too. He'd had ample opportunity…why didn't he follow through? Maybe if they talked about it first, about boundaries. Yes, that might work.

His thoughts returned to tonight, when he brushed up against her while getting the steaks from the refrigerator. Desire hit him so hard he almost took her then and there on the kitchen floor. He wanted to rip her clothes off and taste every inch of her skin. Just looking at her tonight gave him a hard on several times.

He usually found women in bars who were looking for a good time with no strings attached. But he was stone cold sober with her, and he found himself with thoughts all night long about making love to her. So, why didn't he just go ahead and go for it. Two consenting adults having a good time. He was sure she wanted him when they were at the fridge. His thoughts lazily drifted into what exactly he felt for her and why.

Kara was beautiful no doubt, probably the most beautiful woman he ever met, even with her singed off, uneven hair. Her body was perfection. He always liked the smaller breasted women, and her legs, he gulped, those long legs, why they went all the way to the floor. He chuckled at his self-made joke. He was still feeling playful. Body wise she was definitely a ten in his book. He was attracted to her. He couldn't deny it for a minute. It was as if there was an invisible band of energy drawing them together. Plus, he felt like he'd always known her.

He thought about other women. Kara had an aura about her they didn't have. A special something that made him feel her beauty beyond seeing it. The more time he spent with her the more beautiful she became. He didn't understand it. Maybe it was because he was taking the time to get to know her. It was something he'd never bothered to do before.

Perhaps when Kara was released and he went back to his old life, he should make an effort to get to know some other women. On another note, he didn't take Kara for the kind he found in nightclubs.

She wasn't the type to simply sleep with someone for the sake of having sex. Maybe he was afraid of her turning him down. Maybe he didn't want to engage because he couldn't make promises he couldn't keep.

He also reminded himself of the fact she was going to eventually lose her mind. He should perhaps hurry and finish her training so he could get back to his old life. But hadn't Kara put a damper on that as well? He didn't feel the same as he did prior to meeting her and it bothered him. He could return to his old ways as soon as she was gone. He guessed he could wait until then.

He rolled over onto his side, then leaned up and fluffed his pillow, and plopped his head back down. He couldn't get comfortable, and he couldn't quit thinking about Kara. His mind kept going back to wanting her no matter how hard he berated himself. She was just in the other room. He could *feel* her through the walls.

He felt her loneliness, her warmth, and her uncertainty, and surprisingly shyness. She had been engaged. She couldn't possibly be a virgin, could she?

He rolled over to his other side. If he kept this up, he'd be awake all night and he'd be like a steak on the grill, on one side a few seconds then on the other for the same, only he wouldn't be pulled off after the first flip.

He groaned into his pillow. He didn't think any of the women he brought home ever slept in the other room. Yet, there she was, and as far as he could tell, she was the woman of his dreams. No, she couldn't be. *Way to go, DeLucci, quit thinking and get some sleep.*

He grumbled then jerked up and fluffed his pillow again. He laid on his back, putting his hands behind his head and stared at the ceiling. "Thomas." Such a common name. Was it even real? Who were the people who raised her? Why were her powers bound? Where did she really come from? So many unanswered questions. Questions she probably had as well.

At least he knew where he came from. He was Italian and from a family with an old name. He was several generations down from the first DeLucci, and he had big shoes to fill. Every generation the DeLucci's had a strong hard-working man. He didn't know if he was filling those shoes, but he was trying his darndest.

No one in his family had ever been wolf, at least that he knew of, and thanks to Christian he was the first. He laughed about his strict father who wore the shoes he was trying to fill. Wouldn't he be surprised if he saw him now. He chuckled.

Thoughts continued to swirl through his mind as he closed his eyes and finally relaxed. When sleep overtook him, he fell into it deep and restful and didn't wake until his morning alarm.

Chapter Six

Cain awoke with a start. He must have been dreaming, it took him a minute to figure out where he was. He turned and glanced at his clock on the nightstand. 6:00 a.m. He slammed his hand on the top to turn it off and moaned. It was time to get up, he overslept. He was usually up by five, an hour before his alarm went off. Well, not this morning.

He crawled out of bed and dragged himself to the bathroom. He turned the shower on, took care of business, then stepped under the spray. He could hear the water running in the adjacent bathroom and figured Kara was up and getting ready. He didn't get much sleep last night because he kept dreaming about her. Kara as a wolf, Kara as a woman in his kitchen, a naked Kara in bed underneath him.

He must have enjoyed the dream about the latter because there was evidence of it on his sheets. "Damn." He hit the shower wall. He shouldn't have thought so much about her before he fell asleep. He went to sleep with her on his mind, and he awoke with her on his mind, if he kept this up, he'd go stark raving mad.

He leaned his head against the shower wall and looked down at his feet watching the water gather and circle around the drain before taking the final plunge downward. He took a deep breath.

It was pure torture having Kara around, but it was

his fault he was her sire. He changed her. He thought about it for a second. He'd do it again in a city second, he didn't have to think twice about it. His thoughts picked up where they left off last night. Back to how life was when she wasn't in it. He tried hard to remember it, hold onto it, get back into it. He had it made with his lifestyle.

He had his pick of any number of women. He always had a new phone number. Numbers he never saved. Most of the time he'd just throw their number in the trash. He chuckled when he thought about the blonde, what was her name? He couldn't remember, but he sure remembered how her body looked and felt. She wrote her number in permanent marker across the bottom of his favorite T-shirt, but he didn't think twice about pitching it. He could get another favorite T-shirt.

He turned the spray off and grabbed a towel and wrapped it around his waist and stepped on the mat outside the shower. He grabbed another towel and vigorously rubbed his head then threw it around his shoulders. He was on automatic pilot because he was still deep in thought about Kara.

With Kara here, he realized his life with other women had been nothing more than a joke. She made him look at himself and what he saw made his heart drop and displeased him immensely. No, she made him want more, so much more. He wanted a wife and a family and hadn't met the right woman yet, so what had him so bothered?

"What are you going to do, DeLucci?" he mumbled. "Just pick up where you left off when she leaves? How long before you can release her?" She was doing well. The full moon would be the tell all. He had to be on top of his game. Since he'd never been a sire before he was a bit concerned. He barely kept it together himself.

He could ask Christian because he'd been a sire several times, but if he did after telling him all was well…no, nope. He wouldn't involve Christian. He had to do this himself. He needed some time to meditate before the full moon. Prepare himself.

If she passed the full moon test, and one more, he could release her then. The thought made his heart skip a beat. He realized he didn't like that idea at all, he didn't want to release her.

Perhaps his need to keep her around was because he needed to solve the mystery behind her powers being bound, because she was such a conundrum to him. It was like a lightbulb going off. That was the answer, he told himself. He was just purely involved with this mysterious puzzle. Yes, that was it. He loved a good mystery. He smiled. Happy with finally having an answer to his one large problem lifted his spirits.

He found himself whistling as he got his razor and shaving cream out of the medicine cabinet. He set the things down and grabbed his toothbrush, with a quick look at his teeth in the mirror, he smeared toothpaste on the brush and began brushing. He now knew why he felt the way he did, and as soon as he solved the puzzle, he could go back to the way he was and find his true mate.

He spit out toothpaste and rinsed his mouth, then took floss and flossed his teeth.

"You have to be logical, DeLucci," he said to himself in the mirror. "You have approximately four hundred years left, and she has only twenty at the most. You have to quit thinking with the head between your legs and start thinking with the one on your shoulders."

He smiled at himself. He peeled his lips back and looked at all his teeth, satisfied with what he saw, he put his brush and paste away. He closed the door to the medicine chest and looked again in the mirror smearing shaving cream over his cheeks.

Then he thought about Kara going crazy in ten to twenty years. His heart sank again, this time like a lead balloon. What exactly was different about their blood? What Kara said to him about her blood made him wonder. If he could get Reid Dalton to look at the dilemma, they may find a cure. But he was human, did he dare bring it up? He wasn't sure. He had to feel the man out and see what if anything he might know about wolves and the people of the magical kind. There were some humans aware, but they were few and far between.

He finished in the bathroom and went to his closet and picked out a nice cotton button-down shirt. He had to look presentable today because he was taking Kara shopping for a dress and getting her hair done. He was also going to buy a new suit. Maybe he'd take her to his favorite little Italian bistro for lunch. He thought about it and chuckled.

It always made his partner angry to hear him call his favorite little restaurant an Italian Bistro because bistro meant French cuisine, not Italian. So, Italian bistro stuck, and he used it often around Stone, just because it drove him crazy. It was his favorite little spot to eat though, he couldn't deny it. He leaned down and pulled his socks on, slipped into some nice loafers, and looked in the mirror.

"Ready for the day, DeLucci?" With a salute to the mirror and one last look to see if he'd pass in public, he smiled and left the bedroom to go find Kara.

He found her in the kitchen eating a bowl of cereal and staring at the back of the box. "Why is it," he asked, "that when eating cereal people always feel the need to read whatever is on the back of the box? When I eat eggs, I don't read an egg carton."

He pulled out a chair and sat in front of an empty bowel. "Pass me that one, will you?" he asked her, pointing to another box. Without taking her eyes off the box she seemed so fascinated with, she handed him the other one and kept on reading.

She finally looked up and answered him. "I don't know, but I think it is an ingrained habit to always read the back of the box that you pour your cereal out of." She smiled at him, and he thought the whole kitchen lit up. "Good morning."

"Good morning," he said smiling back. "You do remember we are going shopping today?"

"You don't have any work you have to do?"

"I do, but it shouldn't take long. I'm going to meet with the owner of the bar that had the explosives. I just found out he owns the whole block of bars and just rents the others out. It will be interesting to speak with him."

"I'd like to be with you when you see him, if I may."

"Of course, you will be with me. After all, I wouldn't make you sit in the car like an abused child while I interrogate the man."

She giggled over the comment, and it warmed his heart. He really did enjoy being around her. She was fun, and he needed that. He would miss her when she left. He poured his cereal then grabbed the half gallon of milk and poured in a generous amount over the cereal.

"I thought we'd stop by your place if we have time, and you can go through your mother's things. Perhaps you can find a clue to help you find out more about why your powers were bound and why no one ever told you."

She put the box down and looked at him. "I tried using the other power last night," she said soberly.

"And? Any luck?"

"No, I don't believe I have that power. I think whatever happened to you was some sort of residual effect from the spell I was trying to do. I'm not even sure I was doing it correctly."

"Well, it seemed to me you were moving right along through it. I have the bruises to prove it."

"You do?" she asked raising her eyebrows. "I…I'm sorry. I didn't know that would happen."

"I'm just kidding, I have no bruises, but you did slam me up against the wall pretty damn hard without ever laying a finger on me. Pretty impressive if you ask me, and handy if you do have that power. I'm not sure I want to see you at your full potential it could prove to be very dangerous."

He tried hard to keep a straight face as he shoved a spoonful of sugary cereal in his mouth. When he saw the shocked look cross her face he broke out in a grin. "I'm still just kidding," he said quickly. He wanted to wipe away the shock. "I want to give The Oracles back to you, but I need you to tell me that you won't try breaking the spell again. We need to find out why someone bound your powers. I know it wasn't your parents."

"How do you know that?"

"Because they are gone. If it were them, your powers would no longer be bound. No there's someone alive who is keeping your powers bound and the shroud intact so the wolves wouldn't be able to smell witch on you. Whoever it is, they don't want anyone, sorcerer, or wolf, to know you exist. That tells me there is something very important about you. I don't think it's just for you to go through life without knowing your background, otherwise we wouldn't have found The Oracles."

"That's right."

She appeared so forlorn to him that it made him feel bad for bringing it up again, but damnit they had to, they had to find out. He knew she was going to go through a whole lot more before this was over with. He wanted to spare her, but he couldn't, they needed to know.

"We can talk more about it when we go through your mother's things this afternoon. First thing this morning we meet the owner of the nightclubs, then we'll go shopping and get your hair done, and then over to your house. Does that sound agreeable to you. I don't want to plan your life out or anything, but I thought it was a good plan."

"If it's good for you, then it's good for me."

\*\*\*\*

Cain let Kara have the only other chair in the small, cluttered office, but she chose to stand. She had a look on her face that spoke of not wanting to touch anything for fear of catching something. He could relate. He figured there must be a week's worth of fast-food hamburger wrappers keeping half eaten pizza and their boxes company. He looked at the unkempt man shoving things aside on his desk.

"I'm sorry," said the short round man. I'd normally meet you at Mr. Belchamp's main offices, but this was closer. I usually don't meet people where I do most of my work. Mr. Belchamp is currently in New Orleans. I'm afraid I'm all you've got. How can I help you?"

Cain flipped his TITAN I.D. closed and returned it

to his pocket. "We're here about the bomb that was found at your nightclub."

"Oh, that," he said wiping his brow. Carl Jonson looked relieved. Cain cocked an eyebrow. Relieved that he was here about the bomb? Belchamp's accountant quit fidgeting with things on his desk and began tapping his pen. "Well, then how can I help you?"

He wondered how such a nervous accountant could get any work done. He was ready to take the man's pen and run it through his eye. Between the clutter and old food smell, Jonson tapping his pen was driving him nuts.

"Why do you think there was a bomb put on Mr. Belchamp's main nightclub? There was enough explosive to blow the entire block. A lot of people could have been killed if it had gone off. Most of them young adults."

"I can't think of why anyone would want to put a bomb there," said the sweating accountant. "I mean, I'm sure a man of Mr. Belchamp's stature would have some enemies but nothing like that. He is a successful businessman after all."

"Think, Mr. Jonson. There must be something. Anything happen in the last couple of weeks that seemed strange to you?"

"No, business as usual. Hum…there was this…"

"What? Any little thing could be important."

"Mr. Belchamp turned down an offer for all of his clubs a couple of weeks ago."

"An offer on his clubs?" asked Kara. She quickly looked at Cain. "Who made an offer on the clubs?"

"Mr. Belchamp is selling the clubs?" asked Cain.

"No, he's not selling the clubs. He's making a killing on those clubs. Some guy went by his office downtown and gave his secretary an offer. We thought it was a joke until he got a phone call asking if he was ready to sell. I heard it was double what they were worth, but he won't sell. He enjoys his clubs. I don't have a copy of the offer, but his secretary might. Perhaps you should talk to her. I only know about it because I heard Nancy talking to Mr. Belchamp. So, I asked him about it."

"Nancy the secretary?" asked Kara.

"Yes. Go see her. Now if you don't mind, and if you have no more questions, I have work I need to get back to."

Cain reached in his pocket and pulled out a card and handed it to him. "If you can think of anything else, call me."

"Like I told the Police I have no idea why anyone would want to blow up the clubs."

Cain and Kara bid the accountant a good morning and they left. "Do you think the reason they wanted to blow it up was because they wanted to buy the clubs?" asked Kara. She walked along side of him toward the car. "But, if they wanted to buy them, why blow them up? Because they wouldn't sell?"

"Well, if they were blown up, they'd get the property cheaper. I don't know. Knowing who wanted them might give us some insight. I think we need to find out who tried to buy them. That's where we are heading now."

"I wonder why Belchamp had us meet with his accountant instead of his secretary."

"Probably because he knows everything that goes on with the clubs, at least monetarily, or he's just close enough to the guy that he'd be more help than his secretary. Not sure really. I think we should do some background checking on Belchamp and find out who this mystery buyer is."

\*\*\*\*

Kara watched as Cain pulled out his cell and hit a dial button then waited. "Hey, good morning to you too, Stone."

She felt good this morning and she let Cain have some privacy as he talked to Stone. She walked ahead a bit and looked at all the trees on the way to the parked car and noted all the buds. It was warming up and spring was in the air. Cain caught up.

"…background on Belchamp and I want you to look into Carl Jonson. No, I don't think there's anything special about either one of them, but it doesn't hurt to check. That bomb was there for a reason. No, I'm going right now to speak to the secretary. I'll let you know who tried to buy them when I find out."

A cat skittered across the sidewalk in front of them and it took her by surprise and she laughed. Cain almost tripped, glanced at Kara with a frown, then grinned at his own clumsiness. They got to his car, and he hit the button on his keys, and she heard the beep, beep, that unlocked the doors. He opened hers for her and she thought about what a gentleman he was even when he wasn't thinking about it.

"Okay, Stone, get back if you find anything untoward. You bet, you too." He quickly put his cell back in his pocket and got in the driver's side.

"Where to now?" she asked.

He glanced at his watch. "Right on time," he said as he turned the steering wheel hard left. He glanced back in her direction. "To get your hair done." It wasn't long, and he pulled up to park in front of the boutique. He let her out at the front door and said he'd be back in about an hour to pick her up.

It didn't take them long to cut her hair, add some highlights, then wash it. After that they did her hair up in rollers. They sprayed it to keep it wet then led her to one of the dryers. She really enjoyed getting the cut and her head scrubbed. It felt like she was letting go of the past as the locks fell to the floor.

She was getting rather bored, but quickly found herself in a group of upper-class women who probably did this kind of thing on a regular basis. On the other side of the room, where the women sat, was a place to get a foot massage and manicures and pedicures. The group of women were getting their nails done. She noted they must all be friends, the way they talked to each other. They all had some type of alcoholic beverage, and it was still morning.

"I hear Nancy is an addict. Did you know that Jerry took her to a dry out clinic? I feel sorry for those kids."

"I know," said another woman looking at her nails. "Red, don't you think red is the perfect color this week? How about you Sarah? You want red nails this week?"

"I think those kids will all end up doing drugs," said the redhead.

She glanced around the room and sighed. This was the boring part of getting her hair done, so she started drumming her nails on the arm of the chair as her hairdresser pumped the chair up, went too far, and with a whoosh let her down, then threw the dryer over her head and turned it on. She grabbed a magazine, opened it up, but didn't pay attention to what was on the page. She found herself listening to the women. She thought the hair dryer would be loud enough to drown out the other women, but she'd been wrong.

"I heard Danny got caught with cocaine," said the blonde who was getting ready to get her toenails painted.

"If one of my four boys got caught using any illicit drug their father would ground them for a year," said the redhead.

"If any one of my girls got caught doing drugs they'd be grounded for life," said the brunette.

"Well none of my kids would ever do drugs," said the blonde.

Kara glanced in her direction and noted her hair done up in large rollers and the one working on her nails put the bottle of silver down and held up a bottle of red. The blonde nodded.

"At least it was a quality drug," said the brunette. "I heard his friend John got caught with that killer drug that makes you stay awake for days. Both those boys were expelled from school for a whole month."

"You mean Meth?" asked the blonde.

"Yes, Janie, that's the drug. Poor man's cocaine I hear."

"Sounds like you know about drugs Althea. Have you tried any?"

It got quiet for a second and all Kara could hear was her dryer. She strained so she could hear the answer, and why she didn't know. Well, in Rome she thought, she was just curious.

The brunette plopped beside Janie, the blonde. She took the red polish from the girl's hand and picked another red and handed it to her. "I've tried Cocaine. It's not all that it's cracked up to be."

"Why do you say that Althea?"

"I had the most expensive kind," said Althea. "It

came directly from the maker."

"The maker? I heard it came from a plant," said Janie.

"Yes, but the maker cuts it," answered Althea.

"Cuts the plants down?" asked the redhead, Sarah.

"You aren't really that dumb, are you Sarah?" asked Althea. "They cut the drug with something that lessens it's effects, so they have more to make more money, understand?"

"Well, I wouldn't know, I don't do drugs like some people…" She looked at Althea mischievously.

Althea harrumphed. "I never…"

"You never what, Althea?" Sarah laughed. "Oh, come on. Tell us what it was like. Maybe I'll tell Harry and he can get us all some."

"No, he doesn't know anyone," said Althea. "Let Jimmy get it. Wouldn't that be fun? We could all try it. Hey maybe after the gala. Are you going?"

"To what?" asked Janie. "You mean the benefit gala for Reid Dalton and the new hospital? We must go. It's important for Klyde and his company. You going?"

"I am," said Althea. "It's the same for Jimmy. He's representing his company."

"We could meet at our house afterwards and have our own little party," said Sarah. "I'll have Harry get the stuff and we can at least try it."

"No, I'll have Jimmy get it, he has a good friend who knows where to get stuff like that. We can have the kids at my house," said Althea. "I'll hire two babysitters."

"Ohhh," said Sarah with a grin. She rubbed her hands together in glee. "Then while the kids are at your house, you can all come to mine, and we can do it there. Isn't there something so wicked in doing something you're not supposed to do.

"You mean like doing something against the law?" asked Janie.

"I haven't felt like this since I was in high school and skipped out my bedroom window on a Saturday night to go cruising with my boyfriend," said Althea.

"I know what you were doing with your boyfriend, Althea, and it wasn't cruising. Besides when have we ever tried anything like this?" asked Sarah.

"Well, never," replied Janie.

"It'll be such fun," said Sarah.

She'd heard enough, and if someone didn't come and get her soon, she was just going to leave. She couldn't believe these women. The girl who was working on her came and pulled a lock of hair from the roller. She turned the dryer off and hit the pedal at the side of the chair that let her back down.

"Follow me," she said with a smile. It was back to the other room to have her hair combed out. Soon she'd see how her hair turned out. She was quite excited.

She looked in the mirror at the bob cut. The highlights were perfect, and she had to admit her hair looked great. She put her fingers in her hair and fluffed it out. She wanted it as natural as she could get it without a great deal of hairspray. There was just enough highlight to add to the shine of her dark hair. She stood up and turned around just in time to see Cain come through the door. His smile widened as he saw her.

"You look great." He handed the woman his credit card. He took her hand and pulled her closer to get a better look. Then he walked around her. "Do you like it?"

"I love it, Cain, thank you. I never had highlights before, but I think I like them."

"They look great, and I couldn't tell you had them until you mentioned it."

"That's the way it's supposed to be," said her hairdresser. "Just enough highlight to show off the true color. The rich chocolate brown she has is gorgeous and her hair is so thick."

Kara blushed. "Thank you, both of you."

He signed the credit slip and added a tip, then handed her back the receipt and she gave him a copy.

"Thanks," he said. "We'll be back for sure."

"That is what I like to hear," said the hairdresser.

"Are you hungry?" he asked as they left the boutique.

"I'm famished."

"Do you like Italian?"

"I love Italian."

"I know this great little Italian Bistro. It's by Cherry Creek and not far from the Botanical Gardens. Have you ever been?"

"No, I can't say as I have. My parents didn't take me out very much. We would eat at the mall and fast food, but that was it."

"You, my dear lady, are in for a treat."

They didn't go far, and they were there. He parked and led her into the restaurant.

As they sat waiting for their food, Kara asked, "Did you find anything out from the secretary?"

"I did, and they did offer a mighty big sum. I looked at the offer myself. Looked professional enough."

"Who was it?"

"I don't know, some big company. R & D Enterprises. I'll have to look into it. You ever hear of them?"

"No, can't say as I have. Probably some large company wanting to come into to town. Happens occasionally."

"Yeah, but Denver is pretty tight with their people. Old names and money come from here."

"I hear you."

"I also stopped by the office and picked up the warrant and made a quick stop at the country club and got the names of the people who were there for lunch."

"Anyone stand out?"

"Not really, Reid Dalton was there, but he goes there every day. I doubt it was him. I didn't recognize any of the other names. I'll have Stone run them and see if anything sticks out.

The waitress came and put their food in front of them. "Oh, this smells divine," said Kara. Those were the last words said until they finished eating.

He wasn't kidding when he said the food was good, she thought, as she finished off her wine about a half hour later. She pushed her plate aside. She had the Gamberetti and she had to admit the shrimp was exquisite. "How was your lamb?" she asked.

"Well, I ate everything so it must have been good. To tell you the truth this is my favorite place to eat. I never leave hungry that's for sure and they have quite a variety."

"We'll have to come here again. Then she realized what she said.

He gave her a funny look and she felt herself blush. "I me...mean. I will have to come here again."

"No, that's all right, Kara. We can definitely come here again before I release you."

She sat back and looked at him. A feeling of warmth

traveled through her, comforting her. "How long does it usually take before a new wolf is released?"

He put his wine down and wiped his mouth with his napkin. He put it on top of his plate. "Normally we take a wolf through three full moons. Some have been let loose at two but that's rare. It usually takes three because invariably there are some if's in there."

"If's?"

"Yes, what *if* this were to happen, or that to happen. The first full moon we try and go where they are guaranteed not to run into any humans. The second full moon a possible sighting of them. The third to a more public place. We must make sure we can trust a wolf by him or herself. We can usually tell if one becomes wild right away. There are certain signs. But before we do anything rash, we allow for three full moons.

"Unless someone kills a human. That's upright a no-no and taken care of quickly. Sometimes the sire has to stop something like that. They all try to, not always making it. To tell you the truth, Christian told me there were many times someone did the same thing you did, and it was the sire's responsibility to make sure that no mistakes were made. It's hard on a full moon for sires, and it's doubly hard on newbies."

"That sounds reasonable."

They were enjoying their wine and talk when his cell went off. He quickly answered it. "DeLucci."

She watched his eyebrows raise and he gulped. She could tell he wasn't enjoying what was being said to him at all. His brow furrowed and there was a tightness in his jaw. She had a sneaking suspicion she wasn't going to make it to her house this afternoon to go through her mother's things.

"I'll meet you at the morgue," he said, and hit end. He sighed heavily as he returned the cell to his pocket.

"Bad news?"

"Yes, it seems a group of kids overdosed last night."

"A group?"

"Yes, a group from Commerce, Lochbuie, and Central West Denver."

"Are you saying a group from all those places got together and OD'd?"

"No, three different groups. They were all from the low-income areas of the city. A group from each place. Fifteen kids in all. Damn Ansen Horn. He brought that shit here."

He slammed a fist to the table then quickly looked around. He appeared to remember he was in a quiet restaurant. He grabbed his jacket off the back of his chair and stood and she followed suit. She noticed his locked jaw and could tell he was fuming angry. If Ansen was anywhere near him now, he'd be a dead man. He quickly paid, and they left.

When they got to the morgue, they met Christian and Stone near the front door. They were just getting there themselves. Christian was talking to the coroner.

"Thank God you got rid of the P.D." said Christian. He turned and saw them enter. Hi, Cain," he said with a nod. "Kara."

Cain said hi to everyone and introduced the coroner to Kara. "Let's go have a look at these kids."

The coroner walked them to a large room where all the kids were in the mortuary cabinet being kept cold, but the drawers were open, and one was on the table. The coroner had completed at least one autopsy which was evident when they walked into the room.

"Yes, I know it was an overdose. I think whatever they took made their hearts explode. When I get the results back from their blood tests, I'll be able to tell you more. Whatever drug it was, it took out anyone who did it. It must be a new drug floating around."

Cain pulled back a sheet over one of the kids and under it was a teenager. Her eyes were bulging out and her mouth was shaped in an O. It must have been quick, but she must have realized something was terribly wrong by the expressions frozen on her face. Kara looked at her torn and dirty clothes and noticed her hair was in knots. She didn't think the kid had bathed in a week, she saw lice come crawling out from her bangs and stepped back.

The coroner noticed her quick step back. "They haven't been processed yet," he said, as if he was trying to explain the lice away. Lice didn't scare her they just took her by surprise. The poor kid was probably homeless and maybe seventeen or eighteen. She could hazard to guess what the place looked like where they were found.

"They didn't have time to call E.M.S.," said the coroner. "It was a friend that went there at 3:00 a.m. and found them all dead. It was two hours after that another group was called in and thirty minutes after that the third group was called in. I'm not sure there won't be more before the day is over.

"Dr. Ganton?" interrupted an orderly.

"Yes, What is it, James?"

"I found this in the pocket of one of the kids." The young orderly walked up to the coroner and handed him a tiny baggie.

"Thank you, James. Check the clothes on all the others and see if there is any more." He took the bag and walked over by a desk and held it up under the light. "It appears to be some sort of speedball. I'll have this checked out. He dropped it from his gloved hands. I'll have P.D. analyze it."

Cain looked at the baggie the coroner was holding and noticed a smiley face on the baggie. "Get a load of that. There's a damn smiley face on the baggie. Who in their right mind would put such a thing on it?"

"A really sick person," said the coroner. "A really sick person."

"When you find out what it is, please call me," said Christian.

"You know the TITANs are going to have to work with P.D. on this. They know too much, have too many questions, and they aren't going to stop. You may as well get used to the idea of working with them. I'd get in there now so you can have some control over them and what they do. They aren't going to go away."

"Yes, I know," said Christian. "I have an appointment with the police chief this afternoon." He looked at his watch. "I think I should get over there now. Today has just flown by. Cain get out there and see what you can dig up. Talk to relatives of these kids. Well, you know what to do, get on it. You too, Stone. Divide the counties up between you and see what you can find out."

"On it," said Stone.

"I'm out there," said Cain. She followed him out the door and after he and Stone discussed where they were going, they left.

Chapter Seven

Cain and Kara spent the rest of the day talking to people. She got to see Cain at his finest. He was gentle with family members, and he asked a question in such a way, they didn't feel uncomfortable answering him. One name kept coming up. Terrence Oliver. Terry. He evidently kept the kids in drugs. He stood on the same corner selling the stuff. He could be found after dark.

"We really should be out as wolf tonight," said Cain when they'd finished with the last family. "But I feel it's more important to find this kid Terrence."

"I agree. I don't think it will be bad missing a night. You've taught me a lot the last couple of nights."

"Maybe we'll find him early and we can still get some time in. Tomorrow is the full moon. I hope you have been thinking heavily about that."

"I've had some deep discussions with myself," she answered with a grin.

"Seriously, that's what it takes. Oh, look, I think that's our kid right there." He turned the corner and went around the block. "I'm going to park back here, if you want to come in on the other side of him maybe we can catch him."

"Sure, I can do that."

"Do you have a gun?"

"I do, but not on me."

"Shit, you should have a gun. Grab the 22 out of the

glove compartment."

Kara opened his glove compartment and grabbed the Rugger SR 22 pistol.

"Yes, it's loaded," he said.

"Just checking." She clicked the safety off. He parked and they both got out. She saw an alley in between the buildings and turned down it. Cain went around the building to the left. She nodded at him when he glanced back at her. Once he saw her positioned, he continued toward their target.

"Terrence Oliver," shouted Cain.

The kid took one look at him and started running toward her. She came out from beside the building and tripped him as he went by. She placed him in a headlock.

"I just want to talk to you," said Cain.

"What the hell you wanna talk to me for?"

She released the boy from headlock and held him by his arms. She could tell the kid was high on something himself just from his fidgeting. He was sweating and she could smell an odd chemical odor on him. He was scuffing his feet on the sidewalk and motioning quickly with his hands. He must do the drugs he sold.

Then suddenly the kid started breathing hard and he grabbed at his chest. Cain took ahold of the boy. "Breathe. Take a deep breath."

The boy started shaking then went into a seizure. "Call 911."

Kara pulled her cell out of her back pocket and called for help while Cain started administering CPR. They waited until the ambulance arrived, but it was too late. Even with CPR Terrence still died. They couldn't revive him even with the use of a defibrillator. They finally called it, put him on a gurney, pulled the sheet over his face, and left to transport him to the morgue.

"Another kid down."

"I should have been able to do something. I found this on him." He held out a large Ziplock bag full of tiny baggies resembling the same substance they had found on the bodies at the coroners. "There's the smiley face. All together there's maybe a half ounce here." He shook it and then frowned. "Damn I should have been able to save him."

"Cain, you didn't know. It wasn't your fault he took the drug. I'll bet it was the same one those other kids took. Sure, looks like it."

"Probably, and I know where it came from. It probably wasn't Ansen that distributed it, but it was damn sure him that brought it here. What the hell is he trying to do with shit like that?"

"Maybe he didn't know it was that lethal."

"Well, someone did, and I want to know who."

"We'll find out."

"In the meantime, people are going to die. Mostly kids."

"Yeah, kids that don't know any better. Kids looking to have a good time."

"Or trying to hide from reality."

"Well, there's that," she said.

## Chapter Eight

Cain drove to a remote spot, but neither of them felt the joy they'd experienced the last couple of nights. He spent the night teaching her the things she needed to know to be wolf. She learned more about halo's, about the habits of different animals, and how they smelled. How to spot a habitat and judge which ones were more dangerous than others. She learned to notice certain paths of the animals.

From small squirrels to the birds in the trees and ducks in ponds. She learned about beaver dams, ground moles, and other various critters. By the time morning was about to show itself they made it home and fell into bed tired and worn out. Since it was Saturday, and Cain didn't have to work, neither of them set an alarm.

It was ten o'clock the next morning when they both woke up. Kara hit the shower and so did he. When she came out rubbing her hair with a towel he was sitting at the table in a housecoat, slippers, and reading the morning paper.

"There's fresh coffee," he said without looking up from the paper. He couldn't get what happened to those kids out of his mind. He was feeling anxious. He wanted to put his hands around Horn's neck and squeeze until dead, but he knew he'd never do it. He just couldn't wait until he had enough evidence to put him behind bars for life.

He was so preoccupied with the case. It had never taken him this long to get what he needed for an arrest. He sighed heavily and caught himself still staring at the article as if something could jump out of it and give him what he needed to know.

"Oh, that sounds wonderful." She went to the cupboard and pulled out a cup and poured herself some coffee. "Tonight's the full moon." She grabbed the cream from the fridge and swished it around a couple of times. "We need more coffee creamer. Can I do some grocery shopping today?"

"Yes, sure you can," he said and glanced at her. "Sixteen deaths in one night because of the drug." He still had his nose in the article. "Sixteen kids we could have saved if Horn was where he should be. Jail."

"You will get him, Cain. I know you will."

"I will get an audience with Reid Dalton. He'll help, I'm sure of it. We need someone who knows how to get on the inside. Someone inconspicuous. He has people. I know it."

"Aren't you afraid he could be targeted?"

"No, he knows how to keep his hands clean. He'll stay far enough away where trouble won't find him. He didn't get where he is today by being careless or stupid."

"No, I suppose not."

He put down the paper and picked up his cell phone. He punched in a number then waited. "Hi Stone, have you found out anything?" He leaned back in his chair. "That's a start. Where do they think it came from?"

Kara glanced his way then put the cream container in the trash. He got up and went to a cupboard, opened the door, and pulled out a container of powdered coffee cream. He handed it to her, and then pointed to a sugar container on the counter. She mouthed thank you and poured some powdered cream and sugar into her cup. She pulled her house coat tighter around her and leaned back on the counter, crossed her legs, and took a deep drink of coffee.

He shut his cell down and laid it on the table.

"Did he find out anything?"

"He did. It seems instead of cocaine in the heroin, they used meth. The heroin was stronger than ever and with what the meth does to your heart it was a lethal combination. It seems its cheaper to combine those two drugs and leave cocaine completely out. It makes it more accessible to kids as well."

"I can see why that'd be a lot cheaper. But also, a lot deadlier."

"Yes, cheaper and deadlier. They are calling the drug Black Beauty on the street. Something named after some black diet pills that used to be sold as an upper"

"We should have the news put out something about the drug, maybe kids will stay away from it."

"It's definitely something we can do, but it won't keep them from using it. But it might make someone who's never tried it before not go down that road."

"Great, I'll call one of the stations and have them run a segment on it."

"Maybe all the stations. One good thing about this month's full moon…"

"What's that?" she asked and sipped her coffee.

"It falls on a Saturday, and I don't have to work tomorrow."

"Don't you kind of work when you want, and don't have to other times? I didn't get the picture it was a nine to five."

"It's not really, but I try and put in a good week."

"I bet you work more than that." She smiled then set her cup down on the counter went and grabbed the pot and poured another cup. "Work seems to be your life."

"My other life is my clan. Right now, things are quiet. If something goes wrong over the full moon, I'll get a call, then we have a meeting. It's been quiet lately with the wolves. Sometimes it gets hectic juggling both my job and being the alpha male of the Silver Sables. Just depends on what is happening. Thank God they're all quiet right now because being a sire is more than a nine to five as well."

She looked at him and frowned, then realized he was just making fun and she smiled. "Tell me what it entails, being the alpha male."

"Well, I take care of boundaries, mundane business, clan squabbles, and any problems we have with any other clan. I find most of it is petty stuff and handled quickly. If there's a death or a murder that's a whole other story."

"I see."

He stared at her and again was drawn in by how beautiful she was. Standing here in his kitchen she looked like she belonged. He wasn't sure his life could go back to the same way it had been. He glanced at her new haircut. She looked stunning to him yesterday when he picked her up from the boutique, and she looked just as stunning this morning with her hair wet and in a bathrobe.

She wasn't wearing any makeup and she appeared just as beautiful without it as she did with it. She never wore much, but what little she did enhanced her beauty. She had sparkly green eyes, high cheek bones, a small, rounded chin, and thick, shiny, dark chocolate colored hair. Something he'd thought about running his fingers through many times. Tall and slender he'd noticed her rounded butt an unhealthy amount of times. Even with their visit to the morgue, thoughts of her had danced through his head. He didn't understand himself. He never let himself be distracted at work, especially by thoughts of women.

He wondered what it would be like to wake up to Kara's naked body pressed up against his. With that thought something began to grow. *Dammit, Cain get rid of that thought.* He thought about Ansen Horn and that cooled him off. But she sat down across from him and as she bent, he caught a peek of cleavage, which just sent his thoughts right back to her and what he'd like to do with her.

"We will take it easy today and get ready for the full moon tonight. We can go shopping and I'll cook on the grill again. We have to be out there before dark because once the moon comes up it doesn't matter where we are, we will turn to wolf."

"We have no choice at all in the matter? Can't we just say the magic words?"

"Those words will do nothing tonight, at least trying to return to human. We will be wolf until morning light hits."

"Where did those words come from anyway?"

"They are very old words, and they only work if a wolf uses them. They are just words to ordinary humans. Christian told me that a very long time ago the first wolf showed up amidst the Vikings in Norway. They moved from there into Scotland. So, goes the history of the wolf.

"Something about a curse. He said a man fell in love with a beautiful woman and the clan leader, her father, wouldn't allow them to marry, but he stole her away anyway. When the woman's father finally found them, he killed his clan and took the man prisoner. He had a witch with him and for punishment he turned him into a wolf, but the witch put a twist on the spell she used. If a wolf bit a human, they in turn would turn into a wolf. The leader of the clan didn't know that." He cleared his throat, folded the newspaper up, and laid it once again beside him on the table.

"The woman he was in love with was very frightened of wolves, had an unhealthy fear of them, and when he turned the man into a wolf, she would have nothing more to do with him. He was angry at her father with what he did, so he attacked him. Instead of killing him, the bite turned him to wolf.

"The daughter would have nothing to do with her father after that either. They tried to kill the man, but he didn't die. He left and no one saw him after that. It is said she committed suicide by jumping off a cliff into the ocean. The father went crazy and continuously attacked young men. The only thing he accomplished was to make a great many wolves."

"Interesting story," she said with a giggle. "He must have really loved the woman. Not the father, the man."

"Yes, I guess he did. He went to great lengths to try and keep her. Christian could embellish the story quite well."

"So how did an Italian end up as a wolf?" she asked playfully.

"We are all over the world now. You could just think of us as a different nationality."

"You're something different all right."

"I'm not sure how to take that," he said, with a grin.

For some reason he thought he'd love to take her to the floor and tickle her, naked. He had all kinds of thoughts about what he'd like to do with her and none of them involved him releasing her. He wanted to make love to her. In the worst way he wanted her. This was going to drive him crazy. She was going to drive him crazy.

Perhaps it would be best to teach her everything he could as quick as he could, release her, and get back to living the way he wanted. *And just how is it you want to live your life, DeLucci? I am not having that conversation with myself this morning. No, nope, not gonna happen.*

"What do you say we get dressed and get this day started?"

"Sounds good, but uh, Cain. I have a question. It's kind of personal." Kara chewed on her bottom lip. He watched her face turn beet red.

He sat back down. "Sounds serious."

"What happens if I turn wolf and I'm, uh, you know, and it's that time of the month?"

He was usually a fast thinker, but this stumped him for a second. "Oh, oh, you mean *that* time of the month. Are you close to being finished with it?"

"Nope. A day and a half into it. I usually last three days."

"Christ, Kara I didn't think there could be anything else to pile on top of our problems. If you still are by tonight, you will turn wolf in heat. If that is the case every wolf for miles around will catch your scent and come looking for you. They will all want you to choose them as a lifelong mate." What if he couldn't control her wolf?

He thought he could control his well enough, but he

wasn't sure about hers. And what was he to do with a wolf in heat? He knew damn well he'd be one of those wolves trying to vie for her. He'd found himself in a similar situation once and he wasn't nice to the other male wolves. She quickly broke into his thoughts.

"I'm sorry, Cain. It seems the cards are stacked against me."

"No, don't say that. We take one problem at a time and deal with it. Let's just hope your wild wolf is under some control." He could be hopeful, couldn't he?

True to his word, they spent the day taking it easy. She got the shopping done she wanted to do. They had lunch again at the Italian Bistro then they strolled through the botanical gardens. He thought about taking her to her house so she could go through her mother's things but decided against it. He knew she wasn't emotionally ready for it, and she was worried about the full moon and what she might do. He didn't want to overload her.

****

Cain went over rules with her late in the afternoon. So much so, she was tired of hearing the same thing over and over. He fixed steak on the grill, but she started dinner earlier, she wanted to make something that was one of her father's favorites. Her mother called them twice baked potatoes.

She had to bake the potatoes till almost done, dig out the middles, mix cheese, broccoli some garlic and onion with the potato, refill the holes she'd created, cover with cheese, and then bake them till golden brown.

They were time consuming, but worth the wait. She thought they'd go great with the steaks and salad. Cain commented a lot about them and said they were his new favorite kind of potato. He helped clear the plates and clean up the kitchen. Afterwards, with a good hour of daylight left, they were ready to go.

It seemed like he drove forever, and the more he drove the more nervous she became. "Where are we going?" she asked.

"Where there's no chance in hell we will run into any humans." He took yet another road or what seemed like a path deep into the mountains. "Well, there's always a chance we can run into one, but the chances are slimmer the deeper we go. There are signs all over that there's no hunting or camping on a full moon, but that doesn't mean everyone pays attention to them." He pulled into some brush and parked. "I don't think anyone will see the car here."

"I'm not sure I can see the car here," she retorted. She glanced around at her surroundings. "Very pretty here. There seems to be a lot of daylight left."

"There's a reason for that. There's a couple of things I didn't mention before that I need to mention now." He paused. "We are in mountain lion territory."

"Good lord, why did you bring us here then?"

"Because I'd rather we deal with a mountain lion than a human. If you killed a mountain lion, which I'm sure won't happen, and more likely it will be the other way around, you won't get in trouble. However, the mountain lion is protected, but if you had to kill one to protect yourself, you wouldn't be penalized."

"That's just great, on top of everything else I have to worry about a mountain lion."

"Between the both of us we can ward one off. The other thing…about your monthly…"

"I know, wolves in heat are like dogs in heat. I can

fight the males off." She hoped so anyway.

"Some maybe, but not all of them, and not all at once. If one should happen to get you, I don't want you to be worried. They can't impregnate you. It just doesn't work that way."

"I don't let men near me, you think I'm going to let a wolf?" she asked surprised.

"You have to remember your wolf will be completely wild tonight. You will only have snippets of human thoughts, emotions, and feelings. If it does happen, don't be embarrassed or worried over it. You are no longer completely human. You have to understand that."

"And I have no choice about tonight?"

"I could chain you up, but then you'll hurt yourself trying to get free. It would be a nightmare for you, and it will prolong your training another month."

His words rang through her brain. He didn't want to be stuck with a half breed. He didn't like having to be a sire. He was doing everything for her. She had to let him get back to his life. "If it's the last thing I do, I'm going to clear tonight with flying colors," she said finally.

"Good, then I'm ready when you are."

"I have a question. Doesn't the female wolf have say-so over what male is to mate with her? I thought you said wolves mated for life."

"They do mate for life. I'm saying you may choose one while your wild is in control, or you may just want to do the dirty with him. Sort of the way humans are. We don't know what you'll do or won't do until the time comes. As far as a mate, you probably won't choose a wolf who is wild all the time, at least it's never happened before. One usually chooses from their pack. If you choose a wolf from another clan, the male moves to that clan. In our case you'd probably choose one of the Silver Sables, and I doubt any will be this far out tonight.

"There's a couple of places we gather where the whole pack runs together. I can't take you to them until I release you though. Females usually choose their mates during their heat cycle and the alpha male chooses the alpha female and vice versa."

"That's why you haven't introduced me?"

"That's right. When I release you, you become part of the pack, not until."

"Is there an alpha female in the Silver Sables?"

"Yes, Casandra."

"Did you choose each other?"

"Yes, and no. Not as lifetime mate anyway. As wolf there have been times, we have…"

"I see."

"Casandra has also had other male wolves. As humans, she would be the last one I'd ever choose for a lifelong mate." He cleared his throat. She could tell he didn't want to get into the story of him and Casandra. "Ready?" he asked.

She nodded, got out of the car, and started stripping down. He got the duffels out of the trunk, and in a few seconds, they were ready to go.

"We don't have to wait until the moon turns us. We can speak the words and become wolf now. On a full moon you needn't say the words to change and it's the same way come morning, but that wouldn't happen until the moon comes up. There's maybe a half hour left of daylight."

She did just that, and he followed suit. She took off running into the trees and he followed. They played and ran, pounced on each other, nipped, and laughed.

She was running at top speed when she ran out of the forest and into a clearing. They ran past a small herd of deer bedded down for the night. She passed them and hardly gave them a second look. She wasn't hungry, but she was very thirsty. She needed water. She could smell a nearby river, and she headed for it. The moon rose and it was brilliantly bright out. The trees in the forest cast long shadows and milky white light filtered through the trees. The forest was stark, but it was beautiful. When she arrived at the river, light danced along the top of the water glistening, disappearing, and reappearing.

She loved it and felt more at peace than she ever had. This was right. This was her life. She was beginning to think this was the best thing to ever have happen to her. She only wished she could hang onto it for more than twenty years. She would think about that later, tonight was for fun. She looked behind her and saw Cain. Then everything changed. The wildness took over.

She reached the edge of the water when a male wolf came toward her. Cain growled. The large male growled back creating a standoff, until the other male peeled back his lips showing his teeth. Cain growled and charged him.

She didn't want the wild male at all, and she let it be known. Cain was her mate, and she sent the other wolf a clear image. He got the message, pulled away, and took off running back into the forest. He was an alpha wolf like Cain, but not her Alpha.

She lowered her head and drank heavily. She was standing with her front paws in the water and enjoying her drink when a new smell hit her nose. She jerked her head up and breathed deep. The scent invaded her senses and she felt fear fill her. She looked for Cain. As she caught sight of him behind her a very large mountain lion ran by.

It didn't stop or try and engage or fight. She trembled in fear...then she heard it. A shot rang out. She knew that sound and it wasn't good. Her head snapped to attention and her eyes darted to where it came from. A human with a rifle stood not far from them.

"God damned wolves. I've been hunting that mountain lion for days. I had a perfect shot until you showed up."

It was mumble jumble to her brain, but she saw the man raise the rifle and instinctively knew she was in danger. Cain came running toward her at lightning speed, then she heard a shot. Cain leapt between her, and the human and she knew he was trying to protect her. He dropped at her feet, a large hole in his chest, bleeding badly. His breaths came in shallow gurgles. There was blood coming from his mouth and nose. She nuzzled him and he didn't move. She licked his face, but he was motionless.

Turning to the human anger overtook her fear. She lunged after him and another shot rang out, just grazing over the top of her back. *Kill, kill, kill.* Tear the human apart. Adrenaline surged through her body. A voice sounded in her head. *Human. Avoid. Human. Avoid.* A picture of her running away from the human ran through her mind. Did it come from her mate? No, he was wounded. Bleeding badly.

The man raised the rifle again. She took off in a dead run toward him. She wanted desperately to kill him. She was frightened, angry, and hungry. She snarled. *Human avoid, human avoid* repeated in her mind. She leaped through the air and clamped her teeth down on the human's arm holding the rifle. He dropped the weapon and screamed.

She felt the bones crunch beneath her teeth. She clamped harder, breaking skin and bone. She let go, snarled, and growled. She stood over the weapon used to hurt her mate. Gun, she thought. He mustn't use again. She pawed the ground, and the man took off running, screaming loudly and holding his injured arm.

She picked the rifle up with her teeth and drug it to the river and dropped it in the water. She returned to Cain. Her mate. She chose her mate and now she might lose him. She crawled slightly over the top of him and rested making sure the bulk of her weight was off him.

*Protect.* She looked about, no wolves, no humans in sight. Then she heard the large growl of the mountain lion at the edge of the woods. It was coming back. Her mate. Protect mate, still breathing, heart still beating. *Protect, protect.*

She had to keep the mountain lion away. How? There were pictures forming in her mind of hungry wolves. Three words filtered through her pictures. *They are hungry.* She instantly thought of the animals being very hungry. She knew how to avoid the lion. She didn't see the mountain lion, not yet anyway. She quickly ran to the forest toward the resting deer.

Most jumped up and ran in all directions, but she caught one. Clamped hard on its neck until it died just like she saw her mate do. Then with all the power she had she dragged the deer to edge of the clearing where she could protect her mate and see the lion. Then she ran back to her mate. She sniffed first to make sure he was still alive.

Fresh blood oozed from his nose and mouth. She nudged him to see if he would move. She crawled just over the edge of him and laid her head between her front paws where she could see the dead deer clearly. She watched and waited. Then she saw the lion creep forward, low to the ground, from the edge of the forest. It growled low and grabbed ahold of the deer and drug it away. She knew the lion was taking it to a secluded and safe area to eat. Then she thought of other creatures coming. There would be more. They would smell the blood of her mate if she didn't deter them.

She checked her mate once more. *Still alive, but barely.* She quickly got up and began tracking the deer she frightened. She followed them down river and caught sight of them gathering near the water. They began lying down trying to bed down for the night. She saw one at the end of the herd and ran after it. The deer fled again, but she caught up with the slower one and in one giant leap brought it down.

When it died, she began dragging it back. Close to where her mate lay. It was heavy and she had to stop and change her bite. She strengthened her grip and began pulling again. When she finally got it where she wanted it, she dropped it, and quickly returned to her mate.

She once again crawled alongside him. It didn't take long, and she heard the howl of a wolf, then several wolves followed suit. She rested on top of Cain, panting, exhausted after transporting the deer. She glanced to where she heard the howls. Several wolves came out of the forest. The males caught her scent and ventured forward. She growled at them. She sent the males a picture that she had a mate.

The wolves sniffed the ground and got closer. A

large male nipped at the others and snarled at them until they backed up. It was obvious he wanted her. An image from the male showed that her mate was dying, as good as dead, and she was fair game. She howled.

She tried hard to send pictures of the deer she dropped. One wolf had located it and howled telling the others there was meat. The male watching her was the alpha. He trotted to where the deer lay and growled at the wolf who was feasting. He nipped him and the wolf begrudgingly left the deer and sat down near it. The rest of the pack circled the deer.

She stood and sniffed Cain. He was still breathing but not very well. She crawled back on top of him to protect him and watched the wolves eat the deer. When they finished, they all went back into the forest and left her with her mate. Time passed, an owl hooted, then it grew silent, and she fell asleep.

****

Cain awoke in tall dewy grass with pain in his chest, but he was alive. He opened his eyes and felt a heaviness across his body. Kara lay naked on top of him. What the hell happened? The last thing he remembered was the mountain lion and the man taking aim at Kara. He ran toward her to get her out of the way. Then he remembered. He heard the shot then felt a searing pain shoot through his chest.

"Kara," he said gently. "Kara, wake up." A little louder. She moved but she fell right back into slumber. He reached to grab her shoulders to move her and touched a nice round soft breast instead. He left his hand there for a second while wild and crazy thoughts went through his mind.

"Wha…what?" she asked opening her eyes. "Where

are we?" She quickly sat up and rubbed her eyes. "Oh my God, you're naked."

"Oh, my God, so are you," he said devilishly. He squeezed her breast and she yelped and not because it hurt. She smacked his arm and quickly got off him. "You're alive." she exclaimed. "I thought for sure you were going to die."

"Nope, the only thing that will kill me is a silver bullet through the heart or severing my head. The bullet wasn't silver."

"Oh, my God you were shot through the heart?"

"Not through it, just grazed it, but I managed to heal. It took all night. How did you fare? The last thing I remember was being shot. You didn't kill the human, did you?"

She wiped her eyes again, brushed her hand over her face, and sat cross legged beside him. "No, I didn't kill him. I really wanted too, though. Two words kept going through my mind. Human and avoid. I bit his arm, and he dropped the gun."

"He didn't try to shoot you afterward, that's surprising."

"I sort of crushed his bone. In two," she said, a grin crossing her face. He moved to sit across from her. "He took off screaming holding his arm."

"Did he still have the gun?"

"No, after he left, I drug it to the river and threw it in."

"Whoa, wait a minute. You had that much control over your wolf?"

"I guess…"

"What about the mountain lion and other wolves. Did you see the mountain lion again? Did you choose a wolf for mate?"

She looked away and her face turned red. He surmised she did something with the wolf she chose.

"I did, but we didn't do anything."

"What do you mean? Usually, you physically seal the bond when you choose your mate."

"Well, I couldn't, he was incapacitated." She quickly looked away again.

He realized what she meant. "You chose me?" his voice squeaking in surprise.

"Yes, and I told the other wolves so."

"They would know I was injured, and they would still have tried to get you."

"An alpha male did. But before they showed up, I did what I did with the mountain lion."

"What about the mountain lion?" He couldn't believe his ears. Was she telling the truth?

"Other words kept going through my mind. Let's see, there was avoid humans, mate, gun, and oh yeah, they are hungry. I killed a deer and left it where I heard the mountain lion last. She came and got the deer and pulled it away to eat or at least that's what I presume. I think she had cubs, I don't know how I know that, but I do. Maybe her scent?"

"Yes, you're learning and that's what they do with their meal. They take it and hide it. Sometimes up in a tree. So, you are saying you killed a deer for the mountain lion and the wolves?" He asked unbelievably.

"Well, I had to find the deer again. They were down river and getting ready to bed down again. I had to drag one quite a distance to get it near you."

"That's unbelievable, Kara. I'm so proud of you." He took a moment and looked in her eyes, then gently leaned over and kissed her. Passion enveloped him and it was evident during the kiss. He deepened it, and she responded in kind. Then she pulled away.

"I ca...can...I'm still...it's that time of month," she said finally. Her face turning beet red.

He felt his face heat. He had forgotten. He stood up and took her hand and quickly changing the subject, said, "We should be getting back. Uh, thank you, Kara, for saving my life. You stayed with me all night, didn't you?"

"Yes. I couldn't just leave you. Besides you saved my life first, that man was going to shoot me. The bullet you took was meant for me. I really was afraid you'd die."

"I can't wait to tell Christian this story. It will be one that will go down through our pack for generations to come. As far as I'm concerned, I can release you today."

Her face turned down, and he could swear he saw tears gather, but she quickly got ahold of herself and looked away from him. What was the matter?

"Oh, okay. When do you want me to leave? Today?"

"I was thinking about that, Kara, a great deal. I really would feel better, if you stay with me until we find out about your powers and why they are bound. I don't think you're safe, and I'd like to make sure nothing happens to you."

"I've been taking care of myself for a long time, Cain. I'll think about it. Right now, I'd like to go get dressed."

"On it." He pulled her to her feet. "I don't think the mountain lion is around, but it would be good for us to leave anyway."

They hurried to the car, dressed, and he drove home.

During the trip he questioned her about how she'd felt when she was wolf. He wanted to make sure she knew what she was doing. When they reached his house, she mentioned taking a shower.

"I'd like a shower myself. But I think it wise we rest before the gala. I want to be at my best when I meet Reid Dalton. I must convince him to help us and the type of healing I went through exhausted me."

"I don't know if I'd speak to him at the gala about that."

"Oh, I wasn't planning on it. I just want to set an appointment with him."

"He'll probably have you get with his secretary about it."

"Not if I can convince him to meet with me. I think it would be harder going through her."

They both agreed to shower then rest for a couple of hours.

\*\*\*\*

Kara was worn out and she knew Cain had to be because his body spent the night healing. They hadn't eaten since last night, so she decided she would mix up something for them to eat before they left. Benefit dinners were known for leaving the guest hungry. It was more for show than anything. With her plans in mind, she went and took a shower, then crawled in bed and quickly fell asleep.

Chapter Nine

Kara finished her hair and got her new black dress on for the dinner. After they awoke, she made sandwiches, and warmed up twice baked potatoes. It was just enough to take the edge off their hunger. She looked at her little black dress in the mirror. After going through several shops, she found what she wanted in a little place in Cherry Creek.

The dress was called the Infinity High Low Dress and she had to admit it looked pretty smashing. It was low cut and tight around the waist then flared out from her hips and flowed down to her ankles. The front was open, scalloped, and overlapped. When she walked it would open just above the knees giving a peek of her legs.

One thing she appreciated on her body was her long slender legs, and it seemed men did as well. She'd bought some plain black heels to go with it and a thin shawl, to drape around her back and over her arms. She wished she'd thought to bring some jewelry from home, but it never crossed her mind she might need it. The amethyst studs in her ears didn't really match but they'd have to do. Cain knocked on her door.

"Ready?" he asked. "I don't want to be late."

She opened the door, he stood speechless, then he gave a cat whistle. "Everyone is going to think I'm the luckiest man alive. You look absolutely stunning."

She smiled and felt a blush rise on her cheeks. She was glad to have taken the extra time to do her hair. "You clean up pretty good yourself." He had on a white tailored suit jacket, black pants, and a black shirt with a white tie. He really did look handsome, she almost choked when she saw him.

"Wait right here." He left and came back a second later with a long shallow box in his hands. "I got these for you to wear tonight. I didn't think you'd remember anything from home, and besides…I just wanted to get you something nice."

"But, Cain…" She took it and noticed her hands shaking. When she took off the lid she gasped. The box held a teardrop emerald necklace and matching earrings set in gold. "This is gorgeous!" She couldn't believe it, no one had ever given her such a nice gift and it wasn't a holiday or her birthday. She quickly collected herself and looked at his face.

"Like you. The green reminds me of your eyes. Here let me…" She handed it over in trembling hands.

He took the necklace out and she held her hair as he put it around her neck and clasped it together. She stood in front of the mirror. "This is perfect." She took out the earrings and replaced the ones she was wearing. Then she turned to him and twirled in a full circle.

"Stunning. Kara, you are stunning. I have no other adjective, perhaps beautiful, or smashing might work, but no, you're just completely, *lavishly,* stunning."

"Thank you." Without thinking she reached up and kissed him. She meant for it to be a soft quick kiss, but it didn't end that way. He grabbed her around the waist and pulled her to him for a more intimate kiss and she did nothing to stop him. She opened her mouth and accepted his tongue.

Their breath mixed, their tongues danced, and she swooned. She had never felt anything like it in her life. The now familiar feeling of bees buzzing through her blood took over. She wanted nothing more than to rip his clothes off and taste every inch of him. She'd never once felt this way for her fiancé. The thought of Cain naked gave her a little shiver. She was lost in him when he pulled away. She had to remember what it was they were doing before the kiss. She stood back and touched her lips with her fingers, speechless.

"Are you ready, miss, for an evening out?" he asked in a deep husky voice. He put out his arm and she took it and giggled.

"Of course, dear sir, more than," she said finally, as they walked into the great room. He picked up her shawl and put it around her shoulders and she let it drop to her arms, then he handed her, her small black sequined handbag. She turned to him. "Do you have the invitation?"

He patted his suit jacket. "Thanks for reminding me." He left and came back quickly shoving it in the inside pocket of his jacket. "We work good together." He smiled as he buttoned his jacket.

"Yes, and we look good together too." She smiled back. He got a funny look on his face, and she quickly lost her smile. When was she going to learn? She always made everything sound like they were a couple. They weren't, and never would be. It depressed her, but she wouldn't let it get to her or spoil the evening. She would enjoy him for as long as she could, no strings attached. "Well, are we ready?" she asked quickly. "I am if you are."

They pulled up to where the benefit gala was being held and got out. They were greeted by a valet and Cain handed him his keys. "No scratches my man," he said.

"No, sir, if there are any complaints R.D. would skin us."

"R.D. huh, is that what you call your boss?"

"No, sir, we call him Mr. Dalton, sir."

"Well, I like the term R.D. so I won't tell on you." He smiled.

God, she loved his smile. It twisted her insides up into an awful mess, or was it a good mess? She waited for him as he craned his neck around to watch the kid park his car. If it were her car, she'd be the same way. It was a hell of a nice car. She almost chuckled, perhaps someday she'd show him her car in the garage. He really would drool. He trotted up the steps and took her hand. There wasn't a line, which surprised her, but then again, they were quick and efficient here.

The building itself was an old ironworks dated 1903 and it kept a great deal of that ambiance. Everything from formals to pregame parties were held here. The place could house up to twelve hundred guests. The custom chandeliers were enough to make one amazed. She glanced upward at them. There was a winding staircase that went up a few floors with chandeliers that stair stepped through the middle. The place was beautiful. She remembered her father telling her about it one time although she had never been inside.

Three people stood at a podium just inside the doors. A handsome man in a suit took their invitation. "Name, sir?"

"I'm here in Christian Keller's stead. Cain DeLucci, with Kara Thomas."

She watched as he found Christian's name and marked it off. "Mr. DeLucci, Ms. Thomas, Cameron will show you to your seat."

A man nodded at them, and they followed him to one of the tables. As they sat down a hush fell among the crowd. Up on the stage at a podium was Reid Dalton talking to two men and a woman. Behind them bulletin boards held before and after photos of all the different buildings Dalton had restored in the city. On a larger bulletin board was a colored pencil drawing of the proposed hospital complete with landscaping. Kara looked about the room and could smell the money. The richest people in Denver sat in this place tonight. She figured maybe a hundred and fifty people. Clearly out of her league, but she didn't feel any of it. After all she got used to that when she had to be a bodyguard for different dignitaries.

A waiter came to their table carrying a bucket of ice holding a bottle of Champagne. She knew enough about wine to know this one cost at least five hundred a bottle. The waiter had a towel over his left arm, and he put down two wine glasses next to their water glasses. "May I interest you in a drink before dinner?"

She noticed the dinnerware and the glasses of fine crystal. She was afraid to touch anything for fear she might break something. The only place she'd ever seen this dinnerware was in a catalogue. She would love to have some. In fact, she and her mother laughed about owning such pricy dishes, but she couldn't help it, she loved them. Five pieces cost over a thousand dollars. This man didn't hold back on anything. She glanced at Cain.

"Yes, please," said Cain. The waiter opened the

bottle and poured a touch in the bottom of the glass, swirled it around a couple of times and handed it to Cain. He sniffed it then tasted it. "Very good." The waiter poured them each a glass and put the bottle back in the bucket of ice and sat it on the table. She looked about the room and it seemed there was a waiter for every table. She glanced at the small group of musicians playing chamber music. She especially enjoyed the harp. It fit.

The waiter pulled out a pad and pen from his jacket pocket. "Sir, ma'am, we have prime rib as our main course for those who enjoy meat. If you are vegetarian or vegan, we offer Vegetable Biryani, and whole roasted Cauliflower with Zaatar sauce. What would you prefer sir?

"I'll have the prime rib, please."

"You, ma'am?"

"I will also have the prime rib." Then she snickered and looked at Cain, daring him to say one word. "The Biryani and Cauliflower sound divine, if I were vegan, which I used to be, I would love it." She felt her face going red and decided to stop blurting right there. "I'll just have the prime rib," she said in a quiet tone.

The waiter raised his eyebrows. "Very good," he said and left.

Their table was set for eight and she wondered who they'd be sitting with. She didn't recognize any of the names on the place cards. It didn't take long for her to find out and she was shocked when she saw their table mates.

The three women from the boutique came striding in with their husbands and made their way to the table. They were introduced as the Wilson's, Henderson's, and Patterson's.

"Hi, I'm Janie Henderson," said the blonde, "and this is my husband Klyde.

"I'm Althea," said the Brunette, "this is my husband, Jimmy. We are the Patterson's."

"I'm Sarah Wilson and this is my husband, Harry," said the red head.

"Nice to meet you," said Cain. "I'm Cain DeLucci and this is my date, Kara Thomas. They all nodded their heads.

"Say," said Janie. "Don't I know you from somewhere? Do you belong to the P.T.A. at Dalton elementary, Mr. Granson's class?"

"No, we haven't met," said Kara. "At least not formally. But I did see you at the boutique where I got my hair done."

"Oh, oh," said Althea. "I remember you. You were under a dryer while we were getting our nails done!"

Kara smiled. "That's right."

Then she watched her turn white when she remembered what they had talked about. "You can't hear a thing under those darn dryers, can you?"

She was acting like it was small talk, but Kara knew why she asked. "I suppose you could if you were listening, but I'm afraid I had a lot on my mind that day." That seemed to appease her. One thing she didn't want to do was make her shy away. This evening was going to be very boring if she had to make small talk all night. Maybe she could talk the women out of their idea to use drugs after the gala. She wished she could tell Cain what they had planned, so he could help.

"We own Paterson's Pet Store, the chain of stores throughout Colorado," said Jimmy.

"I'm in investment banking," said Klyde.

"Same for me," said Harry. "Klyde and I work together. What is it you do Mr. DeLucci?"

"I'm a TITAN officer. My friend here has been asked to join. She was a M.P. sergeant in the military and just finished with the local police force."

The three women looked at each other and their faces turned red. Kara could almost laugh. She knew they were all thinking about what they talked about at the boutique sitting across from her.

"TITAN aren't you like SWAT?" asked Jimmy, glancing at Harry and clearing his throat.

She could tell by their expressions they must have gotten ahold of some type of drug. They were all too nervous not to have.

"Actually, it is harder to become a member of TITAN than it is to be a member of SWAT."

"Excuse me," interrupted their waiter. He stood waiting with two other staff members holding buckets of ice and three more bottles of Champagne. He explained the menu offerings again and everyone told him they wanted the prime rib, except Sarah.

"Please try the prime rib, Sarah. I know you are trying to be a vegetarian, but I thought you'd be over this kick by now," said her husband.

"No, I want to be healthy. I'm on this diet for a reason. I'll have the vegetable dishes," she said to the waiter.

He finished pouring everyone a glass of champagne and took out his little book. "Very good," said the waiter. He wrote it all down and left.

She wasn't paying attention to the waiter. She was thinking more and more about what these people planned for after the party and it scared her. She had to do something. She remembered she was connected to Cain through thought, although he never seemed to communicate with his mind outside of being wolf, she'd give it a try. He had a wall up, which was natural, she always felt hers up, but she could push on it.

*"Cain, can you understand what I'm thinking?"* She tried probing his thoughts and she felt a flutter. *"I need to tell you something important."*

He raised his eyebrows and looked at her in surprise. She felt something give way, like he let down a wall, or opened a door, and when he did, she could read several of his thoughts. His thoughts about being bored the rest of the night mirrored hers. She chuckled. *"My thoughts exactly."*

*"Why are we doing this now?"* he asked raising his eyebrows. He glanced back to his wine glass and picked it up to take a drink.

*"These women were planning on having Jimmy, Althea's husband, get some drugs that they could try after this gala. They plan on using them tonight. She talked about getting cocaine."*

Cain was just taking a drink of his Champagne, she knew her thoughts hit him like a bulldozer run amuck and cocaine was at the forefront. He spit out his drink and coughed. He quickly picked up a napkin and held it over his mouth and coughed a few more times. Then turned to Kara and stared. Kara reached over and slapped him on his back.

"For some reason that went drown the wrong pipe," said Cain. "Please excuse me." He coughed slightly again. *"For Christ's sake, Kara, if they got ahold of that new drug, they're all dead."*

*"I know that's why we have to do something."*

"That's okay, my man," said Klyde. "It happens to me at least once a week, but usually when my lovely wife Janie tells me something that the kids did."

That comment made everyone at the table chuckle, except for Kara and Cain. She knew she looked worried. Cain winked and she settled down somewhat, but quickly felt her blood pressure rise thinking more about their plans. The women had planned an evening away from being housewives, something different and adventurous, they just didn't know the danger in what they had planned.

"May I have your attention please?" said Reid Dalton. He stepped up to the microphone on the stage. He tapped it a couple of times. "May I have your attention, please." It got quiet and all eyes turned to him.

She and Cain put their thoughts on hold to listen to him.

"I'd like to thank you all for coming to this very important gala. I won't bore you with a speech right now as some of the finest chefs prepared an excellent meal for you. I will just welcome you and ask you to enjoy your dinner. I will say a few words while your dinner settles, then a very fine group will entertain you with music, so feel free to dance afterwards. Again, welcome, please enjoy your meal."

Everyone clapped and she followed suit. She admired Reid Dalton and so did Cain. She picked that up in his thoughts along with his hope to get an audience with him. She turned to him and smiled. She mouthed *you will* with the strong thought behind it and he smiled back.

*"We need to deter these people from trying any drugs. Are you sure that's what they are going to do?"*

She acted like they were just sitting there quietly, but she couldn't help but glance his way as she sent her thoughts to him. *"It was evident at the boutique. All the women wanted to try cocaine. They talked about it the whole time I was under the dryer. There's one thing we can do. We can talk about the kids who died."* Cain nodded, and Kara cleared her throat.

"Have any of you watched the news lately?"

Everyone turned toward her. The women were all ears. It seemed even the men liked a good story.

"Sixteen kids died of an overdose in three different subdivisions here in Denver."

"My God no," said Janie. "What happened? Tell us."

"Cain, it was your case would you care to elaborate?"

He looked at her confused, after all she'd been there too.

*"They'll listen better coming from a man. They will take it more seriously. I don't agree with it, but it is just a fact."*

"It's true," he said. "The drug is called Black Beauty. It's supposed to be a speedball. Cocaine and heroin. Only they aren't mixing cocaine with the heroin, they are using meth. It's a very deadly drug. Cocaine and heroin are also very dangerous to mix, but this other drug is flat out deadly. I would warn anyone not to take illicit drugs, but I would especially tell them to stay away from this one."

She noticed the couples, especially the women, looking at each other with fear on their faces. Then Althea smiled.

"Not all drugs are the same," said Althea. "It really

depends on who you get them from."

"The only good drugs are the ones you get from your doctor," said Cain. "Those kids thought they were out for a good time, what they got was dead, and by the look on their faces, it was excruciatingly painful for them."

Kara noticed Althea's husband Jimmy staring at Cain. He was the one who was supposed to buy the drugs and it was Althea who pushed the idea on the others. Maybe, not push but she embellished the idea of taking the drug. Her thoughts were broken into as the waiter came to their table with food.

She was famished and everything smelled so delightful. It was quiet as they all ate, once in a while a comment was made about how good the food tasted. She had to admit the prime rib was excellent. She took a drink of Champagne.

After they finished the waiter came by with coffee for those who wanted it. One of the bottles of Champagne was empty and he removed it and opened another. Another server took the dishes and empty bottle and put it all on a cart.

"The dessert will be out shortly," said the waiter.

"Oh, what will that be?" asked Althea curiously.

"We will have many different deserts to choose from," said the waiter with a smile.

"Yummy," said Althea. "I may want two." Kara noticed Jimmy nudged her. "After I have my first one, of course," corrected Althea.

"I need to find the little boy's room," said Cain.

"I know where it is," said Jimmy. "I need to use it as well. Follow me."

The two men got up and left.

\*\*\*\*

"It's over here," said Jimmy.

Cain followed him through the door and started when Jimmy locked the main door behind him. "Is anyone in here?" asked Jimmy, then waited.

When no one answered he continued, "Good. I need to speak with you Mr. DeLucci, privately."

He was hoping the man had come to his senses. "What can I do for you, Mr. Patterson."

"Please, call me Jimmy. Our wives got it in their heads that they wanted to have a little party tonight after the gala." He cleared his throat then hesitated.

"Go on."

"They wanted to try cocaine. There's this guy I know who supplies different drugs to the upper echelon, I guess you could say, so I purchased some for tonight. I was going to give everyone their share after the gala before we get to Sarah's place. They wanted to see it. Anyway, your story frightened me. Here, take these, I don't want anything to do with them." Jimmy pulled three small baggies out of his pocket and handed them to him. "I don't want to get arrested or anything. Please don't do that. We didn't take any of it yet."

Cain rolled the bags over in his hand, then took one and held it up to the light. He immediately noted the smiley faces on the baggies. "If I had to guess, I'd say this is the drug that has been killing young people. I recognize the baggies. Do you have more?" Damn, it looked like the stuff he saw in the morgue. "This isn't cocaine, Jimmy, it looks like the stuff that killed those kids. What did the guy tell you it was?"

"All of his drugs were in baggies like these. He said this is better than cocaine. That it had some type of opiate, heroin, to counteract the jitters you get taking cocaine and he said you could go to sleep with it. I opted for this. He had several different drugs."

"Did he have a name for it?"

"Yes, he called it Black Beauty. Which is why what you said frightened me."

"Who was the man you got it from?"

"Oh hell. I don't wish to get him in any trouble. He's a friend."

"Your friend is going to end up killing someone with these drugs and he will end up in prison for it." He knew there was a law that protected pushers for murder because they didn't force buyers to take the drugs they bought, but he didn't want to tell Jimmy that, he wanted to frighten him. "You could help him by telling me. I won't have you arrested if you tell me who you got this from. For Christ's sake man, kids are dying over this stuff."

"I'm sorry, I can't give you his name."

"You better think hard on that one, Jimmy." Cain got in his wallet and pulled out a card and handed it to him. "Think about it and call me if you change your mind. I'm not going to arrest you because you came clean with me. My friend and I knew your plans thanks to the talk the girls had at the boutique. You have kids, and you don't normally do drugs, so I won't penalize you for it. But seriously, call me.

"On another note. Is this everything you got?"

"No, I have one more at home. I bought it for Althea and me. If we liked what we did tonight we'd have a night to ourselves. We just wanted to try something different. Life can get boring doing the same thing every day, so I try and keep Althea entertained. I love her and I want her to be happy."

"Do you think she'd be happy if you did an illicit drug and died? Think man, you can't just go putting things in your body that you don't know what it will do to you. The coroner said it was like the kid's hearts exploded."

He was getting frustrated, but he knew he couldn't pry the guy's name from him. He'd give him time to think about it and if he didn't call him, he knew he could find him well enough. He leaned against the sink, the mirror imaging the look on Jimmy's face. Cain glanced over the urinals, then thought about the kids. "Do you have it in a safe place at home? I need to get it from you."

"Yes, it's under lock and key."

"Good, you don't want to take the chance any kids could get into it. Thanks, Jimmy. You probably saved all your lives tonight."

"God, I don't want anything to happen to Althea, or my friends. They will be angry with me, but I don't care. Thanks, Cain."

Cain slapped him on the back. "No problem."

"Here is my card as well. You can call me anytime," said Jimmy.

"I will, I want to get the other package you have. It's important to get it off the streets and out of people's hands. We should get back to our ladies."

"I couldn't agree more."

They did their business and left the restroom.

****

Once he was seated, Kara looked at him expectantly *"Jimmy gave me the baggies. It looks like the same stuff, but I won't know for sure until its tested."*

*"That's great. How did you manage that?"*

*"He listened to what we said about the kids, and it*

*frightened him. He has more at home we need to get."*

Kara glanced at Cain and smiled. "The dinner was great and the champagne superb," she said for the benefit of everyone at the table.

"I thoroughly enjoyed it," said Althea. "I wonder if he's going to speak now."

"Mr. Patterson?" asked the waiter. He was behind Jimmy.

"Yes," said Jimmy.

"Your babysitter has been trying to call you. It seems there is an emergency at your home. Do you wish to speak with her on our phone, or do have one you can call her with?"

"My cell. I had it turned off for the dinner. Thank you, I'll use that," said Jimmy.

"Very good," said the waiter. "I will tell her you will call. She sounds pretty frantic, and it seemed there was a great deal of commotion."

"I'll call right now." He pulled out his cell, switched it on, and called home. He waited a second then spoke. "Maddie, what's wrong. No, no slow down. I can't understand you." He put it on speaker.

*"Stand back,"* came a man's voice loud enough for everyone to hear

"Who's there?" he asked.

*"It's...it's the EMS. They are trying to revive Jimmy,"* said the babysitter.

"What do you mean revive him?"

*"Come home now,"* she sobbed.

Cain was trying to hear what was going on in the background. He could hear snippets and it sounded hectic. *"Clear,"* came the male voice.

"Althea, we have to leave immediately. Klyde,

Harry you may want to come too, your kids are there. I'm not sure what's going on, but something is wrong with Jimmy Jr."

Cain leaned over to Jimmy. "Would you like us to meet you there?"

"No, I don't know what's going on at home. I'll call you tomorrow." Jimmy was already trying to rush Althea. He put her wrap on, and the rest were on their feet.

Kara looked at Cain. *"They may have gotten into what he has at home."*

*"Yes, I'm afraid of that. We'll know tomorrow."*

*"Shouldn't we go?"*

*"No, we don't know what is happening. We'd only be in the way. It could be something simple. I need to stay and speak with Reid."*

That was all he could say because right then Reid Dalton stepped on stage.

"May I have your attention."

Kara looked at the man. He was younger than she pictured him. Handsome, she thought. She hoped they could get an audience with him.

"I called you all here and I appreciate you've all come. You know why we are here. The wealthiest people in Denver. We've had good fortune, better fortune than the average person, but it's those average people we need to think about, those who work for us. Without them we wouldn't have our fortune. This is our way of saying thank you to them.

"I'm sure all of us here have the best health care anyone could ask for, but the average working person has little or none. Ensuring their good health makes for a happier, healthier person and thus makes for a better worker. It's up to us to make sure our fine city is well taken care of.

"These people not only work for us they are also our friends. They are important to us. Their families are important to us. For us to maintain our companies, our businesses, our schools, and our hospitals, we need them as much as they need us." He cleared his throat and continued. "We all know that this is a fundraiser for our new hospital. I make this vow now, that whatever your contribution is, I will match it."

People clapped and he held up his hands to still them. She noticed it was quiet when he spoke. The people admired him. Everyone hung on his every word.

They listened intently to his speech and clapped enthusiastically. When he finished people lined up to shake his hand. The band was setting up their equipment for the dance, and Reid took a second to speak to everyone individually. She and Cain were fourth in line.

When it came their time, she let Cain do all the talking.

"Mr. Dalton," said Cain shaking his hand. "I'm Cain DeLucci and this is my date, Kara Thomas. We are here in Christian Keller's stead. He regretted not being able to come but said to inform you that his contribution is in the mail."

"He's a busy man," said Reid. "It's nice to meet you, Mr. DeLucci." He shook his hand then turned to Kara.

When he took Kara's hand, he paused. Kara had an uneasy feeling go through her, but it left as quickly as it had come.

"Do I know you?" Reid asked.

"No, we've never met," she replied smiling at the tall man.

"Yes of course," he said. "You remind me of someone I knew long ago. It's uncanny your resemblance to her." He turned again to Cain. "Well, I do hope you enjoy yourselves this evening."

"Mr. Dalton, I need your help."

Reid instantly looked bored and looked to the person behind Cain, until Cain said his next words.

"Our people are dying, and Ansen Horn is behind it. I know it, I just can't prove it. Please I'd just like to set an appointment with you to plead my case."

Reid's eyebrows shot up. "You say people are dying?"

"Yes, I've been working on this for three years. I could use your help."

"Well, we can't have that, can we. Meet me tomorrow at noon. I usually go to the club for lunch, but I'll skip it and have something made at home." He looked behind him. "Terry come here, please." The woman that was on stage with him earlier stepped up. "Change my calendar for tomorrow. I'll be staying in for lunch. Pen me in for a meeting with Mr. DeLucci, please."

"Yes, sir," she stepped back. "That's my personal assistant, Terry, she makes and breaks appointments for me. So, I will see you noon tomorrow. Oh, and Mr. DeLucci, bring Ms. Thomas with you. Do you know where I live?"

Kara's first thought was that everyone knew where Reid Dalton lived. "Yes," he replied. "I do. I'll be there."

That was it, Reid immediately went on to the next person, dismissing them quickly, but Cain got what he wanted, and it showed. He was happy and that made her happy. He took her hand, and they went back to their table, and waited for the music to start.

They left work out of their conversation for the rest of the night and talked while they waited. She was having a great time, and she knew Cain was too. When they started playing music, they by-passed the first dance. By the second song, people were on their feet dancing, and they joined in. Cain took her hand. "My lady," he said as he smiled wide.

She nodded her head, stood, and followed him to the dance floor. It was a relatively fast song and they danced well together. He swung her around and they moved to the beat. She found herself laughing, watching his wide grin, and was enjoying herself immensely.

The third song was a slow dance, and he didn't give her a chance to leave the dance floor. He pulled her to him and wrapped his arm tightly around her waist. He bent his head to the side of her face in her hair and she forgot to breathe. She was pressed against the full length of him, his hard body tight against her.

"Relax," he whispered in her ear. "I certainly can't do anything to you on the dance floor."

His warm breath teased the side of her neck like a light feather, and she shuddered. She didn't know if she could do this. She started to pull back and he pulled her tighter. She finally took a deep breath and felt that feeling again. Her blood was buzzing through her system like a swarm of bees, dizzying her, and she heated. She brushed against him and felt him, wanted him, and knew he was feeling the same.

Every time he brushed against her, her stomach did a little summersault, then clenched. She was completely taken by his body. Her body wanted him as much as her mind did. God she'd never felt these feelings before.

What was he doing to her?

She wished they were alone, their clothes felt foreign and in the way. She wanted desperately to touch his skin, and the way he smelled…like a touch of the best cologne and a forest after a good rain.

Then she remembered her death sentence. She was destined to go crazy. He may want her, but nothing would ever come of their relationship. Sadness overtook her, she was happy having him in her life on a daily basis. She wanted him. She wanted him sexually, and she wanted his heart, because she was definitely losing hers to him. She was wolf now and she was coming to accept it. In fact, she loved being wolf. It was one good thing. Somewhere along the way, being wolf helped heal her of all that she had lost, and she wondered when that happened.

Cain broke into her thoughts. "I want you, Kara," he whispered into her ear. His voice was husky. His warm breath traveled down her neck and made her shudder again and this time she knew he felt it. He pressed tight against her and slid across her. "I can't deny this any longer. I want you; I need you." He moved his hand and she noticed it trembled. Good God, she thought, she might just melt into a puddle of mush in the middle of the dance floor.

She leaned back and looked in his eyes as he stepped back and twirled her. He quickly brought her back close to him. She was still staring at him and noticed his eyes turning a warm deep amber color. His dark hair glistened in the dancing lights. She'd seen this look before. Just before he kissed her on the couch, and during dinner, and many other times. But the questioning look on his face was purely sensual. She'd never seen anything more seductive. She gulped and he put his hand just at the top of her hip and gave a gentle squeeze. Then pulled her tight to him and again leaned into her hair. "Kara I…"

He didn't finish because the cell phone in the top pocket of his jacket vibrated.

"Kara, I…Kara I…Damnit, I have to answer this. Someone keeps calling me, and I think that someone is Christian.

He pulled out his phone and put it to his ear. "Hello. Let me get to a place I can hear you. I said I can't hear you! I'll call you back!" Slipping his phone back into his pocket, he quickly led her off the dance floor and back to their table. He grabbed her wrap and put it around her shoulders. "I think we are going to have to leave. The only two words I could understand were '*get there*'. I have to find out where."

When they made it out the door waiting for the car to be brought up, Cain called Christian back. "Christian, yeah" he said, then paused and put it on speaker.

*"There's been another overdose, I need you to get there and take over. The P.D. is there and I want them gone."*

"Where do I need to go?"

*"Jimmy and Althea Patterson's house."*

"Oh, Christ," said Cain, and rolled his eyes. "Damn it. Look I just got some of the drugs from Jimmy Patterson. It's a long story, I'll tell you later. I'm on my way over there now."

*"Good, I'll text you the address. Keep me informed."*

Cain clicked off and put his cell in his pocket. They were standing outside near the front doors. "Come on. We have to get to the Patterson's."

**\*\*\*\***

Cain didn't waste any time. He put Jimmy's address in his GPS and made it there in record time. They got there just as they were bringing out a gurney with a body covered by a sheet. Cain stopped them.

"We're with TITAN." They stopped for a second. "What happened?" he asked the E.M.S.

"Overdose. Three kids, two of them weren't even teenagers yet. All boys."

"Did you find the drugs they used?"

"No, did not. Weren't looking for any, just trying to keep the kids alive."

Cain's lips thinned and he blew out a large breath as he pulled the sheet back and mumbled. *"Jeez us friggen Christ!"* He pulled the sheet back up and nodded at the E.M.S. to continue on, then turned to Kara. "Let's go see what happened."

Once inside they went to the cop in charge. "Hi again, Jeff," said Kara.

"Hi, Kara. Seems like we are running into each other a lot lately."

"I wouldn't call twice a lot. What happened?"

Cain glanced around the living room. There were papers, left over medical equipment laying all over from the E.M.S. working on the children. Two more gurneys were headed for the door. "Jeff," said Cain. "We'll take over from here. My boss is meeting with yours to discuss this situation, but for now, it's under our jurisdiction."

"Are you sure about that?"

"Yes, I just got off the phone with Christian. I've been working three years on something bigger than the P.D. can handle. We will keep you in the loop, use you if we need you, and like I said, at the very least keep you informed. Did you find any of the drug or drugs they used?"

"No. We just got here ourselves. The women are torn up, and so are the men."

"Understandable."

"Hey Gary, Dave," shouted Jeff. "We're out of here. Wrap it up, TITAN is here." Cain watched the two police officers come striding up. "While you guys are talking, I want to take a look at the other two kids." He walked over to where they were getting ready to take them through the door. He pulled the sheet back on one then the other. "Looks like the same drug. Has me baffled."

Cain was getting more worried. He looked at Kara who glanced at the kids and looked like she might start crying. He could relate. So young. He continued his quick assessment. There were two babysitters and seven other children running around. The younger kids seemed unaware of what had happened, and two young girls were chasing each other. He counted them, seven in all. They were all hyped up from the E.M.S. and the police being here. The noise had them all excited. He walked over to Jimmy.

"Show me where you had it stashed, Jimmy."

Jimmy was a mess, eyes red as hell, his hair was in all directions like he kept pulling his hands through it, and to prove him right, he did it again. He motioned for Cain to follow him into his office. The middle drawer of his desk was pulled out, and some keys hung from the lock. "Looks like he found the keys to your desk." With that comment, Jimmy broke down and cried.

"Jimmy Junior, only thirteen years old," he said, and sobbed. "I'll tell you who I got it from, Cain. I won't hold back on anyone. I'll help you in every way possible."

"Good, that's good, Jimmy."

"His name is Axel Stellan. He works where I work."

"I want to talk to you about our next move, Jimmy, and how you can help when you are up to it. Not today, but in the next few days. All right, Jimmy?"

Jimmy nodded. "I'll let you and your family have a few days. You need to be together right now."

They walked out of the office, and Cain noticed Kara talking to the parents. She had a pad of paper and was writing things down. As they walked through the living room Cain noticed a little girl of around three sitting behind a chair with something in her hand. She was about to put something in her mouth. He moved quickly to stop her.

"No," he said raising his voice. He took what was in her hand. "It's a damn good thing this kid didn't eat this, or you would have another dead child on your hands." Everyone stopped talking and looked over at him. The child broke out in tears, and he watched Sarah rush up to them.

"Samantha," cried Sarah. She quickly went to the girl and picked her up. "My God, Samantha," she sobbed.

He looked at the little baggie in his hand. The same damn smiley face on it. It was open and the white powder was falling out. "Sarah, you may want to wash her hands. She probably has some of this powder on them. I'd also change her clothes."

The doorbell rang and Jimmy let in two men.

"Hi Stone, Kylo," said Cain. "Christen send you two over?"

"Hi Cain, yep, called us about fifteen minutes ago. Do you want Kylo and me to process the scene and get the info?"

"Yeah, that'd be great. Hey Stone, come here. I need to speak to you."

Stone walked over to a corner where they could have some privacy. "Listen, Stone," said Cain seriously. "Jimmy got the drug to try with his wife and he gave most of it to me at the gala. I know he could go to prison for it, but I think losing his boy is enough. Don't go down that road with him.

"He didn't have this with him, or he would have given that to me too. It was locked in his desk drawer. It's a damn shame his kid knew where the keys were. I want to protect him from facing prison time after losing his son. Jimmy is also going to help us get the guy who sold it to him. You know what I'm saying? I want to keep him out of it."

"Gotcha, boss," said Stone. "Too bad, it's a horrible thing to lose your child. He'll be paying for that for the rest of his life. Probably destroyed him."

"Yeah, damn shame, he's angry enough now he's going to help us."

"Was it our guy that sold it to him?"

"No, his name is Axel Stellan. Ever hear of him?"

"No, I can't say as I have. I bet he got it from Ansen."

"My bet is the same. Well, process the scene. He glanced over at where Kylo was standing next to Kara. She was writing in a little notebook. He shook his head. "Get the names of the deceased kids, ages, and parents' names. I want to know who belonged to who. Get the rest of the kids' names as well."

"Why?" asked Stone. "All the kids?"

"I want to know if Jimmy has other children. Help

heal him. Same for the other two families."

Stone nodded. "I see."

"I'm seeing Reid Dalton tomorrow at noon."

Stone raised his eyebrows. "Really? It'd be great to use his resources. Bets were going around the office on whether you would get some time with him."

"Did you bet for or against me, Stone?"

"I'll never tell," he answered with a grin.

"You son-of-a-bitch, you bet against me and lost."

"Like I said, I'll never tell. That's like askin' a man who he voted for. You can't do that."

"Yeah, well, you lost. I got a meeting with him tomorrow at noon. I'm looking forward to that. Okay then, I want to say good-bye to Jimmy. Bring Kylo up to speed and make sure the P.D. don't arrest Jimmy for buying the drug."

"You got it. On another note, how is it going with your wolf? Did the full moon go well?"

"Damn, Stone, I have an amazing story to tell you about that. She did great. I think you'll be impressed."

Kara walked over. "Hi Stone. How are you?"

Stone gave her a large smile and his eyes lit up. Cain caught the look and Stone's response. He knew she was drop dead gorgeous in her dress and heals. Hell, any man would fall all over her. He felt jealous. He could almost hear Stone's thoughts. He had to come clean about her being a half breed, but not yet. He felt very protective of her. He liked working with Stone, even called him friend. He didn't feel very friendly right now, instead he wanted to knock him out.

"Do your job, Stone." He turned to Kara. "Come Kara, we're leaving now."

"I could stay longer with the women if you'd like.

Try and calm them down…"

"No," he said very quickly and forcefully. "Stone and Kylo are going to process the scene and get back to us. What were you writing down?"

"What time it was when the babysitter first noticed the boys overdosing. Where they were. The kid's names who died and who they belonged to, and the other kid's names and ages."

"That's so funny," said Stone. "Cain just asked me to do the same."

"I don't think it's so funny," said Cain. "She's smart and she thinks like me. Do exactly what I told you to do and do it now." He watched Stone raise his eyebrows and wink at Kara. "Great seeing you, Kara, you look ravishing tonight, by the way. Did you do something to your hair?"

Kara blushed. "Why thank you, Stone, and yes. Since the fire singed most of my hair, Cain was kind enough to take me and have it done."

"Cain, my boss, Cain? My alleged partner with seniority?" he asked. Stone seemed to be playing him, and he didn't like it.

He gritted his teeth. "I said, get to work."

"Gads, what crawled in your panties, DeLucci?" He obviously saw Cain's face. "I'm going to work now. Have much to do. Bye now," he said as he backed away. He held his hands out in front of him like Cain was going to attack any second.

"See you later, Kylo," shouted Cain. He walked over to Jimmy. "I'll call you in a couple of days. I know you have a lot to do for the funeral. We probably won't do anything until after that. Are you okay with that?" He looked at the man's red rimmed eyes and his heart went out to him. He put his hand on Jimmy's shoulder. "I'm sorry for your loss. I know it doesn't help, but I am."

"Thank you, Mr. DeLucci...Cain. I know what you are doing for me. I know you're keeping me from being arrested."

"Did you tell the police you bought the drug?"

"No, they didn't make it into my office, thank God. You guys arrived. They were only here a couple minutes ahead of you. They arrived while they were working on the boys, so they were more concerned with that. I said I didn't know where my son got it. I know what the implications would be if I told them the truth."

"Good job, Jimmy, smart. The P.D. will be asking about it, probably even other kids at school. Just don't back down, stay silent. They won't find anything but dead ends, so keep it that way, okay? I think you've paid enough."

"Thanks, Cain. I'll help you get Stellan, and maybe he'll tell you where he got it."

"I'm hoping. I'm hoping. We'll work that angle and I appreciate your cooperation." He nodded at him then and patted his shoulder. Then he took Kara's hand and led her out of the house.

As they were walking back to the car, Kara said, "That was nice of you back there, Cain, I know some people would have cuffed him immediately. You really do have a big heart." She squeezed his hand as she said it.

He glanced down at her. "Yeah," he said with a smile. "Don't tell anyone else that or you'll destroy me." Kara laughed.

The drive back they were both quiet thinking of the children lost to foolish drugs.

\*\*\*\*

Once they got home and through the front door, Kara was hoping to return to the feelings she knew they both felt on the dance floor. She turned to Cain and waited, excitement bubbling up once again and running through her. She wanted him to make the first move. She knew he wanted her. Maybe now she'd have a chance with him. She wanted him like she'd ever wanted anyone or anything.

Was he just a friend? She wanted more, but she knew she couldn't have it. Tonight, however, she would gladly settle for a night of sex with him.

He was silent as he took off his jacket and loosened his tie. He laid his jacket gently over his arm and turned toward her. He finally looked at her.

"Kara, I…I…" he said, gazing at her. He pulled his hand through his hair. He looked at the floor then back up. "I…uh, it's late and I think we should get some sleep," he said quickly.

That was the last thing she expected. Especially after their dance and what he said to her. She was sure they'd share a bottle of wine and see where it took them. This was such a surprise. She tried reading his thoughts and got a wall. Well if that's the way he wanted to play it, she put hers up too. She quickly collected herself slamming her wall shut. "Yes," she replied. "I am tired."

He turned and went to his room. She stood there for a second, staring at the spot he had stood in, then went to her bedroom. She was sure neither of one of them would sleep well.

## Chapter Ten

The next morning Cain went for a run. It was a beautiful morning, and he planned to enjoy it. He hadn't had much sleep because he kept thinking and dreaming about Kara. She dominated his thoughts all the time now. Why was that? He thought he might be the one going mad. He knew he was sexually attracted to her. Maybe he should just enjoy one night with her and move on. After all that was how he operated. Two consenting adults, no problem.

He could just release her and let her go on her merry way, but no. That thought made his heart skip a beat. He didn't want to release her, he wanted her near him. Maybe he'd become used to her, and he'd lose the desire he felt. Maybe he just enjoyed her cooking. Of course, she had a say, and he'd respect her feelings, but he knew she wanted him last night. He was as confused this morning as he was last night and the night before that. He had to stop this nonsense before he really did go mad.

He needed to find out why her powers were bound then let her leave. But what if she went to work for TITAN? He'd see her almost daily. He thought about Stone and how he looked at her. If he didn't claim her, Stone would. He was a Silver Sable too. He could try for her. You better shape up, DeLucci.

Don't make something out of it that it isn't. Let Stone know that she's destined for madness, and he won't try anything. That would put a stop to it right away. Yeah, just like it did with you, huh? He sped up and turned a corner. He was two miles into his run and hadn't broken a sweat. He also hadn't figured a damn thing out. His thoughts traveled to the kids who died. Damn that just straight pissed him off. He turned a different way and opted for a longer route. Hell, he damn well needed it.

She was going to look at The Oracles this morning and he was going to do some work on his computer. He had to fill out a report about the three families and the kids. Damn he hated doing those reports. He'd rather have teeth pulled. Although he wasn't sure what that was like. He chuckled to himself because he never had any teeth pulled and he never wanted to. People and their sayings, he thought as he ran.

His thoughts went back to Kara. Why didn't he take the opportunity to take her to bed last night then? He knew he could have her. She made that clear to him. So, what was wrong with him? Again, they were two consenting adults. What was wrong with having some fun? He wanted answers and wasn't getting them. This run was frustrating him and wasn't solving a damn thing. Maybe a cold shower would shape him up.

He kept going back and forth in his thoughts. He could have just taken her. Why didn't he? Because you're not an asshole, Cain. Kara's not like that. If she went to bed with you, she'd do so with meaning behind it, and you can't give her meaning. She knew they would never have a relationship. Yet she still wanted him. So, why didn't he do what he wanted so desperately to do?

His thoughts sped up with his running and too many things began to tumble through his brain. He turned another corner and started his trek back. He might have to do this run twice this morning. He was going to have to introduce Kara to the pack soon if he was going to release her. He was also going to have to reveal she was a half breed at some point. He wasn't sure what his punishment was going to be, but he would be punished in some form. The leaders of the six clans that lived near each other worked together as a town and community. The leaders would hold court and let him know their decision. Usually, he'd be in the court helping to make that determination, but not this time.

She was a hero in wolf form and the pack needed to know what she did on her first full moon. He couldn't wait to give the report. He'd never in all the time he'd been wolf ever heard of anyone having such control over their wolf. He was damn proud of her. Then he reprimanded himself, did he thank her for saving his life? No. He shook his head. Sometimes DeLucci you are such an asshole.

She chose you, Cain, as her mate. What does that say about her? She chose you when she thought you were mortally wounded and knew you couldn't protect her. She then was able to think human thoughts and formulate a plan to save you. Do you even hear yourself, DeLucci?

He slowed his pace. Maybe she only chose him for the night, in order to keep the other wolves at bay. Did she know what she was doing? To say she chose him as mate, did she mean for life? If she truly did, then in wolf form he'd have to either accept or not. Could he have her as mate as wolf but not have her as his human mate?

He'd always had an idea about his future partner. She would be his mate on all levels, in human and wolf form. He somehow always saw himself with a tall blonde. Kara was tall and gads her long silky legs had been wrapped around his body at least a thousand times in his thoughts. The thought made him grow hard. It felt complicated and he was getting a headache. Kara had come into his life and turned his whole world upside down.

On his way back to the house, he pushed all thoughts from his mind, picked up his pace and ran. When he got back, he was sweaty, and his muscles hurt. He opened the door to the smell of another good breakfast. He was famished.

Perhaps he could talk to her at breakfast and see what she was feeling and get this whole thing straightened out. He knew he was going to release her from being her sire, but he did want to keep her around until they had answers. He sensed she was somehow in great danger, and he didn't like that. He could use that though to keep her around and then they could have sex. With that in mind…he smiled.

He pulled his running jacket off and threw it over the back of a chair and walked into the kitchen and stood stock still. He forgot about all the planning he'd done on his run and just stared at her.

"Good morning." She stood holding a spatula like she did the last time she cooked breakfast. Her eyes sparkled and his heart fluttered like a flock of butterflies taking off all at once. He wanted to swallow his tongue and every word he was going to say went right out the window. All he could think about was how beautiful she looked standing in his kitchen, robe on, hair wet from a recent shower, raw and beautiful.

What was wrong with him? All the other women that stayed the night woke up and wanted to hurry into the shower, so they could paint on their morning face. Some of them didn't spend the night and that was always okay with him. But this woman looked like she belonged here. That was a realization that shocked him to his core. He shook his head of his thoughts.

"Good morning," he said automatically. He sat down. "Something smells wonderful." He continued to stare at her. He shook his head again. Damn, DeLucci, you do need to get yourself laid.

"Eggs Benedict, in hollandaise sauce, with Canadian bacon, on an English muffin. You don't have a poaching pan, so I have to do it the old-fashioned way and drop the eggs in boiling water. Hope they turn out."

"It smells divine." Could she look any more like she belonged, he wondered? He thought about mentioning his release of her as her sire. Then suddenly he was frantic over the thought of her leaving. What if she wanted to leave right away? Maybe he shouldn't mention it. He started thinking of excuses to keep her near him, yet she was everything he said he didn't want. Dumbass, he told himself, she was doomed to go crazy in ten years. He stared at the back of her as she cooked. All thoughts of what he wanted to do being tossed through his brain like shards of broken glass cutting all of his well laid plans to pieces. He was silent and couldn't look away from her.

She turned around and set a hot cup of coffee in front of him and he caught a glimpse of beautiful breast and a whiff of fresh hot coffee. "It'll be a few more seconds and breakfast will be ready. I hope you're hungry," she said with a bright smile.

He quickly tried thinking of something to say. "How is it that you always cook?" He managed to ask. Was that a dumb question? He was thankful when she didn't notice and started speaking.

"I love to cook." She turned back to the stove. "I love my career as well. Cooking is a hobby for me. I mean really good cooking. I can cook the traditional meat and potatoes meal, but I also like to delve into other recipes. I thought seriously about culinary school, but opted for the military, and I'm glad I did. I learned a great deal while I was in the service. Plus, I love our country. She turned to him with a smile. Do you have any hobbies outside of work?"

He was quiet for a moment. "Oh…uh…I used to like to build things. My father was a carpenter and I worked with him for a while, but TITAN keeps me busy. I love my job. It would be hard to do both, but I do miss the smell of fresh cut wood and other smells that come with building, and there's something to be said for having your hands busy." Everything seemed to fall into place. He enjoyed talking about his work.

She turned around with two plates in her hand. She placed two eggs and Canadian bacon, on an English muffin, in front of him, then turned around and grabbed a pan and poured golden sauce over them. He felt his stomach growl. Did the same to hers, turned, and returned the pan to the stove then sat down across from him. "Dig in. Or they are going to get cold."

He caught himself staring at her and quickly looked at his breakfast. "This looks fabulous." He cut into it and took a hefty bite, closed his eyes, and moaned. "This is really good." He said and meant every word.

"Ever have eggs benedict before?"

"Not like this, this is amazing."

They both went to talk at the same time. They both

stopped and looked at each other.

"You first," said Kara.

"No, you first."

"I've been thinking, Cain, and it's time I went home. If you are releasing me as wolf, then I have that option."

After all the thinking he'd just done. She says this? "No," he said a mite quickly. He was shocked that she'd suggest such a thing. He thought he wanted her to go, but now that she said it, his heartbeat sped up, and he felt an urgency to keep her with him. He tried hard to slow his pounding heart and answer with some semblance of decency. "I think we need to find out who bound your powers. You also need to get inoculated, so you won't go crazy in ten years." He stated as if to stop her.

Instead, she laughed. "You are so good to me, Cain, and I appreciate it. But I need to go home. I can get the inoculation myself, and I can find out about my powers. I can read the book. I know you want to get back to your own life. We both know it. I can't take up your time any longer. Besides, I'll be joining the Silver Sables so I will see you as wolf. It's not like we won't talk and be around each other. I'm thinking of joining TITAN."

His first thought was how Stone looked at her yesterday and his heart began to pound furiously. Would Stone still want her if he knew she was doomed? Maybe he'd just want to take her to bed. That thought made his heart pound even harder. He didn't want Stone to touch her, and he certainly didn't want her to leave. In fact, he didn't want any man's hands anywhere near her.

He went into a full-blown anxiety attack over the thought. Something that never happened before. He desperately wanted her to stay, but he couldn't keep her either. So, he opted for a plea. "Please Kara, stay. At least until you find out why your powers are bound."

"No, Cain. I have to go, get back to my life, and you need to get back to yours. I appreciate everything you've done for…"

"Don't say it Kara, please, think about it. There are still a lot of unanswered questions. Besides, I can't release you until you've been out at least one more time on a full moon." He lied. "I have to make sure you'll do all right."

"You said you'd release me now."

"I was so incredibly proud of you Kara that I spoke too quickly. But I have thought it over and that could have been a fluke. I have to make sure."

"When did you decide this?"

Good God, he thought. You just decided this. "I thought about it during my jog this morning. I doubt Christian will let you go."

"Why would Christian have anything to say about it?"

He knew he was now grasping at straws. "Well, he doesn't on that, I do. But he will insist before he brings you into TITAN. He would think it crazy if I release you now. It's just one more month. That isn't that long. We can go out any night now together, or we don't have to if you don't want to."

"No, Cain. I've made up my mind. After we meet with Reid Dalton today, and after I cook dinner, I will pack up my stuff. I'll be here one more night, besides there's one more meal I'd like to prepare for you. Sort of a going away meal. Something I'd like to do for you to say thank you."

He didn't want to hear that at all, so he tried to pull himself together, and politely said what he thought he should. "What would that be?"

"I can't tell you it's a surprise. While you dropped me off to grocery shop the other day, I got all the things I needed for what I want to make. I think you will enjoy it very much. I will be in the kitchen after we get back from Reid's and I won't leave it until after dinner and you are to stay out. That's an order."

"Order huh?" He grinned. "Okay, Sergeant Thomas, I will stay out of your kitchen." *Your*, he thought. He just gave her his kitchen. He shook his head like he was getting rid of cobwebs. That is, for today only, he thought. But then didn't believe it.

She didn't pick up on it, he thought. Good. He didn't want her to leave, but after all it was her choice. Maybe it was for the better. He certainly didn't want her to stay if she didn't want to. He wasn't that kind of person. Although he did think about kidnapping her. Seriously though, what he did have was tonight to convince her to stay. He could do that. He could have her another month. He was sure of it. Then he'd let her go. This was such a conundrum he thought. Right now, he didn't want any more thoughts, so he sat and quietly ate his delicious eggs benedict.

## Chapter Eleven

They were a bit early to Reid Dalton's. Once Cain told the butler who they were, he let them right in, and showed them to a sitting room. He looked around. It was a huge place. The room he was in was bigger than his house, well maybe not that big, but it felt like it. Everything stunk of money. He was afraid to touch anything. He noticed a Ming Vase and recognized it as a dynasty porcelain dragon vase.

He walked toward a glass case that he couldn't help but look in. It held some incredibly valuable items. He was glad they had tags at the bottom that told what they were. A small gold object's tag read, 'Lydian Lion 600 B.C.E., it was round like a coin and had a scene carved into it. "These things belong in a museum, if they are real," he said to Kara.

She walked over to see what he was looking at. "Oh my. That's incredible. Look at this one. It's a tablet and it's in Sumerian, 3500 B.C.E. Look at the gestures, pictographs. The oldest known language. You are right these belong in a museum."

"You are in a museum." Reid Dalton said as he entered the room. Behind him was Terry his personal assistant. Cain thought the energy level increased ten-fold when he spoke.

"I take these objects seriously. They have cost me a great deal and are very important to me. I have very expensive safeguards for them so they cannot be stolen. The cases are fireproof and temperature controlled. They cost a great deal and it costs a great deal to protect them."

"If I had any of those," said Cain. "I wouldn't be able to sleep at night. I'd be afraid of touching one."

Reid chuckled. He walked over and shook Cain's hand. "Nice to see you again Mr. DeLucci, and you as well, Ms. Thomas. You both remember my personal assistant, Terry. You brighten this dull place up immensely with just your presence, Ms. Thomas." He took her hand and held it for a moment and stared into her eyes.

Cain watched him closely and he didn't care for the way he looked at Kara. He felt uneasy looking at him, almost like he was a predator. There was something about him, something hidden, something about his face. Why in the world did he have these feelings about the most admired man in Denver? He didn't feel this way at the gala. He thought his sixth sense was wrong, but he couldn't deny there was something strange about him.

He breathed deep to see if he was wolf. He didn't have the olfactory senses his wolf had, but ever since he was turned, they'd become twice as good as an ordinary human. He couldn't smell wolf or warlock on him. So, what was making him so nervous? He was obviously human. He took a closer look as Reid held Kara's hand.

Reid stared right into her eyes. His eyes were a sharp green, intelligent, striking. He wanted to punch him. He could see the lust falling from Reid's eyes. They smoldered and he thought if he hadn't been there Reid might try to take advantage of Kara. Jealousy surged through his system.

Just as he was ready to do something, he knew he'd

regret, Reid let go of Kara's hand and smiled. "You so much remind me of someone I knew long ago. I can't get over how much you remind me of her."

Remind him of her? That's more like it. But who did she remind him of? His mother? Sister, cousin, aunt? Now he was curious.

"Who does she remind you of? If you don't mind my prying."

Reid turned to him and narrowed his eyes then smiled. "I had a woman working for me years ago, unfortunately she died in a car accident on her way back from shopping. She was beautiful, smart, and she was my lover. Unfortunately, my wife at the time didn't take to that very well."

He turned again to Kara. "But the poor girl never had any children, and she didn't have any family. We were all she ever had. I met her in Colombia when I was there to pick up an artifact. She was young and homeless. I always enjoyed being around her." He got a faraway look in his eyes, if Cain didn't know any better, he'd say Reid Dalton was very much in love with one of his employees. He certainly didn't like the way he looked at Kara.

"Well, Mr. Dalton, Kara Thomas is not your employee." He couldn't keep his damn mouth shut.

"Are you employed?" Reid asked her.

"I've been…"

"She was in the service," interrupted Cain getting rather angry. "She was Military Police, Sergeant Kara Thomas, anti-terrorism. Then she worked for the P.D. Now she is considering a job with TITAN."

"Really Cain, I can answer for myself," she said a little miffed, but he didn't budge.

"Impressive, Ms. Thomas. But I thought wolves didn't work for the P.D. I have need of a new bodyguard if you're interested. In my line of work with the amount of money I accrue, it can be very dangerous for me. I would pay you double what TITAN offers you. Just think about it, I don't need an answer today."

His statement shocked Cain. He was stuck on what he said about wolves. "Did you mention wolves?"

"Also, in my line of work it is important to know everything I can. I know about wolves, and I know about sorcerers. Terry here is a witch and it's fine for you to speak in front of her. She knows almost all of my workings. It's too bad that back when Paganism was thought to be the devil's work, the Romans tried to eradicate them all.

"During the reign of Constantine the Great, they began tearing down temples and killing everyone who opposed the church. Under his son's reign common Christians could pillage and plunder anyone they thought pagan. That included killing anyone. Of course, through their knowledge of magic, most stayed alive. Although so many innocent people were killed during that time."

"Sounds like you know a lot about it, Mr. Dalton," said Cain.

"You did say you needed my help, something about an Ansen Horn?"

"Do you know him?" asked Kara. "There are a great many deaths because of him."

"How so?"

"Through drugs and guns," answered Cain. "I have been working on this for three years and I can't seem to tie him to any of it, but I know he's behind it all. He's tied up from the west coast to the east coast. He met with a Colombian drug lord in Florida in the past few weeks."

Reid raised his eyebrows. "How do you know that, Mr. DeLucci?"

"I have my sources."

"Listen, if I am to help you, I need to know everything you know. That's why I've stayed alive for so long. This may be a surprise to you, but I also know you and Kara are wolves."

"How do you know that?" asked Cain.

He walked away from them and stretched his arms way out. "I know everything about Denver. I love this city, it is mine, and I make it a point to know everything about it. I love the people of this city, and I'd love nothing more than to eradicate the filth that crawls over our streets. I know about the National Forests, and the Silver Sables," he said and turned to him. "Aren't you alpha of the Silver Sables?"

Cain couldn't deny it, to do so would look foolish, and he did want Reid's help. "Yes, aren't you human? How do you know this?"

"Like you, Mr. DeLucci, I have my sources.

"But as I was saying…Ah, yes. Denver still needs a great deal of cleaning up and I will do that before I die. I will see this city clean and the people happy and unafraid. Everything will be peaceful."

"You've certainly done a good job so far, the schools, the library, and now the new hospital. It's very generous for you to match what others donate."

"Excuse me," said Kara. "Do you have a restroom that I may use?"

"Oh, of course," said Reid. He opened the door for her, smiled, and motioned down the hall. "Turn right and at the base of the stairs make another right and take that hall and it's the second door on your right."

\*\*\*\*

"Thank you." She really needed to use the restroom. She headed down the hall as the door clicked behind her once again ensuring privacy for Cain and Reid. There was something off about Reid Dalton. She had a very uneasy feeling when he took her hand. One she didn't like at all. She couldn't put her finger on it.

She didn't like the way he looked at her either. She felt there was something very predatory about him especially in the way he stared at her. Which made her feel cold and clammy. She did not like him undressing her with his eyes one bit, but perhaps she was just imagining things.

She got to the side of the stairs and looked to her right at another hall. She was about to turn and go down it when she heard a low echoing whistle. She quickly turned but didn't see anyone. She looked up the stairs and halfway up was a rope cordoning the upstairs off. It had a metal sign that hung from it that said, "*No Admittance*".

How strange. She heard the whistle again and she looked further up the stairs. At the top and barely visible stood a petite old lady, hunchbacked with white hair. She smiled down at her. Then the old lady took her hands and clapped them together and opened them like a book. She did it three times then shook her head. Kara stared at her. "Do you need help?" she asked.

The woman shook her head no, smiled again, and did the same thing with her hands. She was motioning like opening a book, so Kara did the same thing back. The old lady shook her head yes, with a wide grin, then held up three fingers. "Three?" asked Kara. She shook her head, yes. Kara held up three fingers and it delighted the old woman. Then the old woman held up four fingers. What kind of game was the old lady playing?

Maybe the woman was senile. She started to walk away. When she turned, the old lady whistled again. Kara turned back. She made the gesture again of opening a book, held up three fingers, then four fingers. Kara did the motion with the book, held up three fingers, then four. This seemed to make the old lady very happy. So, she did it again. The old lady shook her head vigorously yes, then pointed to her. Kara put a finger to her chest pointing to herself, and the old lady shook her head again.

"What? I'm opening a book and three and four what? Three and four times, three and four pages?" she asked.

The old lady shook her head no. She gestured opening the book again then held up both hands showing three fingers on one and four on the other.

"Seven?" asked Kara.

She shook her head no and frowned. With one hand she showed three then four.

"Three, four," said Kara. "Three, four. Thirty-four. Thirty-four!"

The woman again pointed to her. So, she pointed to herself, and the woman shook her head yes. "I'm opening a book to page 34?" The woman smiled so wide this time that she could see she didn't have any teeth. Then she turned around and hobbled away disappearing into a room. Kara just stood there, kind of awestruck.

She was supposed to open a book to page thirty-four. What book? Perhaps the old lady was senile. Why was there a sign on the stairs that said no admittance?

Was the old lady sick? She was probably senile, and the staff was supposed to leave her alone. If that was the case who took care of her, and who was she? She shook her head. Perhaps she'd ask Reid who she was. She walked to the restroom, quickly took care of business, then hurried back to the room Cain and Reid were in.

Cain looked at her with some surprise.

"I thought you fell in," said Cain.

She chuckled. "I haven't heard that one in a while. My father used to say it."

"You seem to love your father very much," said Reid.

"I did, I really did." she said. She could almost feel tears at the back of her eyes thinking about it.

"Did?" he asked.

"I'm afraid he and my mother are gone now. It's just me left."

"I'm sorry to hear it, you don't have any siblings?"

"No, my mother and father couldn't have children."

"You mean after you were born."

"No, I was adopted." Saying it aloud made her feel weird. And what made her blurt such a personal thing to a stranger? She was usually more guarded.

She looked at Cain and found him looking at her questioningly. She felt violated somehow. That was the feeling Reid gave her. She felt strongly it was a trick question. As if Reid was trying to pry information from her but doing it in a polite way. He was slick, she'd give him that. His eyes held intelligence and knowledge. She could see how he could get anything he wanted. She was curious about his love for antiquities.

He seemed to enjoy that idea as much as he did for the people of Denver. She decided that she didn't care for him. Didn't know why, but she didn't, no matter how much she told herself he was great for the city and its people.

"I see," said Reid.

"Well, I think we are finished here," said Cain. "We can see ourselves out."

"Yes, Mr. DeLucci, and I will get some people on what we discussed right away. Everything you know, I should know, that way we don't have to go the extra mile and we can stop this before it eats up our city. Don't be afraid to use my personal number either. I will always answer, at the very least return your call promptly." He smiled, but she didn't trust his smile.

Cain took Kara's arm to lead her out. "Don't forget, Ms. Thomas," continued Reid. "The offer of a job at twice the pay as TITAN is offered to you, and if you come to work for me, you'll reap great benefits. Ask Terry here if that isn't the truth of it." Terry nodded her head but didn't speak. "Think hard on it. People who work for me are treated very well and with the utmost respect."

"I'll think about your offer, Mr. Dalton, but I'm pretty sure I'm going to work for TITAN." She turned her head back around and they left.

## Chapter Twelve

When Kara got back to the house, she set to work right away. Reid Dalton and the old lady were completely gone from her mind for the moment. Cain had business at TITAN and needed to see Christian about his meeting with Dalton, so she had time to work on the dinner she planned. He mentioned a little of what he and Reid talked about while she went to the restroom, but it wasn't much. She already knew what they would be discussing.

She started humming and thought about putting music on. It had been quite a while since she had the time to cook and bake and she really enjoyed it. She pulled out her cell phone and turned on her favorite playlist. She hummed as she set all the ingredients out for dinner.

She found the roasting pan for the ham and set it in. Then she set to mixing the honey and brown sugar glaze, the secret ingredient being mustard, then basted the ham with it. She opened a small jar and poured out some cloves and pushed them into the ham forming a pattern. Then she set it aside.

She turned on the oven before she went to work on the pies she was going to make. It had been a while since she made pies. In fact the last time she did, it was with her mother for Christmas dinner. She thought of her as she mixed ingredients for the crust. Lard made the best pie crust, she had told her, it makes it flakey and tasty.

She missed her mother. She was glad she bought a rolling pin because Cain didn't seem to have one.

There was a store next door to the grocery that sold organics and rare items and that's where she found the golden raisins. She was afraid for a minute when she couldn't find walnuts, but one of the workers showed her to them. It felt like this dinner was meant to be because she'd found everything she needed. She even found fresh blueberries, unusual for this time of year.

She set to work and a half hour later she put two pies in the oven to bake then quickly cleaned up the flour mess. She sat at the table and began snapping fresh green beans for the Lemon Feta Green Beans she was going to make. When she was finished, she set them aside and began peeling potatoes. By the time she had the scalloped potatoes ready to go in the oven it was time to take out the pies. She put more glaze over the ham and set the ham and potatoes in the oven to bake. Then she made the shaved Brussels Sprout salad.

Last but not least she cut the carrots for her mother's famous Parmesan Carrots with lemon and parsley. She was really enjoying herself, and she was really making a mess of Cain's kitchen. She put three bottles of wine in the fridge to chill. Her mother mentioned it was the best wine to pair with ham because it had a touch of sweetness to offset the salty ham. It also had plenty of acidity and bold fruit taste to go with it. She just plain liked the wine, and she hoped Cain would too.

After she cleaned up her mess, and checked the ham and potatoes, she looked at the clock. It was four o'clock. She still had an hour before Cain came back. She took off her flour covered apron and rolled it up. It too was new from the organic store. She giggled when she looked at the mess on the apron, blueberry stain, flour, and she wasn't sure what else. She'd certainly broke it in.

She went to her bedroom and put the rolled-up apron in a pocket of her suitcase. She'd wash it when she got home. She quickly changed into her new outfit and took a quick look in the mirror. She fluffed her hair a little, turned and looked at her back side, and sighed, not bad. All in all, she liked the look. She put on just a touch of makeup, not much because she didn't like to feel she had stuff caked on her face. Glanced at her teeth and thought everything was how she wanted it. With one last glance in the long mirror, she decided she'd do.

She then decided to bring out The Oracles and look through it while she waited on the food to bake. She'd quickly leafed through it before. Now she wanted to take her time and look at each page. Each spell was on the right side and on the left was an explanation of the spell and its history. There were also warnings of possible repercussions. She ran her hand over some beautifully illustrated drawings of mostly the leaf or bulb being used in the spell.

Blood spells had the biggest repercussions. Some shouldn't be used unless it was a dire emergency. She read a little about each spell and went over the one she tried to use before Cain stopped her. When could she unbind her powers? She thought about her biological parents. Who were they?

She was humming along with the music, turning pages, when one stopped her in her tracks, causing her heart to skip a beat.

There was a page with a mixed up jumble of letters. They looked like they formed words, but the letters didn't spell anything she understood.

Then she looked at the page number. It was page thirty-four. A coincidence? Her heart skipped a beat again. She thought of the old lady who kept repeating herself. Did the old lady know her? What spell was this? What was she supposed to do? How was she supposed to figure it out?

She wasn't good at puzzles. She didn't care for them. "Huh," she said, and closed the book. She couldn't think about that now, she had a dinner to check, and she had to finish the carrots and string beans. She returned the book to the bedroom and went back to the kitchen to finish dinner.

She had the table set with two tall, tapered candles that she'd purchased for just that purpose. She found the leaf to the table in the garage. She cleaned it and put it in so all the dishes would fit on the table. She looked everywhere for a tablecloth but couldn't find one. She hadn't thought to purchase one and she wished she had. It looked all right, she thought, it'd have to do. She was just setting the last dish down when Cain came through the door. Just in time, she thought, and smiled. She was so excited she couldn't wait to see his face.

"What is that delicious aroma I smell?" he shouted.

"Get in here and find out," she hollered back. She couldn't help it she was giddy with excitement. She flattened out a couple of invisible wrinkles on her new outfit and wondered how she looked. Cain came around the corner. When he saw the meal laid out on the table his eyes grew as big as saucers.

"My God, when you said you were going to cook dinner, I had no idea that I was coming home to a five-star meal. God the smell," he said, leaning his head back. He drew in a large breath, then looked at the table again.

"This looks fit for a king and makes my mouth water just smelling it, let alone seeing it. Is that ham I see? I haven't had a good ham in years. He turned to her. "Kara, you did all this for me? Wow, you look great. I must be the luckiest man alive. I was not expecting this."

"I wanted to make you something special. I know as a bachelor you probably have steak on the grill at least five days a week. I wanted to make you a great going away dinner, and a thank-you dinner all rolled into one."

He gave her a funny look, then the smile was back on his face. "I'm so hungry I could eat a whole cow, or I should say, pig, and this looks absolutely scrumptious."

"Please, sit. It's all ready." She brought out the opened bottle of wine and poured some in both their glasses.

He sat down and piled his plate so high, she had to laugh. "It's a good thing we aren't in public."

"Why?" He took a large bite of ham. "Oh my God this ham is out of this world." He leaned back, closed his eyes, and moaned. It made her giggle. She was happy and she was proud. She was the first person who would stick up for women's rights and not wanting to be labeled domestic, but damnit she really enjoyed cooking.

She could be so many things, and do so many things, that she was grateful she had been taught it all. She didn't get her packing done, but she could do that in the morning. Tonight, she was going to enjoy Cain in every way possible and right now she was really enjoying watching him savor his meal. She wanted to make this night very special.

When they finished dinner, he helped her clean up. She started the dishwasher and turned to him. "Now for the piece of resistahhnce!" she drawled. She walked over to where her pies were cooling and brought them to the table. "Which would you like first?"

He groaned. "I'm so damn full, but damn, is that, is that..."

"Yep, golden raisin pie," she answered proudly.

"And homemade blueberry?"

"Yep."

"And you made them?"

"Yep. Which would you like first and there's also vanilla ice cream if you'd care for à la mode. Good Ice-cream."

He smiled and grabbed her and pulled her in for a hard kiss which lasted inordinately long. He finally pulled back. "The dinner was wonderful, the pies are wonderful, you are wonderful. I'd like a piece of both?" he asked as he released her.

"You're asking me?" She laughed. "You can have all of both pies if you want. I made them for you. I just hope they are better than the ones you buy."

"I already know the answer to that after the dinner I just ate. I have room for two pieces not a speck more. I'm so full, but I must taste both. Golden raisin first."

"Ice cream?"

"Only with the blueberry and that's next."

After he ate two pieces of raisin pie, one piece with a touch of ice cream, and one of blueberry with a hefty scoop of ice cream, he finally called it quits.

"Kara, I haven't eaten like that since I was eighteen years old when I could eat a whole cow, and I have never in my life tasted a meal better than the one you fixed. I will remember this meal for the rest of my life. The pie was extraordinary and believe me when I say it won't have time to go bad in this house. I'm also hiding it if I get company. Let it be written in stone, I'm not sharing."

She laughed. "I can always make more pie, Cain. My home isn't that far from yours. I'm just on the other side of the city, sort of."

He put his arms around her and looked at her smiling. "I'm so full that the only thing that will relieve my overgrown stomach is to go to wolf and do some running. Would you like to go for a run? We don't need to stay out long. I've taught you everything you need to know. The rest is experience. What say you a couple hours? Then I think we should drink those other two bottles of wine, or perhaps you'd care for a different one. I have a few to choose from, your choice. In all of it."

"You know, that sounds wonderful, and fun. Sure, where are we going?"

"Right out here. There are some beautiful sights around my home. There are other homes around the lake and some farther up that are Silver Sables, but I trust you now. If you run into another wolf, it would be one of the Silverbacks. This is our territory."

"You trust me to run into other pack members?" That humbled her. She wanted to be accepted into their pack and hadn't realized how much until now.

"Of course, I do. You'll do fine." He smacked her butt. "I'm the first one out." He headed to the sliding doors. He began taking his clothes off on the patio looking out over the lake.

"You are like a little kid, Cain DeLucci. You forgot to say Na, na, na, na, na, naaa." She laughed. She'd barely got the last na out, and he did just that. She slipped out of her clothes and left them lying on a patio chair. She no longer felt embarrassed being naked in front of him. He'd seen her every which way, even on her monthly, which thank God was over with. He was wolf before her because she was a bit behind in getting her clothes off.

She did a double take as she looked at him. She gazed at the beautiful dark-haired wolf staring at her with yellow eyes, and she fell in love. Perhaps she'd always been, but she really felt it in that moment. He was large, sleek, and majestic and she could see why he was the alpha of the pack. She could see intelligence in those golden yellow eyes.

She couldn't help it, as a human she went to him and he stared up at her, his mouth open, and tongue out panting. She reached down and petted him, then leaned down and kissed the top of his head, and he licked her face. She giggled then stood back and said the magic words and felt the change. Fully changed she took off running.

They traveled around the lake and further up, chasing each other, nipping at each other, laughing together. They were fully open in their thoughts with one another, and she felt good. She snorted a couple times in laughter, and he had plenty of fun with that. A snorting wolf he thought to her, and she felt the humor in it.

They went up a small hill and into some trees, above them were some rock formations. She wasn't watching where they were going when they ran into two silverbacks. She knew right away they were male, but they acted funny when they saw Cain. They dipped their heads and immediately looked away heads down.

"*Derik and Danny. I can tell by your actions you are doing something you shouldn't be.*" Then they heard a cry come from between two trees and out bounced a lion cub. "*Weren't you two just in trouble for playing with the lion cubs?"* The cub went up to one of the males and licked his face.

*"This one really likes us,"* said one of the two.

*"Derik, you are going to get yourselves killed. Where's the mother?"*

*"In the den with the other two cubs."*

*"She's going to know this cub is gone and come looking for it. Do you two dumbasses have a death wish? Put the cub back now. I'll see you two at the meeting."* One of the two picked the cub with its teeth around its neck and headed toward some boulders.

Cain turned to her. *"There's probably a small cave in those rocks and that's where her den is."* He turned and sprinted away, and Kara followed. She would ask later about the two males.

They went into the forest and played hide and seek then came to a clearing that led to a river. She ran fast toward it. She was thirsty and Cain was right on her tail. They reached the river and drank their fill then rested. Cain lay down near the river and she next to him. He put his head on her stomach his muzzle resting on her chest. *"Kara?"*

*"Humm?"*

*"You chose me as your mate the night I was shot. Did you mean that, and do you remember the meaning of it? You were full wolf the night of the full moon."*

*"Of course, I do. When one chooses a mate, they choose them for life, and of course you'd have to choose me back. I didn't just do that because I was trying to get the other males to leave me alone. I mean, I wanted them to leave me alone, but that's not why I chose you."*

*"So, you know fully what that means."*

*"Didn't I just say that? I mean think that. I forget*

*sometimes that we communicate through thought."*

*"I want you to know, Kara, I choose you as my mate. I accept you. As wolves we are mated for life."*

She hurried and put up a wall because she didn't want him to know what she was thinking. She thought about what he said, and it made her extremely happy and extremely sad. She wanted to be his mate as wolf more than anything, but she wanted him as a man as well.

She wanted his heart. She wanted all of him. She quickly hid those thoughts and dropped her wall and let the excitement of being his mate come to the forefront. She'd think about the other later. She turned her head down to his and licked his face.

*"I think that's the best wolf kiss I've ever had."*

She chuckled.

*"You do know that Cassandra will fight you as she is the alpha female of our pack. Now you are alpha female because I've made my choice. Since I'm the alpha it makes you the alpha, but she will want to fight you for it."*

*"Does she love you?"*

*"It's different in the wolf world. I'm alpha and I haven't chosen Cassandra, she fought her way to the alpha position. It's true we've had sex as wolves when she was in heat, but she also had a great number of the males."*

*"Is there ever any jealousy that develops because the wolf might have another?"*

*"Oh, yes, there's been jealousy in the wolf world, ergo fighting for your place within the pack. When one gets more attention than another it can cause jealousy. If you look at domestic dogs in the human world you can see it. When a person has two dogs, and the owner, the*

*alpha, pays attention to one dog the other gets jealous and pokes his nose between them vying for the owner's attention."*

*"Oh, I see."*

*"Yes, it's the way of the wolf. Come, I'll race you back."* He jumped up and so did she. The chase was on. They followed the river for a distance and came out around a clump of bushes and into another wolf drinking from the river. The wolf looked up and Kara caught its thoughts. The wolf was female and recognized Cain. She ran to him, and Kara caught that she was excited, and it showed on her face. She was a blue-eyed wolf, Silverback, and after licking Cain's face she turned to Kara. She must have heard the news because her thoughts were a question about her being the newbie.

Cain answered her questions. The female wolf growled at Kara and Kara growled back. She didn't like the female wolf at all, and she bared her teeth. Everything was happening strictly by instinct. She was catching pictures here and there and it wasn't long before she figured out the female was Cassandra.

Then Cain let it be known that Kara was his mate for life. She felt the jealousy come off Cassandra in waves. She turned to Kara and snarled, bared her teeth, and attacked. Neither Cain nor she, saw it coming.

Kara didn't back down either. She was a well-trained human, so she used it in her fight against the wolf. Some of her actions were purely instinctual, primal. Cassandra wasn't holding back either, this was not just a squabble, no, it was an all-out fight. Cain kept throwing out orders to stop, but neither female listened.

Cassandra bit the side of Kara's neck and Kara spun around to break free, and on her return, grabbed the side of Cassandra's neck and pulled the wolf to the ground and kept her there. She stood growling and snarling over the top of her. This showed Cassandra that she won and took the place of alpha female. Then Kara let her intentions be known to the wolf on the ground. *"Cain is my mate you are to leave him alone."*

Cassandra conceded, but she thought to Kara. *"This isn't over by a long shot."*

Kara let her up and she took off. Cain turned to her. *"Are you all right?"*

*"I'm fine, she's not though, she's pissed."*

*"She will come at you in human form too. Just so you know. Cassandra, for lack of a better word, is a bitch."*

She laughed. *"Of course, she's a bitch, that's what you call a female wolf."*

*"You are funny. Let's go home."*

She quickly erected her wall. Home, she thought, is on the other side of the city. She ran alongside Cain all the way back.

Once back on the patio they both said the words to change back. They were silent as they got dressed. Cain opened the sliding door. "How about some wine?" he asked smiling.

"That sounds great." She paused. "Cain?"

He turned to her. "Yes, what's on your mind?"

"I have the distinct feeling that Cassandra loves you."

"You got that while you were fighting with her?"

"Yes, very much so. She was hurt you chose me as your wolf mate. Especially so quickly after meeting me. She always thought of you as her mate. Tell me Cain because this is getting very complicated for me. What happens now? If you find a human you want to marry and she's wolf too, will she then fight me for the right to be alpha, and if she wins, what will happen to me, because wolves you say mate for life."

"I don't know. I guess we'll know when or even if the time comes. Usually wolves that mate for life, also marry as humans." Cain gave her the strangest look then. Then half breed went through her mind. She wasn't going to be alive for long compared to how long a wolf lived.

Five hundred years is a long time compared to her life expectancy of ten to twenty years. He probably just gave up ten years of having someone to marry. He was going to stay single until she died then find his mate. She wondered just how old Cain was.

"Cain?" she asked following him to the fridge. He opened the door then turned to her. Both had their walls back up.

"Uh, hu?"

"How old are you?"

"I was a young man in the navy stationed at Pearl Harbor when it was bombed. I survived. It was after the war that Christian approached me about the change. I met him in Pearl Harbor, he was also stationed there."

"Pearl Harbor?" she asked, then gasped. "You survived the bombing of Pearl Harbor?"

"I was nineteen in the navy. I was on shore at the time of the bombing. We lost most of our crew from the Arizona. I lost a great deal of my friends."

She mouthed wow, and he grinned.

"You're hanging out with an old man tonight. How do you feel about that?"

"That would make you a little over a hundred years

old. I think I have a million questions."

"In the werewolf world, I'm young."

"Oh, well that makes it a hundred percent better." Which made her giggle. He had to chuckle to himself while he pulled out a bottle of wine.

"You want this…wait, wait. I forgot. I have something very special I've been saving. I think tonight would be the best time to celebrate with it." He put the bottle back in the fridge, left, and came back with a different bottle of wine.

"I hope you like this." He grabbed a corkscrew from a drawer, opened the wine, and set it out. He went to the great room and put some slow, sultry, music on. She liked it and felt it went well with the ambiance. Then he lit a fire in the fireplace. He returned and poured some wine and handed her a glass. "You kicked Cassandra's ass tonight." He smiled and it warmed her heart. "I wish you could have seen yourself." He took his wine glass and held it up in a congratulatory way. "You acted like a seasoned wolf."

"She gave me no warning. I didn't know she was going to attack me. As a kid would say, she started it." She tapped her glass to his then took a sip of wine and smiled.

He chuckled. "Well, she might have started it, but you certainly finished it. You are going to meet her soon, and she is going to be royally pissed."

"What does she look like when she isn't wolf?" She took a seat on the couch. He followed and sat beside her.

"Oh, I don't know, blonde hair, lots of makeup. She is kind of loud mouthed sometimes, or I should say she can become heavily opinionated. You'll meet."

"When is the next meeting? Will I be going?"

"Of course, you will, I am releasing you. You are the first to be released after the first full moon. Your official release will happen at the meeting, and you will then join the pack of Silver Sables. Hopefully you will join us at TITAN."

"Is that wise to let me go so quickly?" she asked.

"Under the circumstances I'd say yes. You had to have massive control over your wolf to have done what you did."

"I only did what came naturally," she said with a blush.

He saw her blush. "How's that?"

"I was only protecting my mate who was mortally wounded," she said honestly. "I just knew I didn't want any harm to come to you. I instinctively knew and felt that."

He took a sip of wine. "I don't want you to go home tomorrow, Kara. I want you to stay with me."

"How so?" Her heartbeat sped up and she was hoping with all hope he'd say something to her, anything that would tell her he felt even close to what she was feeling for him. She wanted, no needed him to say something other than mentioning her bound powers. She was damn tired of hearing it.

"I'm worried about why your powers are bound."

Her heart sank. She felt the comment sealed their fate. If he would have only said he cared for her, he didn't have to say he loved her, and it would have been enough to keep her here. "I'm sorry Cain, but I have to get back to my life. I have to figure out where I'm going to go from here."

"You should have a place here within the Silver Sables."

"Can't I just come here when I am wolf? I can drive Cain, I know how. I can go to the protected places. I don't live far, just across town. Besides, I love my home, I don't want to leave it. Aren't there people who live outside of the boundaries?"

"There are some."

She couldn't tell anything by his expression, but he had the strangest look on his face, and she couldn't read it. He was bound and determined not to have a woman that was sure to go crazy and she knew that. She didn't want to talk about it anymore. She told herself earlier she was going to enjoy him to the fullest tonight and that is exactly what she was going to do. Tomorrow would be a different story. So, she made the first move. She moved closer to him.

"I don't wish to discuss it further, Cain. Can you please fill my glass? It seems it's empty."

"Mine too." He poured wine for them both, and they each took a sip quietly. Then she looked into his eyes, her lips parted, and he leaned closer. Her heart sped up and all she could think of was how good he smelled and how mesmerizing those golden eyes staring into hers were. The now familiar feeling of bees buzzing through her veins returned. She wanted nothing more than for him to kiss her again. She knew how much he wanted her, and she wanted him back. Desperately. Her breathing quickened with her heart rate, blood rushed through her and heated, and he softly kissed her.

She got lost in an ocean tide of feelings, his kiss drowning her and taking her to a place of pleasure. He put his arms around her and pulled her closer. A warmth gathered somewhere in her stomach and ventured down. She again felt the feeling of an all-encompassing connection, the love that opened her heart and left just her and him in the world. His tongue opened her mouth and sought out hers and she obliged and journeyed off to a different place. She sunk deeply into the passion she felt.

She put her arms around him and put her hands under his shirt and slid her hands up. She brushed her hands over the warm hard lines of his back feeling his hard muscles ripple beneath her fingers. He stopped kissing her and put his lips to her neck and pulled her tighter. He nibbled giving her little shivers which only inflamed her blood even more.

He brought his hands to her breasts and cupped them over her bra making her moan. He took his fingers and gently went up under it until he found the soft mounds he was looking for, then cupped them again and gently squeezed.

He pulled back. She looked at him half lidded. "Don't stop," she whispered. "Please, don't stop."

He smiled and pulled her to her feet. Hand in hand he was leading her to his bedroom, and she stopped him. "Not your room," she said with finality.

He raised his eyebrows and looked at her questioningly.

"I don't want to go with you to where all the other women went. I won't lay with you in the same bed. My room."

**** 

He quickly changed direction and they went into the room where she slept. He didn't care where they went as long as he could go to a place and undress her. He didn't think he'd had sex with anyone in this room. In fact, before her, no one had ever slept in the bed or even touched it for that matter.

He took her to the queen size bed and sat her down. He kneeled between her legs and began unbuttoning her blouse. He pulled it open and unclasped her bra and pulled it aside and gazed at her breasts. Her dark nipples puckered in front of him and with one hand he covered one and with his mouth sought out the other. He flicked her nipple with the tip of his tongue then sucked deep and she leaned her head back and moaned.

Cain had waited for this forever. His blood roared through his veins and plunged below his belt, his heart pounded in his chest, and he became painfully engorged. If he didn't have her soon, he was afraid he'd lose his ability to ever have sex again. He desperately needed this as it had been a while and he knew in his heart of hearts that no one else would do. He needed her, desperately.

He took his hand and rubbed gently between her legs over her jeans, feeling the heat coming from her. He could only imagine how good she'd feel with her pants off. The warm dampness of her soft folds beckoned him. Just thinking about sinking deep within her made him want to rip her clothes off.

He held back and went to her other breast, enjoying the taste and texture. All the while rubbing between her legs. He wanted so bad to drop his pants and push himself home. He stood and she raised her head and halfway opened her lids. He pulled her to her feet and gazed into her eyes. "I want you, Kara, like I've never wanted anything before."

She gulped. He gently took her blouse off, and she let her bra fall to the floor then she pulled his shirt off. She brushed her hands over his chest as he opened his jeans. She loved his smooth skin and the dustiness of the few hairs on his chest and the ripple of his hard muscles as he moved and worked his hands. She took the edges of his jeans and pushed them down and he sprung free. He still gazed at her as he opened her jeans and pushed them to the floor.

The second their clothes were off he took her in his arms and kissed her. Not gently this time, but desperately. He was like a wave washing over her and she welcomed it. He pulled her to the bed and went between her legs and pulled them up. He quickly lowered his face and took her in his mouth, and she arched up.

The oral sex she tried with Cal was nothing compared to this. She'd almost married someone she didn't truly love. She loved Cain. Earlier she thought she might, but she knew it now without a doubt. He was the missing piece of her. She arched back, gulped, and lost herself in the feelings he created.

Oh God, how good this felt. She moaned as his fingers danced lightly over her skin. It felt like a soft breeze tickling a calm ocean. Then she felt something she never felt before. Inside of her something opened, she felt herself unfurl like a flower for him, her body beckoning him. Her soul was inviting his as if it knew him. Their souls were joining, becoming one, doing the age-old dance of love. She could feel it and understand it. She had never felt such connection and desire before. Not with her fiancé, not with anyone she dated. It was like they joined in a warmth of knowing. She felt she knew this man, but what she felt more was the love she had for him. She wanted him more than anything.

What she felt for Cain made her realize that she had never really loved Cal. She had cared for him and would always mourn his loss, but this feeling, this love, outshone anything she had ever experienced. The heat between her legs increased and she opened her legs wider. He leaned up and took her nipple in his mouth and sucked, and she thought she'd lose it. Sinking her fingers in his soft dark hair, she pulled his head in tighter and closed her eyes.

She was headed down the road of no return at a runaway pace. Cain was pulling her there and she couldn't stop, didn't want to stop, instead welcomed these new emotions and feelings that exploded within her. She held her breath as she breached the precipice of a feeling so overwhelming, she could die and do so happily.

Then it happened and she hit the stars. She never felt something so wonderful or so powerful in her life. But she wasn't finished either. She wanted him inside of her. She wanted more. She wanted to feel him deep within her. She grabbed his shoulders and pulled him up.

****

Cain felt her release and it excited him. He stopped when he thought he'd taken her as far as she could go. He reached up looked into her eyes as they darkened even further. They were at half mast, her lips swollen and wet and slowly she parted them. He leaned down and drew his tongue lightly down her, from the middle of her breasts to the juncture of her thighs. Then he leaned up and blew down her, tapping his fingers lightly down behind the path he made with his tongue. She arched under him, and her nipples tightened.

"Please Cain. I want you; I need you."

He moved up and positioned himself just barely at her juncture. He felt her moist heat and he trembled trying to keep it together. He slowly pushed and blanketed just the tip of himself in the most incredible heat he'd ever felt. With how slippery she was, he knew if he went any further, he'd lose it. She was so wet and hot he couldn't believe the heat coming from her. God, he did not want this to end, not so quickly.

He held back and moaned and silently prayed to the gods that he could last at least a few more minutes. He felt like he had no restraint and if he wasn't careful the best thing to have ever happened to him would be over. But more than that, he was falling for this woman, head over heels, down a steep, slippery slope. He was falling in love. It was a shocking revelation. Most of the questions he'd had for days had been answered with that one thought.

The thing that surprised him more was that he was gloriously happy knowing it. He felt like he was on a runaway train with no end in sight. This was more than just sex to him, and he knew it. Maybe he always knew it and that is why he resisted letting himself take her before this. He was making love, not having sex, and he was *in* love.

He didn't know why he didn't realize it before. He was falling so in love with this woman that he couldn't bear the thought of being without her. He caught himself thinking of her almost every second of every day since he met her, and he couldn't stop looking at her when they were together. She didn't have to touch him for him to sexually want her. Clothes or not, didn't matter. So many times, in the morning when she was just in her robe, he dreamt of tearing it off her.

He lusted after her an unhealthy amount of times during the day, and he knew without a doubt that when and if he did get lucky and have the chance to be with her, it wouldn't satisfy him. He wanted her always. Half breed doomed to become crazy be damned. He would find a way to find a cure. He could and would cherish each and every second with her and not regret a second of it. With that thought he understood and admitted the truth to himself. He wanted more than her body he wanted her heart. With each tiny little second of being around her, he was losing more and more of his own to her.

He wanted desperately to ram it home, but he enjoyed the feeling of filling her slowly, fully. He pulled back and pushed in. He felt something for her he had never felt for anyone else. Love. He could wake up in the morning with her, be wolf with her, have deep conversations with her and enjoy it all. And the sex…oh my God what he was feeling… He wanted to wrap himself around her and keep her forever. He grunted and pushed himself home.

She let out a giant moan and the look on her face made him pause. He tried to pull out, but she grabbed his buttocks and lunged over him further and shouted out his name. When he felt her release, wet and hot, it was his undoing. He arched back, shut his eyes, and let himself go. When he finally came back to earth, he opened his eyes and looked into hers. She smiled and wrapped her arms around him. She pulled him down for a deep kiss. When he pulled away and collapsed on top of her, he whispered in her ear.

"I hope you aren't finished, because I'm just getting started."

"I was really hoping you were going to say that." She wrapped her arms around him and pulled him closer.

\*\*\*\*

Somewhere in the early morning hours Cain fell asleep in Kara's arms. After making love countless times and exploring each other fully, they were finally sated and ready for sleep. She breathed deep as he fell asleep with his head on her chest. Her hand rested on his head, her fingers tangled in his hair, her breathing finally evening out, and for the first time in her life she felt whole.

She knew what he was feeling. There was no way she could feel this way and he not feel the same. He never said words of love, but she felt it. He mentioned her needing to stay because of her powers again. It made sense, but she wanted more.

He kept saying he wanted to protect her, which didn't make any sense because she'd been protecting herself for the last few years and they both knew it. No, she needed for him to admit what he felt for her.

She couldn't go through life with someone who lied to themselves. He had to know, he had to come to terms with what he was feeling. She couldn't have it any other way. This crap with him protecting her was getting old.

He would protect any woman in his pack. But she wasn't just any woman and she refused to be. By what she saw in his eyes and felt in his touch, she knew she was the woman he loved. She would have to go through with her plans and pack in the morning unless he said something that could make her stay. He'd either come to see it, or he'd never see it. Either way, she wouldn't settle for less.

She was willing to give her heart completely to him, and he had to be willing to do the same, or it wouldn't work. Was there a possibility she could lose him? Maybe, but she believed in their love. She had to. She finally closed her eyes, took a deep breath, and fell asleep.

## Chapter Thirteen

Cain yawned, then opened his eyes. He looked at the ceiling and didn't recognize it. He remembered last night and grinned. He'd never felt better in his life. He loved this woman and he wanted to scream it from a mountain top. Why couldn't he tell her last night? He told himself it was because he didn't know if she loved him back. He reached for her, and his hand hit an empty spot and the sheets felt cold. She'd been gone for a while. He could feel her, but where was she? She was near but he didn't hear the shower.

He sat up and looked around the room...no Kara. He jumped from the bed and went in search of her. He checked the bathroom...no Kara. He ran out to the great room and through to the kitchen. He stopped dead in his tracks. There she stood in a robe pouring coffee. Her hair was wet, and she looked drop dead gorgeous. His heart slowed but not by much.

He wasn't sure why he loved this time of day with her, but he really looked forward to walking in the kitchen and seeing her there in her robe, wet hair, and even better after spending the night making love. He was sure now. He loved her, he couldn't deny it any longer, and he couldn't wait to tell her. She turned to him.

"Good morning." She smiled wide. "It seems you forgot something," she said looking the length of him.

He glanced down at his naked body. "Oh, right, be

right back." He quickly left and returned tying his robe shut.

He slowly sat down at the table. She was leaning back against the counter, her legs crossed, and drinking coffee. Good God, he could take her again right there on the kitchen floor. Could she look more radiant or beautiful? He didn't think so. She moved and poured another cup and walked over and handed it to him. He wanted to blurt out how much he loved her. He wanted her to know. He opened his mouth to do just that, but she spoke first.

"It won't take me long to pack. I just have a few things, if you could drop me off this morning, I'd appreciate it." She turned around and put cream in her coffee and then put it back in the fridge. He couldn't see her face or read her. She was acting very cold and distant. He thought after last night she'd be very happy. What the hell happened? Was it something he did or said? He couldn't think of anything. He thought if anything they had a wonderful, meaningful night together.

Did he mean that little to her? Was what they shared last night so meaningless to her? It seemed it was. Is this how the women he'd brought home felt? He hadn't taken her as that kind of person. He felt angry. He'd never given his heart to anyone before. Didn't she feel it? He damn sure felt it.

He tried to get into her thoughts and probed the edges of her mind. He felt a wall that would take a stick of dynamite to penetrate. He withdrew because it wasn't worth it. Perhaps it didn't matter, she didn't want to stay. She had her fun and was ready to go. He wouldn't invade her private thoughts. His heart dropped to the bottom of his stomach like a lead ball.

He swallowed hard, then spoke. "Yeah, sure, I can take you whenever you are ready." He took a drink of hot coffee to try and keep from shaking. He didn't want to be angry with her, but he was. She didn't care, she mother fucking didn't care. Might as well take his heart and put it in a vice. "I have to be at work this morning, so probably the sooner the better," he said evenly.

He stared at her as she took her cup of coffee and without turning back to him, she left the kitchen. When she got to the hall, she stopped and yelled at him. "I shouldn't be too long!"

He didn't know what to say so he blurted out. "Take your time. You don't want to forget anything." He told himself, he sounded like a child. He shook his head and got up and took his coffee to his bedroom. He laid out his clothes for the day, sucked the rest of his coffee down, and hit his shower mumbling to himself. He'd better get ready, because 'Ms. I'm Up Early' wants to hurry and leave. Surprisingly they were both ready rather quickly.

****

Neither one spoke on the way to her house. Kara had to keep from crying when she'd got her coffee and she told him she wanted to leave. It took all her strength and willpower. She didn't dare turn around and let him see her crying. She would have lost what little willpower she had to leave. If he would have given her one word of encouragement other than he wanted to protect her, she would have stayed, but he didn't. She felt like he was ready for her to go. She thought it would be easy, but it wasn't, it hurt like hell. She couldn't quell the mounting tears festering behind her eyes. She caught herself swallowing fast and she choked a couple of times on the tears she was holding back, but she managed to keep them from falling. Her stomach was tied up in knots, and she felt like she was going to be sick. It felt like someone had plunged a knife through her heart and was now twisting it.

Perhaps she'd made the wrong decision. No, she chastised herself, if she'd learned one thing from the army it was to make an informed decision and stick by it. Well way to go, Thomas, she made the wrong decision. Did she though? She wouldn't be happy only having half of Cain. And she would never consent to being his weekend plaything.

That would drive her insane especially if there would be a weekend that didn't involve her. She saw the handwriting on the wall. She'd be sick all weekend thinking he was with another woman. Better to never know at all. She sighed to herself. She had to quit thinking about it.

Riding in the car without talking or smiling hurt her too. She chanced a quick glance his way. His jaw was tight. This wasn't the Cain she'd come to know and love. She felt really low and wondered what he was thinking. If this was how he treated all the women he went to bed with, it was no wonder he was still single.

The trip to her house seemed to take forever. When he finally pulled up, he got out and opened her door. She looked at him, but he quickly looked away. She went to the back to get her suitcases and he was right there. "I'll take them in for you."

"I…I can get them. I need to unpack the suitcase you loaned me for all my new clothes."

"I said I'd take them in, and you can keep the suitcase. He grabbed the suitcases with stiff rugged motions. She sensed he was angry at her for not staying. All he had to do was say something…let her know she mattered. "I am a gentleman," he said through his teeth.

"You are that." She took out her key and went to unlock the front door, but realized it was already open, it pushed right in. The shock must have shown on her face because he dropped the suitcases to the ground and in an instant, was beside her.

"What?" She pointed at the door, and he put his finger to his lips telling her to be quiet. She nodded in understanding, he quickly pulled a gun from his back and pulled the safety. He held the gun in front of him and motioned with two fingers telling her he was going in. She knew the signals. She stepped back as he came from the side and gently pushed the door fully open. Then he spun around, gun ready. It seemed like an eternity before he said, clear.

"Cain don't go in until I get a gun," she said heading back toward the car.

"I'm going in."

"Please Cain, don't do this to me." The fear for him escalated and all the tears she held back earlier pushed to the front, filled her eyes, and tumbled over. It seemed time stood still.

He glanced at her then and nodded; good he'd wait. He motioned for her to get the gun. She ran to the car, grabbed his 22 out of his glovebox, and hurried back. She mouthed thank-you, and nodded her head letting him know she was ready. She unlocked the safety and gripped it tightly.

He swung around and into the hall and quickly entered up against the wall, she followed suit hugging the other wall. He glanced into the living room. "Clear," he said. She followed him down the hall and through the dining area into to the kitchen. When they got to the back door, they saw a broken window and they'd left it partially open. "This is how they got in," said Cain."

"Do you think they are gone?"

"We haven't checked your father's office, or the upstairs yet, but since the front door is open, I'd say that's how they left. They just didn't close either door tight."

"What do you think they wanted?"

"I don't know, so far everything is okay. Let's check the rest of the house."

She followed him to her dad's study, and they didn't need to open that door. It was wide open and the room completely trashed. The lock to his desk had been picked and the contents of every drawer were strewn across the floor. They'd drilled through the lock in the safe and its door stood wide open.

"Good thing we took everything from the safe with us. Your sixth sense was dead on, Kara." He looked over at her and noticed her bottom lip trembling and tears gathering in her eyes. She was staring at something on the floor. He moved in the direction of her gaze and found a pocket watch. Someone had stepped on it or dropped it hard and broken the face. He went and knelt and brushed the broken glass off. He turned it over and saw the insignia, and picked it up and handed it to her, then he took her in his arms and held her while she cried.

After she was spent, she looked up at him and he tenderly wiped her eyes. "Who would do this, and why?" she asked. "There isn't anything of great value anywhere in the house. What could they have possibly wanted?"

"I don't know, but I promise you this, I'm going to

find out if it's the last thing I do." He brushed the side of her face and cupped her chin. "I'm taking you back with me, you aren't safe here."

"I've taken way too much of your time, Cain. I can't ask that of you. Besides we both know I can take care of myself."

"You aren't asking and I'm telling you, you are coming back with me."

Tears formed again and spilled over. Everything was more than she could take. There was just too much bottled up. She jerked out of his arms and stepped back. Everything rushed through her mind, her fiancé getting killed, her crew dying, her parents gone, her father's keepsakes destroyed, but most of all, Cain not admitting to loving her, it was all too much, and she'd had enough.

"Why, Cain, why?" she blurted. "Is it because you enjoy my cooking? Is it because you must watch me as wolf over two more full moons, so I don't do something stupid? Why, Cain? Tell me the truth. Just don't lie to me, just don't tell me it's to protect me when we both know I'm heavily trained in defense, in hand-to-hand combat. You've seen my credentials. I was a sharpshooter top in my class, I know about guns and how to use them. You are saying you are worried about me?

"Hell, Cain, I'm probably more trained than you are, and you know it, so tell me what is it really? Is it a fling you are interested in because I'm not interested in one-night stands, two week stands, or even months? I'm not going to wait around until you get tired of me, I'm not that way. My heart couldn't handle it." Tears flowed down her face, and she didn't even bother to wipe them away. She could no sooner quell them than she could stop the water going over a broken dam. Her own dam broke, and she didn't bother to try and stop it.

He put both of his hands on her shoulders and tilted her chin up until she focused on him. His eyes sparkled. She could almost see tears form on those golden globes as he stared right at her. "I have never once lied to you Kara. Yes, I want to protect you, I will always want to protect you. It's the way of the wolf to want to protect its mate. Do I enjoy your cooking? Immensely. I feel you belong in my kitchen. There's never been anybody that's belonged in my kitchen before.

"In fact, you look damn great in it, especially early in the morning wearing your robe, hair wet, and drinking coffee with me. I feel that is when you are most beautiful, and I enjoy that a lot. Kara, you look damn great in every room of my house. It's like you belong everywhere with me.

"Are you a one-night stand, two nights or one month? No, never have been and never will be. I have too much respect for you. Since I've met you, I have yearned to take you to bed. God knows I wanted to, but I couldn't do that to you. I had to be sure about how I felt. Yes, maybe I didn't understand it all at first, I've never been in love before.

"And yes, I have laid awake at night and imagined every way possible that I could make love to you. I go to sleep thinking about you, I dream about you, and I wake up in the morning thinking about you. But I never once thought of you being a one-night stand. I want you to go home with me, so that I can, yes, protect you, if it were anyone else with your qualifications, I'd let them stay, but it's not, it's you, and you are the one I want to protect.

"I must have that as a man, as a *man*, Kara. Do you understand that? It's also the way of the man who loves a woman as passionately as I do you. You are the one and only one. I've fallen madly in love with you and want to be with you every day of my life. In fact, I can't think of a second of being without you. So, yes, please come back with me. He paused and turned away, then turned back. "But if you want to stay and tell me so, after what I've said, then I can't force you, I won't force you, but I will beg you. I love you do you understand?"

Her tears spilled over, and her bottom lip trembled. She threw her arms around him and sobbed. "I love you too Cain. I just needed to hear it from you. I needed to know that you loved me, or at the very least, cared for me. I'm not stupid Cain. I know you could have your choice of any woman you wanted, and that's okay, I'm not faulting you, I just can't be that woman, I won't be. I can't share someone I love. That's just not me. I couldn't stay any longer if you didn't love me, it would have hurt too much. I knew after meeting Cassandra, even if she was wolf. What I felt from her was her pain, Cain. It would kill me to live that way. Maybe she hid it well from you all this time, but she didn't hide the fact from me." She looked into his eyes managing to stop the tears.

"I have known for a while that I love you, but I also knew you didn't want a woman that was doomed to go crazy in ten years. Even if I could squeeze twenty in, it's still way too short of a life span compared to how long you will live. I know you desire a family and deserve it, and I couldn't promise you that. So, I felt I had to let you go. I love you that much. I want you to have what you want and what you need."

He put his hands on each side of her face. "What I *need* is you. God Kara, half breed be damned. I'll be beside you, finding a cure. We'll work together to find one, and if we can't, we can't. I love you, Kara, and I will love you for as long as you let me, for as long as I can. There are no promises in life, so I will cherish every day that I can be with you." He leaned down and softly kissed her and she could feel his love. He not only said it, she felt it.

He pulled away and smiled. "Now I just hope there's no one upstairs or they got an earful. We should check out the rest of the house. Then we are going to see Christian. But tonight, I want to be with you, all of you. Will you come home with me? Will you stay with me?"

She half smiled. She loved him and didn't want to be without him…but she still wasn't sure about how being a half breed was going to play out. On the other hand, she couldn't leave him with children and have him take care of her while she went crazy. "Cain, children… I…I'm not sure…"

"Do you love me, Kara? I think you do."

"Yes, of course I do, Cain, I told you I did."

"Then be with me. You are worried about a cure. Let's try and find it together. Come home with me and we'll take one problem at a time."

She paused for a second chewing on her bottom lip. She finally looked up at him. "Of course, I will go back with you."

"Come on then, we'll check the upstairs, find something to put over your back window, lock up, and go back. We can come back later and clean up."

She nodded her head, and he took her hand and led her out of the study. Once they got to the stairs, they both raised their guns again and went up. There were two bedrooms that had been ransacked, her bedroom, and her mother's and father's. The three spare rooms were left alone. They were basically empty anyway. When she got to her mom and dad's room she began crying again and Cain held her for a bit. "Come, Kara," he finally said, "let's get the hell out of here. I promise we'll be back."

She nodded. She showed him where her father's tools were, and the scrap wood they kept around. She helped him board up the window on the back door then they locked the front door and left.

On the way to the car his cell phone rang. He didn't get a chance to see who was calling. "DeLucci," he said answering. "Christian? Yeah… what? Are you friggen kidding me? Where?" He paused. She looked over at him and saw the shock on his face. What now she wondered. "When? Okay, we will be right there." He clicked off.

"What?" asked Kara.

"They found Ansen Horn dead this morning, been shot through the heart and left face down floating in the South Platte River."

"You have got to be kidding."

"Nope, and I have a sneaking suspicion who was responsible for it."

"Are you thinking Reid Dalton?"

"I'm thinking he has the power to do it. I think he called for it. Whether or not he was doing it for the city or for some other reason, I don't know. He may have thought he was doing us all a favor. Either way, if he did do it, or had a hand in it, it was wrong to do. We don't need a vigilante, and if it was for other reasons, I'll find out. And damnit he was our only tie in finding out who's behind it all."

"What if it wasn't Reid?"

"Well, there's that too. It could've been by the hand

of someone else. I don't know if the police chief leaked anything Christian told him…Hell it could be any number of things. Let's go see Christian, then to the morgue, then home. That okay with you?"

"Sounds good to me," she said taking his hand.

****

Once they made it to Cain's office building, they found Christian pacing and fuming. Kara had never seen any icier eyes than Christian's. Everyone sitting at desks working on computers were quiet except for the hum of a printer. Kara had the distinct feeling everyone was walking on eggshells. He kept pacing.

"If he was in charge," said Christian, "then it could be over, but most likely someone else will rise up. I'm worried about this Cain," he said, stopping and turning. "At least we knew it was Ansen Horn who was responsible for running those drugs, and his ties to anyone is lost with him dead. I hate to say it, but I think you were right, there is someone else behind it all, or at the very least involved."

"I won't say I told you so, but if he isn't the mastermind, I wonder who is. We know there were a great deal of other people involved, but they were pawns in someone's elaborate game of chess. How many do we have behind bars now? Twenty? Twenty-five? Three years and we have put away twenty-five people responsible for drugs and guns, and they aren't at the top, they are at the bottom. They are the ones that won't talk no matter what. Perhaps Reid Da…"

"Don't say it," interrupted Christian with a huff. "He's done nothing but good for this city. Besides that, we are friends for Christ's sake. I can't believe you were even thinking such a thing."

"All I'm saying is maybe Reid thought he was doing something good. I find it strange I had a meeting with him yesterday, and today Ansen Horn is dead. Don't you find that coincidental? At any rate he is no longer. That *should be* a good thing."

"You're right, then you tell me, why am I so fuming mad? Don't answer that." He put his hand on his chin and stopped dead. Then he began again. "I'm angry because I don't know who the hell killed him or why. Get out there and find out, Cain. Go to the morgue. They should be done with the autopsy by now. I damn well don't want to wait for the report. Talk to the coroner right away. I don't care if he was shot. See if you can find out anything strange about his death." He stopped for a moment and looked at Kara. "Oh yeah, you said you had a story to tell about Kara. I'm sorry I'm so wrapped up in this case."

"That's okay it can wait for a better time," said Cain. "I will tell you this, she did exceptionally well. So well in fact, I've released her."

"Really? Well good, good, now you can come work for us."

"I'm still thinking about it. But I do appreciate the offer. I'm not saying no, just not sure yet."

"Well Cain, make her sure, will you? Now get to work."

Cain smiled and took her hand and they walked out. When they got to the elevator, Stone was coming out.

"Well, hello boss," said Stone. "You heard the good news? Your man is dead." He stuck out his finger like a gun then made the noise of a gunshot. "Right through the heart man." He turned to Kara. "Kara, what a very pleasant surprise." His words dripping with honey. Cain saw how he looked at Kara and jealously flooded his veins. "Put your eyeballs back in your head Stone before I rob you of them. Kara is my woman. I won't have you drooling over her every time you see her."

"Can't help it boss. Besides you aren't married, she's single."

"Keep it up Stone and you will be holding that heart of yours in your hands, or better yet that thing in your pants. Do you understand?"

"God, testy much? All right, all right. Man-o-man." He quickly left the elevator shaking his head.

"Stone would eat you alive," he said after he left.

"You forget Cain. I believe I told you I could take care of myself. He'd never get a conversation with me let alone get to first base."

He chuckled. "I can believe that."

The coroner didn't have anything to tell them. Cain pulled the sheet back and looked closely at the body. "First time I've seen this bastard up this close. I could smell him though. I've chased him so much for so long I'm not sure how I feel about him being dead." He pulled the sheet back up. "There's nothing here. It had to have been a silver bullet that killed him. Did anyone find the bullet?"

"No, the bullet wasn't found," said the coroner. "Clean shot through and through, up close and personal. He was shot somewhere else then dropped in the river. There wasn't any water in his lungs."

"Uh, huh," said Cain. "Then we need to talk to head of the executioners to see if they have any missing bullets. Although occasionally there have been homemade silver bullets used before. That wouldn't be unusual. It could be any number of things."

Kara was busy staring at the dead man in front of her and barely heard Cain talking to the coroner. Their voices became a low hum in the background, and she seemed to be standing in a fog. From the second she saw him lying there she got snippets of memories involving him. But they were a whirlwind, just flashing around her. It was like she was standing in the middle of a kaleidoscope and instead of colors moving past her it was images.

The dead man, the old lady, Reid Dalton, and each time she saw them their faces were distorted. She had never had anything like this ever happen to her before, and it was making her dizzy. She had her hand on the edge of the drawer and it was the only thing steadying her, but now she felt sick.

When Cain pulled the sheet over his face it all stopped, and she was released from the storm. He put his hand to her shoulder, but he was still talking to the coroner about something. She wasn't sure what. She needed to get her bearings and figure out what happened.

"Are you all right, Kara? You look white as a sheet." He pulled her back away from the drawer as the coroner shoved it back into the refrigerant. The coroner was still talking and didn't seem to notice her.

When Cain turned toward her and saw her face, he was instantly worried. "We need to go doc. Call me if anything changes."

"I will, Cain. I will finish my report by this afternoon and have it sent to Christian."

He took her hand and led her out. Once they were in the car, he turned to her. "Are you all right? What happened in there?"

She put her hand to her forehead as if the gesture

would get rid of the cobwebs floating around in her brain. "The strangest thing…It was like I was in a kaleidoscope and snippets of Ansen, Reid, and the old lady went through my mind. They were distorted…"

"What old lady? You never mentioned an old lady."

"I didn't? I thought I had. It didn't seem important at the time. When we were at Reid's house and I had to use the restroom, I bypassed the stairs and heard a strange whistle coming from the top. So, of course, I wanted to investigate. I went to the bottom of the stairs, looked up, the first thing I saw was a no admittance sign in the middle of the stairs, but at the top was a very old woman, hunchbacked, no teeth, and she wanted to play charades."

"Play charades?"

"That's what it looked like to me. I thought her crazy and tried to leave and she whistled at me again, so I stopped. I don't think she could speak. When I figured out what she was trying to tell me, she turned around and went into a room."

"What was she trying to tell you?"

"To open the book to page thirty-four."

"What book?"

"I don't know, but the weirdest thing happened while I was making you dinner. I got out The Oracles while I was waiting on everything to get done, and I just happened to turn to page thirty-four, and whatever is on that page is a mixed-up jumble of letters that doesn't make any sense. I'm not even sure the two go together."

"Why didn't you mention this before?"

"I thought I had, about the old woman anyway. But while I was looking at Ansen Horn, pictures of the three kept going around and round. I have never had that happen before."

"You better believe that's important. Now to figure out what it all means. I'd like to look at it when we get back." He sat back, started the car, and pulled out.

"Sure." She sat back as well but couldn't relax. She stared at the scenery all the way back but didn't see a thing. It all flew by her in greens and yellows and the occasional color that didn't belong to nature, but she didn't pay attention to any of it. She was too deep in thought.

**** 

When they got home, they had a quick lunch and afterwards Kara brought The Oracles out and sat it on the table. Cain poured them each a glass of wine and sat down beside her.

"Let me see this page thirty-four," he said solemnly.

She took a sip of wine, leaned down, her brow furrowed, and opened the book.

"Have you tried any of the spells in here since the other day?" he asked curiously.

"No, with my powers bound, I didn't think anything would work. I have a question that's been running around in my brain since we were there. Why do you think there was a barrier on the stair that said *No Admittance*? Why would Reid not want anyone up the stairs and *who* is the old lady?"

"I don't know. Lots of questions that need answers. I'd like to find out if Reid had anything to do with Ansen's death. I still find it funny that the day after I see him and talk to him, the man I've been following for three years, winds up dead. Regardless of what Christian thinks."

"He could be trying to help."

"No one is above the law. No one. If he is responsible, that's murder. If Horn was captured and put through the courts he would be imprisoned, not murdered. He may have supplied the drugs, but the courts wouldn't get him for murder. He didn't put drugs in the arms or the mouths of the people who took them. There is a law that protects drug dealers, and it is that they can't be charged for murder if someone dies because they took their drugs. That law doesn't help, but it's there."

"Well, here's page thirty-four."

He looked down at it. It was a mix of jumbled letters. He glanced at the first few lines.

*Nllmyvzn rm iryylm uzoo*
*Kozxv Nrhi vbv*
*Rm pvbslov dzoo*

There was a full page of these letters. It made no sense to him. Then he looked at the last three. They were still jumbled letters, but they were the same on each line.

*"Hl nlgv rg yv"*
*"Hl nlgv rg yv"*
*"Hl nlgv rg yv"*

He looked closely at the page in front of him. "Look at the bottom," He pointed to the last three lines. It's repetitive, so it is saying the same thing three times. There must be a correlation here. But what it is, I have no idea." He rubbed his chin and got up and began walking around the kitchen. He pulled his hand through his hair.

"What? You look like you know something or like you're confused, and I can't tell which."

"There's this…there's this thing my brother and I did when we were younger, but that was about a hundred years ago. We had a thing where we wrote notes back and forth to each other when we were grounded and when we didn't want our parents to know what we were talking about..."

He stopped and turned to her like a light bulb went off. "Try this. Hang on a second." He walked over to a drawer and pulled out a tablet and a pen then handed it to her. "Write down the alphabet and on your second line leave enough room to write underneath each letter."

"You know what it is, don't you?" She grinned.

"I'm not sure, but maybe. We'll have to try it and see."

She wrote down the full alphabet. "There. Now what?"

"Write under the Z with an A and run through the alphabet backwards under each letter."

"Oh, oh I see where you're going with this. Easy enough." In a matter of seconds, she had it done.

"Now take just a couple of the letters and see if they spell a word. Like those two there." He pointed to the ones he was talking about.

"Be," she said excitedly, "It spells be. I'll try a larger word."

She did and found they'd cracked the code.

He smiled. "You'll be busy a bit, so if you don't mind, I'll let you work while I do some paperwork of my own."

Her forehead was furrowed. She leaned down to focus on the letters, barely paying attention to what he said. "Um huh," she said automatically not bothering to look up.

He chuckled. "When you are finished come and get me. I'm curious what it has to say."

She looked up. "Are you going to call Reid and ask him if he had anything to do with the murder?"

"Yes, and no. I'm going to call him and make an appointment to see him as soon as he's able, but no, I won't ask him on the phone. If I do, and he was responsible, he won't tell me. I doubt he'll tell me in person, but I want to see his face when I do ask him."

"Okay." She leaned down and transcribed more letters.

He quickly left her to her own devices and headed to his office. He couldn't believe someone used the same code he'd used as a kid. His parents had probably figured it out and never said anything. Whoever wrote it down should have known it would be easy enough to figure out, so why go to all the trouble? He shook his head.

He sat at his desk and turned his computer on. He wanted to see what Stone came up with at the Patterson's. He didn't find out anything new. The Patterson's lost their oldest son but had two remaining children, a boy and a girl. The other two families each lost a son, but also had other children. The Wilson's had three other children including the baby who had almost ingested the drug. He shook his head, clicked off his computer and leaned back. "Damn shame," he mumbled. "Those families sure are paying for it."

He picked his cell up off his desk and pulled a card out of his wallet then called Reid.

"*Dalton,*" answered Reid.

"Reid, this is Cain Delucci."

"*Yes. I figured you would call. I heard the news.*"

"I need to see you."

"*Let's see, I'm really tied up tomorrow, but I can see you at lunch again the day after. Will that work for you, or is it urgent?"*

"No, no, important, but not urgent. I can meet you then. Where?"

*"It's probably not a good idea to meet at the club. Here at the house around noon?"*

"Sounds good, see you then."

*"Yes. See you then. Oh, bring Ms. Thomas with you again."* Reid hung up without waiting for a reply.

Cain leaned back, plucked a pen from a cup, and tapped it on his desk. He couldn't bring himself to work on anything else. Something was bothering him, and he couldn't put his finger on what it was. Something about Dalton. How the hell did he know about Horn so quickly…unless he had a hand in the murder?

There was something else bothering him too. He didn't like how Dalton looked at Kara. She may have reminded him of someone he once knew, but Kara wasn't that mystery person. Could Kara be related to someone from Reid's past? He wanted to find out. He pushed in his keyboard drawer, shut down his computer, and stood up. He wanted to see what Kara came up with.

"I have an appointment with Dalton day after tomorrow," he said entering the kitchen.

Kara looked up and smiled. "Good. I figured out the puzzle, but I have no idea what it means. You want to see if you can make sense of it?"

"Sure." He sat beside her. "Let me see what you have."

She pushed the book back and laid the tablet over in front of him so he could read it.

Moonbeam in ribbon fall

Place Misr Eye in keyhole wall

Upon the alter the Apis bull will rise

In fire he cries out and opens his eyes
Release the souls corner eye sees all
Rise from the fires and answer the call
"Release them all"
"Out from their cage!"
"Release all, Amsu, Adom"
"Release all, Abasi, Akil"
"Release all, Amon, Amenhotep"
"All distant and still"
Only one bullet harry hand unfolds
Only one bullet the gun must hold
The blood of your blood the trigger and point
As the Apis bull burns and the moons out of sync
As the eye sees all in smoke you will rise
Dissipate mist amongst screaming and cries
"So, mote it be"
"So, mote it be"
"So, mote it be"

He finished reading the text. "It doesn't really sound like a spell. It's more like the release of something or someone, or the breaking of a spell."

"If the old lady at Reid Dalton's knew what she was doing and wanted me to look at page thirty-four then does she want me to do something? I don't understand."

"Well look at the deep meaning of most of it. It's Egyptian. The *Misr Eye*, that stands for Egypt. It's Arabic. Egypt was called the *Misr Eye*."

"How do you know that?" she asked impressed.

"I took an Ancient Civilizations course in college. I don't remember a lot of it, but some things stuck with me."

"Well, what are we supposed to do about Egypt?"

"I don't know. The only other thing I know is that

the *Apis Bull* was an Egyptian God, and I believe the names toward the end where it says, *'release all'*? I think those are Egyptian gods as well. Release all of what? That sounds a bit dangerous, especially when we don't know what it's releasing. Could be anything."

"Cain, I've been thinking…" she said, letting out a long breath. She cleared her throat.

"Yeah?" he asked raising his eyebrows. He didn't like the way she was looking at him. He had the sneaking suspicion she was going to say something that he wouldn't like.

"There's something weird going on at Reid Dalton's place. The old lady, the book. I've been thinking, and the more I think about it the more I think I should."

"Should what? I'm not going to like what you're going to tell me, am I." He had a sneaking suspicion he knew what she was going to say, and if she did, he knew he wouldn't like it.

"I think I should take him up on his job offer of being his bodyguard."

"You what!" he asked standing. Bingo, actually as he thought, but when she gave voice to it, the idea rolled through him like a time bomb ready to blow. *"You* are going to *protect him* against harm, who's going to protect *you*? I don't trust that guy as far as I can throw him. Did you see the way he looked at you? Kara, I don't think that is such a good idea. He's cunning in every possible way. I don't trust him. Not at all, especially with you."

"I didn't care for it either, but please, let me finish. I was thinking of doing it as a trial period, say for a month. Four weeks, enough time to do some snooping around and watch him and see what he does, where he goes, who he sees. If he killed Ansen Horn maybe I can find out."

"Kara…"

"Cain, I'm trained in protecting myself. I don't have anything to worry about he's human."

"Babe, look, I know you're trained. I personally wouldn't want to go up against you even with the strength I have from my wolf. That's not the point. Reid Dalton is smart, and he looked at you as if he could eat you alive. I didn't like it. He's the kind of man that doesn't stop till he gets what he wants. And I'm positive he wants *you*."

"Well, I didn't much care for the way he stripped me down with his eyes either, but I've been around men like him before. I'm not afraid, Cain. Unless you have a better idea, I kind of like mine. You and I both felt uneasy around him. We both feel something isn't right. We need to find out what is going on."

"I've been thinking too, if he did kill Horn, why? What was his reason? That's what I want to find out. Speaking of which, tomorrow is pack meeting. I must be there, and you need to go too. I've released you and it's time you met everyone."

Kara got a faraway look on her face, and she frowned.

"What?"

"I kind of feel like a young kid getting ready for my first day at school. Wondering if they are going to like me, and what they are going to say or do when they find out I'm a half breed, a Gundi?"

"Please don't call yourself that, Kara. It's derogatory, and it doesn't fit you. I used it against Ansen, but he deserved it. I don't even like the term, never have. Not even sure where it came from to begin with. It's like you are cutting yourself down."

"Cain, I am that person, I'm a half breed, and Gundi is a term that could be used for someone who's gone mad. That part fits. I'm going to go mad, period. If what you told me is correct and every half breed experiences it, then I'm no different. You and I both have to face the truth."

"There's always hope for a cure. Bane's labs are studying blood and trying to find a cure. They've made some leeway, just haven't got a cure *yet*. Dalton Labs have at least found a formula that will allow you to have twice the time. As soon as I report that you are both species, I will make an appointment for you to get inoculated. I must speak to the board to get you the shot. They keep close watch over half breeds. We're close, Kara, don't give up hope because I haven't. I refuse. So, please don't ever use that term again when speaking of yourself."

"All right, if you feel that strongly, but I bet there are others who will. I can think of one in particular."

"Cassandra?" he asked, knowingly.

She smiled. "Yes. There's one other thing, Cain. There are a great many spells in this book. If I had…"

"No, Kara don't, not yet, please. I really want some answers before you do that. I feel we are close. Your father and mother wouldn't have saved that book for you all these years just for you to get it and not be able to use it. They also had to have known your powers were bound for a reason, so just hang on for a while longer. You'll get to use them soon enough I wager. I just know there's more to this than meets the eye."

"You mean the *Misr Eye*?" she asked jokingly. She giggled at her joke.

"That's another piece to this crazy puzzle."

"Do you think the old woman's senile?"

"I don't know, I didn't see her."

"I wonder why she couldn't speak?"

"Maybe she just enjoys playing charades," he said playfully. He grinned at her.

She sighed and pulled the page from the tablet. She shoved it into the fold of the book she had been working on, closed it and then looked at him. "Are we going out as wolf tonight?"

"I thought you'd want to take a break after the last few nights."

"Well, not really. I enjoy being wolf."

"So do I, and since you do, then yes, let's go out. Do you have any place you'd like to go? Any that we've been to?"

"I'd like to go out around my house on the fifty acres. I think I've ridden my horse around most of it, but I think I'd like to experience it as a wolf. There are some beautiful places I would enjoy showing you."

"We haven't cleaned up your place yet, Kara, are you sure you want to go there?"

"Yes, I'm okay. I want to look in my mother's room."

He looked at her worriedly.

"Cain, really, I'm all right. It just took me by surprise to find my father's things violated. I'm all right. I'd like to stop at the grocery and pick up some things and spend the night there and clean the house tomorrow."

"All right," he said. "If that's what you want to do and where you'd like to go, then let's go."

Chapter Fourteen

Kara just finished showing Cain through the barn where she'd kept her quarter horse, Star, for eight long wonderful years. She brushed dust off her brown saddle and pulled the stirrup down and let it hang as she spoke animatedly about her life growing up on the ranch. The saddle was the only remnant left of her years with her best friend. It was settled over the wooden pummel horse where it was always kept, and she lazily leaned against it.

She glanced up where the bridles used to hang and other than an old leather strop, there was nothing on the hooks. She was feeling nostalgic as she reminisced fondly of her early teenage years. Cain grinned as she vividly told her story.

"When was the last time you rode?"

She stopped talking and thought back. "Two weeks before Star got caught in a Conibear trap breaking her leg."

"Did you have to put her down?"

"Yes, her leg became infected. We never found out who set those traps either."

"Someone else set the traps?"

"Yes, dad never trapped. Someone was running traps upriver and when Star and the rest of the horses were put to the north pasture early spring we found them. We had plenty of signs for no hunting or trapping but as you probably know from the signs in the National Forest, not everyone pays attention to them."

"You miss riding, don't you?"

"Very much. When Star died, I lost interest. It's when I began thinking about my career and the service. When dad had his heart attack mom sold off the livestock. They talked of turning the third floor of the barn into a small apartment and hiring someone to take care of the animals, but in the end, they just sold them off. I wished they could have kept the stock, but it wasn't up to me."

"I can tell by the way you talk about them that you loved the animals."

"Very much. I also had a pet pig named Homer."

He chuckled. "Homer the dirty pig."

"Actually, they are quite clean if taken care of properly and very intelligent. Homer used to come into the kitchen looking for food. Mom always fed him lettuce and carrots and I had to give him a bath once a week. He ended up being a house pet and he slept on the back porch on his favorite pillow."

"Would you still want animals? If you could find a way to take care of them of course."

"I would, and you're right I do love animals. That's why I became vegan. Every time I ate bacon I thought of Homer. So, I quit eating meat all together."

"I see. Speaking of animals…it's getting late. Are you ready for your wolf?"

She smiled. "I am."

"You do know that here we are in Arctic Pride territory?"

"I meant to ask about that. I thought maybe there would be some Lycans here. Is that going to be a problem?"

"No, they are a great bunch. But if you live here, you will have to go to some of their meetings. We have rules and laws for all Lycans, but each pack varies on some issues. You wouldn't belong to their pack, but you are in their territory, and you'd have to know their laws and abide by them while you're here."

"What if someone marries into another clan? Does that happen?"

"Occasionally. When that happens the male always follows the female. They become a member of their pack and are no longer tied to their original one. They get a brand, which is painful, but necessary. Their fur tells of their original pack, the brand shows the pack they've joined. It is so other packs know which pack they belong to."

She played with the concho's on the side of the saddle. It was a habit she had long ago. She flicked it again, and where the leather was rotted, the concho fell off. "Oh, no." She bent down to pick up the silver piece, and when she did, she noticed the marking on the back. "Hum…I wonder what this is."

"What?" He moved to look at what she had found.

"This is the same marking we found on the medallion at the burned warehouse." She rolled it around in her hand and handed it to him.

"It's a rune sign. Another rune but look at your saddle Kara. Look at what was underneath.

She bent down. "Another rune sign. Two different signs tucked against each other. Snapped together they made the concho."

"I believe they are." He looked at the other concho's. He took out a pocketknife and picked at another one until it gave way. He popped it off in his hand and turned it over. On the backside was another rune sign and up against it was another one. He began removing them all. "My God, Kara, every one of them has a different sign. I wonder what they mean."

"I don't know anything about them. I wonder if mom and dad knew."

"My guess is they did because your saddle was obviously never sold. This is really going into the bizarre," he said picking at the last one. As soon as he removed the last one, they all lit up with a blue light. They could only stare in amazement. They rose in the air and circled her.

"What's happening, Cain?" she whispered stumbling back. She watched them until they became a blur. A flash of light shot from them, and she felt everything go black, and she fell to the ground. Images filled her. She could hear men and women alike praying for their queen's return. They were all hurting. Who were they? There was so much and the prayers so heartfelt that she cried for them. What did it mean? What was she supposed to do? Was she to find this queen? She was in the kaleidoscope again and she was feeling nauseated. She called out to them. "What do you want me to do?" No answer. She listened and saw all these people swirl around her then they went faster and faster, and their voices became a hum. Then it all stopped. The runes fell from the air and landed next to her.

****

Cain quickly knelt and picked up her head. "Kara, can you hear me? Wake up." He wasn't sure what to do. "Kara, wake up." He jostled her shoulders. Finally, she moved and moaned. Her eyes snapped open, and she looked at him.

"What happened?"

He stumbled back as if in shock and fell on his butt beside her. "Your…your eyes," he said, pointing to her. "No…no pupils. Ah…ahhh…all white.

"What are you saying? I can see you perfectly."

He gently took her face in shaky hands and looked closely at her.

"Oh my God, I've never seen anything like this. The color is returning to normal, the beautiful green… your pupil… but honestly Kara, there was no color whatsoever in your eyes. When you opened them, they were pure white. Scared the shit out of me, thought you were blind or that they rolled to the back of your head. Thought for a second your head might spin."

She laughed. I think you are talking about that old scary movie."

"What happened to you? Anything strange?"

"Remember when I told you about feeling like I was in a kaleidoscope in the morgue?" He shook his head yes. "Well, it was like that again, but I saw and heard all these people…thousands of them. From distant past to now. They were all praying for the return of their queen. I'm not sure, but I think I'm supposed to help them find this person. Was I crying?"

"I didn't see any indication of that, no. You lay on the floor shaking and I was trying to revive you."

"Then it was in my mind. Cain, I felt strongly for those people. I tried talking to them, and they didn't hear me. I even shouted to them. I could only hear them and not everything either. They were all praying. I felt love for them all, that's all I know. I just don't know what any of it means." She felt the tears slide down her cheeks and

Cain put his arms around her and held her. She leaned into to him, sitting there on the floor of the barn, and he rubbed her back and just held her saying soothing words while she cried.

When Kara stopped crying and finally pulled away, Cain was unsure of what to say. He was speechless over what he witnessed but he knew in his heart that something highly unusual was happening and he was a bit frightened of it. Mostly for her. He was deeply concerned. She went to flick her hair out of her face and as she did the saddle flew across the room. "What the…" He glanced over in surprise.

"Well, that went beyond the bizarre," said Cain. "I'm not sure, but I think you just unbound your powers, or those conchos did. Your hand looked like you motioned toward the saddle. What were you thinking?"

"Actually, I was thinking about moving the saddle. At least a few weeks ago I was going to do that and clean this place up. I was just thinking about it again."

"You certainly moved it," he said laughing.

"What? Where did it go?"

"Into a pile of old hay. Well, you can't see it. It's buried. I think you are going to have to be careful from now on with what you think, say, and do. I was right you can move things with your mind. At least we know another of your powers are back. Maybe all three are there now, but your eyes…" He shook his head.

"I don't think I like this much. Perhaps we better skip our wolf tonight."

He leaned down and sniffed the air.

"What are you doing?"

"I still can't smell witch on you. Your powers are unbound and yet I still can't smell you. I can't smell wolf either."

"I'm probably more baffled over this whole thing than you are. At least you knew we existed before, I'm one and never knew it."

"Look I have a good friend in Florida, he's a warlock. I'm going to give him a call, send copies of these different marks and ask him what it all means. Damian works for TITAN there. If he knows anything, he'll tell me."

"Where'd you meet him?" she asked leaning against the door to a stall. She threw a concho into the air and caught it.

"I should take pictures of all these rune signs," he said glancing at a few he picked up. "Oh, where'd I meet him? I met him in the service. It's also when I found out about sorcerers. He put us in a bubble when we were attacked in Pearl Harbor. It was he who introduced me to Christian and the rest is history. It wasn't long before I was released from the navy, and when I was, Christian approached me. Somehow the two of them knew each other."

"So, you have some sorcerers in TITAN?"

"Yes, they do special things. They are very powerful people, Kara. Intelligent, loyal, and sensitive. They've been ridiculed, executed, and people just don't understand. Back during Christ's time, a lot of them were killed in many sufferable ways, most captured, and burned at the stake, and they were tortured."

"I remember the history lessons," said Kara.

"All true and more. So, they don't like people knowing about them, and I don't blame them. It was a strong man in the fifties who began to bring them all together again. I can't remember who Damian said it was, or perhaps he never told me. Anyway. There's over a million and a half that reside in America alone. I know because Damian told me some things. There are some who are extremely talented and strong, and they have their own special force within TITAN."

"Is Damian the one who taught you about sorcery?"

"Yes. The thing is, Kara, sorcerers and wolves are different, and most don't talk to each other about their individual traits either. It's an untold courtesy. Wolves and Sorcerers, all know about each other, but it is similar to us not speaking to humans about who and what we are. It's complicated. But I'm sure Damian will talk to me about this. I have to ask him. He's the only one I can think of."

"You could ask Reid Dalton."

"Good God no, he's the last person I want to ask anything about anything. Besides he's neither, he may have people on the street to tell him things, but other than that he's human."

"I see, and you are right. I really wouldn't want too either. I'm hungry. Why don't we go and find something to eat?"

They went into the kitchen, and they opted for sandwiches and chips because they were quick and easy. She was glad they stopped and got supplies before coming here. She'd cleaned out the fridge and emptied some old boxes of stuff from the cupboards and replaced them with new. When they finished lunch, Kara wanted to go to her mom and dad's bedroom.

"It's about time I go through mom's room," she said, as she threw the paper plates away. "I'll start some coffee and we can go up."

"Good idea," he said as he popped his last chip in

his mouth. "Coffee sounds good." He watched her put on a pot of coffee, and then they went upstairs to the bedroom.

She found her mother's jewelry box pried open, broken on the floor and all her jewelry strewn about. Cain gave her shoulder a squeeze in reassurance and started to help her. She began picking up the necklaces. She couldn't help but remember when her mom got each of them. Usually from her father on special occasions. She came across the garnet necklace Kara had bought for her last birthday. The chain was broken but the garnet was still on it. She picked it and the jewelry box up. The clasp was broken but she could still put the jewelry back in it.

A photograph of the three of them taken five years prior lay broken on the floor. She wiped the glass off and looked at it. She was in her uniform, and it was just before she was promoted to sergeant.

"You look good." Cain peered over her shoulder. "Yes, sir, Sergeant!" He saluted her and tried to make light. He was trying to cheer her up.

"It seems like it was a lifetime ago." She shoved some broken glass from a vase into the trash basket and put it back on her mom's dresser. She looked around the room. Most of the books on a small bookshelf had escaped damage. Her eyes caught a book. "Oh, this book was my favorite when I was a little girl. Every kid should have this book. I made mom read it every night. It's a quick read, but a great little story."

She pulled it out and opened it. When she did a photograph fell out of it. She bent down and picked it up. It was an older photograph of a woman who looked just like her. Her hands began to shake. She turned the photo over. Someone had written, *Mariana De la Fuentes, Kara's mother. For Kara.*

She couldn't help it; she began to cry. Cain sat on the bed and put his arm around her.

"You've never seen this before, have you?" He held the book in one hand and something in his other. "Here, you may want to see this also. He handed her a folded document. "It fell on the floor when you went to pick up the photo."

She unfolded it and read it. It was her birth certificate. It had her birthdate, her time of birth and mother's name on it. Father unknown. She was born in America. She looked at the seal. She was born in Denver. Her legal name was Kara Thomas. "How can this be? My mother's name was Mariana De la Fuentes. Why don't I have De la Fuentes as my last name? Why does it have father unknown?"

"She probably had paperwork already drawn up for your adoption. Perhaps she didn't want to involve the father."

"I wish mom and dad were still alive," she said through tears. "They could tell me."

"They wanted you to know, Kara, that's why they did this. Was it random for them to put these in your favorite childhood book? I think not, they knew you'd look through this particular book. At least we are getting some answers. I have the sneaking suspicion…"

"What?"

"I better not say yet. I could be wrong, and I don't want to hurt you further if what I'm thinking isn't right. Let me do some digging around. Christian is Reid Dalton's friend. He might know the name of the woman who worked for him. Let me go through him first. Please don't go asking Reid any questions just yet. Promise me."

She looked at him through watery eyes. "I promise, Cain, but I am going to take a month's trial of working for him. There's more there than meets the eye and I want to find out what."

"If that is what you wish to do, I won't disagree. I don't like it, not one bit, but I won't do anything to stop you. If it looks like anything could turn dangerous, I want you out of there. Promise me that."

"I can handle myself," she said without promising. "I feel I need to do this."

"I want you to stay in touch with me through the day. Text me, message me, call me, okay?"

"I will." She smiled up at him. What time is the meeting with the Silver Sables?"

"Tomorrow at seven, then we usually all go out after the meeting and run as a pack together."

"That's good. We have time to clean this place up?"

"Sure, let's get busy, we can start on it tonight and finish it in the morning. Kara?" He looked at her very seriously.

"Yeah?"

"I still don't want to mention you are a half breed, not yet. I don't feel comfortable with that at all. I want to talk to Damian first."

"Okay, if you feel that strongly, we won't mention it yet. Don't you want to tell Christian though? He deserves to know."

"I may when I ask him about Reid. I want to feel him out. If I don't feel comfortable, I won't."

"Okay. I'm ready for a hot cup of coffee before we finish up, you?"

"Sure," he said and slapped the bed. "Let's get some good coffee. It will get us in the mood to clean."

She laughed. "You don't like cleaning. I remember what you told me."

"I don't mind helping you with it. It is mostly just stuff strewn about. I'll ask you before I throw anything away."

"Okay, I'm ready, but before we get started, I would like to show you something. I think you'll appreciate it."

"What?" he asked with a grin.

"Come follow me."

He followed her outside. She slapped the side of her new Chevy 4X4. "This here is my truck, but my real baby is over there," she said grinning. She pointed to a barn shaped three-car garage.

"It was my first car, and I've kept it pristine. I think you'll be impressed. He was surprised to realize she was gloating. When she opened the garage door and he saw what was inside, he could understand why. He lost his voice.

"Is…is that what I think it is?" he asked in a squeaky voice. "Why, Kara, no wonder you knew what my car was."

"Yes, this is my 1969 Mustang Boss 429."

"What engine?" he asked. He was so excited his hands were shaking. Don't tell me, it has the…"

"820-S NASCAR engine."

"Jeez Us Friggen Christ. That's a super rare car. It's worth at least a half a mil."

"I've been offered seven hundred fifty thousand for it, and I won't sell. It was a gift from my dad on my sixteenth birthday."

"Wasn't he afraid of giving you such a fast car?"

"No, not really, I had my head about me. I was so afraid of scratching it that I always went slow, at least until I got older." She grinned from ear to ear. "I've been known to push the speedometer a little bit."

"How much is a little bit?"

"I've been known to get it up to 120 mph. I know some straight roads around here. I've never drag raced it though. It was a year before I took it to school. My senior year I drove it the last day. Amazing all the guys that came out of the woodwork. They were instantly interested in me." She laughed. "I still had braces and I was kind of lanky, not many boys ever asked me out back then."

"Their loss for sure. I'm glad you never married anyone else. I wouldn't have you to myself now if you would have."

"Wanna take a spin in it? You can drive."

"Oh my God, you trust me? I get going pretty damn fast in my car. No wonder, Kara…" He shook his head.

"What?"

"I thought it funny you knew about my car. You've been keeping secrets my little wolf."

"When I got my car, my dad used to make me change my own oil. He showed me how to rebuild carburetors and do other mechanical things. Of course, nowadays everything is computerized. I couldn't work on my Chevy truck. I thought all girls learned how, then I found out I was the only one. That was okay though, I'm glad he taught me that."

"Your parents sound totally amazing."

"They were for sure. They gave me all their love and attention. I couldn't have asked for better. Even if my biological parents were together and married, I still would have loved the parents I had. I was glad for them. Come on, this baby hasn't been out in a while."

She went to the garage door and pulled a little stool over and stood on it. Above the garage door was a key hanging on a nail. "My spare key," she said looking down at him. "Saves going back into the house." She hopped down and pulled the stool out of the way. "Here. You drive." She tossed him the keys.

He got in and couldn't believe his luck. His little vixen had secrets. He shook his head and snickered. She had a love for muscle cars...he was ecstatic. He turned the key and it fired right up. "Good battery."

"A lot of cold cranking amps. I haven't taken it out in a while, but I still occasionally started it just to keep things moving around in the engine."

He smiled. He took off rather slow and was careful with the car, but damn the engine was just rumbling underneath him. He was twitching wanting to step on the gas. "Any way in particular?"

"Make a right at the end of the drive, go about three, four miles and there's a road to the left. Not highly traveled and a good stretch to let her have her head."

"Are you talking about your horse, or your car?"

"My car is a mustang. Last I checked, mustangs were horses." She laughed. "It used to be a joke between dad and me."

He followed her directions. When they came to the road, she told him to floor it.

"You don't have to tell me twice." He stepped on it.

"I believe your words were, this car will shit and git," she said laughing. She put her hand on the dash and held on. "In about a mile there's a curve, take it at seventy, it's an easy seventy."

"What's the signs say?"

"Fifty-five,"

"Yeah, you're right an easy seventy." He punched it down and they were getting up to a hundred M.P.H. then he backed down and took the curve at seventy-five.

"It's straight about three, four miles. A good place to let it go."

He quickly got up to a hundred M.P.H. then pressed it to a hundred and ten, twenty, thirty, then out of nowhere came another muscle car coming straight at them. "Damn. It must be the day for muscle cars. That looks like…that looks like a Mercury Cougar coming our way. Another beautiful car." It flew past them and when Cain glanced in his rearview, he noticed it was braking. So, he did too.

"I know that people used to use this road for drag racing. I've never done it, but I heard they do it."

"That guy is backing up." He slowed way down until he came to a stop. The guy in the Mercury pulled alongside and put his window down.

"Damn," said the guy. "That is what I thought it was. Does that mustang have the NASCAR engine in it? If you tell me, it does, I'm liable to shit my pants."

"Did you bring an extra pair of pants with you?" asked Cain with a chuckle.

"You're shittin' me," said the guy.

"I thought that's what you were doing."

"I'll drag race you for the car," he said seriously.

"I bet you would. This isn't my car so I can't do that. In fact, it is my girlfriend's car."

Kara leaned over Cain. "Hi. I don't race my baby."

"That's a damn shame. Do you ever come to the drag races out here?"

"No, we never have."

"I bet you could win some cars with that one."

"You probably shouldn't be telling us stuff like that. We work in law enforcement."

"Shit. Can you forget I said anything?"

"From one fast car lover to another, I think I can let it slide. Besides you didn't tell me what day or time you drag race out here. I will say to be careful though, I don't think any of our comrades would be as easy going. Hear me?"

"I hear you," he replied. "Nice car, damn would I ever love to have it."

"You and me both. Have a good one." He took off then and left the guy in the dust. Got it back up to a hundred M.P.H. then came back down. He began going the speed limit.

"Done with your fun?"

"Yep, I had my thrill for the day."

"Well, that's disappointing."

"It is?"

"I thought our nights together were pretty thrilling."

He laughed. "We have to get back. We've got a lot of work to do. Doesn't mean I wouldn't like to take a day's drive with this baby. I would."

\*\*\*\*

Kara and Cain spent most of the night cleaning up Kara's mother and father's bedroom. He finally figured out a system that worked for them. A pile for things to throw away, maybe save, and the definitely save. Then Kara would go through the piles quickly and agree with most of what he did. He really didn't want to throw away anything that might be important to her.

There was a bank statement that was in the red she

wanted to keep and when he asked about it, she said it was something bad she did when she was a teenager. Her mother wrote her a check for shopping at a bazaar her school held. She crossed out what her mother put on the check then made it for more because there were several things she wanted. The total came out to more than what her mother gave her.

Her mother was angry at her and the school for accepting such a mucked-up check, but in the end, she was the one who paid for it, and for all the overdraft fees that went along with it. It took her all summer to make it up. She never did it again. Kara laughed about it when she told him the story.

There were several things that brought Kara good memories. He was just glad that the crying ended. He always hated to see a woman cry. He was surprised she didn't do more of it. He also didn't mention it when she did cry, instead he just held her when things got rough.

He remembered when his parents and brother died. He didn't cry a lot, but he damn sure mourned their deaths. He loved them very much. He had distant cousins now, but he never kept in touch with any of them. Being wolf he really couldn't anyway. He wasn't born one, so his family didn't know about them.

When it came time for bed, she picked a spare bedroom to sleep in. One of the rooms that was untouched, she changed the sheets for fresh clean ones, and they got ready for bed. They would have to finish the cleaning tomorrow. That night he made slow love to her and showed her how much he loved her.

When he heard her call out his name and felt her body release beneath him, he let himself go and rode the waves along with her. He wished he could take all her pain away, but time was the healer for that. He would just love her all he could along the way and be there for her when she needed him.

The next day they continued cleaning. It took them most of the day. She made fried chicken, potato salad, and baked beans for dinner. Said it was a feel-good supper. It certainly made him feel good. He patted his stomach and looked around the kitchen. They sat in front of the picture window where they could look out. It was beautiful here and he liked it very much.

He probably felt more at home here than he did at his house on the lake. This place was totally secluded. His home, although on an acre and somewhat secluded, had neighbors. All around his side of the lake were neighbors, but across the way was all nature where they could hunt. He liked all his neighbors but there was something to be said for the seclusion here.

He also felt at peace here. He knew he wanted to marry Kara, but he wanted to wait until she was ready. She was still processing her losses and he didn't feel right asking her yet, but when she was in a happier state of mind, he would. He was going to shop for a ring and plan something special. He wasn't sure yet what, but he wanted it to be spectacular when he asked her to marry him. Something they would both remember forever.

Maybe he'd throw out some ideas to Christian and he could help him think of something. Right now, they had a pack meeting to go to. As it stood, there were forty-two adults in his pack, and thirty-one children. The children under fifteen wouldn't be coming. Arctic Pride had fifty-four adults, and he didn't know how many children. Christian and he tried to keep up on the number of wolves amongst their packs.

Kara was ready and dressed to go to the meeting. "How do I look?"

"You look beautiful as always. You could wear a burlap bag and you'd still look beautiful." He watched her blush and thought he'd never get tired of seeing it. Sometimes she seemed so innocent to him. There were so many things he loved about her, and all of them were different. She was not like any other woman he'd ever met.

He also admired her strength. If ever there was a partner, he would want in his corner fighting anyone, it would be Kara. She was damn intelligent, and he was drawn to that. "Come on," he said grabbing her hand. "Let's go bowl them all over with your beauty."

"Am I going to have to speak?"

"Since I'm releasing you so early there will be questions you will have to answer. Mostly repeating what you felt and remember about being wolf on a full moon. How you felt about the man trying to shoot the lion. Just be honest and you'll do fine."

Once they got there, he sat her in a chair beside a podium. "I have to bring the meeting to order," he told her. He could tell she was nervous. He sat beside her as they waited for everyone to arrive. He touched her hand every so often to calm her nerves. It seemed to make her feel better. When he thought everyone was there, he nodded to a guy positioned by the door. He watched the guy close the inside door and take a seat.

****

Kara was nervous and she watched as Cain stood and took a few steps to the podium. He cleared his throat. "I'd like to bring this meeting to order. Charles the roll call please."

A man that was seated on the other side of the podium stood up with a pad and pen. He called roll and marked off those who were present. She looked out over the crowd and her eyes stopped on a blonde woman with a lot of make-up staring daggers at her. She figured it must be Cassandra. Kara gave her a big smile. Cassandra didn't look away but continued to stare. She didn't give her any more thought and finished looking out over the crowd.

After roll call, Cain cleared his throat and began. "Old business. Carl, did you finish the fencing on your side of the property? We don't want hunters in there."

She assumed Carl was the man who stood. "The fencing is finished. I have a small herd of sheep that are along that line, and I've marked it well."

"Good enough, Carl. Carlton twins, are you here?"

"No," said a large man standing. "The boys are home doing their chores."

"John, no disrespect for your fathering, but I caught those boys with that lion cub again while I was out. They should be here. I told them to be. I expected them to show. They haven't been wolf more than six months. It's got to stop before one or both of those boys get themselves torn to shreds by a mother mountain lion. I know neither of us want that."

"Shit, Cain, they didn't tell me that. I'll make sure they are at the next meeting, until then, they will be punished for disobeying and playing with that cub again."

"I know they are having fun and they are just boys, but they won't get the best of its mother if she happens on them with her cub. I'm not sure they understand the ramifications."

"I'll take care of it," said John.

"See to it you do, then see me afterwards."

"I'll call," said John, then he sat down.

She thought of the two wolves they met while out at the lake and how they deferred to Cain. They were handsome young wolves, she felt they were probably handsome children as well.

"Stacy did you find out if we can take on twenty more acres south near the river? Our clan is growing."

A pretty woman from the second row stood. "Yes, I got the okay, but I also got a lecture about watching our growth."

"They tell us that every time we take over more land. We actually do them a favor by taking care of it, and they know it. Less work on their part. Did you get with the surveyor and the county commissioner?"

"Yes. We might have a small problem with the water table and where we can put the buildings. They might have to be moved on paper."

"It shouldn't take a lot to rearrange the buildings if we have to. Good work. Keep me informed." Stacy sat down with a smile.

Kara looked from the crowd to the building itself. It was state owned but made available to the pack for meetings. Made of metal it had many windows and a basement with a kitchen and some tables for refreshments. Cain said some of the female pack members arrived early to put coffee on and fill the fridge with soda and set out snacks and probably catch up on local gossip as well. Men that came with them early shot the breeze up-stairs. It was a big building, all open, filled with folding chairs, and the podium at the front on a stage. Two men sat on one side of the podium, Cain and she sat on the other.

"For new business..." said Cain, bringing her attention back around. "We have a new member to the Silver Sables, she is the alpha female, and my mate as wolf, and my girlfriend. Please welcome, Kara Thomas."

Everyone clapped and he held out his hand. Good God, she thought, she had to get up in front of these people, these wolves? She stood and walked over and took Cain's hand.

"To save her life during a brutal fire, I turned her, and I'm damn glad I did. I released her on her first full moon because she was able to do things no other wolf to date has done. There was a hunter and he shot me through the heart. He was hunting a mountain lion. I lay close to death and my body went into overdrive to heal. Needless to say, I was incoherent and unable to look out for myself. She was able to catch not one but two deer. The first to lure the mountain lion away from me, the second to lure other wolves away from me."

"I don't believe that for a second," shouted Cassandra.

"You're just jealous," said a man behind her. "She took your place as alpha female."

"We need to fight as wolves for her to prove that," said Cassandra.

"I think we already did that when I met you out on the land as wolf. If I remember rightly, I took you to the ground and kept you there," said Kara.

People laughed. She hadn't meant to make people laugh at the woman, but she also wanted it known she'd fight to keep her place within the pack and with Cain.

"It wasn't an official fight. I demand we have one. I've been alpha female for ten years. I won't give it up that easily."

"Jealous, Cassandra, you are just jealous," said a man sitting close to her.

"You're mad because you've been trying to land Cain for the past five years and you couldn't do it." said another man and then laughed. The whole place laughed. "Everyone knows you have fallen hard for Cain."

Kara kind of felt sorry for Cassandra. She knew in her heart Cassandra loved Cain, but he did not return that love.

"You attacked her," said Cain. "I watched you do it. She won the fight and did as she said and took you to the ground and held you there. My word is good, and you are out of line. You are no longer alpha."

"Your word is because you think you love her. Anyone could say anything when they think they love someone. I demand a full fight in front of the clan."

"I'm saying that's not necessary, again out of line. One more time you get a demerit."

"No, no, I accept the competition as such. I don't mind," said Kara interrupting the banter. She felt she should show her dominance here, but also some respect for Cassandra who had been alpha so long. Cain glanced her way questioningly, but she wanted this fight. This was a new feeling. Ordinarily she wouldn't want to fight anyone to just fight but as a wolf it was different. She wanted to prove herself.

"See," said Casandra, "she doesn't mind. Set a date."

"How about the day after the next full moon?" asked Cain. "Should we vote?"

Mumbles went around. "If that day is good for everyone raise your hand. Charles?"

Charles stood and counted. "Looks like everyone is in favor of that day."

"Okay, May twenty-ninth, at the old oak tree. Night after the next full moon. Got that Charles?" he asked and turned toward the other man.

"Got it Cain," said Charles. Then he scribbled it in his notebook.

"For other new business. The other ten acres we have acquired will be a park for the children and a new meeting house for us. That way we can quit borrowing the states. Is everyone in favor of that?"

Kara sat back down and glanced at Cassandra. She had a smirk on her face and the devil in her eyes. She wondered what the bleached blonde had planned for the night after the full moon. She wasn't quite sure she liked the smug look she wore. The meeting was finally adjourned, and they all met for refreshments in the basement.

Everyone came and talked to her, most welcomed her to the pack. Cain stood beside her the whole time. Cassandra came over, didn't say a word to her, but dripped sarcastic remarks to Cain. She didn't pay any attention as she was busy talking to other people. She did notice when Cassandra ran her hand down Cain's chest. A simple gesture really, but it immediately angered her.

"You may want to leave your hands off my mate. Or you might find our fight happening tonight instead of after the next full moon."

"Eweee, she's jealous," said Cassandra.

"She's right," said Cain. "That was uncalled for Cassandra. I want you to know, like I've always told you. I wasn't interested in any relationship with you."

"You said you weren't interested in any relationship

at all," said Cassandra. "Have you changed your mind?"

"Yes, I have. I'm in love with Kara, and I don't care who knows it, especially you," he said. His eyes narrowed and Kara could see he was on edge. He really didn't care for the woman at all she could tell, but she didn't think Cassandra could. She guessed any sexual encounters between them must have happened a long time ago, because by his look he'd been disgusted for a while.

"Well, I've had my share of you, Cain. I doubt that will stop. You may be in lust now, but I've never known you to be faithful to anyone."

"Kara isn't just anyone."

Kara smiled. She knew what Cain felt for her and nothing Cassandra could say would make her feel otherwise. She trusted him fully and she knew without a doubt she always would. She also knew in her heart of hearts she was going to marry him, and she felt he knew it too. There was an unspoken bond between them. It may have taken him a bit to realize it, but he did.

They made more small talk, and she helped the women clean up. She really clicked with a couple of them. Stacy was single, and Carla was married with two kids. She enjoyed both women and talked quite a bit to them. They invited her to drop by anytime and swapped phone numbers.

Some of the men, especially the single ones, drooled over her and flirted. Cain seemed to put his arm around her every time an eligible bachelor came along. She thought it endearing and made her feel good. She noticed Stone hadn't been in attendance. She'd ask Cain about it later.

Cassandra didn't seem to hang out with anyone, and

Kara noticed most shied away from her. She also noted Cassandra flirting with most of the eligible men. The younger ones enjoyed it, but the older ones who had her number didn't pay attention. She saw what Cain meant about Cassandra sleeping with many of the men in the pack, and figured the woman did the same outside of the pack as well. All in all, she liked everyone she met. Everyone but Cassandra. She'd felt sorry for her the other night, but she wasn't feeling as generous tonight.

When they finished with the cleaning, they all changed into wolf. She felt amazement as she gazed at the pack as a whole. They were gorgeous as a group. Much like their human forms their wolves differed in appearance. She noticed a white wolf with a mark on his shoulder and remembered what Cain told her. He had to have belonged to the Arctic pack at one time. Cain out shined them all. At least in her book. She was extremely proud to run alongside him. Running with the pack was one of the best times she'd ever had. They welcomed her in wolf form just as they had as humans.

By the time they made it home and into bed it was midnight, and she was beat. They went to Cain's house because it was closer. She'd brought her suitcases back with her just in case they ended up there. She'd forgotten to pack her robe from here, lucky for her. If she kept this up, she'd have to go shopping for clothes to leave at his house.

She didn't mind, it was kind of fun. Having two places. His place was like having a lake house and hers was home. She wondered how Cain felt about it. What he wanted to do. She'd wait for him to bring it up. Officially he still hadn't proposed.

She thought she was exhausted when they crawled

into bed, but one touch of Cain's naked body next to hers and she found energy she didn't know existed. She was lost in another world. A world where only she and Cain existed. They curled into each other when finished, truly exhausted but sated, and fell asleep in each other's arms.

Chapter Fifteen

The next morning Kara awoke unable to tell if it was mid or late morning. Cain was out of bed. She thought he'd gone for a jog, but she found him in his office on the phone.

"Yes, I'm sure. Those marks were around her horse's saddle. Of course, you can come, we have a spare room. Why?" He paused.

She wondered who was on the other end.

"Important, how important? No, no just let me know your flight number and I'll pick you up. Okay, any way you want to do it. If you want to rent a car, go ahead. I'll see you when you get here. Just call so we can let you know where we're at. All right, bye." He laid his phone down, turned to her and smiled.

"Good morning. Who was that?"

"Damian, I talked with him earlier and then I sent him the pictures I took of the conchos."

"He's coming here? Why?"

"He said after looking at the rune signs, it was amazingly important. I tried to get him to tell me why, and he wouldn't. He said he was going to get a flight out tomorrow. Beats me, and since he won't tell me I'm curious as hell. He said to keep it to ourselves for now. He wanted to see them for himself. I guess we'll know when he gets here."

He stared at her for a second, stood up, grabbed her,

and kissed her hard. She fell into the kiss, and he didn't break away until her lips were swollen.

He led her back into the spare bedroom and showed her what a truly good morning it was. They hit the shower together where they lathered each other up, played, and kissed, and washed off the previous night's activity. After their shower they drifted into the kitchen for some much-needed coffee. Since Cain was up first, he had a pot made.

"We'll have to hustle. We have to be at Reid's in an hour. We don't have time for breakfast," he said.

"Darn, I'm starved."

"How about we go to my favorite restaurant after we're done at Reid's?"

"That's good with me. Italian sounds great. I think it's my favorite restaurant now. I really like it, the food, the people, and the atmosphere.

"It's always been my favorite. Come to think of it, you are the only other person besides Stone that I've taken there."

"Then I feel very special."

\*\*\*\*

When they got there, Cain wasn't sure what to think as they were led into the same room as their previous visit to wait for Reid. He had so many conflicting emotions concerning Reid Dalton. He wandered back to the glassed-in cases that held the numerous artifacts.

A square stand stood nearby, it's top empty of whatever treasure it once held. He wondered what used to be there. There wasn't a plaque or engraving to tell him. He tried to move it, but it wouldn't budge. It was bolted to the floor, strange, he thought. He was pondering what it meant when Reid came in.

"Good afternoon," Reid said as he entered. Terry his personal assistant and a very large man followed behind him. "This is Mitka Petrov, my right-hand man. He's been out of town for the last couple of weeks, that's why you haven't met him. These are my friends, Kara Thomas and Cain DeLucci."

Cain nodded at the trio. Petrov didn't budge from his spot by Reid, and he felt the large's man stare. Cain noticed he didn't change expression either. He wasn't sure how he felt about the man, but a good bodyguard should be a bit scary.

"By the looks of him you don't need a bodyguard," said Kara.

"No, he is my second bodyguard. You would be my sharpshooter...my first bodyguard. You would also always be by my side unless it was a private meeting. Then you would join Mitka outside the door. So, you've thought about it then?"

"I have, and what I'd like to do is a trial run for a month. At the end of the month, I will tell you whether I will remain with you. I'm still considering going with TITAN."

"Well, I suppose if that's all I can get from you then that's all I can get. At least it gives me opportunity to convince you stay." He smiled at her, and Cain didn't like it. The smile didn't reach his eyes, it was purely fake, and he didn't trust fake at all.

"When would you like me to start?"

"Tomorrow morning, five a.m. we can go over the plans for the day. Sound good to you?"

"Sounds a bit early to me," said Cain.

"I'm up at 4:00 a.m. every morning, Mr. DeLucci, my day begins at five."

"I'll be here," said Kara.

"Make sure you are, I dislike tardiness."

"I said I'd be here."

Cain had to hide his smirk. Kara gave back as quick as Reid put out. He was glad she stood up to him. He had a feeling most people didn't. He wished she wouldn't take the job. He felt very uncomfortable with the setup. He hated that he couldn't put his finger on why. By all appearances the man was a saint to Denver, and maybe that was it. His father always told him, if something seemed too good to be true, it usually was.

"What is your business day usually like?" asked Cain. He didn't think he'd get much but he wanted to hear what Reid had to say.

"Like most days, cleaning up this fine city." He spread his arms wide. "This city is like gold and as such should be polished daily. That means keeping the riffraff out. The dirt cleaned away."

"What do you consider riffraff, and dirt, if you don't mind me asking?"

"The grungy, lazy people. People who don't think, or people who can't think."

"Perhaps they aren't lazy. Maybe they just can't get a job or do what they wish to do. There can be all sorts of reasons," said Cain.

He glanced at Kara and noticed that Petrov was moving closer to her. He didn't like that. He didn't like the Russian. He didn't like the feeling coming off him. He couldn't smell warlock or wolf on him, so he must be human.

"No, Mr. DeLucci, these people are the scum and parasites of our great city. They don't stand a chance of doing anything, because they don't wish to do anything, if they did, they'd be doing it. When I'm finished with Denver, my home, I will begin outside of the city limits. If I can, I will clean up the country. Did I tell you I was thinking of running for office?"

"No, you failed to mention that."

"I'll be governor first then work my way up into the presidency. I feel I would make a fine president. After cleaning the city what better way to clean up the country?

That sounded almost Hitlerish. He didn't like the fact he talked so much like a dictator. What did he have planned? What did he mean clean up the city? Many homeless were sick, or disabled, mentally, physically. Many were war veterans. There were programs to help them and people trying to help, but even with the effort many fell through the cracks. He didn't like what he was hearing at all and worse the whole city loved the man. He did at one time, but now that he had met him...

"I'm here," he said interrupting Reid's rant, "because they found Ansen Horn dead floating in the river. Coincidentally it happened the day after you and I spoke. You know anything about that?"

"I'm afraid you have me mixed up with someone else Mr. DeLucci. If you are trying to insinuate, I had something to do with the murder, I'm offended."

He knew he was stepping on toes here, but he didn't care, he wanted to see the man's reaction. So far it was just as he imagined it would be. He didn't say whether he did or didn't know anything about it, just that he was offended to be thought of in such a manner. Smooth.

"I didn't insinuate anything, Mr. Dalton, but I find it odd you knew about it the same time the cops did."

"I knew about it because I have people on the street. How do you think I find out about the people of the city?

The cops are my friends don't you think that as such that they wouldn't have called me? How do you think I know everything that goes on in Denver? I work diligently on this city, and I put good money into helping the good people that live and work here."

"And you think this city, Denver, is yours alone?" He knew he was taunting Reid but didn't care. Kara did though, she brushed up against him and he knew she wanted him to tone it down.

"It is my city. I own more than half of it. Most of the people work in my companies. Tell me that it's not my city."

"I did not say it wasn't yours, I said you feel this is your city alone. However, I will say it now, it is not. This city does not belong to you, it belongs to the people. This city is made up of a diverse group of people. We are all created equal. We all make up Denver, and it's what makes Denver…Denver. I feel you have somewhat of a dictator attitude."

"Yes, I do," he retorted back. "It is the good dictators that make for a better town, city, or country. I will be the first person in Denver to say so when I am elected, and make no mistake, I will be elected. And I agree we are all created equal. It is up to us to make something of our life. There are those who do not. The ones who push drugs, and the ones who do them for instance, they deserve each other. We are on the same side here, Mr. DeLucci. We both want the drugs off the street, we are just of differing opinions on how to do that. Getting rid of the pushers doesn't stop one from doing drugs. There will always be someone pushing, as long as there's people buying drugs. Do you see my point?"

"Perhaps a little too clearly." This conversation was

going nowhere, but he did have a much clearer picture of Reid Dalton, something Christian failed to see in him. He could also see why people loved him. He was right, if he ran for office, he'd win hands down. He didn't like that prospect but bantering with him would get him nowhere. He felt he had his answers. He was done. "I think we are finished here. Do you have any questions, Kara?"

"No, I don't. I will be here at 5:00 a.m. sharp."

"Great, Ms. Thomas. I shall see you then."

"We can show ourselves out," said Cain.

"Very good," said Reid. He felt the man always had to have the last word. He'd let him have it. He wasn't about to play that game. He took Kara's hand and led her out.

It wasn't until they seated themselves at the bistro that they began to talk. He was gathering his thoughts all the way there, and figured Kara was too.

"What was your take?" He waited until the waiter dropped water off before he asked her opinion.

"Probably the same as yours. He really is a slime ball. Dictator, my ass. I'm going to find out as much as I can. He may have eyes on the street, but he certainly can't see everything. It was a little too coincidental that he knew about Ansen as quickly as he did. Stuff like that has to filter down. I'm sure I'll learn more about him as time goes on. If he is connected, I'll find out."

"My thoughts exactly. I hate to say this, but what if Dalton is behind all the drugs coming into the country. He even mentioned drugs, although that could be because my original appointment with him concerned drugs. He has the power and money to do it. Hell, everyone looks the other way with him because he does so much for the city, and they'll continue to look the other way no matter what he does. I have to say, if he is responsible, he has an unbelievably great cover, and if he makes governor..."

"I hear, my thoughts exactly. How did he make all his money anyway? The stuff in his house had to cost a small fortune. I don't think the pharmaceutical companies gave him that massive fortune, could have, but I just don't know."

"He has other companies as well. I wonder what his total worth is? Millionaire, billionaire? Could very well be the latter. Not to change the subject, but what are you having to eat?"

"I think everything." She gave him a gigantic grin.

"Why, I believe I will too." He grinned back. He was holding the menu in one hand and held out his other for her to take. There was something comforting in being able to just touch her. Cain thought it uncanny how they seemed to always be on the same wavelength. The looks they exchanged spoke of love and understanding. Except where Reid Dalton was concerned, and he had to voice it.

"I'm worried about you being with Reid. I know you are going to tell me you can take care of yourself, and I don't doubt it, but I'm worried about what he will put you through. He's slick, smart and methodic. The man has patience for what he wants."

"I've dealt with his kind before. He won't be the first to try and get things over on me. I too can be very diplomatic. I was specifically trained in it."

"Just please be careful with him."

"I promise, I will."

They stopped talking then and ordered. After they

were finished eating and settled in the car, he looked over at her. "Where to, your place or mine?"

"I don't care, but I'd like to stop at yours and pick up The Oracles. I'd like to spend some more time with it."

"All right. He put his car in gear and backed out. They headed to his place. "No," he said out of nowhere. "I really don't feel comfortable with you at Reid's. I will shut up after this, but I have to at least plead my case one more time. I think it would be good to leave the man completely alone. If he is mixed up in the deadly game of drugs, he has no compunctions with killing and Ansen Horn's death made that clear. The more I think about it, the more I think he's the one that had the trigger pulled. There's something not quite right with him. What I'm really surprised about is Christian hasn't seen it."

"He does hide behind all the good he does. Sometimes people see the good and it's so good, they overlook the bad."

"Well, he won't even let me mention his name in the same sentence that includes anything accusatory."

"I think I can help by working for him, Cain. I am good at snooping. I'll be careful."

"Okay, it's your call. I've said my piece now I'll shut up about it and stand behind you and support you. Perhaps we should stay the night at your place since Damian is coming in in the morning. He wants to see the runes. I should have taken the pictures before I took them all off so I could tell him which ones went with what. I don't remember, do you?"

"No, I don't remember. I don't know what any of them mean."

"Well maybe Damian can tell us." He headed down

his drive, and even though he didn't want Kara anywhere near Reid Dalton, he did in fact trust her. It wasn't a matter of trust he told himself, it was a matter of her getting hurt, and she'd been hurt quite enough lately. That was what worried him the most. He headed toward the garage when Kara stopped him.

"Look, Cain. That isn't good. I thought you locked up."

"I always lock up. He squinted and looked toward the house. They got closer and he saw the front door wide open. "Jeezsus friggen Christ." He slammed on the brakes, threw it in park, and jumped from the car. Not bothering to close his door he took off toward the house. Kara right behind him. She followed him through the front door and right into his back.

He stared in shock. A floor lamp had been knocked over; the shade bent. Throw pillows and cushions thrown on the floor, the T.V. laying on its face, broken. The living room was trashed and so was the kitchen. Cupboard doors stood open. There were pans, broken dishes, and food strewn across the floor.

He walked through a pile of spaghetti noodles to the sliding doors off his breakfast nook and saw the broken glass. Whoever broke in hadn't bothered to pick the lock they just smashed one of the sliding glass doors. The curtain had been pulled on, the rod bent, the curtain trailing across some debris.

He went to his bedroom where he found his clothes all over the floor and drawers pulled out. In the bathroom he found broken bottles of cologne, shampoo bottles on the floor, and the towels pulled from the rod. His bathroom smelled like a whore house on Saturday night. He coughed, his eyes watered, and he quickly shut the door behind him.

"Oh, shit, my office!" His heart went to his throat and beat frantically. He ran to his office and even though the door was closed he knew what he was going to find, and sure enough when he opened the door everything from his desk lay on the floor. The thing that pissed him off the most was his computer was gone. They stole his friggen computer. He pulled his cell from his pocket.

He came out and ran smack dab into Kara coming in. She had The Oracles in her hand. "They didn't get this."

"Where did you have it?"

"Under the mattress pushed to the middle. My room was trashed as well, but at least they didn't get that. I'm surprised they didn't check there. I wonder what they were looking for?"

"They took my computer. I need to speak to Christian pronto. If they break my passwords and get into TITAN that's bad."

He punched in Christian's number. "Hello Christian? Shit it's his damn answering machine." He hung up without leaving a message and punched in another number. "Stone, you at work?" He hit the speaker button so Kara could hear.

*"Yeah what's up?"*

"Listen, you need to get into my files and save them to yours. Someone stole my computer and trashed my house. Where's Christian?"

*"I don't know, hasn't been in all day. Why would someone trash your house? Damn Cain, that sucks."*

"That's weird, he's always at work. Did he call in sick?"

*"Not that I know of. Hey you guys,"* shouted Stone.

*"Did Christian call in sick?"* There was a pause, then Cain heard him move his phone around. *"No, he didn't call in sick, no one's heard from him. Probably ran into something important."*

"He would have called me. I'll check my phone. I did have it off earlier. Stone get me out of the system for now. I don't want anyone to be able to get into TITAN's files. Wipe my computer clean. I know you know how to do that."

*"Right this second?"*

"Yes, right this second!" He shouted raising his voice. "Damn it Stone. Didn't you hear what I said? They stole my friggen computer! What's so important you ask that?"

*"I'm backing through R&D Enterprises, the one you asked me about. So far, I'm through a Swiss bank account and still going backwards. I should have your owner by the end of the day."*

"That's got to get put on hold for now. Get me out of the system before someone hacks through." He pulled in his anger because it wasn't Stone's fault and became more civil when what he really wanted to do was scream. No one violates his space. Hell, he was still angry about Kara's place being trashed.

*"Gotcha, boss. I'll put some extra protection on too. There's this new software…"*

"Great," he said, interrupting Stone. "Good, do that. I'm going to try and reach Christian."

*"Okay, I'll call you when I'm finished."*

"Good, later Stone, thanks," he said in more cordial voice.

*"No problem,"* said Stone and he heard a click.

He looked at the mess around him and threw his

phone. "Fuckin A!" What the hell were they looking for?"

"Do you think they may have been looking for this?" She held up The Oracles. "Ever since things have been unraveling for me it seems more trouble keeps popping up. I'm sorry Cain. If this is my fault, I'm so…"

"No, Kara stop that, nothing is your fault. We have to figure out what's going on."

"My saddle! What if they are looking for those runes? Did you hide them well? I forgot all about them."

"I think I did. The spare bedroom we slept in. A drawer. We need to get to your place. I can't very well board up my sliding door. They are going to have to be replaced. I'm pissed."

"As well as you should be." She went and picked up his phone for him and handed it back to him. "I hope it still works."

"It will, but you know since…"

She raised her eyebrows. "What, Cain?"

"Ever since I went to Dalton for help, we've had nothing but trouble. Don't you find that odd?"

"Perhaps, if he is involved, he didn't know anyone had been tracking him for three years. Once you mentioned Horn, he knew you were getting close."

"I'm beginning to think more and more along those lines. Come on, we need to get to your house. Whoever was here had to have known I would be gone this morning and for a certain amount of time. Sound strange to you?"

"Very," she said and followed him out the door.

His phone went off just as he pulled the door shut. He pulled it out and noticed it was an unavailable number, but he answered anyway. "DeLucci."

"Wait, what? I can't understand you." He looked at his phone and put it on speaker, then put a finger to his lips. Kara sidled up next to him to listen with him.

*"Go to the warehouse, 1220 Hawthorne drive, north, in the business district. Repeat the address."*

"It's hard to understand you, you have that voice changer on, and you mumble. Repeat it again for me."

*"I'm only going to say it one more time. 1220 Hawthorne drive, north, in the business district. The warehouse. You'll find your boss there."* He heard a click. He looked at his phone and tried the call back. Nothing. He couldn't get anything.

"This has gone beyond bizarre. Come on," he said jumping in his car. "Did you get the address?"

"Yep, 1220 Hawthorne drive, north, the business district."

He sped all the way there. He grabbed the red cherry from the back and popped it on top. He had red lights and a license to run them, and he did, all through Denver as fast as traffic would allow. He almost passed the address. He slammed on the brakes and fishtailed all the way to a stop.

Kara hung on to the dash all the way there but didn't say a word. There were big bays with large garage doors on the warehouse, but it was the little door that stood wide open. He pulled his gun then motioned for Kara to get the other out of the glove compartment. She followed his motions, pulled the safety, looked closely, then pulled it back.

"Ready," she mouthed.

He got out and went to one side of the door, she to the other. They both came around the same time. He stepped into the darkened doorway and felt along the wall, Kara right beside him. Off in the distance was a faint yellow light, other than that it was dark as sin. He could use his flashlight on his phone to see better, but he wasn't sure they were alone. He let his eyes adjust to the darkness as he slowly walked toward the only available light.

The place was open with some old abandoned machinery scattered about. He could tell at one time the place had been full of machines. It was an old factory that had seen better days. It smelled heavily of old grease, dirt, and oil. He motioned with two fingers for her to head toward the other side, and she immediately stepped aside. They came to the doorway where the light was, Kara on the left side, Cain to the right. He stayed up against the wall, took a deep breath then swung around to the opening, gun ready to fire.

Nothing, no sound, no movement. He figured the worst. Whatever was done here, was done and over with. He broke out in a veritable sweat. He wanted to rush in, and he wanted to shout Christian's name, except he knew better, but it was damn hard not to. He was his best friend.

Chapter Sixteen

Kara was worried for Cain. She could tell his nerves were stretched tight. She didn't like the sound of the phone call and thought the worst had probably happened to Christian, but she wasn't about to voice her thought. She knew he was smart enough to think the same thing, but by looking at him he didn't want to believe it. He was waiting to see it with his own eyes.

Cain took a few strides in, and she followed, then she saw him drop his gun to the floor and take off running. She glanced up and saw what he was running to. She bent and picked up Cain's gun and hurried after him. Her heart dropped to the pit of her stomach, and she thought she'd wretch. Her stomach somersaulted.

Christian was tied to a chair, the ends of his fingers cut off, his shirt was sliced open in numerous places along with his skin. On the floor lay the cutter that was used to remove his fingertips, near it was the tips of his fingers. His eyes were both bloody and swollen shut, his jaw broken and crooked.

"Oh, God no!" shouted Cain, as he dropped to his knees. "Fuck an A, no!" He tore open Christian's shirt and saw the hole through his chest. There was stippling from the gun, so he'd been shot close range. He felt for a pulse, any pulse, and there was none. "He could be healing." He choked on a sob. "He could be healing! God damnit," he yelled, "tell me he's fucking healing!" He dropped his head and sobbed.

She put two fingers to Christian's neck just under his chin over the carotid artery. There was no pulse. He wasn't bleeding anywhere either. He was beat to hell but what killed him was a bullet through the heart, a silver bullet. When Cain was shot, she could still hear his heartbeat, he was still warm, and while his breathing had been shallow, he was breathing. Christian was still. She knew Cain knew it too. He was dead.

"It had to have been a silver bullet. I'm sorry Cain, but he's gone."

Cain's head dropped to Christian's lap sobbing, and she went and put her hand to his back in support. She wasn't sure what Cain needed, but she let him know she was there for him. Tears streamed down her face, some for the man she just met and liked, but more for the man she loved. He was totally torn up.

She didn't know Christian all that well, but the few times she saw him, she liked him immensely. She could see why he and Cain were such close friends. Right now, she had to be strong for Cain, even though her heart felt it was being squeezed in agony for him.

"Give me your phone, Cain," she said, finally.

He looked up through a tear-stained face. "Huh?"

"Give me your phone, please. I'm going to call it in. Not, to the P.D. I'm going to call Stone. His number isn't in my phone. I'll give you a few minutes with Christian."

He fumbled around his back pocket, stood, and pulled out his phone. His tears stopped and his face changed expression as he tried to pull it together. "You're right, Kara, this needs to be called in. I can do it."

"If you want some time with Christian, I don't

mind."

He handed her the phone. "There are some things I'd like to check out." Passcode, 5764."

Kara took his phone, punched in his passcode, and looked for Stone in his phone's directory. She hit the button."

*"Yeah, Cain, I found out…"*

"It's me, Stone, Kara. Listen…"

*"Cain all right?"*

"Yes, yes, Cain's fine. He got a weird call, someone disguising their voice. Told us to come to 1220 Hawthorne drive, north, in the business district to a warehouse for Christian. Cain and I got here as quick as we could, but someone murdered Christian."

*"Someone what!"* he shouted. *"Are you friggen kidding me? Did, I just hear you right? Christian's dead?"*

"Yes, I'm afraid so. He was beaten up then shot through the heart. It had to have been with a silver bullet."

*"Where's Cain now?"*

"I'm giving him a couple of seconds with Christian."

*"I'll get a team and be right there. 1220 Hawthorne drive, north, business district."*

"Old warehouse. You'll see Cain's car. See you in a few."

She heard a click and knew Stone hung up. She walked back toward Christian and Cain. Cain was a little more together. He was using a pen to move Christian's clothing and look at various parts of his body. He walked around the chair he was tied to. They'd used wire to tie him, and parts of the wire were embedded in his skin, in his lower chest and abdomen where part of his stomach hung out. The wire was also embedded in his arms where they tied his arms to the arms of the chair.

Cain bent down and looked at the wire wound tight around his ankles. She could see what he saw clearly. She couldn't speak. This torture had to have been unbearable for Christian, and she knew Cain saw the same thing. It had rubbed through his pants and into his skin. Whoever did this, also took a long slice over the inside of his thigh and nicked his femoral artery. There was blood everywhere. Cain picked up his hand where the ends of his fingers were missing and looked beneath the palm.

"They tortured the hell out of him," he said, his voice breaking. "Why?"

"They probably wanted information and Christian was stubborn enough not to give it."

"Other than this spot right here near his feet, there's no sign of struggle. That tells me, Christian knew who did this and trusted him. There was another chair here in front of Christian, so someone sat across from him. Whoever it was, was probably asking questions. There are scuff marks around the chair, and there's somewhat of a footprint in the dust, but it's smeared.

"It's a damn big footprint though. Probably from the one who tortured him. There was someone else here too, standing off to the side. He walked over to where there were more prints. "See there? I don't want to get to close because I don't want to destroy any evidence. We should stand back now and wait for the crew to get here."

"What do you think time of death will show?"

"For as cold as he is, could be five to eight hours, hell I don't know, have to wait for C.S.I. on that."

He no sooner said that than she heard the sirens and speeding cars coming up out front. He went to greet them, and she followed. She heard Stone's voice just before going through the door.

"Hi Stone," said Cain.

"I'm sorry, Cain, I know how much you two cared for each other."

"Yeah. There were at least three. Who's processing?"

"The coroner's coming in, and so is our crime scene investigators.

"I'm sorry, Cain. P.D.'s coming too. I had to call the chief since they were working together. I also very quickly looked at the file…"

"Are you talking about *the* file? The one that if anything were to happen to Christian file?"

"Yeah, had to know if there was someone taking his place."

Kara listened intently to their conversation piquing her curiosity.

"Yes, just a glance, didn't get through all of it, you are officially our commander in chief now. Christian left specific orders and corporate agreed with him. Also found where Christian highly recommended Kara for a job with us. So corporate will be all over Kara to hire her. You know how Christian's word was. He didn't use it often, but when he did…" Stone whistled. "And because of all your commendations, you are to take his place."

"Jee zusss," said Cain.

"My exact sentiments. I'll be getting a new partner, and I don't think I'm even used to you yet and we've been together for the past five years. Now I have to deal with a new partner, and you as my real boss, boss. I guess you will always have seniority over me."

"Shut up, Stone."

Kara could tell Cain didn't want to argue with Stone right now, or banter or joke. It wasn't the place or time. She figured Stone maybe had a habit of joking when nervous, at least that was her opinion. To her Stone appeared white as a sheet when he looked at Christian. She thought he might get sick to his stomach. He wouldn't be the first, and sadly he won't be the last.

"Shutting up. Sounds like the militia's here."

Cain tilted his head and listened to all the sirens for a second. "It's too damn bad I have to wait for everyone. There's someone I'd like to go kill right now."

"Do you know who did this?" asked Stone raising his eyebrows.

"No, but I have my suspicions. Stone, if I give you my phone, do you think you could locate an unavailable number? The person who called me?."

"Man or woman?"

"I don't know they used some sort of voice changer. It was low and echoey."

"Most of the voice changers are like that. I don't know let me take it and see what I can come up with."

Cain handed him his phone. "I need it back asap, Damian's flying in in the morning."

"Damian? Florida Damian?"

"Yeah, and while you're at it get a crime team out to my place and have them look for prints. I doubt they will find anything but do it anyway. Please?" he said and pulled his hand through his hair. He moved from one foot to the other, not able to stand still. Kara thought he looked like he was crawling out of his skin. Sort of the way she felt when her fiancé was shot and the ensuing aftermath. She could relate, a lot was probably going through his mind. One thing she was pretty sure of, was who Cain wanted to go kill, and he was right, they couldn't prove a thing.

His house being ransacked, Christian being killed, that all happened simultaneously while they were visiting Reid Dalton. What better alibi? Reid could have been here with Christian earlier than their appointment and then possibly someone else take over so he could make the meeting on time, and he could have hired someone to tear up Cain's house. She rubbed the back of her neck. She felt a headache coming on.

She thought they should probably go to her house, to heck with her clothes, she had some at home. Her other clothes were strewn across the floor at Cain's. She'd also brought The Oracles with her and left it laying on the front seat of Cain's car. She didn't know why, but when she thought of the book, she got a funny feeling. She went running out of the building.

Just when she got through the door, she noticed a cop heading for Cain's car. She felt the need to stop him before he got any closer. "Hey," she yelled, sprinting toward him. "That's Cain DeLucci's car." She stopped in front of him. "Can I help you? I'm his girlfriend." She glanced at the car and noticed Cain had left his door open. She made it a point to stand in front of the cop. He leaned trying to look past her to the car. "What's your name officer?" she asked.

"Why?"

"You're new, I just got off the force, and I don't remember meeting you."

"I am new, just hired in from D.C."

"Cain is commander of TITAN, Central Division,

and you are?"

"Officer Demming. I was just going to shut the door to the snazzy muscle car."

"I can get the door to that snazzy muscle car, especially since I forgot to get something out of it. Thank you for the effort though."

The officer gave her a strange look.

"You should go check the scene inside." Suddenly, the man was enveloped in a red haze. She blinked hard then looked again. It was still there, a deep, dark red haze following his every movement. She could tell he was angry at her. Why? He didn't appear to be angry. What the hell did it mean? Her brain felt weird like it was zinging like it was firing in double time. She was still able to speak all right it was just a strange experience. She just knew she had to get him away from the car.

"Well," she said, holding out her hand. "Welcome to the force Officer...what's your first name Mr. Demming?"

"George," he said, "George Demming." He took her hand and shook it lightly. She remained where she was at, and finally he turned and followed the others through the door to the crime scene. She let out a breath she'd been holding and quickly went to the car. Her book was still on the front seat. She felt frantic to get to it. She noted the keys still in the ignition. She grabbed them, threw a small blanket from the back seat over her book, opened the trunk and put it in, and locked it. She double checked that all the doors were locked. Then put the keys in her pocket.

When she left the car to go back in the building, she saw Demming standing in the doorway staring at her. She didn't think he could see what she had because of the blanket, but the look he gave her unnerved her. He quickly turned and went inside. She had to find Cain and get him out of there. She'd keep an eye on officer Demming too.

When she reached the scene, she found Cain speaking to Demming. She interrupted their conversation. "Cain, I need your help, quickly please."

"Anything I can do to help you Ms. Thomas?" asked Demming.

"I don't remember giving you my name," she said tight lipped. She had had about enough of the officer. She didn't like him at all, and he was still sporting that weird red haze and it was getting on her nerves.

Just then a man in a white lab coat came over. "Hi Cain, is this how you found him?" the guy asked.

"Yeah, Jason, the only thing we touched was the skin on his neck for a pulse. The footprints in front of him are mine, Kara's, and whoever else was here. There's another print about two feet to the right of him where someone stood watching. There was also a chair across from him. Probably for the interrogator. The chair must have been dragged away at some point. I figure three people in all. I guessed time of death early this morning."

"I'll take an internal temp. and let you know."

"Please do, thanks."

"You seem to know your stuff, Mr. DeLucci," said Demming.

"I don't think I've ever seen you before."

"No, I'm new, just in from D.C."

"Cain, I need your help for a second, please," she said again.

"Sure. Sorry, I got sidetracked." He took her by the

arm and escorted her away from the scene and activity.

"Cain, whatever you do, don't say anything to that new cop. I'm not sure what's happening to me, but I see this red haze covering him, and I know he's angry because I stopped him from going to your car, and I don't like him at all."

"My God, Kara, you can see his aura?"

"That red haze is his aura?"

"Yes, some witches can see people's aura's very well. Damian told me about it. You can tell different things by the color of someone's aura. Not sure how it works or what red means, if I had to guess, anger maybe, don't quote me."

"The weird thing is, I had a very strong urge to save The Oracles. I had a feeling someone was going to attack it or take it. I hurried out and found that officer heading for your car. He said he was going to close the door, but I don't buy it, not at all."

"All right then, let me tell Stone we're leaving, and I'll have him keep an eye on him till we're gone. Then we'll go."

"Good, that cop gives me the creeps."

"I didn't notice it, but if you did, then we better listen to how you feel."

"I did, I do, and I want to get the hell out of here."

"Okay. He took her by the hand. Stick by me and I'll be quick."

They went back inside, and Cain pulled Stone aside. "We're leaving. Process everything and take note on everything. I'll fill out my report later. See what you can find out about my phone and get back to me as soon as you can and don't forget to get a team to my place. I'll be at Kara's. Drop it by there when you're done, I'll text you her address from her phone. Someone really trashed my place. I have to get someone out there to replace the sliding glass doors and make arrangements for cleanup. I'll try and have that set up for tomorrow after they process the scene. Also, be very leery of that new cop. He's nosey in a bad way."

Stone raised his eyebrows but didn't say anything. "On it, boss. It shouldn't take more than a half hour, hour tops, after I leave here. I'll let our guys know about the new cop, and have a team sent to your house. No questions now, but later… Got any clues as to who trashed your place?"

"I have my thoughts, when I know for sure, I'll let you know."

"Okay, see you," said Stone. He saluted then left.

Once they got to the car and Cain was ready to open his door, he looked at Kara. "Kara, will you drive?"

"Sure, if you want me to. I have the keys, you forgot them in the ignition."

"Thanks, I have a lot on my mind. I'd feel better if you drove."

"No, problem, Cain,"

She unlocked his door and let him in then went and got in the driver's side.

Cain was silent all the way to her house. She was really worried about him. She glanced at him. His eyes were on the road in the front, but he wasn't focused, and his jaw was tight. She saw the silent tears run down his cheeks. She could also tell he was very angry. She tried seeing what his aura showed but couldn't concentrate and drive at the same time. She didn't know how it worked anyway.

When they got to her house, she thought it might

have been ransacked again, but it wasn't. She put her purse down then she went back outside to the trunk to get the book and carried it inside.

When she got back, she found Cain on her phone. "What's your passcode?" he asked. She told him. "I have to text Stone your address. What is it here?"

She told him and he punched it in then sent the text to Stone.

\*\*\*\*

A few seconds later, her phone rang. Cain recognized Stone's number, so he answered.

"Yeah, Stone?"

*"A couple of things,"* said Stone. *"Damian kept trying to call you, so I finally answered for you. I just got your text before he called. I knew Kara's phone number then, so I gave it to him, hope you don't care, he was insistent on speaking with you. So, he's going to be calling you in a sec. The other thing? R&D Enterprises? Reid Dalton owns them. Has a huge account in the Swiss banks, millions. Very hard to find him connected. I had to go through some pretty tough channels to get there. He could have accounts other places as well, I don't know. I can probably find out for you later if you want. I thought you'd like to know. He was the one trying to buy the businesses. Can't tie him to the bomb though."*

"I know," he said, angrily. "I can't tie him to any damn thing…yet. I will though."

*"You think he is the one behind everything? Christian seemed to think the world of him."*

"I don't think Christian ever saw the side I've seen," said Cain. "I'm not saying anything, yet. But I will get the big fish behind the drugs, and I will find out who killed Christian, and Horn. Hey, gotta go, I think Damian is calling." He hung up with Stone and answered the call.

"Hello?"

"*Cain*?" said Damian.

"Yeah, it's me. What's up?" He hit speaker.

*"I did some scrying, Cain. There is some really bad mojo around you. You have to keep Kara safe."*

"What are you saying?"

*"She's not safe, not at all. I will tell you more when I see you tomorrow. Please, watch out for her. She's extremely important, and she's an extreme target. I can't tell you everything over the phone. I will be there at 7 a.m. and I'll rent a car. Where should I meet you?"*

"I thought you would…"

*"Don't,"* he said interrupting. *"Don't say anything over the phone. You'll know why tomorrow. I think Kara is all right for the time being, but there is a large dark cloud heading her way. That's all I know, and that usually means something bad, evil coming after her. I'll tell you more tomorrow. You didn't mention anything to anyone did you?"*

"No, I haven't. Sounds serious, Damian."

*"It is. If what I think is true, which I'm pretty sure is, I'm very serious."*

"All right, I'll text you the address, put it in *maps*, she's in the country."

*"Okay, tomorrow then."*

"Tomorrow." He hung up. He was sitting on a chair in the kitchen. He bent and put his elbows on his knees and pulled both hands through his hair and down the back of his neck with his head leaned over as if he could find answers that way. "Think, man. You have to find evidence."

Kara left while Cain was texting Stone but just

walked back into the kitchen. "You look like you've just seen a ghost."

"If I'm not careful, or you aren't careful, that's what you are going to be. I just got off the phone with Damian. He said he did some scrying, and you are in extreme danger. There's a black cloud heading your way. Please, Kara, for God's sake don't go to Reid's."

She pulled a chair in front of him and sat in it. She put her hands in his. "Look at me, Cain."

He looked at her and knew he wasn't going to like what she had to say.

"I'm okay, I'll be okay. Yes, there may be danger, but I feel the need to do this more than anything I've ever felt. The old lady is tied up to me, or this book. I just know it. She knows something and I aim to find out what. I will get information on Reid, and whatever he is guilty of, and I will get the hard evidence to prove it. Please trust me. It's our only way in. It's our only chance to stop him. I feel in my bones he's guilty and he's laughing at everyone because he thinks he's invincible. We'll get him, so please back me on this. I need your support. Please."

"Kara, I swear to God if anything…"

She put a finger to his lips. "Shush. Nothing is going to happen to me."

"At least give me a couple of weeks. Kara, call him tell him you will start later. We have Christian's funeral to go to," he said choking on his tears. "I'll have to make the arrangements. I'm the only one he had that was even close to being family. I don't feel mentally stable and up to my game. Please wait a few weeks, if you wish to still go in there, then fine. I'll be in better shape to watch over you. I *need* that from you."

She bent her head down. "I'm so sorry Cain, how very thoughtless of me to do that to you. Of course. I'll call him right now. I'm sure he won't mind me starting after the funeral. I will still go in then. Just so you know."

"I know you will and thank you. I will feel better then." She grabbed her cell and punched in Reid's number and hit speaker so Cain could hear too."

*"Reid Dalton, speaking."*

"Mr. Dalton, this is Kara Thomas, I'm afraid I can't start work for you tomorrow. Cain's boss, Christian, was killed this morning. They were very close friends. I will be spending my time helping him with funeral arrangements. If me starting in a couple of weeks or more is unacceptable to you, then I apologize and will have to refuse the job all together. If it meets with your approval, I will still do the month trial period. It's up to you."

*"My goodness, I'm sorry to hear about Christian. Are there any leads as to who would do such a thing?"*

"Not at this point."

*"He was my friend as well. Please keep me informed, and yes of course you may start at your convenience. Call and let me know, or we can talk at the funeral. I'll surely attend. Please give my regards to Mr. DeLucci."*

"I will, and thank you," she hung up.

"You know, I feel better about starting then. I'd like some time just with you. We could both use it. No worries, just take a step back, and breathe. Besides I can help you with all the arrangements." She kissed his forehead. "I'll make a list of what needs done if you want to make a few calls about your house getting fixed, or I can."

"No, I can do that. I need to do something."

"All right then later I'm going to make us dinner."

He looked at her without smiling. "I'm not really hungry."

"Oh, no you don't. You must eat to keep up your strength. I'm making dinner, and you're eating it. It's farm cooking for me tonight. Pork chops, mashed potatoes like your mother never made, and fried cabbage with onions and carrots. A real feel good meal. It'll be great, you'll see."

He glanced over at her. "Well since you put it that way…"

\*\*\*\*

He really didn't think he was hungry until much later when he came in the house. He was over the initial shock of Christian's death and more able to function. He still had his tearful moments but if he kept busy, he was okay. He actually ran out of phone calls to make and really needed to do some manual labor. He couldn't face the office yet, he just couldn't, so he opted for cleaning the barn. Kara seemed to know he needed something to do so she showed him where brooms were and other things he asked for. She said she needed to go inside anyway to do some domestic things. He wasn't sure what. He finished with that and was now on the back porch taking the trash out. Picking it up he stopped and sniffed the air.

He could smell whatever it was she was cooking for dinner and a peace flowed through him. He actually felt all right. Something changed in him in that second. He still felt for Christian, but this was just such an unusual feeling. He got the same feeling he had after jogging and coming home to a house that was filled with good smells, and one in particular, very beautiful woman. Kara made his house a home and in that second, he realized, he wanted a family with her. He wanted children with her, not with anyone else. Even if she went crazy in ten to twenty years, it didn't matter, his children were going to have Kara as their mother. In that instance everything came full circle and blew him away.

He thought about it. It all made perfect sense to him, and if he hadn't been so hell bent on her being a half breed, he would have known it sooner. He'd been too caught up in his idea of a perfect woman and family to see what was right in front of him. He knew he wanted her for his wife, but in the back of his mind, he thought he'd never have children with her. That was bunk.

His old ideas of what his future held crumbled like a dry cracker in the wind and something so beautiful bloomed inside him. He was going to propose tonight. It wasn't her and her feelings he was holding back on it was his own! His idea of a perfect wife, and a perfect life. Well, if his old ideas were what was right and perfect, he didn't want any part of them. He wanted children with Kara, and he would find a cure if it killed him, or not, if he couldn't, didn't matter he still wanted a family with only her.

Yep, he'd propose right now. Damn, he didn't have a ring. He'd make one. Suddenly, he felt like a little boy. He was happy, he was damn happy. He threw the trash in the bin beside the barn and headed back toward the house. His steps were light. It was like a weight was lifted from his shoulders. He shouldn't feel this way because he just lost his best friend, he stopped and felt sad, then it was like he could hear Christian laughing at him, and he could have sworn he heard him say, *"Enjoy your happiness, Cain. I'm okay, I'll see you in the future."* He was dead still, as if to listen to him he could catch his voice and hold onto it, then he heard his laughter, and he smiled. That's exactly what Christian would have told him, and his happiness once again bubbled up inside him and this time he didn't stop it. He kind of thought that Christian had a part in helping him see this.

He practically skipped around the yard picking small blooming dandelions. He remembered what he and his brother did as kids making rings out of dandelions. He would use it to propose and get her a real ring later. Childish he knew, but he loved the idea, maybe brighten her day in a funny sort of way. They both needed it with the heaviness of Christian's death hanging in the air.

He whistled as he made two or three rings that were worth keeping throwing the others out in the yard. He strode back into the house. She wasn't in the kitchen. He found her in the living room fluffing throw pillows. He grabbed her hand and took her to the couch and sat her down.

"What in the world has gotten into you Cain. What's that grin for? Are you drinking?"

"No, I'm not drinking. I'm completely sober and that's the nice thing about it. I don't need to drink to take you to bed, Kara. In fact, I enjoy being completely sober and having all my senses clear to enjoy all of you."

Kara tried to get up, but he held her down. "Wait a second, please."

"Oh, okay," she said and smiled at him. "What is it?"

He got down on one knee and pulled his hand from behind his back. "With this ring, or rings, I'd like to ask for your hand in marriage."

Kara looked at the bent twisted up dandelions and couldn't help it, she laughed. "That is the silliest, funniest, cutest, most endearing thing anyone has ever done for me, Cain."

"You have to pick which ring suits you best, I couldn't decide. I'm afraid there's about ten more lying in the yard that didn't make the cut."

That just made her laugh more. She laughed so hard, she couldn't quit, and she hiccupped.

"Do you think you could quit laughing long enough to at least give me your answer? My knee's beginning to hurt."

He noticed she was just beginning to gain control when his words caused her to begin all over again.

"I'm so happy to be the brunt of your amusement," he said and chuckled.

She had tears coming out of her eyes, and through hiccups, he could tell she tried to get a yes out. She was having so much trouble it made her laugh harder, so she shook her head yes.

"Are you having seizures?" he asked.

"Sto...stop it, Cain, I'm going to pee my pants. Yes of course (*hiccup*) I will marry you. (*hiccup*) That's the sweetest thing (*hiccup*) anyone has ever done for me." (*hiccup*) She bent toward him, threw her arms around him, kissed him, and hiccupped at the same time.

"Carful, you are going to ruin my rings. Pick your ring so I can put it on your finger. I want the world to know you and I are going to get married and have a family together."

Her laughter died immediately. "Did you say family? As in children? Cain, I ca..."

"Don't say it, Kara, yes you can. There is no other person on the face of this earth that I want to have children with, only you. That's what I couldn't get through my thick head Kara. This damn half breed thing.

But, in the mornings after jogging coming in to smell breakfast, seeing you in your robe with a cup of coffee in your hand, standing there so raw and beautiful. I would get this unexplainable feeling. I never wanted to see a woman in the morning, I mean I didn't make them leave after a night of sex, but I couldn't wait for them to leave.

"I can't wait to see you in the morning. It's my favorite time. You are the most gorgeous to me then. I get so turned on with seeing just a peek of cleavage, and your raw beauty, with your wet hair, and a cup in your hand, makes me want to throw you on the floor and make love to you. I want to feel your naked skin against mine, put my nose in your hair and smell you, kiss along your neck and down until I find your breast, and put myself inside you and make you mine.

"When you said you were going to leave me the other morning, I had an anxiety attack. I didn't know how to keep you with me. Tonight, when I stood on the back porch, I realized something. I feel at home, here, or at my house, with you, and that's because wherever you are is home. I can't see myself with anyone else. I can't see having children with anyone else.

"If you go crazy in ten to twenty years, if God forbid, we don't find a cure, I will take care of you *and* our children. I will raise them to remember you. I will plaster photographs everywhere and kill them with all the stories of the memories we are going to make together. I love you Kara, I truly love you."

Her mouth hung open and tears filled her eyes and spilled over. "Everything you said was perfect. We can make memories, Cain." He knew they could do that, they really could.

"I will marry you, Cain DeLucci, and I will have your children, and I will be your wife and their mother for as long as I possibly can. God willing, together we'll find a cure." She held out her hand. "Well?"

"Well, what?" he asked.

"Aren't you going to put the ring on my finger?"

Cain looked down at the poor wilted flowers, he picked one that seemed to stay together, and he carefully put it on her finger. He looked at her with tears in his eyes, and could not believe his happiness, he could not believe his sorrow. His emotions were in turmoil. She stared like it was a diamond and held her hand out in front of her.

"It's perfect, it's beautiful. I love you Cain." She wrapped her arms around him and sunk into a very deep kiss. She drew back. "We have everything we need except the marching band," she said with a laugh.

"A marching band?" He raised his eyebrows.

"Oh, it just reminded me of something between my father and mother. When I was little and they didn't want me to know something about their special occasions, my mother would say, *'That sounds wonderful, we will have everything but the marching band.'* And my father would wink at her and say, *'oh we're going to have the marching band all right.'* Then he'd kiss her, but I never saw any marching band…when I was little, that is. Now that I'm grown, I know what they were talking about and what that meant."

"Did he ever have a real marching band for her?"

"He did and my mother laughed so hard. It was their twentieth wedding anniversary. They marched across our backyard with a banner. They had a party with friends, picnic tables full of food, it was in June of course, but I remember mom saying they were going to have their own little marching band later together. That's when I knew exactly what the marching band had always meant. They loved each other right to the end. A love I feel you and I have…" she paused and put her nose in the air.

"Oh no, the dinner! The pork chops!" She jumped up and ran into the kitchen, pulled the lid from the frying pan, dropped it, and burned her finger as steam rolled out from under the lid. "Shit, shit, shit!" She took a fork and quickly turned them back into the sizzling oil. "Oh. Right on time." She turned to him, smiled, fork in the air, her elbow on her hip like she did with the spatula in the morning, and he had a new snapshot of his favorite view of her.

"I love you, Kara. Thank you for being patient with me. I can be pretty hardheaded sometimes."

"Yeah, I can agree with that statement. Do I love you any less? No, but it is time to eat."

She was true to her word, she made porkchops like he'd never tasted before, mashed potatoes like his mother never made, and fried cabbage with carrots and onions, something he'd never had, but really enjoyed.

That night they forgot about the world. They drank a bottle of wine, made slow passionate love, caressing, touching, and learning each other's bodies while their minds and hearts melded together. Then they fell into a deep peaceful sleep in each other's arms.

Chapter Seventeen

Kara and Cain were still sleeping the next morning when the doorbell rang. They didn't budge, not until they heard the pounding on the door. Cain opened his eyes and glanced at the clock on the nightstand. Seven forty-five. "Who…" then he remembered. "Oh, damn," he mumbled. "I forgot Damian was going to be here early."

Kara rolled over and opened her eyes. "Humm?" she asked.

"I bet Damian's here. Go back to sleep if you want. I'll get the door."

Her eyes snapped open, and she quickly sat up and swung her legs over the side of the bed. She brushed the hair off her face and hopped up. "You get the door, and I'll get the coffee." She was so excited. Damian was going to tell her about the runes. Maybe something about who she was. She couldn't wait.

"Deal," he said pulling his robe on. He went out the door and closed it. She pulled her house coat on and was right behind him. She quickly went to the kitchen the back way, while Cain took the front stairs to meet Damian.

She could hear them talking in the foyer about Christian. Damian was giving his condolences. She had the coffee on and looked in her cookie jar for cookies to put out. It was empty, but she remembered there were sweet rolls and doughnuts in the cupboard. She quickly arranged some on a plate and placed them on the table. Then she went back to check on the coffee. It was almost done. She decided to go out and meet Damian. She wasn't sure why she was so nervous about meeting him, but she was. Maybe she'd get some answers. She went to the foyer and heard them in the living room talking.

When she walked in the living room they immediately stopped talking. She looked at the man and was going to greet him but the way he stared at her made her pause. She shrugged it off. "Hi, my…"

Damian got down on his knee in front of her and bowed his head. "My queen," he said.

"*Yo…your what*?!" she squealed. "You are mistaken…Mr…please stand up, you're making me nervous."

Cain quickly grabbed his shoulder. "Damian what is with you? Are you all right?"

Damian looked up at him. "You have no idea Cain. We've been waiting centuries for her. You know what this means? It means the prophesy that has been handed down for generations has come true. It is true. The original witch lived. She did not die. She did not cast herself into the ocean, but her true bloodline lives on, and she did conceive a child with the first wolf. You should know Cain. The stories…"

"Look man, get up and tell us what the hell you're talking about. I have no idea. Besides you're making my fiancé nervous."

"Oh, oh, I'm sorry Ms. Thomas. That isn't your real name."

"I have no idea what you are talking about. Besides I was adopted."

"Of course, you were. It was the only way to save us

all."

"Do you want to let us in on what you know?" asked Cain.

"Yes, please. Sit down and I'll bring us coffee."

"You should have a servant for that," said Damian as he got up. "I see your aura, it's white, you are our queen. Your eyes did they…ever…whit…never mind. I don't wish to alarm you. Everything must be so new to you."

"Please, Mr.…."

"I'm sorry," said Cain. "You two haven't been formally introduced. "Damian Aldane, this is Kara Thomas. Kara, Damian."

"Nice to meet you, Damian," she held out her hand.

"You can't believe how nice it is to meet you. I'm the first to know you exist. We've been waiting centuries for you. So many didn't believe the prophesy, thought it was heresy. I believed. Our grandmasters will be so pleased. You are the cure."

"I'm the wha…what?"

"The cure to the illness that befalls wolves and sorcerers. Let me begin with this…."

"Wait. Let me bring in coffee and sweet rolls so we can at least wake-up."

"Would you like some help?" asked Cain.

"No, I can get it, you sit with Damian and talk."

She left and returned with a tray holding cups and the pot of coffee sitting them down a little shakily. "Do you care for cream and sugar or vanilla cream Damian?"

"No, black for me is fine, thank you."

She set down the tray and went back to the kitchen and grabbed the plate of sweet rolls. She was so excited to hear what he had to say…and so terrified. Damian and

Cain were already sipping coffee. She set down the rolls and three little plates. "Chose your rolls, guys."

Cain and Damian grabbed a roll while she poured herself a cup of coffee and added her cream. She sat next to Cain on the sofa in front of the coffee table, Damian across from them in an easy chair.

"Do you know who my parents are?" she asked.

"No, except that their last name is Raigon."

"The father of all wolves?" asked Cain.

"Raigon was the father of wolves. The mother of all sorcerers was Eiris."

"Are you talking about the first man wolf?" asked Cain. "Raigon was the one who fell in love with the woman. They were Norse, Viking."

"Correct. Raigon fell in love with a witch who was also a Viking from another tribe, and they wanted to marry. He was at that time human. Eiris' father refused the man. So Raigon kidnapped her. When her father found out, he searched for her until he found her. He killed everyone in Raigon's village and cursed him to turn him wolf. This is where the story differs some from the actual prophesy. I'm just giving the short version here.

"The story goes that Eiris was frightened of the wolf and that she refused to see him, and she killed herself by jumping from a cliff. That is untrue because in the prophesy they have a child. However, Raigon in his anger against Eiris' father, attacked and bit the father, turning him then to wolf.

"The father became mad and attacked many young men, making more wolves. The latter is true. No one knows what happened to the father, but the prophesy says that Eiris continued to love Raigon, and they begot a child. That child was the first born wolf and warlock. As you know if a sorcerer is bit and becomes wolf, they go crazy after so many years, but sometimes you can't help who you love. However, the spell that was used was a very dark blood spell, and all dark spells have repercussions, some severe. In this case, the reason for the madness after ten to twenty years. That was just one of them.

The witch that put the spell on Raigon, was Eiris' twin sister. For as good as Eiris was her sister was opposite. The jealous sister gladly performed the dark spell against Raigon to turn him to wolf. Eiris, wouldn't have allowed such a spell.

"The Prophesy states Eiris and Raigon had a child, and the child was male, but because of the curse, he was born of evil. He was both wolf and warlock. It also states that he in turn shall have a daughter, who is made of goodness and light, she too is born of wolf and witch, and she shall destroy the evil that is her father and lift the curse. This frightens the son, so he refuses to have a child, if any become pregnant by him, he destroys the child. Except for the child of the prophecy. A child that is born without his knowledge."

Damien paused to take a drink of coffee before continuing. Kara looks at Cain who is sitting there openmouthed and she realized she was probably the same. Kara cleared her throat. "Go on."

"She is kept from him and grows up to destroy him. In the story his own mother denounces him. To keep him from finding or knowing his daughter, the child's powers are bound until she is strong enough to face him. She is hidden away with another family until the day her one true love finds her.

"He will be wolf and he will bite her to save her life which begins the journey of her learning about her powers and opening the door for the great fight between good and evil. If she wins the curse on the sorcerer and wolf is lifted. They will no longer go crazy. This makes everything come full circle."

Cain coughed. "So, you believe that the daughter is Kara, that when I bit her this all started?"

"I do indeed. I not only, believe it, it's true. Those runes are listed in the prophesy. They are the ones that bound Kara's powers. Didn't you say something happened to Kara when you found the runes?"

"Yes, when the last one came off, they lit up, bright, white," said Cain animatedly. "They flew around her, and she fell to the floor. I had trouble waking her, but when I did...when I did..."

"What Cain, what did you see?"

"The pupils in her eyes were gone. Her eyes were white, nothing else. I didn't know if they went to the back of her head or what. She said she could see fine, but then slowly the color returned, and her eyes looked normal."

"Now I know it's true. When you meet the grandmasters, you'll see that their eyes are almost white, but the only one to have ever had them completely was our queen. That means that she doesn't have three powers."

"No?" asked Cain gulping. Kara had to gulp too. She couldn't even speak; she could only listen.

"No, that means she has *all* the powers."

"Jeee zuss friggen Christ," said Cain flopping back against the couch back. "Are you kidding me? She only knows of one, wait two now. She can move things with her mind, and she has visions."

"When and how am I supposed to know all these powers? I just found out about myself."

"I'll help you," said Damian. "They will become second hand to you."

"Do you have the runes on you?"

"Yes, I'll go get them," said Cain.

"No, I'll go," said Kara clearing her throat. "Which drawer, Cain?"

"Top right," he answered.

Kara ran up the steps into the bedroom and plopped on the bed. She couldn't be this person, could she? "It's all so scary," she mumbled. What if she hurt someone? What if…"Kara, you could what if yourself to death. Go face Damian and listen to what he's saying. You aren't a wimp quit acting like one." She opened the drawer, and she shoved some socks around and found a little leather bag. She grabbed it and it felt like coins. She took a quick peek and noticed they were it and ran back downstairs.

"They are of little use now they are just plain conchos," said Damian. "Their usefulness is finished. But it's a good idea to keep them hidden because someone may know how to read them. I have the photos of them, and I matched them to the prophesy."

"So, you are saying I'm the woman in the prophecy and I have to stop my father? Those people lived hundreds of years ago. How can this be true? I thought wolves only lived up to five hundred years."

"Besides," Cain started, "I bit her to save her life. I watched her turn wolf. It was my bite that turned her."

"No Cain, it was your bite that unbound the power that held her wolf captive, you merely let her wolf loose. Because you bit her, she lived. Because her powers were bound along with her wolf, she could have died and been reborn had you not bitten her. Which has probably happened before. Let me ask this…did you smell witch or wolf on her?"

"No, that's troubled me from the beginning. Why is that?"

"You won't smell it on her father either. They are the originals, and none has been born of them since. All other cross breeds as you call them have been made. Created if you will. If Kara has children, your children could very well be born of both. Most likely will be."

"Why is it, then, when a witch turns wolf and has a child with a wolf all the children born turn wolf with seemingly no sorcery in their blood?"

"There can only be one type born of the bitten and because the wolf is stronger the children are born wolf. It's in a book that has been studied religiously over the ages. We have several that have been handed down. However, one born as wolf and witch or warlock produces a child with both characteristics. As I was saying, the father has lived for hundreds of years, honing his powers, but is no match for the purity of the massive white light that resides in his daughter.

"Where he is corrupt and evil, she is not. If she fights and wins it will clear the slate and the curses will be lifted. Trust me, my colleagues and I have been studying everything we can find for years.

"I have the original prophesy but there's been quite a few other findings as well How spells and curses work, etc. We know that if she wins those with the curse will no longer have it. But children born of the blood of the original will be born both. A witch or warlock can be changed to wolf, they won't lose their mind. All of it has to do with the original curse."

"Wait, wait, wait just a minute. How can this even be? The original wolf, the original witch, they lived hundreds of years ago, that would mean my father has been alive for hundreds of years. That's ridiculous. I'm not even thirty years old yet."

"Yes," said Damian. He leaned over and picked up a sweet roll and took a bite. Then washed it down with a drink of coffee. "He was born of the strongest witch and wolf to have ever lived. Our queen, if you will. That makes him incredibly powerful. You wouldn't know him to look at him. Hee probably seems like a normal guy, but make no mistake, he's been using blood magic to stay alive. Which means he's taking lives to do that. What the spell is, or how he achieves it, I don't have a clue."

"How the hell am I supposed to find him?"

"I think your paths are meant to cross."

"What about the ones who are witch or warlock turned to wolf, these half breeds that are going crazy?"

"That's the byproduct of the curse of the same blood spell. Like I said, it was a very dark spell, but her sister who did the spell for fun on her part, made it so if he bit anyone, they would also turn wolf. I don't think she planned on it causing people to go crazy. But then, I don't know what she thought, I wasn't there. I just wouldn't like to think anyone would want to put that kind of a curse on anyone.

"Because it was so bad, it has to equal out, the scales must be balanced, and the only way to do that is to send your father back to where he came. He should have died long ago, but by using a blood spell he's stayed alive. The only way to combat it is through goodness and light, and I'm afraid that is you my dear."

"Does the prophesy say anything about my mother?"

"I'm sorry, no. We believe your mother would have to be a very good person, possibly a virgin, intelligent and strong."

"I know she died giving birth to me. I found my birth certificate."

"Do you have a copy of this prophesy?" asked Cain.

"I do." Damian got up and picked up his briefcase. "It's originally written in the old Norse language, but we've since been able to put it in English."

"We?"

"The sorcerers council. The grandmasters and high priests. Like I said, we've spent years on this very thing. We don't want witches or wolves to go crazy, so we've been trying to figure out how to cure them. Our council has diligently been studying this."

"I see," said Cain.

Damian pulled out a large paper with markings on it.

"Those are the markings on the runes on my saddle. They are laid out in an oval shape two together. If I'm not mistaken, those are in the exact order we found them," said Kara.

"They are, these were written on the back of the parchment that held the prophesy. So, you can see my excitement when you sent me those photos."

"Do you know what they mean?" asked Cain.

"Yes, they were used to bind your powers and keep your wolf from coming forth until you were ready. They also provided protection for you."

"I don't think I like the sound of where this is

going," said Cain. "How am I going to protect her if there's an evil that strong. Plus, he's been working on spells for centuries."

"Cain, Kara is that strong. She said she's had visions of things to come all her life. That's incredibly powerful magic to have because the binding spell used on her was so great. On anyone else it would have completely dampened their power to absolutely nil."

"I found an unbinding spell in The Oracles."

"Oh, my God, you have the Book? Now I truly know you are the daughter we've been waiting for. Eiris wrote that book. She might have lived as a Viking, but it's been said she lived with the Egyptians. She was that old. That unbinding spell might have opened a door for a second for you, but you would not have broken it with that. You would have to have taken the runes apart. Once you separate them, the spell is broken, but if they weren't ready for you, you could have used a jackhammer and they wouldn't have come apart. Now is the time. Things are happening exactly as they are supposed to happen.

"That's also why I'm here. I will teach Kara for as long as it takes. I'm just incredibly proud that the powers that be chose me. It would be an honor if you'd allow me."

"What happens if I find and fight my father and win? What will the council, the witches and warlocks, want of me? You called me your queen."

"You would be, you are, our queen. If any of them find out the prophesy came to pass and you're the queen, every sorcerer from every country will be knocking down your door. You wouldn't want for anything. Once they find out you will most definitely live like a queen."

Kara was quiet for a second and Cain turned to her

and put his hand on her knee. "What are you thinking, Kara?"

"Have the witches and warlocks gotten along all right without a queen?"

"Yes, of course, but do you understand how long we've waited for you?"

"Damian, I'm sorry, I really am. I don't want to be a queen. I mean, I know it is a great honor, but I can't. I want to marry Cain and have a family with him. I want my children to live a normal life. I don't want to go crazy in ten to twenty years, that's a given, but I don't want to be queen. I just want to live in peace with my family. Can you understand? I don't mind fighting for what is right, but I don't wish to be queen to anyone."

"You won't go crazy, Kara, but there are others who will. If you are thinking to not confront your father. Not to mention the lives he's taking in order to do a blood spell to stay alive. The damage he is probably doing is unthinkable."

"No, no it's not that, of course I'd help anyone facing going crazy and of course I want to save lives. I just don't want the publicity. I don't want all that you are telling me that I'll be given."

Damian and Cain were quiet for a minute.

"You wouldn't be able to hide the fact if you fight your father and win that you are queen."

"Maybe she couldn't hide that fact. But perhaps she could hide the fact that she is the one who fought and won. If they didn't know who it was, they couldn't bother her. Does it say anywhere they have to know or that you have to have a queen?"

"No," said Damian looking a bit troubled. "I understand, what you're saying. That's one of the reasons I asked you to be quiet on the phone. Until I could see for myself. We always assumed the one we waited for would want to be queen. Give it some time, Kara. You are frightened by all of it and the powers you have are incredible. I have no doubt you are our queen, and as my queen, whatever you ask of me I will do. I will help you with whatever you need, and I will do all that you ask. I give you my word. No one will ever hear your name from me if that is what you desire. We just have to figure out how to keep you secret, and for how long. Eventually they will find out. You cannot hide the power that you have forever. Just take it slow. I have no doubt you will change your mind in due time. It's inevitable. However, in the prophesy it says the moon splits, guiding everyone to you."

"The moon won't actually split in two?" she asked, horrified.

"I'm sure it is some sort of metaphor, we aren't sure. For now, we should concentrate on you learning more about yourself, and getting to know the powers you possess."

"You better make it quick. She starts a job in a few weeks."

"What job?"

"As a bodyguard for the most influential man in Denver."

"Reid Dalton?"

"Yes," said Kara.

"I've heard of him. He does some great things for Denver. He's made national news several times. Wow, how'd you land that job?"

"My experience in the army."

"I see," said Damian. "Cain if you don't mind, I'd

like to stick around for a couple of weeks to bring Kara up to pace. I have some vacation time. I take it you know nothing of your powers?"

"Well, I threw Cain across the room with my mind, and all my life I've had visions of things happening just before they happen."

"The only true seer I've ever heard about was the one who fell in love with Raigon, and that was Eiris. She wrote many, many, books. It is said she wrote her visions in clarity. There are those who scry and try and sometimes get something, like I did, finding out about the dark cloud coming at you, but that is something that is happening in the moment. I don't know of anyone who can tell the future. That's two great powers, anything else?"

"I don't know. I really have no idea."

"Here, this is the copy of the prophesy," he said and handed it to her.

She opened the large paper and laid it on the coffee table as Cain put the tray on the floor. Her hands were shaking when she opened it and read:

*The Prophesy*
*The witch hath cursed the man as beast*
*He will seed a son, this son shall feast*
*On lives and souls of sorcerers and wolf*
*to curse them all with his own self worth*
*He begets a daughter of which good prevails*
*his life she'll take through misty veils*
*to send him back on the tail of the curse*
*at lightning speed, which he'll traverse*
*leaving peace and abundance on that which was made*
*instead of discord, devilry, for a price that's paid*

*fear not, tho time travels as a distant star*
*do not lose hope, she's not gone far*
*simple and pure of light she lives*
*until such time she rises and gives*
*the moon announces, this day, this hour*
*to split in two to take back his power*
*amongst you she walks knowing not her name*
*ancient runes shall guard 'til the bull in flame*
*takes him back from once he came*
*to burn around him his riches and fame*

It was becoming a little too real for Kara, and she didn't think she had it in her to do what was asked of her. "I don't think I can do this," said Kara. "I mean I will try and do what is asked of me, but I don't think I'm strong enough to fight someone who's been around hundreds or thousands of years."

"It's not a question of how long he's been around, my queen…" said Damian.

"Please don't call me your queen. I am no one's queen. I'm just me. Just call me Kara, please."

Damian nodded. "All right, if that's what you wish, Kara. It's not a question of how long he's been around, it's the power that you have. You are an old soul whether you know it or not. You've probably been around longer. Your spirit is an old spirit and I speak of you being around longer as in living many, many, lives. In each of your lives you've gained strength and wisdom. That does not leave you ever."

"How would you know something like that?"

"Old writings and teachings. Power can only go to one who can use it and is wise enough to use it. You cannot teach a kindergartener calculus."

"Now it is I who sees what you're saying," said

Kara. "But I don't know if…"

"You can," said Damian. "You most certainly can. You just need your doors opened that's all. You'll know what to do."

"I think if you are going to be teaching Kara for the next two weeks that will work out perfectly. I lost Christian yesterday, and I am taking his place. It will take me some time to get everyone acclimated at work, including myself. I also need to make arrangements for the funeral. I'm really all Christian had as family goes."

"Christian had a lot of people at work who admired him," said Damian standing. "I for one. On a brighter note, I'll get my suitcases. Are we staying here or your place, Cain?"

"My house was trashed yesterday. At the moment it's not livable. Someone looking for something, and I think I know who that someone was. In fact, I think I know who Kara's father is. Although there's no proof yet."

"Are you thinking what I'm thinking?" asked Kara.

They both said it at once.

"Reid Dalton."

Chapter Eighteen

*Two weeks later…*

Cain sat in front of the casket that was ready to be lowered in the ground. The past two weeks were incredibly hectic. He not only had the funeral arrangements, he had to go to New York and meet with corporate about taking over Christian's position. Then he had to spend a great deal of time getting things arranged in the offices. He went through Christian's many files trying to familiarize himself with the important things.

He hadn't realized what a job Christian was doing until now. He felt he'd given everyone enough work to last them two weeks and then some. If there was something important, Stone would call him. He had two weeks off. He had eight weeks coming, but he wanted to save some for when he and Kara married.

Now he was sitting at Christian's funeral. All of his comrades from TITAN were here. All of Christian's people. Kara beside him on one side, Damian and Stone on the other. There were people standing everywhere. People had come from all over, others who belonged to TITAN from around the country. He barely paid any attention to the sermon that was being said. He'd never met the minister that was so casually talking about his best friend as if he knew him and was close to him.

Instead, he was going through his own memories. Good times, hard times, arguing, laughter, but through it all they remained the closest of friends. He was going to miss Christian. He was more than a friend, he was a brother. His sadness and his anger built. He didn't know whether he wanted to cry or punch something. Instead, he sat remembering his best friend.

Christian never married, if he had to guess, he'd have to say Christian favored men. They'd never spoken about it, but he picked up on comments that were made. It never mattered to him, he loved Christian as a best friend and as a brother. There had been one awkward moment when they were out drinking and Christian had said, "*if you weren't so straight, I'd give you a go.*"

He'd been too drunk to understand at the time and thought it was a joke. He'd got up and found a woman to take home for the night. Leaving Christian at the bar alone hoping he'd do the same.

He later realized that was Christian's way of feeling him out. He'd never mentioned anything like it afterwards. Maybe that was Christian's way of telling him he loved him. Sometimes he was sorry he couldn't reciprocate those feelings, but they were who they were. Christian would take weekend getaways and when he'd return Cain never asked more than how his weekend went. Christian would give short answers of fine, great or a disaster. He had always hoped Christian could have found a mate and he didn't think he ever had, and that made him sad.

Christian and he had gone on a few fishing trips together and camped and ran as wolves. Those were great memories. Clan squabbles always brought them together and they always managed to work it out without hardly ever arguing. God, he was going to miss him. He never thought in a million years he'd lose him. He'd love to tear Reid Dalton apart like he had Christian. He was sure it was him. He worried about Kara.

He caught something the minister said. Something about Christian serving in the navy and living through Pearl Harbor. He watched as the military came forward and blew a trumpet. When they finished, they shot guns in his honor. It brought tears to his eyes, and they ran down his face. He hardly noticed Kara taking his hand and squeezing it.

They approached him and handed him a folded flag. His eyes teared up even more. He pinched the flag tightly as if he could stem his flow of tears. He thought back to their days at Pearl Harbor and he and Christian under the bubble that Damian provided to keep them safe. They all went in as boys, except for Christian, and came out as men. To him Christian had always been a rock.

He stayed lost in his memories until Kara put a hand on his shoulder. He glanced at her. She motioned with her head toward the casket. All was quiet and he realized they were waiting on him.

He got up and threw carnations on the casket, Christian's favorite flower. He kissed his fingers and touched them to the cold metal then walked away. He stood beside a tree waiting for Kara and glanced back at her. Stone was talking to her. He didn't catch what was being said, but he saw Kara slap him hard across the face. He was immediately by her side.

"What happened here?" asked Cain.

"Nothing, boss," said Stone with a hard look. "Not a thing."

"Kara?"

"Nothing of any importance."

"Damn it, Stone, have you no consideration for

Christian's funeral?"

"I do boss, it's just my thoughts got away with me. I apologize Kara, it won't happen again," he said and quickly walked away.

"What happened?" he asked Kara.

"He told me how sexy I look in all black. I don't look sexy to you, do I?"

"Jee Zuss, Kara, you always look sexy to me. I know what you're asking though. You're dressed very appropriately, if that's what you're asking. Stone just overdoes it. If I would have been here, I would have punched him for you."

She laughed. "Thank you for that." He took her hand and led her away.

As they were walking to the car his cell phone rang. He answered. "DeLucci."

*"Mr. DeLucci? This is Sanderson's Jewelry Shop calling. The ring you ordered has been made, and I must say it is very beautiful. All of us are ecstatic with the way it turned out. What a great idea you had. My jewelry maker had a lot of fun with it. Said he wished he could get more orders like yours."*

He was holding Kara's hand with one hand and holding his cell tight to his ear with the other hoping she couldn't hear the conversation "Thank you for calling about those shipping boxes. I'll be looking for them in the office."

*"The little lady near?"* The man lowered his voice.

"Yes, yes, and if this order pans out our company will order from you from now on."

The man laughed. *"You can pick it up any time, Mr. DeLucci, and we thank you for your business. Oh and by the way, it does come with a box, so you're not technically lying if you're worried about that."* He chuckled again and hung up. Cain had to hide his grin at his last remark. He made a mental note to pick up the ring tomorrow.

They headed back to the farm, as he'd come to call Kara's place. Damian was hanging around longer. He wasn't sure Damian being there was a good thing or a bad. Kara was trying so many things. He came in one day to the vacuum running itself, dishes flying into the dishwasher, and clothes folding themselves. She and Damian were standing together. She had a determined look on her face and was waving her hands in the air. He'd laughed at the time, but he was worried about her. She was under a lot of pressure. She must have felt the same way because she brought it up later in the day.

"I don't want to be queen to anyone. I don't want droves of people flocking to see me or expecting something from me. I want a quiet life as your wife and to plan for our family.

"You don't have to be or do anything you don't want to. The covens have gotten along all these years without you, they can continue to do so."

"That's what Damian said, but how are we going to do that? Especially if I win the fight with my father." Her voice rose as she grew more agitated. "People would notice the moon splitting."

"I don't know. Prophesies are sometimes littered with metaphors. We will figure it all out. Now for our next problem. You start work for Dalton tomorrow. With Damian here, and my work, we didn't have much of a chance to plan."

"I like the idea of you being wolf. I can call you, or whistle for you, like we talked about a couple of weeks ago."

"I want a solid plan. Especially because in three days is another full moon. What is it with you and three days until a full moon?" he asked with a chuckle.

"I don't know, guess I'm geared to them."

"Are you ready to go?"

"Can we get a late lunch at the bistro first?"

"Of course, little lady, your wish is my command."

"Oh, don't say that," she said with a dark look.

Cain laughed.

Chapter Nineteen

The next morning Kara was up at four. They had had
a busy two weeks with the funeral and with Damian
being there, but she learned a great deal about herself.
They said their good-byes to Damian yesterday for his
return to Florida, and the funeral was over, now it was
time to find out about Dalton. She was a bit tired this
morning after all that. She grabbed a quick shower, a
quick cup of coffee, kissed a nervous Cain, and left for
Reid's.

He was up drinking coffee and eating breakfast
when she got there. Mitka was sitting across the table
from him on the terrace reading the morning paper. Terry
was in another chair writing in her ever-present
notebook. They all looked up when the butler showed her
in. Reid stood up.

"Please, have a seat and some breakfast with us,"
said Reid.

"No, thank you, I'm fine."

"Well, then sit. It seems you are ready to get to
work."

"You did tell me not to be tardy." She pulled a chair
slightly away from the table, not wanting to be too close
to them.

"Then by all means let's get started."

She listened to the places they'd be going, Terry
reading off time and places and the people Dalton had to

see. They would be gone most of the day. She was hoping they'd stay in, but it wasn't the case.

The whole day sounded extremely dull. Which turned out to be very true. When he offered lunch at the Italian restaurant, she quickly said no. He stared at her for a second then named a different restaurant. She wondered if he'd chosen the bistro because that's where she liked to go with Cain, or he liked the place. She wasn't sure, but she was confident of one thing. She was sure that he'd been the person responsible for ransacking her and Cain's houses.

They returned to his house after a long twelve-hour day. Nothing eventful happened and she hadn't learned anything new. If he continued in the same vein, she'd never find out anything. She went home and filled Cain in. She'd texted him a few times to let him know where they were going and caught sight of him once. Other than that, he'd remained well hidden. She didn't like where this was all going at all.

The next morning, she again arrived by five. It was another uneventful day, and they were out of the house for the majority of it. She was getting ready to leave when Reid called her over.

"Yes?" she asked.

"Tomorrow Mitka and Terry will be gone. I have a couple of meetings here at the house so we will be staying in."

"I was hoping to have tomorrow off, it's Saturday," she said. She was thinking about it being the full moon. What if she didn't make it back in time? She'd turn to wolf in front of him. On the other hand, she could get some snooping done. Something she definitely wanted to do."

"I have to leave here by five o'clock," she said

"Isn't that the time you usually leave?"

"Well, yes, but I wanted to make sure those were your plans. I didn't plan on working weekends either. We didn't discuss that."

"If you are worried about it, I can pay extra, no problem. I just don't want to be left without a bodyguard."

"Are Mitka and I your only bodyguards?"

"I can call and have one sent, but I like to get to know my employees. Is there a problem?"

"No, no I'll be here."

"Fine, I'll see you in the morning, Ms. Thomas."

"Good evening, Mr. Dalton," she said and headed out the door.

She was almost to the house when she saw Cain pull up behind her. She hadn't seen him all day, but knew he'd been around. She had to admit, he was good. She didn't know how long she could put up with this charade.

She'd watched Reid through a great many meetings. She couldn't believe all the stuff he was doing. She pulled her pickup truck up to the back door and Cain pulled in beside her.

"Well, there's someone to brighten my day," she said as she opened her door.

"I'd say it's been my day that has been brightened." Cain took her hand and she hopped down out of the truck.

"Gads, that man drives me bonkers."

"Another uneventful day I take it," he said, as he followed her into the house.

"That man has his hand in everything that has to do with this city. I can't believe it. Meeting after meeting.

He's damn smart I'll give him that. He has an answer to every problem and he's not afraid to throw money around. Hell, it'd take me the rest of my life to earn what he writes in checks a day. Maybe not that close, but damn."

They got through the back door and on the way to the kitchen she plopped her purse on the long counter in the butler's pantry and threw her keys in a bowl. She kept right on going. "I have to work tomorrow," she said with a sigh. She kicked her shoes off in the kitchen and headed for the living room. Cain followed her and sat down beside her when she plunked down on the sofa and leaned her head back. Eyes closed. "Being bodyguard to that man is tiresome."

"You look tired. I'll fix us some coffee, or would you prefer wine?"

"I'd love wine, but then I'd want more wine, and I have to work tomorrow."

"You know, babe, tomorrow is Saturday and it's a full moon. I thought you had weekends off."

"I'm supposed to, but Terry and Mitka won't be there tomorrow, he has no bodyguard."

"So, let him call in one."

She was still in the same position, eyes closed. "He likes to know the people he works with."

"Were you able to find anything out?"

She raised her head and looked at him. "Not a damn thing. We haven't been at his place at all the last two days. Well, you know, I've texted you the places we were going."

"Is anyone going to be there with you and him tomorrow?"

"I suppose his butler is."

"That bothers me."

"We'll be fine. You like oriental food?" she asked.

"Sure, love it."

"Let's get takeout, I'm too tired to cook."

"Okay, babe, you call, I'll go pick it up."

"Sounds good," she said with a yawn.

**\*\*\*\***

The next morning Kara woke tired. She'd put twelve hours in with Reid each of the last two days. She crawled from bed anyway. At least they weren't going from place to place today they were finally staying in. She just wanted to get something on him that would tie him to the drugs and to murder. She also wanted to find the old lady. She had questions.

Cain was already up making coffee. When she walked into the kitchen, she smelled something burning.

"What are you doing?"

He looked over at her and smiled. "I'm making you breakfast," he said jovially.

"How can you be so happy this morning, and what is that burning?"

"I'm sorry that's toast." He went to the toaster and flipped the nob up. Up popped two pieces of burnt toast.

"How can you burn toast?"

"I don't know, how do I do anything?" He put two runny eggs on her plate and grabbed the burnt toast, buttered it, and placed them beside the eggs. "I'm not a very good cook."

"I can see that." She chuckled. "But I'll eat it. It smells good."

He picked up her plate. "You're lying. It's terrible." He scraped it in the garbage. "You know what we need?"

"No what do we need?"

"A dog, so I can give it whatever I cook."

"I believe it's the thought that counts."

"It won't fill you up though."

"I just need coffee, and you cook that pretty good."

He laughed. "Here." He handed her a cup of coffee and went to the fridge for cream. He poured some in her coffee.

"Aren't you tired?" she asked.

"No, I slept good last night. I believe you had a hand in that," he said and winked at her.

She blushed. Something about today worried her, and she couldn't put her finger on why. She put it down to being tired. She took a long drink of coffee. Then a thought struck her. "Cain, where is that silver bullet that was in my dad's safe?"

"Why? Do you think you need it?"

"I'm not sure. I just have the feeling I should start carrying it. I don't' know who I'm going to run into being with Reid all day. Hell, I don't know about Reid."

"I'll be right back." He quickly left and came back handing her the bullet.

She emptied her gun and put the silver bullet in, put the safety on, and slipped it back into her holster. "There, now I feel better."

"Yeah, but now you only have one bullet in your gun."

"That's all I need in that gun. I have two others. One in another holster, and one on my ankle. I'm good to go."

He smiled and leaned over and kissed her. "Don't forget to text me."

"I won't, you'll be around, won't you?"

"I should be, unless something goes really south at work, Stone has it covered. It's a full moon tonight, don't let Reid make you late. I'll be near his house all day."

"I won't. I'm hoping I can find something that will tie him to the drugs and possibly murder. He has a few meetings today so I'm hoping I'll have time to snoop."

"Just be careful and be aware. I don't trust Reid Dalton. I don't care for the man either. There's just, there's just…"

"Yeah, I get that. Wouldn't know it to watch him conduct business though. He's sharp and on his game concerning business. I also want to find out if he is my father. I don't know how I'm going to do that."

"Well, unless you can get a swab for a DNA test, I don't know how you would."

She glanced at the clock on the wall. "I gotta go, I don't want to be late," she said as she downed the last of her coffee.

"I'm right behind you. I'm going out as wolf and do some sniffing around his place. There's got to be something somewhere. If you're inside and I'm out, we might just find it."

His pager went off. "Shit, it's Stone, something at work. I'll put it on speaker."

Kara turned around to wait to see what it was. She watched Cain grab his cell, punch in Stone's number, and hit speaker.

"Yeah, Stone, what's going on?"

*"I need your help, Cain. There's been massive overdoses all over the city. It's like that drug was thrown from an airplane. I don't have the manpower to send out someone for each case. I need your help organizing everyone, plus P.D. is going to be everywhere."*

"Go," said Kara. "I'll be all right."

"You sure?"

She nodded.

"All right, text me if you need me. I'll get there as soon as I can."

"I will." She smiled and gave him a peck on the cheek and went out the back door.

When she got to Reid's house, he answered the door. "Where's the butler?" she asked.

"He has the day off," said Reid. "Come join me for breakfast."

"I guess, since I didn't get a chance to eat this morning."

"Splendid. I have an excellent cook and she's preparing a great breakfast. Come have some biscuits and coffee while we wait."

She sat down across from him, and he rung a little bell. Out came his cook. "I'm having company for breakfast."

"Very good," said the woman. She left.

"I don't like these little bells," said Reid. "But with my butler gone I use them. It saves steps."

"For you, it does." She couldn't help it just came out.

"That was a bit sarcastic," he said with a chuckle. "Kind of refreshing. So many walk on eggshells around me. As I mentioned before you really remind me of someone."

"I'm curious about that, who?" Maybe now she'd get some answers. She could only hope.

"I thought I told you someone who worked for me."

"I was wondering what her name was. Maybe I've met her." She tried keeping her nervousness out of her voice. Her heart started beating faster.

"I don't think so, she died in a car accident close to

thirty years ago."

"What was her name?"

"What difference does it make? Her name was Mariana De le Fuentes. Have you heard of her?"

She broke out in a sweat. She did recognize that name. It was on her birth certificate. She cleared her throat and tried for as much normalcy as she could. She and Cain might have thought that was the case, but knowing it? Having it right in her face? She didn't dare give herself away.

"No," she said clearing her throat again. "I've never heard of her." She must have managed a normal voice because he didn't seem to notice.

"Of course, you haven't, like I said she died thirty years ago. Now for what we have on our plate for today…"

She had a very hard time listening to him. She wanted desperately to ask questions about her mother, but she couldn't. Was he her father? Her heartbeat pounded in her chest. She looked at him very closely. He had green eyes, she had green eyes. Her mother had brown. Fear sank down into her stomach. If she was right, she was sitting across from her father.

"Did you love Mariana?"

He stopped speaking looking surprised at being interrupted. "Did I love her? I was married."

"You spoke very fondly of her, that's why I ask."

He stared at her, and it made her uncomfortable, to the point where she was ready to squirm in her seat.

"Yes, I guess you could say I loved her," he finally replied.

"Tell me Ms. Thomas, do you love Mr. DeLucci?"

"Yes, very much so."

"But you aren't married yet. Perhaps I can take this opportunity to persuade you to my side. I have taken a fancy to you. Perhaps because you do remind me of Mariana. I have a great deal to offer a woman. I guarantee you wouldn't want for anything. If you enjoy travel, I could take you around the world several times."

"There's more to life than things, Mr. Dalton. I can't be persuaded off Cain for any amount of money, trips, things, or prestige. Those aren't important to me."

"You might change your mind if something were to happen to Mr. DeLucci."

"If something happened to Cain and you had a hand in it, thinking to bring me to your side, you'll only make an enemy out of me and I'll kill you, or die trying."

"If you could prove it, my dear. If you could prove it."

"Let me ask you this, is that why you hired me? Because I remind you of someone you loved? I can assure you; I am nothing like the person you knew."

"On the contrary, you have little habits that remind me very much of her. However, I know that you are not her. I'm not that addle brained, and yes that is why I hired you, although you are highly qualified for the job, but you were right, Mitka is the only bodyguard I need."

Taking a chance, she blurted out, "Perhaps the woman was my mother." Why had she said that? She wanted to pinch herself. If he knew that, he'd surely try and kill her.

"I thought of that myself. However, when is your birthday?"

"June 1st, I'll be thirty years old."

"You see, you couldn't be. Mariana died in a car crash eight months before you were ever born. I know because I was called instantly to the car wreck, and I saw her body with my own eyes. So, you see, you are not her daughter."

She pondered his answer and thought about what her mom and dad wrote to her. Her aunt gave her life and her mother died in childbirth. She realized her mother's sister gave her life for the cause. They were either twins, or they looked alike. Pieces of the insane puzzle were starting to come together. She couldn't wait to tell Cain.

They ate breakfast in silence except for the few things he told her about the day. Right after breakfast three men were coming for a meeting. She was to wait outside the door as the meeting was private. He had another meeting planned for noon. He told her he'd show her around the house after the morning meeting was over. She kept thinking about what she wanted to do.

First on her list was the old lady. She thought about asking Reid about her, but the second she opened her mouth to do so, it felt wrong. Since she'd met Damian, she learned a great deal about herself, one thing was to listen to her intuition. She thought about how she could have used Damian's insight years ago.

"Did you enjoy your breakfast, Ms. Thomas?"

"I suppose, I must have, I ate it." She stood when he stood. Time to get the day started. She followed him to the room he met her and Cain in.

"You see," said Reid, showing her the artifacts in the glass cases. "These are our history. They are important to me. I spared no cost to purchase them. I actually have staff in different countries in search of artifacts for me."

"What do you do with them, Mr. Dalton?"

"What anyone would do with them, appreciate

them."

"Why not put them in a museum where everyone can appreciate them?"

"Because, Ms. Thomas I..." She was waiting for his answer when she heard his doorbell. "Excuse me. That will be my first meeting." He walked out, then back in with three men.

She looked up from an Egyptian artifact to see three shady looking characters walk in. Hit men wearing suits was her first thought. "I'd like you all to meet my bodyguard, Ms. Thomas. Three associates of mine, Mr. Ivanov, Mr. Vasiliev, Mr. Lenkov."

She nodded her head. "Gentlemen." Hmm all Russian. She wondered about that.

"Ms. Thomas," said the man in front.

"If you'll pardon us, Ms. Thomas and please take your place just outside the doors to the meeting room."

He dismissed her and headed for his bar to pour drinks, no doubt. She wanted to shake her head, but she politely went through the double doors and closed them tightly. She would love to hear what they were discussing. She pressed her ear to the door and could only hear low mumbles. She gave them a few minutes to get situated and she took off toward the stairs. If he found her gone, she would say she was using the restroom.

She went at a quick pace to the stairs, and up them past the no admittance sign. She wished she knew what room the woman was in. If she was even there. It was dark in the hall when she'd disappeared the other day. She tried the first door. It was locked. She knocked quietly and waited a few seconds.

When there was no response, she tried the next. It too was locked. She tried knocking again, waiting a few seconds and then turned to leave. Suddenly she heard a couple little knocks back. She spun back around and knocked again. A knock came back.

Was the old woman playing games? She still wasn't sure that she wasn't dealing with a senile old woman. Yet page 34 turned out to be something in the book. She tried the door again.

"Can you open your door? I wish to speak to you." She kept her voice low.

"I can't." The woman's voice sounded old, weak, and shaky. "He keeps it locked on the outside. I can't get out."

She dug in her left pocket and came up with a set of lock picks. She looked closely at the door. Fairly common looking lock. She took her picks out and began messing with the lock. As soon as she felt it give, she opened the door. The first thing to hit her was the smell. Did the woman ever bathe? Did no one come to change the sheets on the bed? Then she saw the open door into a bathroom.

"Well, come in. I've been expecting you, Kara."

She was surprised. "How do you know my name?"

"Why, I'm the one who gave it to you. We've not a lot of time and there is much we need to discuss. I'm Eiris, your grandmother."

Kara's vision narrowed. She thought she was about to faint.

The woman grabbed her arm. "Goodness, child, don't do that, we haven't the time for it. Come and sit down."

Her head swam. If she was really Eiris then she'd know about her mother. She sat down then jumped up again. In the corner was a hologram of Reid Dalton and the three men. "Ho…how are you doing that?"

"Magic, my dear. Look closely toward their feet."

She moved closer to see better. There was a chalk line of a pentagram inside were unfamiliar drawings of some type of Sigle. She watched the men, putting her hand through their image, wiggling it around and then pulling it back.

"He doesn't know I can do this. I have a rug to cover the chalk lines and my rocking chair usually sits there.

"May I ask how old you are? You are the original witch, are you not?"

"Actually, I thought my mother was, I couldn't say for sure, but she didn't know what she was doing and poisoned herself with a plant she tried using in a spell. I was born in 795 A.D. I'm not sure of the day, so I can't tell you exactly how old I am. I can tell you, I'm very tired and ready to go to rest, but as long as my son is alive, I cannot."

"Why? Is he…my father?"

"Yes, my dear, I'm afraid he is. I've waited a very long time for you to come to us. Your mother, bless her, chose the parents who adopted you. Were you happy?"

"Yes, very." She grew quiet, So many questions she wanted to ask. "How does he…you, stay alive so long?"

"He uses a terrible spell to stay so young. He feeds part of that nasty spell to me, not enough to make me young, just enough to keep me alive."

"Why?"

"I am a true seer, Kara. He keeps me alive for my visions. He looks daily for anything I might have written because he knows I write down what I see. He always finds my drawings, my writings. He keeps me locked away up here to serve him. Years ago, I tried to find help to end his rein and I've been locked up ever since, under a spell no less. I'm not allowed to see anyone. He feeds me when he remembers."

"Is The Oracles your book?"

"Yes, I wrote it. Just before he locked me up, I stole the book back from him because he was using the spells. Well, I didn't. But a kind woman did. The very same woman who is responsible for you being here. I've also managed over the hundreds of years to get books I've written to the grandmasters and their council."

"My mother?"

"Yes, Mariana, I told her what was happening. She would sneak food up to me bless her heart. Because I could see what my son was doing, I knew where he kept the book hidden. She began helping me. She made my son fall in love with her long enough to become pregnant with you. He always used protection, and before protection existed, he would kill any offspring he had ."

"Because of the Prophesy?"

"Yes, I helped Mariana put a spell on him. He didn't use protection and she got pregnant with you. He's deathly afraid of the prophesy and as he should be. Some of the visions I've seen have made him furious. I told him, I don't make the future, I just see it."

"You want me to kill him?"

"It's not a question of what I want child, it's what must be done. He's very evil, my son. From the time he was born I sensed cruelty. He used to be brazen about it, then he got smart. He does everything behind closed doors now. He covers his tracks. He's very dangerous."

"Why do wolves that are also witches go crazy?"

"I'm afraid that is from the original blood spell my sister used on the love of my life." She sighed heavily and sat down in her rocker. "Do you understand how we've stayed alive so long? The nature of the magic?"

"I don't know."

"My son also uses a blood spell. A very dark spell that should never be used. The inoculation people get? It contains a spell using his blood. When someone goes crazy, he shoots them through the heart with a silver bullet, filled with his blood. He robs them of many years of life and their souls. He keeps them in his room. He feeds off those years of lives he's taken. He keeps himself young and force feeds me to keep me alive."

Kara stood, she couldn't sit still any longer. She walked over and looked at the scene playing out between him and the three visitors. I don't see any souls."

"There is a false wall in that room. He does all his spells in there. The souls are locked in a cage using the Misr Eye. The Egyptians knew how to do this. He studied them for years and learned it from them. He's smart, my son."

"If you couldn't come out of your room, how did I see you the other day?"

"That was a projection of myself, magic. That is why I couldn't speak to you. I could whistle from in here enough for you to hear, but I couldn't speak, you wouldn't have heard me. It took a great deal of energy and concentration on my part, and I barely had enough left to see it through. I didn't know what I was going to do if you didn't understand what I was showing you."

"Oh, the reason for the charades."

"We haven't much time, dear. The Misr Eye is in that stand near the Egyptian artifacts. There is a small black button you must push to reveal it. He is especially careful of it on full moons, as that is the night he could lose everything, and he knows it. You must make your move tonight. It's the full moon."

"Tonight?!" she gasped. "I'm not re…"

"You have to be ready, and it has to be tonight. He plans on killing off anyone left in Denver who doesn't serve his purpose next week. "Listen," she said and waved her hand.

*"It must be next week,"* said Reid angrily.

*"We aren't ready,"* said one of the three men.

*"You have to be ready. I have it planned to coincide with me running for office. You know my plans. Make sure it happens. DeLucci is out with the rest of TITAN trying to figure out where the drugs are coming from. I want the drugs in and out of this town in a week. Do I make myself clear? I will pin it on DeLucci and the town will more than love me. I'll be elected next governor's term coming up."*

*"Why don't you do something with DeLucci?"*

*"I have my plans for the man, make no mistake. He will be gone shortly. You didn't find anything at his house?"*

*"Nothing of any importance. Not at the girls house either."*

"Oh, my God, he *is* the one who trashed our places," said Kara. "We knew it."

"He's looking for the book and he's extremely curious about you. You look very much like your mother. There are spells in the book he wishes to use. You do have it well hidden, don't you?"

"Yes, I believe it's safe."

Reid's next words took her by surprise.

*"Did you check on the girl's mother? Is there any chance she can be my daughter?"*

The three moved around nervously.

*"Answer me!"* he shouted.

*"Yes, I'm afraid she is your daughter."* One man handed Reid a piece of paper. *"Here's your proof."*

*"What the hell are you saying! That couldn't possibly be."*

*"It could be if the mother had a twin."*

Reid looked toward the ceiling. *"My mother..."* he said angrily. He looked at the paper and pushed a button on the stand. The Misr Eye appeared, and a beam of light sprang from it and landed on the wall revealing a dark spot. *Keyhole wall.* The whole wall raised and receded back into the ceiling like a garage door.

Kara saw a cage, and in it, trapped souls moved about in panic. They appeared ethereal and moved quickly as if trying to escape. She felt as if they screamed in pain. A large mirror hung on the wall behind the cage. Off to the side was a safe.

Reid looked at the document in his hand, then opened the safe, *23, 14, 68.* Kara memorized the numbers. He opened it and put the document on the top of a large stack of papers sitting on some cash. He pulled out a wad of bills and handed some to each of the men.

*"If you can't find DeLucci, I know a way to draw him here. In fact, that is exactly what I'll do. Never mind looking for him. I have something better planned, something even better than what you did to Christian. He'll watch me kill my daughter, his love, then I will gladly take his life."* He laughed. He brought out a gun from the back of the safe. He held it up. *"Full of silver bullets. I'll be ready."*

*"Those aren't marked bullets, are they?"* asked one of the men.

*"No, I have my own. These cannot be traced. Just like the ones I used on Christian and Ansen. I have both of the bullets that were used."*

She saw the evil in him then. The evil she felt but didn't see before. Her stomach sank. "Oh no. He's going to kill Cain. What am I going to do?"

"What you need to do, stop him, dear."

"What about you? You aren't safe." She was frightened out of her wits.

"If there is anything I want, it's to go to rest. If he finally takes my life, it will be a blessing. I was meant to leave this world Millenniums ago, child. I need to rest. The time is for you now. Once he is gone, I will naturally go. I can't and wouldn't want to stop that. I will do everything I can to help you, but you must destroy him. Do you have the silver bullet?"

"I…I do," she stammered.

"He must be destroyed with a bullet of his own making shot through the heart from his own dark spell. It will release the trapped spirits and they move on to where they belong. They don't belong here. Don't worry, things are as they should be. They will work out how they should. Bring the Misr Eye up when the moon is full."

"I will be a wolf then."

"You are an original, Kara. You can take the shape of a man from your wolf. You will be covered in hair, but you can turn back. Use the words they are very powerful."

"Won't I think as a wild wolf then?"

"Did you last time?"

"I did some things that Cain thought was unbelievable."

"You can push aside the wild for short spurts and think clearly. You have to know he will be wolf also and he's had practice on a full moon. You must shoot him through the heart after the Misr Eye is up and you must demand the gods to release the spirits."

"Page thirty-four."

"Yes, do you remember the prophesy? The gods?"

"Yes," she said. "Strangely enough, I do."

"They have been ingrained in you, from spirit. You will know what to do."

"Grandmother, the prophesy, why did you write it backwards. I might not have figured it out."

"You most certainly would have. It was backwards because my son is dyslexic, he can barely read and write. He would have never figured it out. You must leave now. Remember to open the wall and hit the button to reveal the Misr Eye. When you see the split in the moon, you must shoot him with the silver bullet. That is when the moon will be at its peak. It must be then. Now go. His meeting is almost over."

She looked at her grandmother and felt a wave of emotion. Tears gathered in her eyes. She wished she had more time with her.

"That's right, granddaughter. I will leave the world tonight and take my place amongst the great spirit, and I will be thankful for it. We will have time together when it is right. In another time. You'll see. All the proof you need is in that safe, it will not burn."

Kara wondered what she meant but stepped forward and hugged her. "You can read my thoughts?"

"Aye, that I can, and with practice and learning you will be able to do the same. Will you be so kind as to pull that rug over in the corner and put my rocker on it before you go?" She grabbed Kara's hand and looked her in the eye. Peace flooded through her, and she didn't feel as afraid. "Know that all that is good shall be at your disposal," she said. "Do not worry over being a queen. You will be one when the time is right, and you will want to be. Listen to your people. I have heard their prayers since the beginning, It is time for you now. It will work out. Know that I love you."

"I love you too," she said, and meant every word of it.

"Now go, before he finds you here."

She was curious to what she'd done to alleviate her fear but moved quickly to replace the rug and rocker. She helped her sit in her rocker, hugged her again, and left.

She ran down the steps. "What was she to do? She quickly pulled out her cell phone and texted Cain. *"Reid is my father. He knows. Tonight's the night. Need help. You too in deep danger. Careful."*

She sent it, ran to the door she was guarding, and shoved her phone back in her pocket, just as Reid opened the door to let the three men out. He didn't act any differently than he had earlier. She tried not to sweat, but her heart was pounding. She couldn't muck this up. Cain's life was at stake, and she wouldn't fail her mission this time. She couldn't let happen to Cain, what happened to Christian.

"Well, Kara, I see life in the hall was uneventful." He stood beside her as he watched the three men leave.

"I didn't see anyone around."

"Someone would have a very hard time coming into my house unannounced. I would know right away.

"Come and I'll show you more artifacts." He walked down the hall.

She felt funny following him, but she went anyway.
"Do you know how old I am?"

"No. Thirty-five or forty?"

"You should add some zeros to that. Ah, here we
are." He opened a door, and she could see more glass
cases. "I don't show these to just anyone," he said
walking in. She followed, and he stepped back toward
the door. He flipped a switch and laser lights crisscrossed
the room.

"Don't dare move into the lights. Not without
cutting off a limb or two."

"Interesting, you can turn them off now."

"I think not, daughter. You may look at the artifacts
in the case you are standing in front of. Come tomorrow
morning when you are no longer wolf, I'll take care of
you. Tonight, I plan on taking care of Mr. DeLucci. It's
sad that he brought all those drugs into the U.S. I was
going to make Christian take the fall, but I wanted
information from him. I wanted to know what TITAN
knew about me.

"Unfortunately, he didn't tell me anything before he
died. But I've arranged it so TITAN will look bad and of
course, Cain at the front of it. When that blows over, I'll
once again take on the drug market. After all that is how
I make all my money. These businesses here in Denver
always need help, so a great deal of my money goes to
keeping Denver running smoothly."

"Denver is not your city to run." Kara was getting
angry. She almost stepped into the laser light to go after
him but remained in place. Her fear for Cain and what
Reid planned on doing made her see red.

"Ah, ah. You wouldn't want to lose one of those
pretty limbs, would you? More than likely, you will,

once the full moon rises. You won't be able to stand or sit still. You will be...let's see...the one hundredth and thirty fourth daughter of mine that I've gotten rid of. The others were quite young. You'll be the first grown daughter. I wonder..."

"What do you wonder?"

"What it could have been like if that damn prophesy hadn't come about. I never did have any sons. But as it is, I would have quite enjoyed having a daughter to raise."

"I'm so damn happy I had the parents I had. You will never in a million years compare to the goodness my adopted parents were."

"I never proclaimed to be good, Ms. Thomas, or should I say daughter?"

"Don't call me your daughter," she said through gritted teeth.

He laughed and closed the iron door behind him. She heard the lock click. She looked at the crisscrossed laser lights and wanted to sink to her knees. She needed to go after him. Think, she told herself. She still had her guns, and she still had her phone. He didn't bother to take anything away from her. He wasn't worried about her breaking out of the room.

She looked at the lights and carefully sat in the little triangle she had free of the lasers. At least she could stand and sit. She looked at the glass case in front of her. There were more Egyptian artifacts. She wondered what their properties were. No matter she wouldn't know what to do with them anyway. She carefully pulled out her phone.

Cain had texted her back. "*OMW*." Shit he was on his way. She had to stop him. Reid would kill him. She just knew it. She went through all the things Damian had taught her. She knew how to ward. Could she ward herself and go through the laser lights, put a protective bubble around her? She should ward the house, put a barrier around it so no one could get in. No, that would take too much energy and too much concentration.

She should save her energy for tonight when the moon came out. She would do things then. Also, her grandmother said Reid was wolf and warlock, so he would also turn wolf. She had to somehow use that to her advantage even if he did have years of experience. She sat and pondered things for what seemed like hours.

She wondered what she should say to Cain. She didn't want to worry him. She texted him. *"I'm being held prisoner. I'm okay, locked in a room. This is my fight. I have help. Old lady, grandmother. Don't come. He wants to kill you and blame you for the drugs in the city."* She lay the phone down beside her in case he texted back.

She had one thing she could try. She pulled out her semi-automatic pocket pistol, her favorite little gun, government issue, and aimed it at the switch that turned the lasers on and pulled the trigger. It hit once and nothing. It must have imbedded in the wall. She couldn't see where to aim exactly but if she could just get the bullet inside the switch, she knew it'd short circuit and turn off. She aimed again and shot. Nothing.

She had to conserve her nine rounds because she didn't have any more ammo with her. She stopped for a minute and looked around the room. No windows, there was a grate in the ceiling. If she could get up to it, she could leave the room. But first she had to deal with the lasers.

She had her two 9 mm police guns, but one had only the one bullet, the silver bullet. She definitely had to save that for Reid. It was strapped in her side holster on the left, her other one on the right. She always wore a longer jacket covering her guns, but it was open so she could reach them quickly. She put her small handgun back in her ankle holster and pulled out her other one, aimed and shot.

She heard a thud. That did the trick. Smoke came from the switch, and she heard a crackling noise. Then the laser lights went out. Thank God. There was just one small light on in the room, so she couldn't see well, but enough. She put her phone back in her jacket pocket.

She went and stood under the ceiling grate. There had to be ducts that ran throughout the house. She just needed a way to get up there. She looked around the room. There was nothing she could stand on. Damn it. She went to the door and tried it. It was probably padlocked from the outside.

She tapped on it. It was solid, and it was iron. However, the outside had wood on it, probably for aesthetic reasons. Maybe she could scoot one of the glass cases over and use it to stand on. She looked for the smallest one and tried to move it. It moved an inch. She would have to work at it, but she could do it. It was at the end toward the hatch side. At least some luck was with her.

She got a text and felt the vibration at her side. She stopped what she was doing to check her messages. It was from Cain.

"*Almost there. I'm staying as man. I won't be turning wolf.*"

She texted back. "*Please, don't come.*"

*"Almost there."*

*"Stubborn ass."*

She got a smiley face with a tongue sticking out back.

She sighed. Then she got another.

*"I'll be careful, I'm not dumb."*

*"That's not the point."*

She glanced at the time on her phone three minutes until noon. Time was getting away from her. She slid her phone in her jacket pocket. She knew Cain would come. She knew she couldn't stop him, but if he was killed because of her, she wouldn't recover. She couldn't lose Cain. She needed out of this room now.

Wait! She could move things with her mind. How the hell did that slip her thoughts? She drew on the energy around her like Damian taught her. She felt it swell in her solar plexus. It mounted and swirled as she contained it with her mind then glaring at what she wanted moved she gave the mental push. It slid a little past where she needed it, but she could stand on it. Thank God, for that extra power. She wondered what Reid's powers were, did he have all of them also? The same? She still didn't know everything. Damian had told her there were lots more. She wished she knew what.

She could do a spell, but she didn't have the pentagram on the floor, or the herbs and candles she needed. She wondered if the cook was still there. Maybe she could get to the kitchen.

She had several hours to work things out in her mind to get rid of Reid and to save Cain. Neither, she felt, was going to be simple, and neither could a human take on. No, it would take magic. It would have been great to have had years to practice her powers, but she knew why they were bound…to keep her alive.

She climbed up on the glass case. He was going to have a meeting at twelve so people would be in the house. She wondered who he was meeting with. More people to do his dirty work? Did Mitka know what he was doing? She was sure of it. What about Terry?

When she thought about him trying to kill Cain and blame the drugs on him, she became furious again. Anger was not going to help her. She needed action. She pushed on the grate. It didn't give. She stared at it thinking how she needed it to move and gave it a nudge. This time it was easier and used less energy. It flew upward then landed beside the hole half covering it. She finished moving it aside. She smiled. It was a handy power to have.

She pulled herself up and looked around. She was in a maze of duct work. There was some light, but she had no idea which way to go. She put the grate back, then felt in her pocket. She had the lighter Damian told her to carry for spells. She needed to find the kitchen. She could head the way she saw the cook come from earlier.

She moved down the duct as quietly as possible. She should have moved the case back before she shut the hatch. Too late now. She came to a fancy grate and looked down. She could see out the patio door. Reid was eating lunch, but she could barely see him. He had people with him out on the patio. His twelve o'clock?

She was sure it was. She'd lost track of time in the laser room. The only real light she had filtered up through grates that were used for heating. Thank God it was warm enough the heat wasn't on. It wasn't perfect but if she kept heading toward where she saw light, she'd be okay.

She headed in the direction of the kitchen. There were two grates in the ceiling of the room. She looked through the first one and saw the cook below. She should have asked her grandmother about the cook. She didn't think the cook knew what Reid was about but would certainly alert him to the fact she was there. She started toward the second grate, and the metal popped, making a loud noise. She stopped dead and held her breath. The cook heard it and looked up into the grate.

"Who's up there." She swung a butcher knife. Damn she was going to alert Reid.

"Please. Don't alert Reid. He's holding me prisoner."

The cook looked up at her. "You are the one I saw earlier."

"Can you please help me?"

"My goodness, how did you get up there?" She grabbed a step stool and pulled it under the grate.

"Will you help me?"

"I can't very well help you if you're in the ceiling. Come down from there before you hurt yourself."

Kara smiled. She pulled the grate up and swung her legs down, then hopped down. She looked back in the duct and pushed the grate back. "Thank you," she said hopping off the stool. "I have to stop Reid Dalton from killing my fiancé."

"Are you saying Reid Dalton is trying to kill someone? I knew with those ruffians he's been bringing into the house he was up to no good. I won't be privy to a murder. You look so much like Mariana. I was shocked when I saw you there for breakfast, but it wasn't my place to ask questions. I really miss her."

"I never got to know her. She died at my birth."

# Ways of the Wolf

The cook clucked her tongue. "Sad, very sad. You have your father's eyes. I know about your grandmother. I would help her, but Mr. Dalton keeps a very close eye on me. It's not like it used to be when she ran the household. Now he keeps her locked away. Says she's senile and won't see anyone but him. He lies. Mariana used to see her all the time when we had more people working here. He fired most of them when he found out people were sneaking to see his mother."

"You'll help me then?"

"Yes, I'll help you. What do you need?"

Kara gave her a list of herbs she'd need and asked for some candles, preferably black if she had them. Then she waited while the cook began putting things in different baggies. "We used to have almost everything in stock for Eiris and Mariana, but I didn't see the need to keep so much of so many different type plants and roots with just me here now. I wouldn't know what to do with any of them." Kara heard the bell from earlier.

"Mr. Dalton requires my presence. I'll be right back. Don't worry I won't mention you," she said a little nervously.

She wasn't sure about the cook. She seemed nice enough, but there was something... She gathered the crumbled leaves, different herbs, the stack of tapered candles and put them inside her jacket. She opened the back door and left it wide open. Then she tucked the front of her jacket in her pants so nothing would fall out and she went back up into the duct. She remained very quiet and still and waited to see what would happen.

The cook came in mumbling under her breath, and behind her was Reid.

"She was in here, Mr. Dalton. I swear to you. You

393

promised a reward."

"You'll get it Lucinda. It appears she took off out the door." He closed the door. "I'll send someone to find her. She won't get far." He left. She waited until the cook left the room before moving a muscle. She didn't want to take the chance of alerting the cook again.

Good thing she thought to open the back door. No wonder her grandmother didn't have anyone look after her. The ones who cared were all gone. The cook appeared to only look out for herself. Thank God for her intuition. Damian was right.

The cook returned humming and cooking something that made Kara's mouth water. She just hoped her stomach wouldn't growl. She hadn't eaten since breakfast. and she wasn't sure what time it was. Then she felt her phone vibrate. She had turned it down earlier so no noise could be heard. She very slowly pulled her phone from her pocket.

She read Cain's text. *"Where are you located in the house?"*

*"I'm free of the room. I'm in the heating duct in the ceiling above the kitchen."* She hit send.

Seconds later he replied. *"I've been all around the perimeter, I can find no feasible way in."*

"*Hide,*" she quickly texted. "*He thinks I escaped outside. He sent men to find me.*" She hit send, then waited. She felt the vibration.

*"Hidden. 2 men. Different direction."*

She answered. *"Be careful."*

"*U 2,*" he sent back. The cook left and she decided it was safe to move. She wanted to find the room that had the artifacts. She would hunker down there until night came. Unless she could find a better place to hide. She got far enough away from the kitchen that she felt safe.

She felt the vibration again. *"U ok?"*

*"Fine, u?"* she texted back then texted more. *"Waiting for dark. Magic in the room we were in. Egyptian artifacts. I'll be there."* She sent that then thought and pulled out her phone again. *"I'll look for a way to let you in."* She looked down the grate where the patio was and found it empty. Did she dare try and let him in there? Yes, she had to take the chance. She quickly texted. *"There's a patio where they eat. Do you know it?"* She hit send.

*"I saw it. Not far from where I'm at."*

*"I'll let you in there. Hurry."* She moved the grate and dropped to the floor. She waved him in.

He was out of breath and so was she. The whole thing was nerve wracking. He quickly hugged her. "We have to get out of here."

"I can't leave, Cain. I have to take care of my father tonight. He's going to kill off a bunch of people next week. He's behind the drugs and he wants to pin it on you. He was going to use Christian, but he killed him because Christian wouldn't give him information."

"Mother Fucker," said Cain under his breath. "Come on, you aren't safe here."

"I'm staying."

"I know, I'm staying with you."

They hurried down a hall and checked a couple of doors. The first was a master bedroom and then the next a bedroom they figured was for guests. They snuck in and closed the door. The room appeared unused. "Let's get in the closet," he said. "Safer."

The closet was empty. They crawled in and pulled the door shut. Cain reached over and kissed her. "I'm proud of you."

"I don't know Cain. He wants to kill you. If that happens, I will never forgive myself."

"If I get killed it's because I do something stupid, not anything you do or don't do. So, I don't want to hear that." He turned her around and brought her into his chest and put his arms around her. "Rest," he said leaning against the wall. "We need to conserve our energy."

She put her arms around his and leaned back. "I love you, Cain."

"I love you, Kara."

She didn't know how they did it, but they must have dozed off. There had been no sign of Reid Dalton, or his two goons. When Kara awoke, she pulled her cell phone out and looked at the time. Seven-thirty. "Shit. The moon's gonna rise in a few minutes. I have to get in that room where the spirits are."

"The what are?"

"I spoke to my grandmother. He's been robbing years of life from people so he can remain young. Their souls are held captive using the Misr Eye. He is using a blood spell. The inoculation? The shot uses his blood and when they go crazy, they are killed with a silver bullet that contains more of his blood. That's how he stays young."

"I knew there was a reason I didn't like or trust that man. How long has he been doing this?"

"I don't know but my grandmother was born in four hundred something A.D. I don't know how old she was when she had him. Not sure what he did before there were guns. Probably silver spikes. In my book that's as evil as you can get. Come on. I have to stop him and let those spirits loose so they can go to rest, so my grandmother can go to rest."

"She will die when they are let loose?"

"She will die when my father does, and I aim to make sure that happens." She stopped and thought of something. "Cain, what if Damian is right, and I've been born before?"

"Yeah, so?" he asked.

"Then I failed all those people before."

"You can't think like that, Kara. If you were, you are who you are today because of experience. You'll make it this time. I just know you will."

"How do you know that?"

"Because you have me to help you," he said, tongue in cheek. "Get your gun we may need it." He pulled his and she followed suit. She knew she couldn't use the silver bullet until the moon split, whatever that meant. She figured she'd know when the time was right. Cain peeked through the closet door. Nothing. "Clear."

They stepped quietly from the closet, and she peeked out the door. "Clear here too," she said. They stepped out of the room, and she hung close to the wall. She didn't see Reid anywhere. She headed toward the room with the spirits and the Misr Eye with Cain right behind her.

They were almost to the door when the two men looking for her earlier came out of the room and turned directly into them. Kara and Cain definitely surprised them. Cain fired and so did she. Both men dropped to the ground, but it alerted Reid to their presence. He came out of the room, just as Kara pushed her way in. Reid stumbled backwards, but quickly caught his footing then he laughed. Kara used her mind and pushed, and Reid flew backwards into the room. He slammed up against a glass case, not budging it.

"Nice," he said when he caught his breath. He pulled his gun and aimed it at Cain. "My gun is full of silver bullets. Your guns don't scare me," he said with a smile. She almost blurted out she had a silver bullet with his name on it, but the words stuck in the back of her throat.

She held him up against the case with her mind and tried getting past him. Reid shot and Cain quickly moved dodging the bullet. She may have Reid pinned but she couldn't stop him from shooting his gun.

"Let me go, daughter, or your man here will eat one of these silver bullets."

She let go of him. "That's better," he said, still aiming at Cain.

"There's two of us, and one of you," said Cain. "And one of us is powerful. I think you met your match." Cain was aiming his gun at him, and so was she. But she wasn't holding the gun with the silver bullet. She couldn't very well switch at the moment. She had to stall him and somehow open the Misr Eye.

"Ah, but in a few minutes you both will turn wolf and lose your ability to think in human terms."

She had to get to the stand and hit the button. Reid still stood against the case between her and the stand. She gathered her strength and with her mind she raised the glass case behind him, but he felt it rise, and used his mind against hers. The case flew hard across the room hitting Cain and knocking him over.

The case pinned him to the floor and knocked his gun out of his hand. It slid across the floor. Kara screeched and in her anger picked the case up off him and slammed it against the wall where it landed on its side blocking the doorway.

Reid held out his hand toward her. He twisted it in the air and yanked it inward. Her arm twisted up in agony and the gun left her hand and flew to his. He grabbed it out of the air and laughed. "You think to go against me. You don't stand a chance."

"Don't I?"

Reid looked at her in surprise, but quickly schooled his expression.

"You have no idea how to destroy me." There was a window in the room and Kara noticed it getting dark. In seconds the moon would rise. She had to do something. She went to Cain to see if he was all right. The case had knocked him out. When she moved toward Cain, Reid fired a shot hitting her in the left shoulder. It went completely through, burning like nothing she had ever felt before.

"Silver hurts, my dear. It's much harder to heal. I could have aimed for your heart, but this game seems much more fun. I'll play a while longer. Like with Christian, taking pieces is so much more fun. By the time the night is over, you and lover boy will have taken all my bullets. I'll save the last two silver bullets for your hearts.

Cain groaned and opened his eyes, then quickly sat up.

"Welcome back to the party," said Reid.

"You think this is funny?" asked Cain.

"Not funny, fun," he answered. "Both of you get up and go…"

Kara looked up and just caught the moon coming up. She felt the tingle and her body began the change. She glanced at Reid and saw him turn into a silver wolf. Cain changed and he growled.

Reid dropped the gun as he changed. Her first thought was *kill, kill, kill*. She watched the silver wolf leap over them and the case and out the door. She stood next to Cain who continued to growl. She got snippets of his scattered thoughts. They were still connected mind to mind as wolf. She was hungry and she wanted to hunt, she felt confined in the space, and she leaped over Cain and the case and flew out the door. She wanted a way out, but there was something in the back of her mind. She was a troubled wolf. Then it came to her…mate.

She turned back to look at her mate. He stood, paw in the air, holding his leg up. He whined. She got pictures of his leg being broken. She felt his pain. She quickly went back into the room forgetting her hunger. *Check my mate*. Then she had pictures of when he lay dying, and she watched over him. *No lion*.

She thought about the other wolf. Hearing a noise, she turned and saw a hairy man. She sniffed the air. Wolf, she thought. Danger. She leaped toward him. *Kill, kill, kill*. He moved as she sailed past him.

A soft voice entered her mind. *"Granddaughter, you must stop him. Look at him, you too can call your man. Do so, or he'll kill you both. You and your mate."*

The voice in her head reminded her of something. The room. The old lady. She liked the old lady. Bad men in the corner. *"Stop him,"* echoed her grandmother's voice. *"Call your man."*

*"Mutatis Mutanda,"* she thought, strongly. Her legs stretched out, her body took form, she stood upright. She looked at her hands. Hair, so much hair. *"Stop him, the Misr Eye,"* whispered her grandmother.

She could think. She looked at her mate. He sat next to her panting. She connected her mind with his. *"Stay."*

Then she heard a hiss and from tiny holes around the ceiling came a mist. "Not good." She quickly raised her hands and called down a ward around her and Cain. She felt it.

Again, she looked at the wolf that was her mate. She gave him the order to follow her. She had to keep him close, to stay within the protective bubble she had around them. She knew the mist wasn't good. The room was becoming foggy. She could barely see. She put her hand to Cain's head. *Follow me.*

His thoughts were scattered like broken glass, or more like wild wolf, but he followed her. She found her way to the stand that held the Misr Eye and felt for the button she should push. She found it and the hissing stopped. She pushed it and up came the Misr Eye. It shot a beam of light into a keyhole and the wall went up. She looked at the cage that held all the spirits. She wanted to pounce on the cage and break it.

No, she shook her head. She had to think straight, not like a wolf. She saw a ribbon of light fall across them, and across an altar.

She glanced at the floor and saw the pentagram and remembered her herbs and roots. She looked for her jacket and saw it ripped upon the floor. The mist was dissipating, the deadly air clearing. She reached down and grabbed her jacket. Cain whined. "*Stay,*" she commanded. He sat next to her panting favoring his leg. She felt his pain from his broken bones and knew it was healing.

As the ribbon of light moved across the floor it headed toward the alter. She felt frantic. She had to do something. The Apis Bull. She quickly grabbed the herbs and root, but her fingers were long, and claw like, with hair, she had to rip the bag to let out the contents. They fell upon the alter. Light, fire, she thought, she must light it. She was hungry. Hunt, she thought and looked toward the door. No, she couldn't, must finish.

She looked for the piece of her jacket that held the lighter then leaned down and grabbed it. "*Come*," she commanded Cain. He stayed close and whined. Then he growled loudly and leapt from her side. She turned to look at what caused his attack, and in the doorway stood the other wolf. Wolf man, bad, must destroy. Cain leaped toward him and in the wolfman's hand was a gun. He shot it and it hit her mate. She howled. "No!" she screamed. Cain fell to the floor panting.

"You can't stop me," said the wolfman, and howled. His voice gravely. Cain lay panting on the floor and his head went down. Instant pictures went through her mind of him being shot the last time when she stayed by his side the whole night.

"He will dieee," hissed the wolfman. "Silver bullets."

Silver bullets went through her mind. Silver bullets bad, kill wolf. She felt anxious, there was something she had to do. She looked at the lighter in her hand. She quickly went back to the alter and tried the lighter, nothing. She tried again and the flame came up. It frightened her and she dropped it in the herbs, and they caught fire. Up came the smoke and with it an Apis bull rose. It cried out in the flames, and it opened its eyes. It frightened her.

*Must happen, good, this good. Must happen.* She heard the cries from the spirits getting louder and louder and quickly glanced their way. Their eyes were all open and from them came light. They themselves were becoming light. They frantically moved in the cage, their cries hurting her ears, their undulations more frantic. They needed her. She wanted to pounce on the cage again. *"The words,"* came her grandmother's voice. *"Demand that the gods set them free."* The old lady's voice echoed away in her mind.

The words, she must say the words.

"Release the souls," she said in a hoarse gravelly voice. She tried again. "Release the souls!" she shouted. "Rise from the fires, and answer the call, release them all! Out from their cage! Release all, Amsu, Adom, release all, Abasi, Akil, release all, Amon, Amenhotep, all distant and still.

She heard wolfman howl loudly. "No!"

She felt a rumble and the floor and room began to shake. The herbs caught the alter on fire and it was burning, smoke filled the room. She could barely see. Flames frightened her but she stayed. She heard a shot, and a bullet flew by her grazing her shoulder. *Silver bullet*, she thought. Her gun, silver bullet. She dropped to her knees and crawled back and felt around the floor where her clothes lay. Her hand ran into the holster, she fumbled around until she felt it.

Outside thunder rumbled, lightning lit up the room, and clouds gathered. But the moon shown exceptionally bright, and Kara caught a glimpse of it. She finally found her gun, but visibility inside was scarce. The floor rumbled and the pentagram on the floor cracked down the middle. The floor separated and she was afraid. She glanced at the cage of spirits and the cage was disappearing.

She glanced through the window at the full moon, when she turned back, she saw the mirror behind the cage. When the floor cracked open the mirror cracked down the middle, splitting the full moon in two. She glanced at the split reflection of the moon and knew this is what the prophesy meant. She was still on her hands and knees and wolfman couldn't see her, but she could see him. The ribbon of light draped across him. She saw him raise his arm and another shot rang out and she heard the bullet zing over her. She picked her gun up and fumbled with it, then got her finger on the trigger.

She looked at wolfman, his eyes were glowing red. Bad, bad man, must shoot him through the heart. She leaned back on her haunches and steadied herself as good as she could. She was careful, aimed, then shot. Wolfman went down. The room began to burn, and she screamed from the fire. She ran to her mate. He lay dying. Bad man shot him in the heart. She howled a mournful sound and knew her own heart was dying along with him. She couldn't think. Tears came from her eyes. She howled mournfully again. Then she heard a shout.

"Kara, Cain are you in here?" came the voice.

Kara knew who. He taught her. Magic. It was Damian. "Oh my God," said Damian coming through the door. "Kara. We have to get you out of here."

"Mate," she said and howled.

"Oh my God, look at you...you...are a person wolf."

She howled. "Maaate!"

Damian looked down on the floor and saw Cain. He quickly picked him up and ran toward the door. She followed him out.

Once outside and far enough away from the house, he lay Cain down and checked him. He was barely breathing. "I think he took the bullet to the heart, but maybe just nicked it if he's still alive. If it was a silver bullet..."

She looked at him. "Saaay!" she howled.

"I'm sorry, Kara, but he's going to die. He's barely breathing. Then before their eyes Cain turned back to human. "Damn, Kara, he's really dying. They can only get their human form back on a full moon if they are dying. I'm sorry but his soul is leaving his body."

Kara howled. "No! No, not him!" She sobbed and lay across him like she did in the forest. "No, take me," she begged. "Don't take him. Please take me!" She screamed toward the skies. She lay over him sobbing. She felt the failure in her heart. Snippets of other times went through her mind when she lost others. She couldn't lose him, not him. No...

Then suddenly she felt a sharp pain in her chest getting stronger and stronger. She could barely catch her breath. She rose up and grabbed at her chest and pulled her hand away where blood covered her hand.

"What the hell?" said Damian. "You took his bullet, Kara!"

She howled at the pain in her chest and felt herself dying. Her spirit was starting to leave her body, but she didn't want to go, and as quick as she thought it, she felt herself being jerked back, and the wound in her chest began to close. Until moments later she felt no pain at all.

Then Kara looked up to see a black cloud move over the house and it shot a bolt of lightning so bright it went through the roof of the house and down incinerating the wolfman. She knew because she felt it. She felt the connection to her father. The clap of thunder was so loud and strong the ground shook. Kara and Damian could do nothing more than watch it as it happened. Great winds howled through the trees and more thunder shook the earth. The sky lit up with Criss cross lightning spikes and more thunder roared through her ears. It sounded like an active war zone. Old feelings reeled through her, fears tried to take hold, but she pushed them all aside accept for the feelings she had for Cain.

The house was on fire and the sun started coming up. Cain moaned, then moved. She began losing the hair and her body changed more until she was fully human. Damian beside them, and Cain opened his eyes.

"We're naked," said Cain. Damian quickly took off his jacket and threw it around her.

"You're alive," she sobbed. "You're alive, Cain."

"It appears that way. I thought I was dying. My spirit wanted to leave this body, but I didn't want to leave you."

"I didn't want you to leave."

"Well, we know what another of Kara's power is, I don't think anyone has ever in the history had that power," said Damian. You are the first to have it. Amazing.

They both looked at him. "Damian where did you come from? I thought you were in Florida? What power?"

"I was, but when I scried, I saw that black cloud chasing you. I had to return. Another one of her powers is that she can heal. You healed Cain. I've never known of a healer before. You were going to die, my man. Reid shot you with a silver bullet and it looked pretty close to your heart."

"It nicked my heart," said Cain. "I was shot there once before, and the bullet hit the scar tissue, or I would have bled to death. You saved my heart three times," he said looking at Kara with a grin.

"Three times?" She looked at him confused. "I only remember two."

"It was three, once when I was shot in the forest, once when I was shot tonight, and once when I fell in love with you."

Kara's tears were flowing and through sobs she leaned down and kissed him. Damian coughed and stood.

"I think I'll go call the fire department. We should move back. The house is going up in flames."

"Oh no, the papers." She looked toward the house.

"What papers?" asked Cain.

"The ones in the safe, that prove all the things Reid's done wrong. Proof that he was my father." Then she heard her grandmother's voice. *"The safe won't burn."* She remembered the words her grandmother spoke. Then she heard her voice again. *"Thank-you, my dear."* She glanced up toward where she thought her grandmother's room was. It was engulfed in flames.

Then she could swear she could hear laughter and she saw a young soul of a beautiful woman lift up from the top of the flames and disappear. She knew then she'd see her again someday along with her mother. She smiled. "Never mind," she said. "The safe is fireproof. We'll get it later."

"We better have a good story for the fire department before they get here," said Cain.

"Don't tell them that I'm his daughter. I have to think about it. Just say we were spending the night because I was working late and would have an early morning."

"The lightning caused the fire," said Damian. "I saw

it hit and I'm sure others did too."

"That's good," said Cain. "Did the moon actually split in two?"

"Not that I saw," said Damian.

"I saw it. It split in two when the mirror behind the spirits broke."

"See metaphor," said Cain. "No one else saw a split moon except the spirits and you."

"They're all free now. We have to somehow let it be known that sorcerers and wolves are healed and not to take any inoculation," said Kara.

"We can think of how to do that later," said Cain.

"What do you remember, Cain?" asked Kara.

"Only that you ordered me to sit and stay. A lot."

"That's because I had to put that bubble around us like Damian taught me. There was some kind of gas that filled the room, and I knew it was deadly. He showed up after he shut the gas down."

"It seemed to coincide with the prophesy that was written backwards," said Cain. "Did you find out from your grandmother why that was?"

"Yes," she said. "Reid was dyslexic, he'd never be able to figure it out."

"Well, I think we have most of our story straight."

As soon as he finished speaking, they heard the sirens. When the fire department got there, they insisted on checking the three of them out. Cain told them his TITAN badge number with the dash C after it. Everyone knew that the C meant Commander in Chief. No one would argue with that. They promised to do everything Cain told them to do. They gave Kara and Cain a blanket to put around them. Kara gave her home phone number after Cain said he wanted the safe as soon as they found it. It had important documents in it. She and Cain would have to get new cell phones. Unfortunately, they lost theirs when they lost their clothes. She told them Reid, his mother, and two of his workers were still in the house but the flames were such they couldn't get to them.

They told them she and Cain were sleeping together in a guest bedroom and that she was working for Reid as a bodyguard, and were lucky to get out alive, without their clothes. She was getting pretty good at covering for her wolf and witch. She still didn't like it but definitely understood it.

Damian had his rental car, so he took Cain and Kara to go pick up Cain's car. It was hidden in the forest about a mile and a half away. Unfortunately, her truck was caught in the blaze, but insurance would cover it. The three returned to Kara's house and were exhausted. It was ten o'clock in the morning, but it felt like night and their adrenaline was still high.

When they got inside Cain and Kara quickly dressed then met Damian in the living room. "How did you know to come and look for us?" asked Cain.

"When I couldn't get either one of you on the phone. I knew it was a full moon, and you suspected Reid Dalton. I wasn't back in Florida but a couple hours, and I was worried, so I scried. When I saw the cloud, I knew things were happening now on this full moon. I grabbed the quickest flight back here. It wasn't hard to find Reid's place. I just wished I would have been earlier."

"I'm glad you weren't," said Kara. "He would have killed you for sure. I know he tried very hard to get rid of Cain and I."

Damian shook his head. "His own daughter."

"Yes," said Cain. "He was an evil bastard."

"Well, I'm just glad you both are alive."

"Wolves are hard to kill," said Cain. He popped a bottle of wine. "Anyone for a drink?"

Kara and Damian both said yes at the same time.

Then they, talked, laughed, and got tipsy. Two more bottles of wine later, exhausted, with nothing left to say, but happy, they all crawled to bed. Content that things turned out the way they did.

Somehow once they made it to bed Cain and Kara found enough energy to show each other just how happy and content they were. Hopeful for their future, Cain made slow passionate love to Kara, then spent, they peacefully fell asleep in each other's arms.

Epilogue:

Kara, Cain, and Damian sat going through the papers. They not only found all the evidence they needed against Reid, but they found several other things. Copies of the companies he owned, stocks, properties, several thousand dollars in cash, the document proving Kara was his daughter, and a copy of his will.

They weren't sure if he was being sarcastic in what he did, or if he thought his daughter would deserve it, but he clearly stated that in the event of his death his entire fortune and holdings would go to his daughter.

Kara was blown away by it. It was true, they gave the lawyer a copy of her birth certificate, a copy of the evidence Reid had in his safe her DNA matching his, and a copy of the will. She wasn't sure how Reid got the proof, but it was there in black and white. She was indeed his daughter. The lawyer asked her to come into the office so she could sign all the legal papers allowing her to take over everything.

Kara was also having visions of her people. They were praying loudly and clearly to her, and she was drawn to them. She hadn't wanted to be queen, but the more she heard them, the more she was changing her mind.

She also didn't want to own so many companies. She just wanted to be Cain's wife and mother to his children and deal with who she was becoming. So, after discussing it with Cain and going over it in her head, she decided to give the shares of most of the companies to the workers who worked for Reid Dalton.

She and Cain also discussed the fact they could drag his name through the mud with all the things they had against him. He had a black book written meticulously with the names of all the dealers he bought drugs from. There was also an area with lists of the people that worked for him along with addresses and phone numbers. Even though Reid couldn't read very well he was excellent with numbers. Either that or Terri wrote everything down.

Cain was going to have to go to Columbia and meet with their government about the drug problem, but at least he knew everyone he was dealing with now, and it seemed the drug problem in Denver was little to none. He aimed to keep it that way.

After days of deliberation over what to do about Reid and how people would remember him, they felt they should leave sleeping dogs lie. Especially since everyone in Denver looked up to him. The fact that everyone would find out Kara was his daughter was inevitable. Cain didn't want her name dragged through the mud, so that was the main deciding factor for their decision. She'd been through enough.

He did however find the ones who were responsible for Christian's torture and death. It had been a priority for him. With the names of everyone who worked for Reid, it didn't take him and a few other TITAN officers long to locate them and bring them in. They arrested exactly who were responsible for killing Christian. The two men who tortured Christian finally admitted to it and they faced a firing squad as he watched. The third man died in the shoot-out at Reid's. Kara stood beside him through it all. He'd told her she didn't need to be there, but she insisted. TITAN had its own rules they lived by.

The government nor law enforcement had any say in how they dealt with things.

It made him feel better to know that at least these three were no longer alive to torture anyone else, but it didn't make him feel any better over the loss of his best friend. Reid's assistant Terry seemed to have disappeared. No one knew where she was. They'd find her sooner or later and find out then what she knew about his business, him, and the things he'd done. With her gone the way she was, Cain figured she must know a great deal.

Kara made true on Reid's promise to the people and matched what the donors gave, and the hospital went up with his name proudly displayed on the outside as Dalton Memorial Hospital. She also donated a large sum for anyone who didn't have insurance but was in need of hospitalization with explicit instructions to let her know if they ran low on funds.

They found out he had several accounts overseas, and it would probably take a while to find all of them. His attorney knew of some and turned them over and offered to find the rest, for a fee of course. When all was said and done, she ended up with one hundred and nineteen million dollars, however the attorney would continue searching for any other accounts. He felt certain there were more.

She knew most of it came from drug money, so she set up an account in Denver for drug abuse and rehabilitation programs along with a substantial amount for the coming years ahead. She also anonymously sent money to the families who lost a loved one to the drug called black beauty. The families figured out who it was, although they could never prove it. Jimmy called Cain to thank him, and Cain had to act like he didn't know what he was talking about. Jimmy chuckled over his attempts and ended the conversation by still thanking him anyway.

The thing that Cain and she were most proud of was the center she and Cain opened to help young people struggling with their sexuality. There were counselors and help lines, and programs to address abuse. They offered them a safe place to stay if they had nowhere else to go. They named it Christian's Way and had plans to expand both the buildings and the land.

She donated money to the schools to help with books and sports and whatever else they needed but was unsure of what to do with the rest. So, she put it in a few bank accounts to sit on for a while. She wanted to make sure that she turned something that came from such negative activity into a positive.

She and Cain were happy and made her house home and used his house for a retreat. He knew that when they'd have kids, they would love the lake, so they kept it. Cain had plans to add onto the house since two bedrooms would not be enough when they had children.

That was something for the future. He and Kara never used his original bedroom, their guestroom became the master, and he bought all new furniture getting rid of his old. She hadn't asked him to do it, but he did it anyway, for her. He said it was to wipe out any memory of any other woman ever being in his home. She thought it sweet.

The lake house was also where most of the Silver Sables lived and that's where they all ran together. Kara was fast becoming friends with the women from the pack and she and Cassandra had their fight on time. Kara beat her fair and square in a matter of seconds, she didn't rub it in though, it was embarrassing enough for Cassandra. Cassandra relinquished her position as alpha female, but she kept up her flirtations, with all but Cain after that.

Stacy and Carla became her friends and they spent time at each other's houses. They also went to meetings of the arctic wolves because Kara's house was in their district. Kara knew Cain missed Christian terribly especially when they went to those meetings, luckily, he was friends with the new Alpha male. He'd never take Christian's place in Cain's eyes, but Cain told her the new Alpha was at least a good man.

All silver bullets containing Reid's blood were destroyed and the operation of making them shut down. Damian spread the word that a spell worked, and no one had to fear going crazy. He said he wouldn't tell anyone how that happened, only that it did. It gave him notoriety, something he didn't seem to mind at all.

There was never any mention of a queen, unless Damian was visiting, and he happened to call her that. The prayers from her people though were getting louder and stronger and she knew she'd have to make a decision soon about what to do. She would have to have a heart to heart with Cain over it. Damian visited a lot and he and Cain became very close friends, more than they ever were before.

She knew he'd never take Christian's place, but she was happy they got along so well. To her, Damian felt like a brother. She did not join TITAN but the offer was still there, and she knew in her heart she never would. She knew she would end up as queen at some point, but after discussing it with Damian, she decided to learn all she could about herself before she approached the grandmasters.

\*\*\*\*

Tonight, she was tired, but Cain insisted on taking her to their favorite restaurant, the Italian Bistro. He said he had something to tell her. Well, she had something to tell him too. She smiled as she got dressed. He kept rushing her like they had a strict reservation.

"What's the rush?" she asked. "It's not like you have to have reservations."

"Nothing special. I'd just like to get there."

When they finally got there, they had the best meal ever and Kara's energy returned. They were sitting enjoying a Shirley Temple because she didn't want wine and he joined her. She took a sip and thought of it and looked at him and smiled. "I have something to tell you."

"Oh? May I please go first? I have something to say to you."

She looked at him funny. "Oh, okay," she said, her curiosity peaked.

He got up and she thought he was going to leave but he came around to her seat and got down on one knee. She looked around the restaurant and felt herself blush as she watched all the people get up from their seats and gather around.

"Kara," he said, clearing his throat. "I've loved you probably from the moment we met. I know it had to have been your singed hair that attracted me, or maybe it was your green eyes," he said, making them both laugh.

She knew her face was turning red because the whole place got deathly quiet as people stared at them. It was getting a little uncomfortable. If the whole thing wasn't so endearing, she'd probably crawl under the table and hide. As it was, he was so damn cute, so she smiled brightly thinking it was adorable.

"Anyway, Kara, what I'm trying to say, is that I want you for the mother of my children, and grandmother to their children, but most of all I want you to be my wife." He took a small blue velvet box from his pocket and opened it. Inside was a beautiful gold band that looked like twisted dandelion leaves and at the center on top was a collection of beautiful small yellow sapphires in a gold setting. "This is to make up for the ring I made and has probably rotted away somewhere."

Tears sprang to her eyes. "Actually, I have it drying in my favorite book, *The Giving Tree*. I could have never thrown it away."

"But you could have never worn it either. This is a dandelion ring you can wear, an engagement ring. Will you be my wife?"

She looked at a lady that sniffled and at the faces watching her. "Are you going to answer him?" asked one lady.

She threw her arms around him and kissed him, then wiped away the tears and shook her head yes. "Yes," she said finally. "Of course, I will marry you."

He turned to the crowd and shouted, "She said yes!"

The next thing she knew the entire restaurant began serenading them. They sounded great, like they did it for a living. She looked at him. He shrugged his shoulders. "It's not a marching band, but I thought having these professional singers to serenade us would be perfect."

"Oh, God Cain. It is, it is sooo perfect. I love you."

"I love you." He put the ring on her finger.

The singers stopped for a second because Cain held up his hand. "You said you had something you wanted to tell me? Is it important?"

"Yes, I think so." She smiled. "I'm pregnant."

The place roared and began singing again all standing around them. Cain actually had tears and he picked her up and swung her around then put her back down.

"You happy?" she asked.

"More than," he said, "and later we'll have the marching band to prove just how happy I am." When they finally made it to bed, he was true to his word and showed her just how happy he was. It was two a.m. and fully sated they sat in bed discussing their future together. Cain was ecstatic that all the wolves and witches and warlocks were healed. The term half breed would never again be used. Gundi was going to be a thing of the past for all of them.

They talked about how many children they wanted. She thought four at the most, but Cain mentioned twelve. Her mouth dropped open, but he was serious. She had to think about that. They talked of building onto the lake house and her house. He wanted an office, but he wouldn't take her father's. He said that office was to be hers. They finally fell asleep tangled up in each other's arms, fully spent and happy with their future looking very bright indeed.

## A word about the author…

I was born and raised in a small mill town in the Midwest where the river, lakes, woods, and nature were my playground, and riding my horse was a great pastime. I grew up as an artist, as a photographer my specialty was taking B&W photos of old ghost towns and hand tinting them. I lived near Santa Fe New Mexico for fourteen-years indulging in my artwork. I've always enjoyed storytelling and now I write. I currently reside in Indiana with my husband and my three tiny Chihuahuas and my tiny Cairn terrier. I love to hear from my readers. You can contact me on my website, Cherylstarrmunger.com, or email me at Cherylstarrmunger@gmail, also you can find me on Facebook, CherylStarrMunger, and Instagram authot.artist,

www.ingramcontent.com/pod-product-compliance
Lightning Source LLC
Chambersburg PA
CBHW070801030726
47504CB00003B/654